THE ENEMY ABOARD

Only one threat came to mind. The Arab near the back of the coach. Terrorists had already taken over two airliners. One or more might be aboard this aircraft. The man might even now be coming at them, pistol in hand. Other men, accomplices Tyler had not seen, might be advancing on them, strapped in plastic charges.

"Don't sweat the one guy. Leave the Arab to me. You keep your eyes open for a second guy, maybe a third."

The airline captain put on a tough look. Tyler gave a weak smile. Barney Fife with BO. Tyler figured he was on his own for the actual combat. He looked at RuthAnn. "You up to crowd control?"

She nodded and straightened up to six feet tall.

"Let's go," Tyler said, as he shoved the door open, fist clenched to throw the first blow, gut tensed to take one.

But no, the aisle was clear. All the way back to the Arab who locked eyes with him. Wary, hostile eyes. The eyes of a terrorist, just as surly as every wanted poster Tyler had ever seen of them.

He stopped cold. The airline captain bumped into his back, poking him with the crash ax. Tyler pulled the door toward himself, just enough so he could keep eye-to-eye the terrorist poster boy sitting there in living color.

So much for Plan A.

DELTA FORCE
OPERATION MICHAEL'S SWORD

JOHN HARRIMAN

JOVE BOOKS, NEW YORK

THE BERKLEY PUBLISHING GROUP
Published by the Penguin Group
Penguin Group (USA) Inc.
375 Hudson Street, New York, New York 10014, USA
Penguin Group (Canada), 10 Alcorn Avenue, Toronto, Ontario M4V 3B2, Canada
(a division of Pearson Penguin Canada Inc.)
Penguin Books Ltd., 80 Strand, London WC2R 0RL, England
Penguin Group Ireland, 25 St. Stephen's Green, Dublin 2, Ireland (a division of Penguin Books Ltd.)
Penguin Group (Australia), 250 Camberwell Road, Camberwell, Victoria 3124, Australia
(a division of Pearson Australia Group Pty. Ltd.)
Penguin Books India Pvt. Ltd., 11 Community Centre, Panchsheel Park, New Delhi—110 017, India
Penguin Group (NZ), Cnr. Airborne and Rosedale Roads, Albany, Auckland 1310, New Zealand
(a division of Pearson New Zealand Ltd.)
Penguin Books (South Africa) (Pty.) Ltd., 24 Sturdee Avenue, Rosebank, Johannesburg 2196,
South Africa

Penguin Books Ltd., Registered Offices: 80 Strand, London WC2R 0RL, England

This is a work of fiction. Names, characters, places, and incidents either are the product of the author's imagination or are used fictitiously, and any resemblance to actual persons, living or dead, business establishments, events, or locales is entirely coincidental.

DELTA FORCE: OPERATION MICHAEL'S SWORD

A Berkley Book / Published by arrangement with the author

PRINTING HISTORY
Jove mass-market edition / December 2004

ISBN: 0-515-13657-3

JOVE®
Jove Books are published by The Berkley Publishing Group,
a division of Penguin Group (USA) Inc.,
375 Hudson Street, New York, New York 10014.
JOVE is a registered trademark of Penguin Group (USA) Inc.
The "J" design is a trademark belonging to Penguin Group (USA) Inc.

PRINTED IN THE UNITED STATES OF AMERICA

10   9   8   7   6   5   4   3   2   1

I Four Hours

As army captain Connor Tyler sat in a row to himself aboard United 411 in a steep climb, forty-eight minutes late, from La-Guardia to Las Vegas, he saw a jet strike the North Tower of the World Trade Center.

One moment Tyler is folding his six-five athletic frame across two seats as his flight soars out from runway three-one, up and into a brilliant morning, the sun flashing gold off two million facets of the city. Crisp light, stark, clean, geometric beauty. One moment he feels warm, confident, centered, intent. Like any man on the way home. To his wife. To set things right with her. And Brendan. Just to hold him. God bless a baby, a son, a Brendan. He has only to think his name to smile.

The next moment a speck streaks across the film of one of his pewter gray eyes. His smile freezes.

He cannot blink away the speck and sees it is not a speck after all, but an airliner in a slalom through the skyline glitter of Manhattan. Not above the buildings but among them. The aircraft dips its wings one way, then the other, slashing through

the Lego forest. An aircraft in trouble? Maybe out of control?
About to ditch in the harbor? His smile flags. He senses danger. He wants to call out a warning. But to whom?

He cranes his long neck, pressing one cheek to the porthole to look back and beneath the wing, feeling his pulse
pounding in his throat. His smile a grimace. The plane. It's not
falling. Not out of control. Not trying to miss.

He leans hard left, lending his body language to the craft
below, straining against his seat belt, urging the runaway pilot,
"Turn, *turn*—"

Tyler flinches from the window, his hair whipping across
his face.

As the plane slams into the rhinestone tower, striking a
spark, blooming from a speck to fire. As the explosion punches
through and out the other side, a gorgeous lethal orange blossom inferno. As first a groan escapes his chest, then a whisper.
Oh, dear God.

"Oh. Dear. God." He peels strands of hair from his eyes.

To see the fuel fire belching through the glass walls.
Flames engulfing the top floors of the tower. An Olympic
torch of glass and steel, smoke and fire. Beauty of an ugly,
awesome kind. His stomach clenches.

He smells the hot fuel fumes in the wind blown up by the
blast. Hears the *whoomp,* a gentle sound, for all its fury. Feels
first heat on his face, a hot wind, then a chill as cold wind
blows back to the epicenter. He hears the shrieks of the dying,
shrieking until—

What? No, that can't be. Different fire, different nightmare. It used to visit him every night, but he hasn't had it for
months. Till now. But—

That was a dream, too. Wasn't it? What he just saw? Okay,
what he was thinking? A few seconds ago? Okay, there was
that warmth inside, that certainty, the confidence of knowing
he'd made a decision, a right decision. There was that. A bit of
hangover, yeah, that, not a sick hangover, but a solemn one.
And the guilt for wronging Amy. Sinning yesterday, a dark
chocolate sin—he remembers that, but today he'd make it
right. Yesterday he—

Yesterday?

A jetliner just flew into the World Trade Center? He looks out the porthole. Yes, a few seconds ago.

Dear God. There is no yesterday.

0850 Hours EDT, September 11, 2001—New York City

Flight 11 hit the newsroom of the *New York Times-Mirror* as a phone call. The assistant city editor reacted in the usual way to incredible news.

"The World Trade Center? Get. Out. In broad daylight? No. Way. It's not even cloudy outside." She covered the mouthpiece of the phone and spoke in a smoker's rasp, her lungs whistling beneath the words. "Got a live one here. Guy says an airplane just flew into one of the Twin Towers."

"Finally. Proof. The sky *is* falling." The copy editor at the city desk who said it didn't even look up from her keyboard.

"You know what I think?" reporter Laren Hodges said, fresh back from the vomiteria, balancing a stack of three coffees. "I think it's Evans over at the *Times*. Little shit's gotta rep for pulling—"

"Shut up." The ACE shot to her feet, the backs of her knees launching her office chair at Laren. "Everybody shut up—no, not you, Greenfield—everybody else. Are you sure, Ben? Can you confirm it, I mean physically see it with your own eyes?"

She pressed the phone against her face with one hand and closed her off-ear with the other hand. As she spoke she stared down at her desk. "You see it burning? Ben, this is not second-hand, right? . . . Not some wastebasket fire—okay, Ben, calm down. . . . You don't have to curse. . . . I, we, we, we have to be dead-solid certain. You know how it is around here—the first report is always wrong. . . . No, I'm not saying *you're* wrong. I believe you. A hundred percent, 110 percent. Are you sure it's a plane and not just a bomb?" She held the phone at arm's length, letting Greenfield shout into the room instead of her ear.

She looked over one shoulder to meet Laren's laser-green

eyes. She needed her friend now. This was too much for her to deal with alone. "It's Greenfield," she said. "Our Greenfield. An airliner really did fly into one of the Twin Towers. He's eyeballing it. The World Trade Center is on fire. Again. Not a bomb this time and not in the basement, but up near the top." She shook her head. "Can you believe it? A commercial liner?" Saying it aloud gave it too much gravity. She started to sit in the spot where her chair had been.

"Wait," Laren said. She balanced the stack of coffees in one hand and pressed against the ACE's bony spine so she would not fall on her butt. "Let me get your chair."

The coffees felt hot and good against her breasts. If only she had larger ones. She could have used a pair of cup-holders right now. She looked around the newsroom. Funny. Nobody was gawking at her. She knew she had a glitz about her, tousled blonde hair, daringly short, a look of *Oh-just-try-not-to-look-at-me*. The green eyes, the pouting lips, the stare that invited stares. She'd had a lifetime of getting used to people sneaking stares at her, even women, nothing sexual, just unable to not look. She hardly ever noticed anymore. Except—when nobody stared at her. Like Connor. He never stared at her. It was what drew her to him, that and his titanium eyes.

Half a dozen reporters and editors now stood at their desks, grinding phones into their heads, getting the same news from their own Ben Greenfields. She shoved the chair at the ACE with her foot and saw a scuff on one toe of her—*Goddammit. Brand new Dolces from*—It struck her before she could finish the thought.

The silence, first. In the cubicles and at the copy desks, Laren saw fingers poised over keyboards. For the moment, the cockroach legs stopped clattering over the keys. Everybody quiet, everybody breathless.

Nobody now more quiet than Laren Hodges. A new flutter in her chest, in the center, behind the hot spot of the coffees in her cleavage. Connor. He'd given her the $400 shoes. He'd spent last night with her—

A plane just crashed into the World Trade Center?

Connor? He was flying out today. Right?

He'd nuzzled her ear, what, three hours ago?

"Gotta go, babe. Catch you on the rebound."

"Cut it out, Connie."

"Come on."

"No shit, I mean it. Your breath's like a canna Nine Lives. Go brush your teeth."

"Screw you."

"Not till after you brush first."

"Shit." She choked back a sob that nobody in the news room bothered to hear. Shit. She didn't even tell him she loved him. Told him his breath stunk. *Didn't even tell him she loved him.*

"Shit," she said. "Couldn't be."

"Yes," the ACE said. "A plane. Greenfield saw it the second it hit."

"Not that, Fran. I was thinking . . . I was . . . I have a friend flying out of the city today."

"I know him?"

"Connor. Connor Tyler."

"Your army hottie with the eyes? I never met a man with gray eyes so dark. I tell you if you were to leave me alone with him for just one—"

"Fran. We got a plane crash?"

"Oh, no. Laren? Sweetie, you don't think?" A look of, *Not the guy with those eyes.*

"No. No, couldn't be." A giddy laugh, void of humor. "What're the odds?" Waiting for Fran to tell her a million to one.

0851 Hours EDT, September 11, 2001—Over New York City

Tyler hasn't heard so much as a whimper from the passengers. How could that—

Impossible. People could not keep so quiet. Not if they had seen what he saw.

He throws off his seat belt and kneels on his seat to look back into the coach cabin, banging his skull on the overhead. A couple guys barricaded from small talk behind the *Times* and one behind the *Times-Mirror.* Some people nodding off.

Most already asleep. A black guy with huge ears trying to sub-
due two pillows the size of field bandages.

Nobody else here has seen the crash. In all the world, he's
the only one who's seen it?

Maybe he hasn't seen it, either. Except as a figment. Why,
yes, now he remembers. Just moments ago, in that other lifetime, he was thinking that a major in the Pentazoo had a
vendetta against him. That damned Roscoe Spangler. Putting
on a big act, as if they were pals, allies against big brother.
Patting him on the back with one hand, stabbing him in the
face with the other, that's what he'd done. Army politics.
Spangler was so fond of saying, *You're lucky, Connor. You go
to war, you get killed once. Up here in the land of puzzle-
palace politics, I get killed fresh every day.*

But now he turns back toward the city skyline, fast fading
behind and beneath Flight 411. Forget Spangler. Forget politics. Let this be the dream, *please, God.*

God answers his prayer. The answer is no. The crash is
real, ripening to its full, horrid glory. At the focal point of the
wreckage is that florid blossom, now cooling to black billows.
A mushroom cloud he knows too well, formed by the back-
blow of cold air rushing in from all points of the compass,
bringing fresh oxygen to feed the flames, heat rising, up, up,
the only way it can go. He knows the physics of a crash and
burning. He knows the human toll of a fuel fire, too, for he has
set such a fire himself. Nothing of the scale below, but bad
enough, for his fire killed people, too.

All those deaths. He tries to get his mind around the enormity. Not because he thinks he can grieve for strangers, even
if they died right in his line of sight. Rather, so he can pray for
them. He can be sick for them. That's the least he can do to—

Tyler spins in the seat to answer the touch on his shoulder.

"Sir?" the stew says. "Did you just see that . . . *something* . . . like, back there over the city?"

"Something?" *Don't be stupid.* A jet just bored its way into
one of the tallest buildings in the world in broad daylight.

She is trying not to cry, but. . . .

Her eyes go weepy at what she reads in his face, as if he

has spoken his thoughts. People have called her stupid before. He rises and kneels on one knee again, bumping his head again, cocking one ear closer to her. He should have not been so rude. *I'm sorry. I didn't mean to upset you. I was shaken by . . . that.* He inclines his head toward the porthole. She inclines her head toward him. Willing to forgive.

"Are you all right? The captain wanted me to ask," she murmurs.

The tears spill over, streaking black eyeliner down her cheeks. Shame flashes over him. She does not deserve his insults, spoken or not.

He checks her name tag. RuthAnn, no space, like a Web site, RuthAnn.com.

"Yes, RuthAnn," he says in his best church voice. "Some pilot just flew his plane into the Twin Towers." He hears his own words. Absurd. *How could a pilot do that?*

She winces at the idea spoken aloud. She gathers herself, talks low to him. "The captain told me to see if I could help the passengers. Keep them all calm. 'Keep a lid on it,' he said. Comfort them?"

He leans away and gives her a once-over. *How's that gonna happen?* Her gazelle legs trembling, ready to fold like a wet fawn's. Her eyes oozing black tears, one nasty word away from a deluge. About to pee her pants too, from the look of her.

The plane banks left, she leans right, toward him. She smells damp and musty. He doesn't have to be a dog to smell her fear. He reads a pleading in her soupy eyes. She is the one who needs the comfort. He knows women don't mind being in his space. When a woman is near anyhow, she often edges closer. To let him know it's okay to stand in her space. He leans in an inch, if that will give her solace.

"I'm an army officer," he tells her. The words sound absurd to him, too, the instant they hit the air. They don't do a thing for her. She jerks her head away, spilling tears onto his knee, pelting him with the first drops of a cloudburst. The corner of her mouth tweaks once, the imitation of a smile. *I'm not that stupid, mister.*

"Or maybe, like, an astronaut?" she says, taking a step back.

Right. He knows how he looks. Not Rambo, more Bambi. Women come on to him. Strangers, and to his face: *You a rock star or something? Excuse me for staring, honey, but—*

Not a rock star, not a honey-butt. Most times he'd give them a weak smile. Turn away. He hates his look.

Mister too perfect. Too *GQ,* rock-jawed, eyes the color of a sports car. The rough-cut ends of his too long, too thick hair tumbling over his Brooks Brothers collar. Suit all too hip, too rich, too Ivy. Everything about him too Calvin-in-your-face-Klein, as if he just stepped off a full-page in the Sunday *Times* magazine: *Hey, buy your own damned underwear and stop gawking at mine.* Women liked to be near him, meaning he didn't hate his looks *all* that much. Men wanted to be friends, just friends. Still. His looks were a liability among soldiers. He was an officer, not a friend. What was he going to say to this woman: *I wear my hair this way so my giraffe neck doesn't look so long?*

No, but he might have said, *I'm a Delta Force officer,* breaking his vow of silence on that. *We're allowed to dress any way we want. And wear our hair long, you know, to blend in?* That might have calmed her a moment ago. Not now. She's not buying anything now. She doesn't have time for him. Not so much that she's dismissed him. Just that she has a larger problem to deal with. Her own.

She's zoning into a thousand-meter stare. First stage of shell shock. He knows that look. He has seen it during his own brief moments of combat. No amount of training can teach you how to deal with it.

"Maybe you shouldn't say anything about the plane crashing into the towers," he says. "Might scare people if they knew."

Her lips work over some words. He should say something kind to compensate for his brusque manner a minute ago. He should hug her. He gets ready to hug her, if she needs it.

She doesn't. "Just the North Tower," she says.

"Beg pardon?"

"You said the towers. Twice you said the towers. It was just the one. The North Tower."

"Ah." He nods. She is all but gone.

She nods back. "I layover in the city a lot. Totally the North Tower."

"Right, right." Probably not the kind of help the captain had in mind when he sent her back here. This time keeping his smart-aleck body language to himself.

"I have to . . ." She tilts her head back, trying to remember what it is she has to do. "I have to act all normal, keep up the service," she says, more to herself than Tyler. "You'd better retake your seat and buckle up. Until the captain turns off the seatbelt light. Then you'll be free to move about . . ." Her voice trails off. She turns and staggers up the ramping aisle toward the flight deck.

She won't be back. No service today. A fresh Scotch and soda on top of the ones fermented in his belly didn't sound too early. He regrets it at once, the thinking only of himself. At a time like this. All those people. He slumps into his seat. God.

Still. One drink. To calm the jitters.

Tyler looks out the window. By now the wing on his side reaches for the heavens. All he can see is sky all the way to the end of the universe, sky clean and sterile as Windex. Unreal. No, surreal. All that destruction. How can God allow a sky so blue? He should stop all the clocks and put away the sun—blacken and shrivel it, or at least shroud it in clouds. *Jesus, God. Show a little respect for the dead*.

One-kneed, he checks out the cabin again, this time hunching over to keep from cracking his skull. Thirty passengers, tops. Sleeping and reading still. Still lost in their heads. And that one stubborn guy—not black, after all—some kind of Arab, wrestling with his tiny pillows, trying to pin them to his seat-back with his head. His ears both leathery and hairy, like tarantulas clinging to his skull.

Tyler slumps. He leaves his seat belt off. What? In defiance? What good did seat belts do for all those people down below? So sudden. Three hundred knots to a dead stop in seconds. God. Now only God can help them. He digs into his faith for the right prayer. *May their souls rest in peace*.

The replay takes over his mind's eye. A sickness numbs his heart. How venal he has been in the last twenty-four hours. How trivial in the last few minutes. Yesterday a world away.

Leaving him in the now. To think only of himself. His sin. Guilt. Worry over his lousy looks and his pitiful career. Looking for an escape clause in his marriage vows that would let him ease out of his marriage but stay in his son's life. And, oh yeah, a Scotch his top priority. At a time like this, letting his petty thoughts prowl his head like a pack of rats. For shame, Connor, for shame.

All those lives lost, all those families left to grieve for all those lifetimes. What the hell is wrong with him?

Nothing left to do but pray. He folds his hands. In public, of all things. He feels a hot spot behind his eyes. And a sting of tears.

But he can't get past *Glory be to the Father*.

For the advance of one more rat pack skulking hard by to sit upon his shoulder with the other, darker angels of his nature. That crash. So incredible he can't get it out of his head.

Too incredible?

Could the bad guys do that?

The rats creep from his shoulder to tingle the hairs on his neck and bunch his scalp as they nuzzle at the frayed edges of his mind.

Could it be? *Terrorists?*

0854 Hours EDT, September 11, 2001—New York City

"What time was his flight?" Fran asked. "Your army hunk."

Laren turned her wrist to look at her watch.

"Watch it!"

The tower of coffees toppled. Steam and cream splattered in a six-foot radius.

Both women shrieked when the molten drinks splashed their ankles. Just the spark the awkwardly silent newsroom needed. All hell broke loose.

A plane crash in the heart of the city!

You didn't need a j-school degree to grasp a story like that. People shouted at each other anyhow, to prove they really did know what to do. Everybody doubly excited because the *Times,* a morning paper, was already on the streets, its offices on skeleton staff until midafternoon. The *Times-Mirror,* an evening paper, was already geared up, already grinding at full-staff, full-speed for the afternoon's "Bulldog" edition, the first of the day.

"Stand by to drop the scheduled lead beneath the fold."

"No, inside. Make room inside for the scheduled lead."

"What the hell is the scheduled lead anyhow?"

"Bush's education trip to Florida?"

"Who the hell cares?"

Nobody now.

"Florida again. Did you notice Florida? Poor Bush. First the chads hang his ass. So now he tries to be the education president and ends up he's gonna be the plane-crash president."

"Hanging again like one of those fricking chads."

"Guy can't catch a break."

"Screw Bush. He's going to eat this one, big time. Who's his FAA chief anyway?"

"Garvey."

"Guy's head's gonna roll."

"He's a she, Jane Garvey."

"Bitch's head's gonna roll."

"A plane crash in the heart of the city? No way." In the tone of *We should be so lucky.*

"Turn on the tube—see what the nets got for pics."

Any other day, Laren Hodges would have been right in the midst of it, shouting down the others. *I'm outta here, roger-dodger, over and out.*

Except for one thing. Connor Tyler. Connie's plane had just taken off today. What, an hour ago? But hey, planes never took off on time. Not from Sluguardia. Right?

She grabbed her spattered purse, the smell of cinnamon sweet to the nose, sick to the stomach. She turned to run out of the news room. But to where? What the hell was she doing? *Shit.*

She snatched a phone. Put it back in its cradle. Nobody to

call to find out. Not when you don't even know the airline, let alone the flight number?

She pounded a fist against the side of her head. *Shit, shit, shit.*

Get a grip. Call him on his digital.

She fumbles through the sticky purse.

All the stories she'd ever written about other people's tragedies. She'd known exactly how to act, what to say. Sincerity. Integrity. Perfect calm. Learn to fake those things and you had it dicked. Now it is all she can do to suppress a scream. She doesn't even recognize the inside of her own purse.

Because, *shit,* this isn't her purse. It is Fran's.

She knew panic. Panic was being stalked by a serial killer while she was a writer for an Indiana daily. Panic was finding him in your home, then in the backseat of your car.

That was panic. Not this.

Except, what is this, if not panic?

At last she finds her purse, and, in it, her address book crammed with Post-it notes, scraps of paper, and two or three cocktail napkins with numbers she keeps meaning to transfer to more permanent spots in the book. When she finds time, which she never finds.

Under *T,* behind a scribbled napkin from Jello's Grille and Drink Emporium, and beneath a pink Post-it scribbled on both sides, she finds Connor Tyler's number. She taps it out like Morse code on her desk phone. She should be using her personal cell phone, but she's not going into that purse again. And anyhow, this is an emergency, hell, maybe a story. *For shit's sake, please don't let it be the story of Connie's death,* as close as she ever comes to praying.

"Hello?" A woman's voice.

For a moment, Laren is confused. A wrong number? She checks. No. He's with another bitch?

"Hello?" again.

No. "Sorry, wrong number."

"Shit." Laren slams down the telephone, not once but three times. She has dialed his home number. *Shit.* Not another bitch, but *the* bitch. His wife. *Shit, shit, shit.*

She dumps her purse onto the top of her desk and rummages into the heap of detritus, plucking the cell phone from the pile. Should have used it in the first place. His cell number is on speed dial, and his home is not.

Finally, the telephone begins probing the blind ether for a handshake with Tyler's phone. She looks around the newsroom. Nobody has noticed her frenzy. Everybody in the office, from the tight-assed executive editor to the slack-jawed mail mule, is dealing with the growing, giddy sense of hysteria in her own way.

She catches a glimpse of herself in the mirror on her desk, a framed mirror instead of a framed family picture because she has no family worth picturing. Across the bottom of the mirror runs a cutline, set in type like the caption beneath a news photo: *If you're looking for somebody to blame, look here first*. She called it her Times-Mirror, although she seldom blames herself for anything. Rather, without a word, she will hand the mirror to somebody who had stopped by to give her shit for something she had done or failed to do on the cop-shop beat.

"About time."

The handshake is made. Conn's phone begins ringing.

Sometimes she takes a long, thoughtful look at herself in the Times-Mirror when she needs to rescue herself from the quicksand of self-pity. Other times she merely touches up her lipstick before running out on an assignment. Now she sees a stranger in the Times-Mirror. She studies the look she has not seen for a long time. Not since a serial killer in Indianapolis had stalked her as she wrote the series that led to the job here. On the ninth ring or so, she sees the stranger is wearing a mask of fear. What do people see in her anyhow?

"Come on, Conn, pick up."

She sees the sexy Laren's face brighten.

"Connor Tyler here—"

"Connie. Darling. Where the hell—? *Shit*."

"But if you leave a number, I'll get back to you. If you want to try me at home—"

Done that already, dammit. Her heart pounding, she puts the framed Times-Mirror facedown on her desk and waits for the message to end. It's all she can do to stay her hand from throwing her telephone across the newsroom. She can't, though. She has to leave a message. Tell him to call her back. Tell him what she neglected to say this morning instead of bitching about his sour-Scotch-laced morning breath.

Finally, he shuts the hell up. She leaves her message. And gives in to the news instincts that have been kicking her butt for the last ten minutes.

She sweeps the pile off the desk and into her purse. She's up and on the run.

"Laren," the ACE calls after her.

"Later, Fran, I'm on my way down to the Plaza." Sounding braver than she feels.

"The World Trade Center?"

Laren doesn't answer, except to toss some body into her wild lion's mane. *Jesus, Fran. Where the hell else would the paper's soon-to-be star reporter be going?*

"Bring back some color," the ACE says, loud enough for her voice to squeak. "Not just the vics bawling and blaming, either. Give me something up close and first-personal. I want to feel the fire, smell the smoke. Put me in that building."

"Roger-dodger." What else? Walking faster and faster, trying to work out the jerky feeling in her knees.

"Oh, and leave your cell phone on. So I can get in touch."

Laren, speed-walking now, her butt sashaying left and right, all bully and bravado *look-at-that-end-for-awhile,* holds her phone aloft and flicks it side to side as she bursts through the newsroom doors on the way out. A metronome waving good-bye: *Roger-dodger, over and out.*

0901 Hours EDT, September 11, 2001—The Pentagon

Major Roscoe Spangler muted the volume on his television monitor and phoned his boss. The news goof at ABC had the pictures, but not a clue. One thumb in the mouth, the other up his ass, switching thumbs every minute or so, unable to decide between a bomb or an aircraft accident.

"Douche bag," he said to the news goof. "That's no bomb, and sure as hell—"

"DCTPO, Staff Sergeant Alvarez speaking—Sir? Say again your last?"

"Never mind that, Alvarez, this's Major Spangler for General Bowers." His tactical radio voice. *You haven't already put him on?*

On hold, Spangler hummed a few strains of a morning TV ditty for cereal. Used to be Sugar Pops, a name they couldn't say anymore because of the sugar part, the tune an earworm he couldn't get out of his head. After a few bars, he overheard himself sounding way too happy, so he muted the humming, too. You didn't want somebody to misunderstand and think that you were *happy* happy. Just that you were happy about being so right, so-o-o damned right. Hell, he'd predicted the exact scenario—okay, not exactly this *exact* scenario, but his miss was too close for coincidence. In his Speculative Intelligence Summary, code-named *Cradle of Fire,* not two years ago Spangler wrote that terrorists would be crashing airliners into the Capitol and the White House for sure, possibly the Pentagon. Bowers had laughed outright at that one, and he came positively unglued at Spangler's suggestion that DoD should set up camouflaged Patriot missiles sites and antiaircraft artillery batteries in strategic spots throughout Washington, D.C. "On the Capitol Mall, Roscoe?" the general had bellowed. "On the roof of the Smithsonian? What, surround them with some potted plants like in the cartoons? How're you gonna explain that to the American people? Anyway, who the hell is going to push the button, you? You gonna shoot down a USAir commuter on final to Reagan the wrong way because the pilot got his compass wires crossed? What are you, nuts?" Bowers had shoved the packet at Spangler as if it were a used, stinking bag of cat litter. "Burn the damned INTSUM before it burns you. Hell, me and you both. You're schizoid about this stuff, Ros, schizoid." He shook his head. "But I guess that beats eating alone, huh?"

Spangler didn't laugh. He did disobey. You couldn't burn a SPECINTSUM like *Cradle of Fire,* not after putting in all those man-hours and so much of the man. So he laid it to rest with honors in his vast and growing personal dead file, the Spangler Boneyard.

Who's nuts now, eh, General? Spangler scribbled the date–time group on his PAL.

DTG: *11SEP010902 Hours.*

VIA: *Telecon.*

CONTACT: *DCTPO.*

SUBJECT: Cradle of Fire *reminder. (YWRR! DIYWR!!!).*

You were right, Roscoe! He couldn't wipe off the grin. *Damn it, you were right-exclamation point!* What he wouldn't give to hear Bowers admit it. *Exclamation point! Exclamation point!! Exclamation point!!!*

"Little busy here, Roscoe, what's on your mind?" Lieutenant General Randall Bowers IV.

"You been watching ABC?" Spangler asked his buddy the general, his general the director, his director the main mother in charge of Counterterror Plans and Operations, CTPO—nicknamed C-3PO after one of the *Star Wars* robots, Spangler could never remember which. *Was I right, Randy, was I right?* "You know, the news about the aircraft—"

"The aircraft accident. Yes, it's on all the networks now. That's what I'm busy with." Tone of *So what*?

"Guy flies into the WTC on a day when you can see all the way to Baghdad? It's no accident, Randy." Spangler taking liberties with his classmate at West Point, the general's career on a fast-burn, his own career a burnout ten years ago, now going through the motions, nothing left but the retirement parade. "Remember *Cradle of Fire*?"

Bowers did not catch the name of Spangler's SPECINTSUM. He had cupped a hand over the mouthpiece, making the sound of rough sandpaper on dry wood in Spangler's ear. Spangler could hear Bowers talking to his staff, could hear muffled staff laughter through Bowers's hand. Spangler's skin prickled. They were laughing at him, and he knew why.

Bowers came back on. "I owe you one, Ros. Some smart-ass up here got up a pool on what time you would be calling in a terrorist alert, and I just won ten bucks. You do suspect terrorists, right?"

Spangler knew who the smart-ass was: his friend, the general, the director, the bastard.

"Roscoe?"

"General Bowers, sir. It's my job to suspect terrorists, sir. It's no joke to do my goddamned job. Sir."

"Don't pull that sir-crap with me, Ros. To quote your hero, you're a fanatic on this; you won't change your mind and won't change the subject. Just be glad—"

"Kiss my ass," Spangler said, his voice hushed.

"What? What did you say, Major? Tell me you didn't say what I just—Oh, my. Oh, my. Kiss. My. Ever-loving. Ass."

The roar of a Super Bowl crowd drowned out the general's voice. And not just in the office of C-3PO. Rather, from hundreds of offices in the Pentagon, every office where TV sets monitored one towering inferno at the World Trade Center. As numbed thousands cried out at once to see the same new disaster that brought the epithet to Spangler's lips.

A second aircraft, later identified as United Airlines Flight 175 en route from Boston to Los Angeles, slashed into view on a hundred million American TV screens, striking the South Tower of the World Trade Center, sending metal debris tearing through the building, spewing flames by the cloud-full.

"Good Christ," Bowers said, in the tone of a true prayer. *Don't let this be true*.

Spangler started a new entry on his PAL. He wrote down the date–time group—11SEP010903 hours—and waited for Bowers to assume his mantle as officer in charge of the military's antiterrorism efforts.

You didn't have to be a terrorism PhD or even an over-the-hill major banished to a cave in the Pentagon to study arcane terrorist writings all the way back to the time of Christ to know that a second plane was no accident. The first one, maybe, with a flight crew half-blind and drunk besides, maybe. *Maybe*. But two carbon-copy accidents within minutes of each other? A few dozen meters apart? Never. Flat fricking never.

"Roscoe?" The general was back. As director, C-3PO. "Course of action?" Mockery gone, seeking an old friend's advice, no apology offered, thinking none necessary between old friends and academy classmates.

Not so much that the bastard didn't know what. Just that he liked his battles to come at him from the last war, Desert Storm, all in set piece, all the tactical odds in his favor, a campaign of bombs first, so he could wear down his enemies, mostly political. In that kind of war, Bowers was a master at falling and not getting hurt. This, though, was instant war, coming early on a bright Tuesday in the a.m., no buildup, no warning. Now the general had to think on his feet and he didn't know what to do first, shit or go blind. So he'd try to get Spangler to lay his neck on the stump. That way, if the general fell, Spangler would be the one to get hurt.

Spangler knew a bit of politics himself, learned from a thousand knocks and hard falls that did hurt. Even so, he didn't pull his punch. "Launch an AirCap," he said. "Get the FAA to clear the skies." A course of action with balls. Too risky for the general. "Do it, Randy."

Silence. Except for the thunder rolling through the building as thousands of chairs scraped across tile floors, as hundreds of doors opened and slammed faster and harder than ever. A rumbling in the seventeen-mile-long, coiled bowel of the Pentagon.

As ten thousand heels clopped through the corridors at the double time. Five thousand breaks ended. Two thousand meetings adjourned. A thousand senior officers called a thousand sudden new meetings. Spangler's phone line to Bowers crackled with the surge in demand on the system.

"General Bowers?"

"I don't have the authority to do that, to launch fighter cover. Or go direct to the FAA, for that matter."

"Then talk to somebody who does."

"I'll run it up the flagpole."

"Randy, we're under attack here. You don't have time to sound out the brass or staff it, just get it done. You can't jump the Grand Canyon in two jumps, you have to make the grand leap, take it all at once. Go right to the SecDef if you have to. He's in the building today, isn't he?"

"Right." Pause. "I mean, roger, he's in the building, but—"

"So get his ear before all hell breaks loose. Ten minutes from now, he won't talk to anybody but the Joint Chiefs and the POTUS."

"Right." Wavering. "Get to him before the president does." Thinking it out loud. "That's good thinking." Tone of *Just not for me*.

"Affirm. Do it, Randy."

"I'm on it. Thanks."

Silence. You're on it? The hell you are. Don't make waves that'll wash your fourth star up on the beach of your precious empty career.

"Roscoe? One more thing? That operations plan you wanted me to staff around the building a couple months ago? What was it again?"

"Cradle of Fire?"

"There you go with the Cradle again. What Cradle?"

"Of Fire. *Cradle of Fire*, the SPECINTSUM—"

"No, cradle doesn't ring a bell. The sword thing. I'm talking about the one that hits back at terrorists all the way to—"

"Swift Sword, General. OPLAN *Swift Sword*."

"Right, *Swift Sword*. How far did we get with that?"

We? "You signed off on it." Coward. "But you wouldn't let me staff it." Asshole. "Remember the *FAF* you marked on the cover? You told me to file and forget, remember?" Another paper corpse for Spangler's Boneyard. *You spineless bastard mother—*

"Too sensitive to staff," Bowers said in his own defense.

"So I filed it away. In the Dead File." Limp-dick.

"A thing like that? One peep to the media and we'd all be on the carpet."

"But? But, what? I heard a *but* in there, Randy." A spike of adrenaline went through Spangler's heart.

"But this *Swift Sword*? It's Limited Distribution, right?"

"Roger, TS-CI, Eyes-Only, Lim-Dis." Spangler bit his lip. "And?"

"I dunno, Ros. Maybe I should take a look. No courier. You bring it by, you brief me on it, vis-a-vis. Refresh my memory."

Yes-s-s-s! "Sure thing." Spangler glanced at his day planner, lowered his voice, struggled to keep the gloating out of it. Oh, *yeah,* baby! "I've got my calendar here, General. What date is good for you?"

"Don't be a wise-ass, Ros. ASAP. Fast as you can haul-ass down here."

"Yes, sir."

"Ros?"

"Sir?"

"Anybody else know about this *Swift Sword*?"

"Just you and me."

"I dunno. You think it could get legs?"

I dunno. You think you got the rocks?

"Roscoe?"

"Hell, yes, General. Run with it."

Bowers silent, thinking it over. The general had a rep for being the strong, silent type. Spangler knew better. A sheep in sheep's clothing, the man just kept quiet because he didn't have anything to say. Even a moron can look wise—if he squints one eye and keeps his idiot mouth shut. Spangler heard a tentative intake of air. The general was about to nibble.

"Roscoe?"

"Yeah?"

"It's an ambitious plan. And bold, very bold, right."

"Better than none at all, General. A call for action in a time of inaction."

"Too bold, you think?"

"Man to man, Randy?"

"Yeah?"

"Thing like this? Two planes hitting the World Trade Center? A road map already in place? A plan with balls to hit back at these guys? Hit them where it hurts? I imagine there's maybe half a dozen other contingency plans floating around the building, but—" Spangler gave the general a moment to set the hook himself.

"But what?"

"You just watch. Hour from now, they'll be calling for plans. From the mountaintop. The guy that gets his on the table first looks like a visionary who saw the chance, saw the cause, saw the difference between a small event and a great moment in history. For this guy—" Pause. Make him ask for it. *Ask for it, you somebitch.*

"Go on? For the right guy? What?"

"A fourth star's a no-brainer."

The phone went dead. End of convo-sation. Spangler smiled. You had to smile. Nothing to tickle a general's weenie like the mention of another star.

Spangler gazed at the images on the television. His smile sagged into a grimace. "Crap," He never got to rub in *Cradle of Fire.* Somebitch didn't even remember its name, let alone what it was about.

0603 Hours PDT, September 11, 2001—Suburban Las Vegas

It took all of thirty seconds for Amy Tyler to go from a state of perfect calm to utter panic.

At second one, the baby squawked to remind her that she had muted the TV volume to answer the phone, a wrong number, thinking, Who'd be calling at this hour?

At second two, she caught a glimpse of the TV picture as she went to restore the volume to occupy her infant son. A movie had come on. A disaster movie. One of those *Die Hard for the Tenth Time and this Time Stay Dead, if You Don't Mind* films.

At three, she decided that kind of movie would never do to show her son, even if he was only six months old. Bad enough his father was a soldier. This kid wasn't going to be raised in a world of violence. Not if she could help it. So she changed channels.

And stopped counting the seconds. Because the same movie unreeled at the same moment in time on the second channel.

And the third.

She stopped flipping to read the screen-crawl. To see that this was a live picture. Real-time, as Conn would say. She pooched her bee-stung lips. *A fire in a high-rise? No, the World Trade—*

She dialed up the volume. To hear a solemn newsman's voice telling her, "Once again, live footage of the North Tower of the World Trade Center burning." Then a long, awkward silence of dead air.

"Unconfirmed reports tell us conflicting stories." Pause. "One that it was a bomb." Trying to think. "And remember the World Trade Center was bombed once before." Not much to say. "Another report says an airplane, perhaps a commercial airliner." Making up stuff as the tower burned. "Suggesting a commercial jet has flown into the building."

She leaned toward the screen and narrowed her sea-green eyes, as if that would help her make out details.

Just as a second airplane flew into the second tower of the World Trade Center.

Amy recoiled from the television set.

"Oh my God," the newsman cried out, giving voice to her mouth.

"Conn?"

"That was an airliner," the newsman said, "I repeat, definitely an airliner. I repeat, a second airliner has flown into the second tower, the South Tower of the World Trade Center."

"Connor?"

Amy Tyler felt her world shift on its axis.

She grabbed Brendan from his infant seat. To comfort him. No, to comfort herself. She was married to an expert in terrorism, but she didn't need an expert to tell her what had happened here. Or what might have happened to her husband.

Connor was flying home today. Yes, out of Washington, not New York, but who knew where those two planes had taken off from?

She ran to the phone and tapped out the number of his digital.

Her heart began to race when she heard his recorded message and spoke under her breath to him. "Why don't you ever leave your phone on, Connor?" She smothered Brendan's face with kisses while she waited for his interminable message to terminate. She inhaled his clean, sweet smell, felt his fuzzy hair wisp over her own cheek, her baby a security blanket now. The six-month-old Brendan squirmed, gasped, fussed. She relaxed her grip on him. He smiled, toothless, innocent, relieved.

At the tone she said, "Shit. Connor, call home as soon as you get this message. I need to talk to you."

She ended the call before it struck her. "Shit." She couldn't leave a message like that. She dialed him again, stamped one foot waiting for him to finish his interminable greeting. "Shit."

"Conn, honey, I'm fine," she said. "The baby is just fine. But I do need to talk to you as soon as possible. I love you. Call me, Conn. I love you."

She hung up. *Strange.*

That woman. The one from the wrong number just minutes ago. She had said the same word before the phone slammed down. *Shit?* In exactly the same tone. She had been worried, too. She'd said *shit* and banged the phone down without cutting the line. Said *shit* again, then the *bang* again. *Shit—bang. Shit—bang. Shit—bang?*

Three times in all? Why was she so upset? Upset about what? About Connor? No. Surely, not. But, then again—

Amy had met her husband through a friend. She had broken up his engagement to the friend. Other women, even other friends, kept trying to return the favor during their own short run before they said their vows at last. He'd look at them nice as you please, and they'd fall into his eyes. *Right in front of her.* She'd stopped using her diaphragm to get pregnant, to keep him close at all cost. Her baby her security blanket long before today. *Connor?*

With Brendan clutched to her hip, she pulled out the drawer on the telephone table. Her hand trembling, she flipped pages to the back of the address book. She felt dirty for what she was about to do. Dirty but justified. She had to know.

Brendan began to fuss, picking up her vibe.

In a blank space on the brochure that told how to use the phone, Connor had written his code. She dialed the number and used the code to get into his voice mail.

The first call was from a major at the Pentagon. Spangler. From an alphabet soup office, an acronym she didn't recognize. He wanted a callback. ASAP, he said. "In light of today's events," the major said.

She saved the message and accessed the second call.

"Connie, darling," said a woman. "Laren here." *Laren?* "I heard the news." *Laren calls him Connie?* "I'm worried sick about you. I know you're safe, but I'm worried sick." *She calls him darling?* "Call me at the office so I can make up for this morning? What I said? I love you, Connie. I love you. I love you." *Laren loves my husband?*

The woman's voice—*Connie and Laren making up? For this morning?*—came from far away now. Somehow, the phone had slipped from Amy's fingers. It lay on the floor. Brendan let out a squeal, a mournful cry. Infected by his mother, he began to sob, not in hunger, not in pain, not to fuss about a wet diaper, but from a broken heart. Even so, over the noise of the baby's pitiful cry and from all that way to the floor, she could hear that woman, that Laren. Still calling out to Amy's husband in panic. "I love you, Connie, I love you, I love you . . ."

0911 Hours EDT, September 11, 2001—Aboard United 411

Tyler could not shut his eyes. He did not want to see the replay of that jet flying into the Twin Towers—North Tower.

Then again, he had the Arab at the back of the plane on his mind, too. Enough so he sat cocked in the seat, keeping the nappy head at the corner of his vision. If the guy tried anything, he'd be ready. To do what? He didn't know for sure. He'd deal with it when it came up.

He saw RuthAnn weaving through first class, her eyes on him.

She leaned in close. "Sir?"

He turned his head from her breath, sweet but fetid. Anxiety breath. Besides, he didn't want to deal with the issue of her looking into his eyes.

"I told the captain you were an army officer," she said, glancing past him toward the rear of the cabin.

Tyler squinted at her: *Not an astronaut?* He saw where she was looking? She suspected the Arab, too? Why?

"You are an army officer? That's what you said, right?"

"Yes?" He breathed past her: *Canna Nine Lives.*

"The captain wants to talk to you."

"Beg pardon?"

"You saw the plane all-crash into the World Trade Center?"

"Yes?"

"The captain wants to talk to you about it. Can you come forward with me?" Her voice had grown thin, barely a bat squeak.

"Sure." He stood up to follow her, and knocked his head on the overhead again. "That's the third time I did that," he said with a sheepish grin. "You ought to give me a helmet."

She drank in his smile looking up at him, noticing. "No. It's just nerves. It just that you're so . . ."

He averted his eyes from hers. "We'd better go up front."

She shook her head as if to clear a thought, then checked past Tyler's shoulder. At the Arab. What did she know about the guy with the goofy ears? He looked back to see for himself. The Arab was sleeping. Or else faking it. She led the way forward.

Tyler's stomach pitched as the plane hit a pocket. He felt the aisle tilt beneath his feet. That other jet's wings had dipped before it slammed into the tower. So, why was this aircraft turning now? It gave him a chill to think it.

RuthAnn held open the cockpit door. He looked into her eyes. *Contact.* She noticed him now. As he ducked down and stepped up to the door, she put a hand to his back. She pushed him inside. She was none too subtle about it, her fingers digging into his ribs. She stood close to his back, close enough for him to feel both of her breasts nudge him. Ahead of him, the copilot was flying. The captain was finishing up with the last button on his uniform jacket. Tyler didn't get a good vibe from the man, gray and unkempt around the edges. Wrinkled collar. Flakes of dandruff dotting the blue black shoulders of his uniform. A bit of a rancid breeze from the armpits. Not as much pride in the sky as he once had. Beyond him, through the windshield, the horizon tilted. Tyler saw no buildings here above the tops of clouds. Still, he wanted to know about the banking turn.

He held out his hand as he glanced at the name tag, thumb-worn in a spot just off center from being pushpinned onto his uniform. "Captain Randolph, I'm Conner Tyler," he said, "Captain, U.S. Army."

The captain turned away and reached down and out of sight to the right of the pilot's seat. When he stood up and looked up to face Tyler, he did not smile, did not introduce himself, did not take Tyler's hand. He brandished a short-handled hatchet.

Tyler pulled his hand back. "What's the deal?"

The airline captain looked him up-and-down-and-up and fixed his stare on Tyler's hair. "What are you, Delta Force or something?" His look said he doubted it. "I hope so. Other-wise, you sure don't look very army-officer to me, okay? More a rock star or—" He stepped into Tyler's space. Tyler held his ground. To avoid shoving back against RuthAnn as much as anything.

"Are you Delta Force?" Randolph's powers of observation were sharper than his grooming habits. The question did not catch Tyler off his guard, though. Part of his Delta Force training was to prepare for it. His face went on auto-smile: *Don't be silly.* One of the stock answers they had trained him to keep at hand: "You've been watching too many movies, sir. I've been in grad school at Berkeley for the past two years." He put on his best sincere smile. "But I am an army officer. Combat engineer." He flapped a hand between them, finger pointed at the weapon, like a fireman's ax, with a spike opposite the blade, the handle of fiberglass, not wood. "What's with the hatchet?"

"Crash ax, okay?"

"Crash ax then." Did they teach that anal-retentive stuff in airliner school? "When somebody waves it at you, it doesn't matter whether he calls it a crash ax or a hatchet."

"Sorry," he said to Tyler, "Okay, we're not altogether ourselves this morning. This is a desperate situation, okay?" To RuthAnn, "Okay, is he still in his assigned seat?"

She broke the weld between her chest and Tyler's back.

"Desperate situation?" Tyler wanted to know.

"Yes, sir." RuthAnn's voice trembled.

"What's he doing, okay?"

"Desperate situation?"

"Sleeping, totally sleeping."

The captain looked at Tyler. Rather, at his hair again. Tyler felt RuthAnn gazing at the side of his face.

"We're allowed to wear our hair long," Tyler said. "To blend in with the Berkeley population. What's the desperate situation and why is the aircraft in a turn?"

RuthAnn leaned into his left elbow. She wanted him to look her way. She wanted another sip of his eyes. He would not meet her gaze. He understood. It was a purely a visceral thing, leaning to him for security, finding it in his eyes. An animal thing in the reassuring touch. He had learned that in his classes about hostage rescue. Normal for any woman—any man for that matter. But . . . *Christ, not now, woman.*

"Okay," the captain said, "you saw the first plane go into the World Trade Center?"

"First plane?"

"Okay, a second airliner struck the South Tower a little while ago, okay? We've been ordered to land at an alternate, we're turning back to Charlotte." He gave it a second to sink in. He and Tyler spoke the word at the same time:

"Terrorists."

Tyler's heart found a new gear. It pumped hard and fast, giving him a rush of adrenaline. *Both towers? Good God.*

Randolph pulled a wad of paper from his jacket pocket. "Read this. It came off the cockpit printer."

His hand shook as he handed over a ragged scrap ripped from the printer. Tyler pulled the wrinkles flat. The text, in all-caps, gave a stark, urgent order: SHUT DOWN ALL ACCESS TO FLIGHT DECK.

"Damn." Tyler steadied himself against the cockpit door.

RuthAnn let him have his space back. He stood straight. Don't shake her confidence in him. She could help with what was to come.

The airline captain spoke Tyler's thoughts. "Not a commercial jet jock in the world a terrorist could induce to fly into a building, okay? A pilot might bore it into the ground. Might try ditching in the Atlantic. But fly a plane full of people into the World Trade Center full of people? Never. Okay, I have to think that somebody on board those aircraft took over the controls." His throat worked up and down like a pump cylinder. "After killing the crew."

RuthAnn gasped. Tyler nodded. Yesterday's Scotch whiskeys had dulled his senses today. He was in a combat situation ever since he'd seen that first craft go in. And not in the least prepared for it, either in mind or body. Now he felt an adrenaline kick. His mind began to work on a combat plan. He was a soldier. Delta. The best in the world. Or so they said. He began to think in military terms: the five-paragraph field order.

Paragraph One, the *Situation*, starting with the enemy. Simple. Terrorists were taking over airliners and flying them into buildings. Only one threat came to mind. The Arab near the back of the coach, the guy with the ears.

Paragraph Two, the *Mission*. His fought the instinct to feel shame. A pro shouldn't need two attacks to make the point that his plane was in danger.

Still, he had no time to waste in regrets. Put your regrets into your after-action report, his toughest mentor had said. You don't have time for regrets in combat.

Yes, combat. This was combat. He knew what Randolph wanted. He wanted muscle. To go with the crash ax. To keep the Arab and any of his pals from taking over this plane.

Trouble was, they had closed the door. They had lost sight of the Arab, their enemy. The man might even now be coming at them, pistol in hand. Other men behind the first, strapped in plastic charges.

Paragraph Three, the *Execution*. As they say in the army, *Whaddya gonna do now, captain?* He narrowed his eyes at Randolph and hatched a plan of action into the air. "Go with me. Hide that damned ax. Don't look at the guy. Look to the back of the plane, as if we're going by. Let me handle him when we get to him."

Paragraph Four, *Admin and Logistics.* Simple enough. The ax was all the materiel they had, the only weapon. Except for his hands and feet. His head and heart.

Tyler nodded at the ax. "Don't be swinging that thing around, got it?"

The airline captain gave Tyler a look that said: *Hell with that.* "I'm the captain of this craft, okay?"

Paragraph Five, *Command and Signal.*

"No question about that, Cap. You're in command. I just don't want you behind me chopping cotton. I'm no good to you if you whack me on the head with that thing or hit an innocent, maybe start a riot back there."

Randolph's face went blank. "Okay. Right." He began nodding. "Okay, I'll wait until you give me the word."

"Don't sweat the one guy. Leave the Arab to me. You keep your eyes open for a second guy, maybe a third."

The airline captain put on a tough look. Tyler gave a weak smile. Barney Fife with BO. Tyler figured he was on his own for the actual combat. He looked to RuthAnn. "You up to crowd control?"

She nodded and stood up to her full six feet tall and leaned to him again. Crowd control she understood. She had a role. He had their trust.

"Ready?"

They both nodded. Now. If he could live up to their faith in him.

"Let's go," Tyler said, as he crouched and shoved the door open, fist clenched to throw the first blow, gut tensed to take one.

But no, the aisle was clear. All the way back to the Arab, who had given up the fight with his pillows.

All the way back to the Arab who locked eyes with him. Wary, hostile eyes. The eyes of a terrorist, just as surly as every wanted poster Tyler had ever seen of them. That was not a curious man. It was a fearful man, and ready to fight. He'd seen that face. *What? On an intel brief? Where?*

Tyler stopped cold. The airline captain bumped into his back, poking him with the crash ax. Tyler pulled the door toward himself, just enough so he could keep eye-to-eye with the terrorist poster boy sitting there in living color.

So much for Plan A.

0919 Hours EDT, September 11, 2001—The Pentagon

Spangler laid a file the size of a novel onto his desk, gently, as if it were sheaves of glass instead of paper drilled and strapped with flat metal bindings. His own Great American Novel. Wrapped in a huge Tyvek envelope, labeled: TOP SECRET-COMPARTMENTALIZED INFORMATION, EYES-ONLY, LIMITED DISTRIBUTION.

Copy 0001 of 0001. The one and only *Swift Sword*. When he first handed it over to Bowers half a year ago, he crowed, "I give you *Swift Sword*, an OPLAN as creative as any Tom Clancy novel." Bowers shook his head and said, "As long as I've known you, Ros. And yet . . . and yet . . . you still have the ego to amaze me." *And yet,* in the tone of it, *you have so much to be modest about.*

Bowers gave it a fast skim, his only remark: "Ros, where do you get these ideas?"

"Randy?"

"Bury it."

"But, Randy—"

"No buts. I've got another project to keep you busy." And one more after that. And another still. Keep the Spangler guy busy, busy, busy. Outta sight, outta mind, outta trouble. Busy and silent about terrorist threats. They accused him of crying wolf—or in his case, Jackal—at every glitch in the American way of life. A brownout on the West Coast, and Bowers's staff would give a time hack and wait for Spangler to show up with a theory about a terrorist strike at power lines in the west.

Spangler couldn't just soldier up and do the time. Put in his single-digit months to retirement. Twenty-four years and out. As a major. For a West Point graduate, a disgrace.

And yet, he had to try to keep on trying. And today. This was his finest hour as a soldier. To blink into this brief lime-light. This proof that he was right. This moment of redemption. This act of terror. This America. This army. This *Swift Sword*.

He stroked the Tyvek. *My* Swift Sword.

In the full-length mirror tucked away beside the coat rack. He caught a glimpse of himself and didn't like what he saw. To be sure, not a lot to work with. Hair gray and slicked back. The Nike-swoop-to-the-left nose, the result of a Blackhawk crash and fire. Black-frame specs with black lenses rode crooked on his crooked face. The too pale skin, the result of the fire and infection, a condition that should have kept him out of Desert Storm in the first place, which, if he had minded his doctors, would have kept him from the blunder of his career and the court-martial that followed. The lips, blubbery, wet, and wide. And crooked, turned down at one corner, pulled up at the other like the Joker, for shit's sake, the look of the perpetual wiseass. His body bent at the hips, an injury from the crash. Legs bent by arthritis, knocking knees that made him a poor marcher. Feet too big for somebody who never played basketball, and pigeon-toed besides. Not too nimble, Jack, and not too quick, either.

Even before the crash, he had to deal with his looks. His looks were the reason he owned a German wirehaired pointer as a young man. Always the winner in the ugly dog contest at the spring bird hunts, Ludwig simply let Spangler look better by contrast. Or so he thought. Until they gave him the award the year after Ludwig died, and he had no dog at the hunt. Two lasts: last dog, last club hunt.

Even so, none of these flaws bothered him as much as the smirk on his lips, not entirely due to the scar-pull. He gave himself a rationale. A quote from his personal god, Winston Churchill: *War is a game that's played with a smile. If you can't smile, grin. If you can't grin, keep out of the way until you can.*

True, this was war. But no, this was not the grin of a war-rior. His was a smug grin. People had died, and he felt smug about it? No wonder his Pentagon weenie pals stared at him as if he were an albino idiot. They were right. The thought wiped the smirk off his face. Fine to be right about the terrorists, but don't prove them right about him. Let them think he was as lame in mind as in body. Let them underestimate him. Let them err. Let them see the runt of the litter and never the vein of pure, raw resolve that ran beneath the external flaws. Never let them see the utter ruthlessness, the willingness to strike at his enemy, no matter what the color of his skin or uniform.

He asked the question, his own daily prayer: *Can you kill, Roscoe? Can you kill?*

"Yes, I can," he said to the mirror. *I'm pretty sure.*

With a corner of his hanky, he touched up a smudge on the dark lenses of his glasses without taking them off. Nobody else could stand to look him in the eyes, irises pink for lack of pigment, and right now he sure as hell didn't want to gaze into his own eyes, either. He found his gig-line off and hitched his trousers to the left so his fly, the right side of his belt buckle, and his necktie came into alignment. He tossed his necktie over his left shoulder so he could adjust the line of his shirt underneath. By the time the necktie came down again, he saw that he looked as worried as he felt. Instead of feeling smug about *Swift Sword,* which might take days, if not weeks to implement, he should have been thinking of more urgent actions, one in particular. The bold stroke he'd tried to goad from Bowers.

Can you kill? Can you really?

Yes, dammit, yes.

"Then walk the talk, Roscoe." He locked the door to his cubbyhole. If the general or one of his munchkins were to walk in on him and overhear what he was about to say over the telephone—

Scott picked up on the first ring.

"Scotty, Spangler, I need a second."

"Roscoe? You crazy, man?" Scott huffed into the phone as if in a sprint. "You got any idea what's going down? You seen what's on the TV? Man, I don't have a second."

"Don't hang up, Scotty. This is about the crashes." Spangler could hear other anxious men yelling to each other inside New York's Air Traffic Control Center. "Are you still there?"

"Whaddya got? Quickly, man, quickly."

Spangler read the situation. He knew what was going on in the guy's head. Any second now Scott might yet hang up on the creepy fish-belly white over-the-hill army major with the Stevie Wonder glasses and the red eyes he sat next to once a month at a low-level FBI terrorist briefing with less in substance than Spangler's personal open-source clipping file.

"You know I'm calling from the Pentagon, right?" Spangler said, "From the antiterrorist office?"

"Okay, fine, fine. Whaddya got?" Scott yelled over the chaos in his own office. "Anything I can use in the here and now?"

Spangler hesitated. Friend or no friend, if Bowers ever found out—*Can you really, really kill?*

What the hell. Worst they could do was court-martial him. Again. "Scotty, can you get to a decision maker? Get somebody to clear the skies? We need to put every plane on the ground."

"Overall U.S. airspace?"

"Affirmatory."

"You crazy, man? Must be four thousand aircraft up there."

"Think. Two crashes. It's the work of terrorists." Spangler cringed. If he was wrong, he was dead. Even if he was right, Bowers would put him up on charges.

"Terrorists? For sure? Some of us been thinking, man."

The magic word. Spangler went with the T-word. Might as well go for the gold, the general court. "No thinking to it. We have highly classified technical intel. A-1 source. It's terrorists, pal. There could be more. You may not have a TV where you are, but—"

"TV? Hell we don't need a TV, we got line-a-sight to the World Trade Center. We saw them bore in, man. Both towers, both planes. We're looking at them smoking like—Wait."

Spangler heard his man shouting to somebody in the office: "No, I need this phone, I'm talking to the Pentagon here. . . . Hell, yes, about the crashes. It's the Pentagon, man . . . about the crashes, about . . ."

"Scotty, don't."

"Hell yes, it's about terrorists." Then, into the phone again, "You still here, man?"

"Don't use my name," Spangler said, hissing in his throat. "You can't use my name or say you got this from the Pentagon. I mean, where you got it in the Pentagon."

"Man, why the hell not?" A note of suspicion.

"For chrissakes, Scotty, just revealing what we know so soon would compromise our tech sources for fifty years down the road, man." Now into using Scott's own tone and idiom, mirroring—*We in this together, man.* "Whaddya thinking, man? I mean, the truth's so precious, we have to lie about it." Spangler waited a second to see if his own lie would take. He warmed over with a confident, forgiving, intimate, "But you know that, man."

"Right. Sorry, man. Things are just so—"

"Can you get a boss with the nads to clear the skies?"

"Doubt it. All the bigwigs—"

"Try, dammit, can't you at least try?"

"They already declared ATC Zero, man. They're not going to order something stricter until that's had a chance to take."

"What's ATC Zero? I'm not up on that term."

"Zero flights in the Air Traffic Control Center, practically Boston to Baltimore to the middle of Pennsylvania, nothing in or out of New York City's airfields, flat nothing."

Spangler bit his lip. "That won't cut it, Scotty. You have to get them to stop them all. Set them down."

"Full groundstop? All over the country? You nuts? What the hell can I do? Man, I'm just a controller supervisor—wait, the bigwigs're asking for advice from the floor."

"What's groundstop?"

"Nothing can take off."

"Still not enough. Empty the skies. Set every plane down, every ass on the ground, man."

"You crazy? That's never been done before, not in the history of aviation. They'll think I'm crying wolf." Wavering.

"Tell them, Scotty, for the good of the country. Think of all the lives you're going to save. Tell them, man—"

Spangler realized Scott wasn't listening anymore. He was

shouting. Not at his off-the-wall Pentagon contact, but into the chaos of the Air Traffic Control Center.

"Full groundstop," he shouted. "Stop everything. Just stop them where they are. In case they're terrorists, man."

Spangler hung up on the juiced-up racket Scott's suggestion had injected into the chaos. It wasn't all he wanted, but it was a move. Right or wrong, he had put the issue on the table, stirring it like a nest of fire ants. Now he could have nothing more to do with it. The idea would play itself out at its own pace, and he could only hope that Bowers never found out about his phone call.

One more thing to deal with before—

The telephone rang, jangling his nerves. He came to attention, straightened his glasses, and picked up.

"Roscoe, where the hell are you?"

Bowers! What did he know? Was his phone tapped?

"Roscoe? You there?"

"Yes, sir. I was just reviewing *Swift Sword* in my head so I could brief you on—"

"No time for reviewing. Get down here."

"Okay, Randy, but I need to brief you before—"

"You don't have time to brief me. Get up to my office and bring *Swift Sword* with you."

Bring the OPLAN but don't brief it? "Sir? You don't want me to brief you? You said—"

"Not me, somebody else wants a briefing, somebody special."

"May I ask who?"

"It's X-rated, Roscoe, I can't say on an open line."

The X-Men? Roscoe Spangler briefing the X-Staff? He looked for a place to sit. What next? Condy Rice? Dubya himself?

"Major?"

"Sir?"

"You're not here already?"

Spangler heard the gentle sarcasm in the tone: *Your big moment, and you're not jumping out of your albino blotchy giraffe skin?*

"Roscoe, this might be just the chance for you to trade in the gold oak leaves for silver."

"Thank you, sir." A step up in rank? Nice but—"Randy?"

"Don't say it, Ros. I'm already dealing with one terrorist scare. Don't dream up another one."

"I'm thinking a second wave of attacks. The kind of badasses we're dealing with, that's right up their alley. They smash a couple planes into the World Trade Center for a diversion, then strike a political or military target. Something big, maybe a nuclear power plant, a suitcase nuke, a dirty bomb. Something symbolic. The Pentagon, the White House, a truck bomb parked outside the World Trade Center, to get the rescue crews—"

"I just told you not to bring up another scare, and what do you do? You invent a dozen. Forget a damned second wave. I've got my hands full with the first one. Now, get your ass in gear. I'm overdue at the Bat Cave. You can brief me on the ride over."

"Sir—"

"Haul ass."

Spangler wasn't done. Then again, Bowers knew that. That's why he'd slammed the phone in his ear.

0926 Hours EDT, September 11, 2001—Aboard Flight 411

Captain Randolph talked up into Tyler's neck.

"Okay, what? What's he doing? Is he coming?"

"No. But he's looking right at me. He smells a rat."

The Arab with the jumbo spider-ears sat up in his seat. Alert and tense. Worse, afraid.

Tyler sized up his man. The ears of a boxer. Once you got past the big ears, he was lean of face with black, angry eyes. Short-cropped hair like Velcro loops, some African blood in the mix. Thick black brows over a black stare. Wide, square shoulders filling out a cheap navy blazer and baby blue shirt.

The Arab twitched and reached inside his blazer.

Tyler got another kick in the pulse. He reached back, not taking his eyes off his man. He had to act. He had to act fast now.

"Give me that ax."

"What's he doing?"

"Now."

Tyler felt the cold slap of the hatchet grip in his palm.

The Arab's hand came out of the jacket with a cell phone.

No relief in that. Tyler knew an empty cell case would take enough plastic comp to blow this ship in two. He shoved through the door and strode down the aisle, keeping the ax on his right thigh. He could hear Randolph clip-clop along behind him. He was no coward; give him that.

Plan B: *I'm a federal marshal. Mind if we step to the back of the plane, sir?*

With the pilot at his heels? An innocent man would not resist.

Tyler took in the civilians in one sweep of his eyes. Only a few paid him any mind, two women on the make and one acne-faced gay teen. They were after eye contact. He ignored them. The others had eyes only for the airline captain coming down the aisle behind him. He saw no fear or anger or hatred in any other face. So far, only the one man to deal with. The Arab.

Still thirty feet to go. The Arab still held the phone to one fat ear. Then he flinched, and his eyes went wide. He bared his teeth in a gape of fear.

Damn. More fear was just what Tyler did not want to see. Fear meant guilt. The guy knew he was busted.

The Arab moved fast. With one swift flick of his hand, his seat belt came free, and the arm rest went up.

So much for Plan B.

The marshal plan not an option, Tyler broke into a jog down the aisle. Still ten feet from his man. No way to avoid a fight now.

"He's got a hatchet," somebody yelped. Tyler half expected Randolph to say, "No, it's a crash ax."

The Arab flung his cell aside, to Tyler's relief. No bomb, no weapon. Just a phone.

"Keep your seats," a voice behind him said. Randolph. "This is your captain speaking. Keep your seats, okay?"

Tyler felt his mouth drawn tight into an attack mask. No hope for an easy end to this now.

The Arab slid into the aisle, coiled like a cobra. He planted his feet like a wrestler, then shifted his weight, ready to throw a kick.

Not a wrestler, Tyler saw. A martial arts fighter. God, what was he up against?

He darted at the Arab to close before the kick could get up to full speed, taking the blow on his left shin.

It stung, but he kept his feet. He showed the ax in his right hand. When the Arab winced from it, Tyler drove at him with a left, his half fist aiming for the nose. Break the nose, blind him with tears, flood the back of his throat with blood—right out of the book of manual combat.

But the Arab had read the book, too. He shied left, and Tyler's blow just clipped him. Rather than try to hold his spot, he rolled, onto his back and over, coming to his feet. Again, balanced. *Shee-it.* This was one helluva fighter. He growled to get his doubt under control.

The man was a terrorist, but he was Connor Tyler, a Delta fighter, for chrissake. The best in the world. *Bring it on, Abu.*

The Arab had gained some space with the roll. Tyler had to be wary now of a lethal kick, now that there was room for one.

Blood streamed from the hooked Arabic nose. It gave Tyler a boost of energy, but he doubted he'd broken it. The blow had not felt solid.

He felt an urge to leap in, in case the man had a pistol or a knife. Doubt held him back. Not doubt in himself, but doubt that the man was armed. He would have made a try for a shiv already, if he had one. No, this man's weapons were his feet and his hands. And his terrorist's aim of virgins galore.

Behind him, the civilians began to panic, men yelling their prayers, women crying theirs.

This much he heard. No more did he allow himself. He put all his focus on the Arab.

This guy had done more than swing from hand to hand on the monkey bars as other guys in black sheets did in the one stock video clip that every TV net used every other week. He moved like a cat. A big and deadly cat.

Yes, he was good. But equal to a Delta Force soldier? No way. Tyler reminded himself: he had drawn first blood. The man wiped the sleeve of his blazer across his nose, his jaw slack as he sucked air through his mouth. Nose broken, after all. Tyler held back. Gave him a bit of a wicked, sure smile. *Drown in it, Abu.* Let him feel the panic.

A woman called out behind him, "A bomb. He's got a bomb."

Whoops and cries rose up, in Tyler's ears as well as his own throat. He put them away. No, he could not.

A bomb? A second terrorist, after all? Adrenaline kicked him in the chest. He dared not turn to face a new threat. And he dared not let down his guard on the threat in front of him.

The Arab rallied at the news. He set his jaw and kicked high with his right foot, not so much a blow as a feint. Tyler knew the move. The man wanted him to back up, to get caught between steps. It felt so . . . familiar.

Next in the move, if it was truly the move he knew—yes, here it was—three fast hand jabs, a left-right-left.

Tyler didn't wait for the finish, the left foot coming through to strike him in the knee or groin. Instead of backing off yet another step, he moved inside the arc of the kick. He lifted a knee to protect himself and swung the ax. This swing not a feint.

It ended just as they said it should in the sand pits at Fort Bragg. He caught a second kick on the shin, cutting the arc to his groin. Again it stung. But surely not so much as the ax blade chopping the terrorist at the hairline above his left eye. The Arab threw up his left arm to block the blow. The ax handle struck his forearm. Tyler thought he heard the sound of a bone-crack from the arm. Even so, the blade edge sank into the man's skull. Tyler marveled at the sound he felt more than heard amid the riot going on behind him. Sharp and sweet, like a line drive double to the power alley in left.

The terrorist crumpled to his knees, then fell back. He grabbed at the ax handle, fighting to pull the blade from his head. He and Tyler both pulling at it, Tyler wanting to hit another line drive. But even together they could not dislodge it. Tyler saw the eyes roll up, the sockets bathed in blood. The terrorist fell flat on his back, his legs under his butt. Tyler let go of the ax. Unless he was faking it, the Arab was a threat no more. Tyler grabbed the man's genitals and twisted. The Arab did not flinch. Out cold, maybe dead. There was no lying still for that move. And no time to gloat.

Tyler whirled to face the guy who had the bomb behind him.

0932 Hours EDT, September 11, 2001—The Pentagon

Lieutenant General Randall Bowers IV met his West Point classmate, Major Roscoe Spangler, at the door of his office, west wing, outer ring. The E-Ring. Bowers didn't greet him but held out his hand.

Spangler felt a hitch in his elbow before he handed over the package. This was his plan. He didn't want to give *Swift Sword* to anybody, not even his boss.

Bowers saw the hitch. He grinned and shook his head. "It's okay, Ros, I've got the need to know."

"Sorry, sir."

"Plan's no good if nobody sees it."

Spangler could see Bowers was enjoying this. Needling the toad-man. He knew the guy. He wasn't going to let up, either.

"Nagging the hell out of me to look at this thing. And now you don't want me to see it?"

Bowers took out a pocketknife and slid the blade under the flap of the Tyvek envelope. Spangler saw him flip to the executive summary of the two-inch-thick OPLAN. It figured. Trying to get up to speed in a hurry. A staff officer of his was going to brief the X-Staff, the most important emergency American entity that nobody knew about outside the small circle of X-Men on it and the only slightly larger group of men—hardly ever women—called before it to brief. Spangler only knew about it because he had stood for a sufficient number of dirty martinis to loosen up his boss's tongue.

"Are you ready to brief?"

"You get the word out about grounding civil aviation? About launching an AirCap?"

Bowers, still reading, shrugged. "I passed it up the chain. It's handled."

That was Bowers. A staff action passed is a staff action completed, the Pentagon's version of passing the buck. "Sir—"

Bowers shut him up with a harsh stare. "Are you? Ready to brief?"

Spangler literally bit his tongue to keep from telling General Cowardly Lion he'd already shut down the takeoff part of civil aviation on his own measly major's authority. Ah, what the hell, the easy road is always mined. You had to—

"Roscoe, dammit, are you ready to brief?"

"Yes, sir." He had to brief, of course. Bowers didn't know the plan well enough to do it. Only one man in the world knew it, the man who had written it. Nobody ever expected to use it. It and ten thousand other OPLANs had to be written: nukes against Pyongyang, troops against Toronto. Contingencies that would not come to pass. Still you wrote the plans, three or four contingencies for every occasion, all fleshed out in precise detail so you can jump from one to the other like a cat. Then you forgot them, because, most times, their very existence was too sensitive even to let on.

The United States had plans to use strike forces in every possible situation, on virtually every other nation in the world. Nobody could talk about such plans, of course. The media would eat you alive if it knew Montreal was on a hit list, say, in case French separatists took control of the country, took control of the military—such as it was—and took American diplomats hostage. If they did find out, it'd be: *Pentagon Brass Ready to Invade Canada*.

Still, you had to have such a plan, no matter how improbable the event. Because the rat-bastards would eat you alive if the stinky-cheese-eating French separatists actually did take over the American Embassy in Montreal, and you didn't have a plan: *Pentagon Brass Caught with Pants Down—Again!*

Bowers closed up the plan and slid it into the envelope. Spangler held out his hand. The general tucked it under his own arm. "You brief it when I give you the word."

Spangler stifled a laugh of his own. The man had to carry it himself, at least make it look as if he knew one whit about *Swift Sword*.

Bowers consulted his watch. "Zero-nine-thirty-eight. We go on at ten-hundred hours. Let me get a notepad."

He ducked inside his office, speaking over his shoulder to Spangler. "Nervous, Ros?"

Spangler hid a smile behind one hand. "No, sir." Not as nervous as his general, who did not remember that he couldn't get into the Bat Cave with a notepad. Nobody took notes, he had told Spangler one night under the influence of three dirty Stolys straight up, extra olives. Nobody kept records of what went on there. The Bat Cave was the Area 51 of politics. The X-Men didn't exist any more than ET, not on paper, not on tape, not anywhere but in the minds of people with imaginations run wild. The Nixon tapes had taught everybody in government not to keep certain records of—

"What the hell?"

"General?" Over the general's shoulder he saw a black, opaque shadow flit past the window—no, through it. The searing cloud hit Bowers in the back and Spangler in the face.

0938 Hours EDT, September 11, 2001—Aboard Flight 411

Tyler turned to face an attack from the rear. He saw the airline captain pushing passengers back into their seats, waving his arms like a conductor to calm them. Nobody heard his shouts above the din in the cabin, the screaming, the begging, the praying at full holler.

RuthAnn had regained her composure. She might not have the training to do anything but cry at the news of the World Trade Center attacks, but she knew what to do in this plane. She had trained to handle panic. She and a steward whom Tyler had not even seen before tried to restore order with no great effect. Their own orders and demands were nothing more than pleas and cajoling added to the racket. Terrified by the fight and the sight of blood, the passengers could get out of control and cause a crash.

Still, as he took in the scene, Tyler did not care so much about the disorder. He needed to find the second attacker, the man with the bomb. He didn't see a second threat among the flailing arms and cringing bodies. He saw no eyes intent on murder among the rabbit eyes. Still, he needed help, to be sure. He needed people to be quiet so he could sort things out. He needed one person to point the finger at the second terrorist.

He was an army officer, a Delta officer, for chrissake. He knew how to get order in a group of soldiers, no matter how noisy they were. He took a deep breath, tensed his gut, and cut loose from his diaphragm.

"Listen up! You people pipe down. Now!"

It froze the cabin into silence, except for two souls, one a hysterical man keening on the floor, the other an infant wailing near the front of coach.

Tyler yelled, "I'm a federal sky marshal on antiterrorist duty aboard this flight." He made up the lie on the spot, to answer all the questions about his hairstyle even before they came up. "Where's the second terrorist?"

He looked around. The looks on their faces told him: no second terrorist. *What? What the hell was all the fuss, then?* Two women, their hair so white it was blue, sat hugging each other. They each released one arm long enough to point out their second attacker. They pointed at him.

One timid voice, an older man piped up. "We thought it was you. We thought you had a pipe bomb."

Tyler let himself relax a notch. No second terrorist. He shook his head. Him, a terrorist? With a pipe bomb disguised to look like an ax, for chrissake? He didn't mind civilians. In fact, he liked most of them and loved a few in particular, those with the right eyes. Hell, he would love to love them all. But did they have to be such nitwits?

Spangler went blind. He felt himself flying. Until he hit the wall of a cubicle, then he fell to the floor. The floor bucked him back into the air. He smelled jet fuel—he knew jet fuel, and this was it. He felt the searing heat of jet fuel burning. He heard the roar of the fuel fire and willed himself not to breathe. He dare not breathe. To inhale would be to die. He knew. He'd been in that Blackhawk burning. He'd run away, leaving men to die, men he might have saved. The smell of fuel brought back the moment, but he didn't need a dream. This was a live fire. Again. Christ, what were the odds? Twice in a lifetime? Was God so perverse? Was there a God? Better not take a chance. Better to pray.

Dear God, if there is a god, save my soul, if I have a soul.

Amid the roar of burning, he heard screams. Huge mistake. A waste of life to use up their air at the pain of being burned. For next they would have to suck hard. On flames. He wiped the lenses of his dark glasses and felt a sting as glass shredded the skin on his forefinger.

Shards of glass blown in from the windows. Spikes of it had stuck in the lenses of his wraparound specs. Saving his eyes.

A gust of cool air hit him. So fresh it could only have come from outside the office. The blow-back of the fire. He allowed himself a breath. He had only a few seconds. He tore off his bloodied glasses and looked around. A blinding light from outside. For chrissakes. The morning sun. Terrorists, the enemy at the gates, had breached the walls of the Pentagon. They'd hit the army where they lived. No way, way. How? Could? They?

Too much. Too much. Much too much for him to grasp.

A spate of fear struck him in the chest. *Swift Sword.*

There, lying on the floor in its Tyvek coat, smoldering, the envelope oozing flames as he watched. He threw himself on it. *Swift Sword* no longer his great American novel, no longer his reason to be. This belonged to more than the army. Yes. This was America's reason to be.

A voice cried out to him from the uproar. "Roscoe." Screeching, "Roscoe, help me."

Backlit by the brilliant light from the outside, he saw a figure on the floor, flailing at the flames on his head with one hand, reaching out to him with the other. Bowers. Reaching through the smoke and flames of his own burning body. Bowers smelled like roasting meat. *Dear God (I believe in you, God), I'll never grill a burger again.*

"Randy? God, Randy, you're on fire." His hair on fire, his back stripped of its clothing, bleeding as if he'd been scourged. Somehow he had survived the first blast, back-shot by a cannon load of glass.

Screeching, "Roscoe, help me. Roscoe, help me, help me."

Spangler looked toward the hall. Smoke roiled down the E-Ring from ceiling to floor. He couldn't see flames, but he knew what would happen next, when oxygen got to that superheated cloud of fuel vapor. There'd be no escape down the E-Ring. It would ignite. And it would fry every man and woman in the hall.

He picked up his precious *Swift Sword* and ran toward Bowers.

"Thank you, Roscoe." A screech of gratitude.

The major stepped over the general and ran to the fallen wall. He staggered outside. Into the fresh air he ran, air so fresh and so cold, he couldn't breathe it deep enough. Into the light he ran, light so bright he could only run blind.

Can you kill, Roscoe, can you kill?

Is there any doubt?

To his left he felt the raging heat and saw a shadow so black he couldn't see through it. So he turned right and ran toward the cold light, *Swift Sword* held to his chest. He felt its heat, from the fire. He felt its weight, much too heavy now, from its value. Now that he had chosen it over Bowers, his boss, his friend, the weight of it too much. It dragged him down. He stumbled, fell, and got up again. A secondary explosion blew him across the grass and onto his face. He held onto his *Swift Sword* still. *Swift Sword.* More than his own life, this was the life of the country.

Strong hands picked him up. Shaking voices told him, "You're all right, Major. You're safe now."

The scared voices did not sell it, but Major Roscoe Spangler did not need them to tell him he was all right. He had gone through his trial of fire. God had given him a second run at life. The first time, he had panicked. He had run away leaving men to die in a fire, saving himself.

Not so this time. This time he had run away from a fire, not to save himself, but to save a country, his country, this country.

Spangler felt a shadow and flinched. This time, though, the shadow was cold.

One of the voices told him, "Wait here for a medic."

"Medic? Why would I need a medic?"

"Jeez, Major, just look at your face, your arm."

He opened his eyes against the light of day.

A young black man, himself in sunglasses, recoiled from his look. "Jeez, man, what happened to your eyes? They all, like red and shit, like a vampire or some shit. That happen in the fire?"

"Not the fire. It's a thing I got from—" Spangler shook his head. He wasn't going into that.

"I'm all right," Spangler said. "Go on with your buddy there, see if you can help somebody else."

They turned to leave him in the shade of a tree.

"Wait," he called. "I'm blind without dark glasses."

The black kid pulled his off. "Here, take my cheaters." *And don't be beaming them vampire eyes at me no more.*

"Thanks. I'll try to find you later."

The kid's head snapped away from Spangler. *What for?*

"You know, to return them."

The kid looked at Spangler's bloody, oozing face and shook his head. "Forget that shit, man." He walked away, flapping his hand behind his back, flapping at Spangler. *Stay away from me, man.*

Spangler had seen that move before. From his superiors, the body language not so blatant but just as obvious. He put on the glasses and felt himself ice over. *Forget the people he repulsed.*

Terrorists had breached the walls of the state, had set the

Pentagon afire. Had killed his brothers- and sisters-in-arms. Even civilians. My God. This was it. War. Pearl Harbor all over, another day of infamy.

He had warned of this war. This was the reason he had written *Swift Sword*. Bowers refused to believe him when he wrote this could happen. Bowers. The other brass. The pols. The media, the fucking media. They all assumed the nation could adopt a passive defense, the strategy of a turtle? Stop them from hating us? How? Love them to death? Even the Neanderthals knew they didn't have to arm themselves with pointed sticks for war. They armed for peace. You want a fanatic to love you, marry him. You want him to respect you, grab him by the balls with one hand and put the point of the stick at his throat. *Look here, Mohammed, we're not going to hurt each other, are we?*

He turned away from the tree and melted into a crowd. People barely looked at him, the front of his uniform dotted with blood. Others had suffered, too, many more were hurt worse than he. But not one person on the grounds felt his resolve, his power.

He had hope. He had *Swift Sword*.

An exercise in futility. That's what Bowers had called it. "Wanna know what *Swift Sword* is, Roscoe?" Bowers had asked him once over his fourth dirty martini. "It's a bit of mental masturbation, that's what it is. Not a realistic option, a piece of fantasy. It's illegal, against the laws of this country. Against the laws of war. Against the laws of man. Against the laws of God, that's right, illegal, inhumane, and immoral. Frankly, those are the very reasons you and I like it so much. But they're also the reasons this country will never allow it. Be easier to invade Canada than to take on all of Islam. So file it and forget it."

Spangler heard the words aloud in his head. Once more he held the package to his chest as if it were the Christ-child. He walked until he had cleared the crowds, had put a corner of the Pentagon between himself and the fire. Against the flow of people running from the building, he walked into the Metro entrance.

Laws, Randy? Look at these faces and tell me about laws again. Tell me how to fight terrorists and keep to laws, Randy, you tell me. God . . . that again . . . goddamn, there is no God. How could He be? How could He let this happen?

0939 Hours EDT, September 11, 2001—Aboard Flight 411

Tyler once again heard footsteps behind him. The Arab had recovered? And now he had the ax?

Tyler ducked as he turned, fearing he might lose his head.

To find that the terrorist had not come to, after all. There were no footsteps, either. Rather, foot*stomps*. As two passengers, a man and a woman in their twenties went after the terrorist. The man working over the dead man's face with toe-kicks. The woman going trampoline on the Arab, jumping up and down on his chest with both her heels, stabbing him with her short, sharp spikes.

"Knock it off," Tyler barked.

The man froze. He pulled his greasy hair out of his sweaty face. He looked surprised to catch himself caught in the act, kicking in a man's face, while he was out cold, for God's sake. And he looked glad that somebody had ordered him back to his senses.

Tyler couldn't tell if the Arab was still breathing. Blood oozed from his mouth. He blew bubbles and spatter at each leap and landing on his chest by the woman who did not stop her assault. Her own breath came in grunts and gasps and ragged squeals of rage. She wasn't going to let up, even if the man was dead, until she had spent her fury.

Tyler picked her up and threw her into a seat, planting her so hard her low-riding jeans became thigh-huggers. She tried to kick at him, too, until he grasped her face in one hand and shook it from side to side.

"Snap out of it."

She blinked rapid-fire. Tyler felt her head trying to nod in his grip.

"Now, behave," he said. She blinked. He had to say something to bring her around. "Pull up your pants."

Her eyes came into focus on him, as she lifted her hips off the seat to tug at her low-riders. She was gone, at least in her head, swept away in the murderous rampage in her heart, getting revenge on the terrorist who had tried to kill her in the hijacking of this plane. Her face, screwed up in hysteria, a gargoyle perched on her shoulders. Long, hooked beak. Lips pulled back to her ears. Teeth bared. Concentric lines radiating out from her snout. Eyes vicious as any wolf's.

"Are you okay, miss?"

"Yes," she said, her lips held pursed in his grip, the word hissing between her teeth. He let loose of her face.

And watched her return from the brink of murder. The features softened, lines flattened, eyes went dreamy, lips curled up in the smile of lovingly spent energy, feeling the endorphin rush after her effort. She was brunette, not yet out of her teens. Not as pretty as RuthAnn, but cute, once the monster in her subsided. Tomorrow she'd be sore from her exertions and shamed by her memories of the animal she'd been. She would never forget what that Arab had brought out in her. But now, in this moment, she was sliding down the far side of a dark orgasm of rage. She would forget that she was an animal just seconds ago. Eventually people could forget most anything.

Tyler shook his head.

"Jesus," she said, "what have I done?"

"Good question," Tyler said. He coughed hard to rough up his voice and bellowed into the cabin. "Everybody stay in your seats. If you get up for any reason, you're subject to federal prosecution for aiding and abetting a hijacking and obstructing justice. Any questions?"

Nobody said a word.

Until one of the ladies with the blue white hair called out in a crisp voice, "Thank you for saving our lives."

Blue-hair number two chimed in. "Yes, thank you, sir."

A chorus of thanks rose up like a prayer to Tyler.

"You're welcome," he said, no longer as gruff. "No more

talking for now. Captain Randolph? If you can spare a moment? Will you give me a hand with our prisoner before you get back to the cockpit?"

Tyler kicked the Arab in the buttocks, not out of cruelty, but to test him again on what Delta called the ass-jerk, a reflex that a conscious man could not fake. The Arab's butt jiggled like Jell-O.

Tyler leaned over him. He heard him gurgling in his own blood. He turned him over onto his shoulder and made sure his air passage was clear. The face-kicking had dislodged the crash ax. Tyler lifted it out of the spreading pool of ooze.

Over his shoulder he said, "RuthAnn, some towels, please, and a first aid kit."

She ran forward. Randolph leaned in close. "Why the towels?"

Tyler shook his head. "We need to save his life."

"Ah," Randolph said. "Federal sky marshal? Combat engineer? Mother Teresa? Which is it, okay?"

"We need to question him."

"Sky marshal or not?"

"You wouldn't have believed I was a sky marshal without credentials." Tyler wiped the ax handle dry on the Arab's shirt, so he could get a tight, if sticky, grip on it, in case he needed it again. "The passengers just needed to hear it to believe it."

"You're quick as a gunslinger with just the right lie." Randolph said it as a compliment.

"I've always been lucky in lying," Tyler said. Except when he tried to lie to the one person where a good lie mattered most. "But I guess that's nothing to brag about, is it?"

Randolph leaned in close. "Just between you and me? Are you Delta or not? You and me, okay?"

"Don't be stupid. Okay?"

Tyler could see the pilot mulling his wording. *Stupid to ask what a guy would not answer? Or stupid to wonder if any guy off the street could or would do what he'd done?* He shook his head.

"You are one helluva poker player, okay."

"Right," Tyler said. *From your mouth to Amy's ears.*

"What do you want me to do, okay? I have to get back to the cockpit. Make a report. You know, you're a hero here."

Tyler snickered. Hero. "And you're a genius because you know how to fly a plane?"

"No genius—" Randolph did a take. "Oh, I get it. I'm just doing what I'm trained to do, okay? And so are you. I get it. Okay, let me guess—you wouldn't want me to mention your name."

"I'd appreciate that," Tyler said. "Here, help me drag him farther toward the back."

"Okay. I'll scrounge up something for this guy's wrists and ankles."

He and Randolph hauled the Arab out of sight into the crew cubbyhole at the rear of the craft. Once they had laid him on his side, propping open his mouth so the blood would flow out, RuthAnn returned with a stack of towels.

Tyler patted down the Arab for weapons and found none. He took the man's wallet and tried to wipe his hands dry with one of the towels.

Randolph said, "Remind me never to get into cards with you, okay?" And then he was gone, back to the cockpit.

RuthAnn had also brought two sets of nylon flex-cuffs, the zip-tie handcuffs very like those Delta Force operators carried on body-snatch missions. He raised an eyebrow at her before he took them and placed a pair on the bloody wrists, feeling the broken ends of bones grinding in the man's forearm.

"We carry several sets. For unruly pax. We joke about it."

Tyler finished up on the ankles, pulling the last zip-tie tight. "Joke?"

"Among the crew. Imagine holding them up on the flight briefing? Like the oxygen masks? 'Ladies and gentlemen, if you all-like act up on this flight, a pair of zip-cuffs will drop out of the overhead. Simply place the cuffs over each wrist and pull the tabs tight with your teeth?'"

Tyler had to smile. Not so much that her joke was funny. Rather, that RuthAnn was back. Now that she had put the

World Trade Center tragedy out of her mind for the moment, she revealed a first-class personality. Nice eyes, sharp eyes. A quick smile, and a sense of humor. He liked that in a woman, and if that woman also had legs all the way up to her—

Cripes! A woman he wasn't supposed to be thinking about in that way. Or at all. Even without today's attacks, he already had two women to deal with, one in particular.

But she didn't know that. "So," she said. "Your name is Tyler?"

"Conner." Her eyes caught him. Full of tears they were soft and bottomless, like a doe's. Now dry, they had the look of a hawk.

"Okay, Connor. We're not going home tonight."

"Oh?" He rechecked the cuffs for fit. She was taking a run at him. Happened all the time. He spent a good deal of his time—not all of it, but a good deal of it—sidestepping such offers. And avoiding eye contact. Mostly that. Eye contact was his downfall.

"The alternate airport?" she said. "Charlotte? It's a nice town."

"I know it."

"Oh, right. The army-guy thing. Ever spent any time in the clubs?" she said. *Want to all-like spend some time together?* she meant.

"Oh?" He kept at the cuffs, adjusting them too tight.

"Every airliner in the country has been, like, ordered to land."

"Sounds pretty bad." He loosened the zip-ties, then busied himself with business, frisking the terrorist for weapons and intel. She wasn't giving up so easily.

"I don't suppose—"

He opened up the Arab's wallet. She was past hinting, now on the verge of issuing the flat-out invite. After last night with Laren? And what he had to do when he got home? *Unh-uh.* He made an earnest study of the wallet. She got it at last.

"No," she said, "I don't suppose you would." Finally. "Are you all married or something? Are you—?"

She touched his forearm. "Are you all right?"

"No." he sagged against the stainless steel door of the waste bin.

"What's the matter? Connor? You look like you're all stroking out."

0948 Hours EDT, September 11, 2001—The Pentagon

Inside the Mall entrance a civilian rent-a-cop stopped Spangler, who flashed his ID card and tried to push past.

"I'm sorry, sir, but you can't go back in. We're evacuating the building." The security guard's eyes bugged at Spangler's wounds. "Jesus, sir. Shouldn't you see a medic?"

Spangler held up *Swift Sword,* turning it so the security guard could read the charred cover sheet taped to the envelope. OP SECR ENTALIZED INFORMA—the rest burnt off. The man shrugged. *So what?* Wasn't the first piece of Top Secret that ever passed by, was it? Spangler lowered his glasses, driving his pink-eyed stare into the rent-a-cop's face. The man blanched. Spangler hugged *Swift Sword* to his chest.

"I was on the way to brief the SecDef on this plan," he said, his voice dead flat. The security guard began to nod. *Yes? You were on the way to brief the SecDef. And?*

Hell, Spangler figured, he'd already let a friend die. What did it matter if he told a piebald lie on top of that?

"The blast," he said. "It blew me out of the building."

"I'm sorry, sir. I—"

"Look." Spangler checked his watch—0948 hours. "I've got twelve minutes before I'm late." He rubbed a palm across his forehead and felt spikes of glass. He plucked a splinter from his hairline. A trickle rolled down his forehead, down the bridge of his nose to tickle his upper lip.

He lifted up his glasses and blew a red spray from the corner of the mouth, drilling him with the red-eye: *And you dare to mess with me?*

The rent-a-cop stood aside and waved him in.

Spangler felt a thrill run through him as he blew through the turnstile. He sneered at the panicked people who ran into him on their way out. He'd been ruined as a career officer, found not guilty in his court-martial, but sacked in the silent, deadly court of word of mouth.

Now this. This is what he has trained for. This is the reason his life and career had taken so many twists and turns. So he could be here, a flunky until this day, this moment. Court-martialed so he could be buried in the bowels of the Pentagon. Branded as a coward so he would not want to meet people. Hidden away so he could write *Swift Sword*. Called to brief so he could save the plan from the fire. His plan instead of his general. So he could brief the X-Men. So he could help save his country. No, not help. To flat out save his country.

War is hell? Was that what he was thinking when he slipped past the rent-a-cop? Not exactly. Other, earlier wars were hell. This one was a special place without a name. From a place beneath hell. *There is no God.*

All the time he'd been writing his master plan, Spangler wondered, not about its validity or morality, but his personal put-up-or-shut-up investment in it. Did he have the ability to act as decisively as the words he wrote, words that would commit others to ruthless, lethal action? One thing to tell a soldier to suppress his soul and murder a Protestant gay black Democrat from Albany who's trying to sneak a PVC pipe bomb aboard an airliner. Quite another to do it yourself in cold blood. He had reckoned he'd never know, that he'd never again be in combat to plumb the depths of ruthlessness in himself.

Until today. At his moment of combat. Under attack. When the explosion peeled back layers of Bowers's skin and layers of his own soul to let him see the depths of his personal darkness. As he walked past a man he'd called a friend, a boss, a somebitch, sometimes in jest, other times in earnest. Leaving him to die. In cold blood.

Wanna know what *Swift Sword* is, Randy?

That's *Swift Sword*.

1750 Hours Local, September 11, 2001—Northwest Afghanistan

Gunnery Sergeant Robert Night Runner, U.S. Marine Corps, shook his head in wonder at the disaster unfolding, not just before his eyes, but with his full participation as an accomplice to it. All hell, all in one day, twenty-four measly hours. One of those days when, just as he's thinking the worst thing in the world had happened, something worse comes along and lands in his skivvies with all the delicacy of a badger.

A simple reconnaissance mission into Afghanistan's northwest corner. That's all. In and out, sneaky-Pete style. Look and book, as his man, the fiery Friel, would put it. Test a few high-tech toys, maybe pick up some intel about the fabled cave complexes of northern Afghanistan. With luck, spot some elements or leaders of the Taliban government, maybe even the Al Qaeda terrorist network.

As it happens, the team gets lucky and spots a band of more than a dozen. Better yet, they identify Mustafa Hazzan Abu Saddiq, one of Osama bin Laden's top lieutenants, No. 3 or No. 7 in the hierarchy, depending on whether it was the media poll, which liked 3, or the Pentagon coaches' poll, which went with 7. Either way, on any given Sunday, you make a report, keep your head down, and get the hell out of Dodge.

Trouble was, Saddiq's troops had set up a night ambush. And a group of Uzbeks had walked right into it. Which should have been no problem for the U.S. government. Except that Saddiq's men captured a CIA man and a high-viz TV news reporter traveling with the Uzbeks.

Still, no problem, in theory. The Marine Corps had no interest in a group of people night-hiking into places they didn't belong. Most days, you couldn't tell which side the CIA was on, and you always had to figure the news media was the enemy.

Night Runner knew this woman, the bitch. Nina Chase. Teeth bright as bleached bones, hair sprayed stiff as Brillo. And pretty? Pretty as a coral snake. Make Hillary Clinton look like Mother Teresa. But on this day, the Marine Force Recon team got its marching orders. Snatch Saddiq. And, oh, by the way, while you're at it, pull the CIA man's ass out of the deep sand. The TV reporter? Nina, who? Oh. Well, screw her.

So the marine's elite commandos, a Force Recon team of four, pulls it off, but too well. They snatch Saddiq and free the Americans. Their only casualty is Friel, who suffers a broken jaw, make that a shattered jaw and a concussion that puts him into a walking coma. Space-age duct tape keeps Friel's jaw from flapping down to his belly button. Space-age duct tape keeps his battered head from falling off his shoulders on the run from the littered landscape of Afghanistan toward the littered landscape of Uzbekistan. Still they survive. End of story?

If only. If only the marines snatch Saddiq, make a run for the border, and leave the other two behind. If only the CIA man, Carnes, doesn't get greedy and try to get intel from Saddiq about a possible terrorist strike against America. If only he doesn't inject the terrorist, not with a truth serum, but with a behavior serum that turns him into a staggering drunk, allowing an Al Qaeda rescue force to catch up fully ten miles from safety.

Outnumbered, the marines fight hard and well. To be fair about it, so does Carnes. Even so, the Americans don't have the gunpower. They will die in Afghanistan. The government will tell their next of kin about a tragic aircraft accident. A training exercise. Their loved ones lost at sea. No hope of survival or even recovery of the bodies. They sleep with the sharks.

Except that the Force Recon leader, Captain Jack Swayne, pulls one last, desperate trick out of his battle bag, a close-in airstrike that surprises the friendlies as much as the enemy.

At the end of this ferocious battle, at the moment when the outcome looks certain and certainly bleak, the worm turns, the battle turns, and the Al Qaeda fighters turn and run. Leaving the Force Recon team flush with victory, but not certain of victory until they accomplish one last task. They have to make certain the Al Qaeda leadership cannot rally their men. They have to shoot men fleeing in terror. They have to turn a battle scene into a murder scene, making Night Runner sick to his stomach. He has an image of himself, that of a warrior, in a long line of warriors from the Blackfeet tribe and back, beyond written history, before Montana was Montana, before America was America, before even the continent had a name other than Mother. Perhaps this had to be done, but there is no glory in it, or even victory worthy of the name. There is only survival, a naked, selfish interest to live on.

His stomach already flighty before the killing is done, Night Runner catches a glimpse of Friel, fighting, but no longer against the enemy. His eyes wide open behind a mask of duct tape. Wide-open in terror, as he tears at his face.

Night Runner sees the reason for Friel's horror. Only too glad to give up taking yet more lives, he runs to save a life. As he runs, he pulls his favorite nonissue weapon, a short sword taken from the only enemy soldier who had ever frightened him, the only soldier in any army who ever made him think a warrior better than him might walk the earth.

He draws the blade across Friel's face, cutting the tape, cutting the lips, cutting the cheeks wide open to let out the vomit that would drown his man.

Friel convulses, spraying him. The teary eyes peek through the tape, thanking Night Runner in one instance, bulging in panic the next. As Friel clutches at his throat.

Night Runner grabs him, his jaw open wide as a mailbox door and bleeding, turns him, puts him into a bear hug from behind and jerks his fists into Friel's solar plexus. The Heimlich clears Friel's airway in a gush of stinking breath.

Night Runner's relief turns to fright. Friel does not inhale. Night Runner turns his sergeant so blood will not pour down his throat, he takes a deep breath. He clasps his mouth and hands around Friel's oversized opening and breathes. In and out until Friel picks up the rhythm on his own.

He positions Friel's head so he will not choke again, then picks up his rifle to resume the fight. Seeing the battle is all but over, he steps away from his sergeant so the man cannot see him, and gives in to his own rising gorge.

They win the fight, but lose their reason for fighting it. Mustafa Hazzan Abu Saddiq, mortally wounded, cries his last to the heavens, then joins Allah, meeting his prophet, Muhammed, and the reward he has earned at the cost of his life.

Happily ever after. Virgins to die for.

Not so the marines. They have failed to snatch Saddiq alive, after all. Instead, they had saved the CIA man, of doubtful value, and, of all things, a pretty, worthless asset to the USMC and America, a TV reporter. For shit sake, a toothy, big-haired TV reporter.

All they have of any value are Saddiq's last words. Swayne wants to know what they were.

Carnes never changes expression. Which says, he, on be-half of the CIA, isn't about to translate and tell.

"You sonofabitch," Swayne says.

"Look, it's classified. Top secret. Higher."

"Look around you, you bastard." Swayne points at the gap-ing maw of Friel. "Look at what you've cost us in saving your skin. Otherwise, you'd have been tortured. You'd have given up more secrets to him than us." Swayne shifts his feet. He doesn't threaten Carnes exactly, but the muzzle of his rifle does twitch in Carnes's direction.

Carnes's head sags. He doesn't know Swayne, except for these past hours spent here together on the surface of the moon. A man with his instincts for spook work doesn't worry that Swayne will kill him. Swayne's honor makes him weak in that sense. But Night Runner sees the CIA man give in to Swayne's logic, and perhaps a higher, seldom-seen instinct in himself. He does owe a life. He sighs. "He was raving about the airstrike."

"What about it?" Swayne asks. What terrorist wouldn't rave after seeing a dozen or so of his men blown to bits, the rest sent packing.

Carnes works his mouth like an actor exercising before going onstage. Night Runner wipes a sleeve across his own mouth for the tenth time.

"He must have seen the plane," Carnes said.

Swayne shrugs. *So what?* Night Runner wipes his mouth with the other sleeve and tries to spit out a bitter, acid taste of vomit not his own.

"He was hollering that the airplane was not supposed to be dropping bombs on us. His pilots had picked the wrong targets."

Swayne doesn't get it. "His pilots? What you mean his pilots? That was our plane." Never mind that it was a drone, without a pilot.

"I'm not sure. He said they were supposed to hit the White House—"

"The White House?"

"And the Pentagon, the Capitol, the World Trade Center."

"Al Qaeda has pilots? Al Qaeda has planes?" In our airspace? Against our air force? "Impossible."

Carnes shakes his head. "Absolutely impossible." He keeps shaking his head. To Night Runner, the man is wishing it impossible more than believing it. He knows more than he is telling. It is not in him to tell the truth, the whole truth, and nothing but. Night Runner spits again, this time in disgust.

Swayne won't believe it. But he makes a report anyhow, connecting the communications dots from satellite to satellite to the Force Recon underground command center halfway around the world with his relay of Saddiq's words.

Night Runner admires Swayne yet again. This time for making the report. The captain knows his job is to report possible intelligence information, not to decide whether the information deserves reporting. Even so Night Runner notices that he does not do a good job of keeping the incredulity out of his voice as he passes the news along.

Darkness settles quickly here. At 1826 hours, just minutes after the sun sets behind mountains that define the word *rugged,* the most vile, vicious colonel in the Marine Corps, the one-eyed Zavello, reports back, his voice somber as a chaplain at a military funeral. He tells them the truth about September 11 in America. About the two airliners striking the World Trade Center. About a third airliner smashing into the Pentagon. About half a dozen other aircraft still unaccounted for.

They stand on their tiny and now meaningless battlefield on the moonscape of Afghanistan. Except for Swayne's, *Roger, out,* at the end of Zavello's elegy, nobody speaks. In turn they look at their watches. Subtracting eight hours from local. Finding it is minutes shy of 1000 hours in New York and

Washington. Dark is light. Day is night. When terrorists fly. When New Yorkers die. The moment is beyond surreal.

Night Runner and Swayne search each other's faces as the last glimmer of twilight gives way to night. They have trained together and fought together and together watched good men die for so long that they can communicate without words. Even in the dim light, Night Runner reads the guilt on his captain's face, just as surely as his face betrays his own guilt to Swayne. He is glad that Friel has blacked out. And that Greiner, the junior man on the team, now stands a security post for them. He wouldn't want the youngsters to see him covered in blood and puke and this even more putrid pallor of shame. For failing their mission. For failing their country.

He hears the crunch of gravel. He and Swayne turn as one to see Carnes melting into the black fog of the desert beyond.

Night Runner looks to his captain for orders, asking by raising an eyebrow, *Bring the SOB back?*

Swayne curls one side of his upper lip: *What the hell for?*

It takes a while to patch up Friel and begin their trek toward the border of Uzbekistan. Night Runner, as usual, takes the lead spot. He is glad for the darkness. He doesn't want anybody to see his face at the finale of this day of shame. Warriors are not supposed to shoot men in the back. Warriors are not supposed to eat vomit. Warriors are not supposed to let their country come under sneak attack. And warriors are not supposed to weep.

0952 Hours EDT, September 11, 2001—The Bat Cave

Spangler stepped out of the elevator and onto a train platform. It looked familiar enough, a Metro station in mini. He walked toward the first car he spotted. He felt a spring in his step. How long had it been? Since he had felt worthwhile, truly worthwhile?

"Help you, Major, sir?" A pair of marines came to attention, not out of respect, but to block his path. "Destination, sir?"

His instinct was to say, "To the Bat Cave." Because it might be the only time in his life he could. But he said the acronym, "DEOC," instead.

The marines swung apart like saloon doors. "That car, Major, sir. Leaving for the Defense Emergency Operations Center in a minute, sir."

The train ride felt like any other he took on any day of the week on the Metro. Other military people with briefcases across their laps. Some engaged in small talk. Not him. He only had room in him for *Swift Sword*.

He timed the ride. A bit more than five minutes. The Bat Cave was not beneath the Pentagon as legend had it. It made sense. The Pentagon would be a nuclear target. He stepped off the car wondering whether he was beneath some nonstrategic piece of ground, maybe Arlington National Cemetery. A nice touch, if true. Not even the Soviets would have nuked a cemetery.

Spangler watched the car pull away and noticed three other tunnels that funneled into and out of this station. So, cars could come here from other parts of the Capitol. He glanced at the ceiling. It figured. No bats.

Other commuters, both military and civilian, swept by him.

Out of habit of the subway commuter, he looked around for signs to tell him where to find his destination, the briefing room where he was to reveal the details of *Swift Sword* to people who could order it into execution. There were only two signs, neither of them helpful.

No Smoking brought a smile to his lips. The people who met here only met in cases of natural disaster, nuclear attack, military invasion, or the events of today? Dying from secondhand smoke was not their number one problem. The other sign wanted to warn him about the many restrictions of the area. He didn't have time to read it.

A marine with another clipboard stepped up to Spangler's shoulder. "Major, sir? Help you sir?"

"Yes." He looked around the Bat Cave. Just he and the dozen armed guards that he could see stood on the platform, all cut from the same mold as the one in his face. "I'm supposed to brief, but I've never been here before."

"Your name, Major, sir?"

"Spangler. Roscoe G. Spangler." On reflex, Spangler looked down at his chest. His name tag was covered in dried, blistering blood. He scraped it off with a thumbnail, leaving his name engraved in red.

The guard consulted a roster on his clipboard. "And Lieutenant General Bowers? Your escort?"

"The general's a casualty." Spangler raised his eyebrows and felt the sting of the cold, stiffening wounds on his forehead. "Of the explosion?"

The marine wasn't impressed. "Your ID, Major, sir?"

Spangler flipped open his wallet.

"Remove it from the wallet, if you please, Major, sir."

He handed over his ID.

The marine showed his back to Spangler and led him into an anteroom.

"Randy?"

Spangler turned toward the voice, that of a four-star air force officer he had never seen before.

"General Bowers is a casualty," Spangler said.

"He's supposed to brief a classified OPLAN."

Spangler flashed his envelope. "I have the OPLAN. I regret to say the general was hurt in the explosion upstairs." He remembered he was not beneath the Pentagon any longer. "I mean, in his office."

"Impossible."

"I was with him, general." He grimaced, feeling the dried blood crackling on his face. *Are you blind or what?*

"Not that. Majors don't get access to this briefing area. Not even with a three-star escort." He slammed the door between himself and Spangler.

Leaving Spangler stunned. He looked around for somebody to ask. *What now?*

Before he could pick out somebody to terrorize with his face, the four-star was back. "Okay, Major, listen up," the general said, his mint-breath hot. "You're nothing but a silent fart to those people in the briefing room. They want to hear about this OPLAN and nothing else."

The general wheeled and strode down the hallway. Spangler stumbled after the soles of his huge shoes slapping the floor. "You give your pitch. You answer questions. You disappear. Forget about names, forget about titles, forget about military courtesy."

"Yes, sir."

"You don't listen very well. I said no courtesy, no titles."

"Yes."

"You don't take notes. After today, if you see anybody from this room up on the surface, you don't acknowledge them. You don't know them. You've never seen them before. They don't exist. You don't exist. This meeting doesn't exist. Got it?"

"Yes, sir . . . I mean, yes."

"This is a meeting of strangers. No records, no minutes, no transcripts, no tapes. Why? Because the meeting never happened. There is no public right to know. There is no constitutional inquiry. There is no congressional oversight. There is no media interest, because there is no meeting to be interested in. You follow?"

"Yes."

"To put your mind at ease, this is not an unconstitutional gathering. This is not a shadow government. This is not a secret staff. This is not a decision-making body. It is no more than a coffee klatch, a group of smart people—not including you—getting together to chew the rag. Trade ideas. People and rank and position and party and ideology do not count. Only good ideas count. You're a pissant. But *Swift Sword* is the alleged good idea for the day. We're gonna chat about *Swift Sword* over a cup of Joe."

Spangler turned his head. Swift Sword *a good idea?* Was that a compliment? No.

"Bowers's idea, not yours. You're just the pissant who put the general's ideas on paper, right?"

"Right."

The general stopped at a set of double doors. With his right hand on the doorknob, he pointed a finger into Spangler's face, practically up his nose.

"Now all these smart people you're about to meet?"

Spangler adjusted his glasses, pressing them tightly to the bridge of his nose, hiding his eyes.

"Lose the glasses, Major, you think this is a day at the beach or—Whoa!" He turned away as Spangler looked over his frames. "Is that a medical thing or a genetic thing?"

"Medical."

"Put them back on. Christ, what was Randy thinking? Bringing you along?"

Spangler didn't cower. He'd heard talk like this before. If he were gay, he might have a cause for legal action. But red-eye had no constituency.

"Where was I?"

"These smart people I'm about to meet?" Spangler said.

"Right. These smart people. They might—not necessarily, mind you—but they *might* go back to their bosses and share some of the ideas that came out of this room. They will be speaking as if those ideas are their own. Which they are. Because why?"

"Because," Spangler said, "this meeting never happened."

"I've got to hand it to you," the general said as he turned the doorknob. "You're not as dumb as you look." He pulled the door open.

Spangler took a step forward.

"Mind your manners." The four-star stepped in front of him, taking care to throw a shoulder into Spangler, jostling him off-balance and into the doorjamb. By the time Spangler righted himself and stepped inside the room, pulling the door shut, the general had found a seat and began to intro Spangler.

"Ladies and gentlemen of the X-Staff, speaking to OPLAN *Swift Sword* on behalf of our colleague, I give you this, this . . ."

Not pissant, Spangler prayed.

"Stand-in."

Spangler faced the group and went weak in the knees. He did know the somebodies he was not supposed to know. Four of them. Two he had seen on Sunday news programs, a woman from the White House staff and a bulldog from the State Department who didn't take any crap from anybody when the cameras were rolling. He couldn't remember their names or titles, which was a good thing, because he wasn't supposed to. The third face belonged to a hatchet man inside the Pentagon, a civilian close to the SecDef. The fourth was from CIA, a spook he had seen in the company of the defense guy.

Two other men he did not recognize. Then there was the general, whom he had just met, and would happily forget.

Spangler nodded his head to the group. He noticed nameplates around the table, giving them their designations. The White House woman, X6; CIA, X2; State, X1; the four-star; and two other men, one X4, the other X13. For all the mystery about it, the designations were about the same as in any combat unit from the special, or S-Staff at battalion and brigade level, through general, or G-Staff, for divisions, corps, and armies, on up to the joint or J-Staff staff at the Pentagon.

"You're late," said Defense guy. "Why the hell—"

"You're hurt," said the woman from the White House, dressed in a red blazer, and Defense guy shut his mouth. Spangler knew at once who was in charge.

He nodded to the woman in red. "I'm all right."

He glanced at the four-star. Knots bulged in the jaw muscles beneath his earlobes, knots that made his jaw as wide as his ears. A warning.

Spangler said, "I'm here to brief Operations Plan *Swift Sword*," he said. "It's the brainchild of Lieutenant General—"

Four-Star cleared his throat.

Spangler did not say Randall Bowers's name. "It's America's plan for striking back with swift and deadly force against terrorists, in case the unthinkable should happen." He took a second to relish the irony. Now that the unthinkable had happened.

He looked around the room. He felt relaxed, strong, in charge. He recognized one more face to go with the others, an executive from the FBI. These were not horse-holders, but people with power within their departments. By the end of the day, they would go back to their bosses to repeat his words, his ideas—as if they were their own, Four-Star said. This was his element. No, this was his calling. Till now, a life of failure, a waste of shame, an existence in disgrace. Those things had brought him to this moment of triumph. Against all odds, and

with the ironic help of his sworn enemy, Osama bin Laden, he
had failed his way to success.

Even if he walked out of this room and died of a stroke, or
of infection from these wounds. Or worse. Even if he vanished into the bowels of the Pentagon never to be heard from
again. Even if he never had an existence beyond the four-star's
recognition of him as a silent fart. He had this moment.
Churchill's words came to him: *Victory at all cost; victory in
spite of all terror; victory however long and hard the road
may be; for without victory, there is no survival.*

He looked to the woman in red for permission to speak.
She gave it to him with a nod of her regal head.

"First the executive summary," he said. "*Swift Sword* is a
war plan, written for a war against terrorists. Given the events
of today so far, we are in a war. Make no mistake about it."

"Cut the poli-sci lecture," the four-star said.

"Sorry," Spangler said and launched into his briefing. He
spoke without even cracking the thick plan in his hands, his
confidence growing as he looked from face to face around the
room. He saw they weren't noticing his bent body, the blood,
the sunglasses. They did not see the troll of a washed-up army
major he was. They listened rapt, held by *Swift Sword,* his
words, his plan, even if he could not claim ownership here. It
was his plan.

"To win this war, America will have to fight without self-
imposed limits," he said. "*Swift Sword* envisions taking on terrorists as if it were a knife fight. Just as there are no rules in a
knife fight, we hold to no rules against this enemy. We seek no
glory, no honor, no allies, no fame. Using the simplest of
strategies. Their own weapon. Naked terrorism. Kill the terrorist before he can kill you. Not random terrorism, mind you.
As Churchill said, we will not adopt the tactics of our enemy
to attack the innocent. Strictly speaking, we will not become
terrorists ourselves. But we will seek out the terrorist, no
matter his station. Whether soldier, cleric, diplomat, or head
of state. Man, woman, child, or elder. Black, white, yellow,
or mulatto. Catholic, Protestant, Jew, or Muslim. Taliban,

Al Qaeda, Democrat, or Republican. If he's a terrorist, hunt him down and kill him. If the terrorist is a woman, hunt her down and kill her dead."

He had them. Every eye, every ear.

"That's *Swift Sword* in a nutshell," he said. "Now for the specifics." He opened the plan to the spot he wanted.

"To do this, we gather the best warriors in our armed forces and the CIA, primarily Delta Force. We sort them, train them, test them. From the best of these best, we form warrior units, hunter-killers with the state of the art in weapons, intelligence, and support. These Preemptive Terrorist Teams find the enemy. No safe haven, no place to hide. They strike the enemy. No rules, no quarter. They kill the enemy. No mercy." He couldn't resist. "Until we win. For without victory, there is no survival."

He saw every head, to a man and woman, begin to nod. By God, Roscoe. You're going to blow these people away with *Swift Sword*. Then you're going back to the office and submit your retirement papers. Because this is it. Nothing will ever be better than this. Nothing.

1835 Hours local, September 11, 2001—Northwest Afghanistan

Agent Brian Carnes went no farther than a hundred meters from the battlefield, just enough to put distance between himself and the Force Recon marines. He had to come to grips with his guilt, his personal shame. And yes, his grief. Not so much that people had lost their lives in America. But because he had not stopped the attacks. Not so much that Saddiq had revealed the terrorist intentions after the fact. Hell, if Carnes had known about the Al Qaeda plan a month ago, he could not have stopped the attacks. Nobody in government would dare to target Arabs for profiling and arrests without probable cause, even if they were illegals. Not on his word. And not on his word would they delay the air traffic control system. So he wasn't blaming himself for not stopping the attacks.

Hell, the intel that he did gather, he only got by sheer dumb
luck, after setting up a dog and pony show for a television
reporter, so he could show off the CIA's discovery of new
cave complexes. After wandering into an ambush and letting
Saddiq capture his ass. After the Marine Corps rode in like the
cavalry and pulled his ass out of the fire. Why blame himself?

Let the media do that. Let those overfed faces in Congress
who always stood up to point the finger to lay the blame to
single out Central Intelligence. Maybe not today. Maybe not a
month from now. But two or three years from now? When the
shine was off their patriotism. When they were looking for a
butt to cram blame up.

He didn't have time for such crap as that, no inclination to
think up ways to cover his butt, no need to justify his work or
himself. He had a job to do tonight. After the Force Recon
team patched up the Friel kid, after they headed toward
Uzbekistan and home.

While he waited, he could only regret the one thing. That
he had never even anticipated the diabolical but ingenious
choice of weapons in the attacks. Hijacking airplanes, for
chrissake. Not to blow up, but to use as guided missiles, full
of fuel and people.

All the while all of America and the other few civilized
nations on the never-ending quest to develop weapons that
took the personal contact out of killing for the killers. Smart
bombs. Unmanned Predator drones armed with Hellcat
missiles—he'd seen the prototypes tested in the airspace over
Northern Alliance territory here in Afghanistan. Over-the-
horizon ship killers. Aerial dogfights with a standoff of seventeen miles between fighters. Carpet bombing from five miles
up. Long-range missiles and Tomahawks from a thousand
miles.

All the while the enemy marching in the opposite direction. The low-tech, personal touch. Bombs strapped to your
body. Pick your victims by the size of their noses. The color
of their skin. Their religion or their country of origin. In short,
anything but what was taboo in America. Walk right up to

them. Spit into their faces. Blow them to hell, even as you blow yourself to terrorist heaven to collect your virgins. Even young women doing it now. Did those Arab chicks even stop to think? Where in heaven were they going to find seventy-two virgin men?

All of which proved that Arab men were the same as Americans. Dying for sex, dreaming of sex in heaven, and finding heaven in sex. My kingdom for a whore. On earth, only the Arab royalty could afford the whores. All the peasants could do is dream of virgin whores. No wonder Westerners weren't winning the war against terrorism. Landing troops in the Middle East was a terrible move. The way to win the war was to land a boatload of whores and pass them off as virgins. Drain all that religious fervor in a single night. Kill them with the clap.

But, dammit, he had never taken today's strategy to its logical, horrible conclusion. Strap on a bomb the size of a jetliner. Fly it into the most visible target you can find. Utter genius, utterly evil. Worthy of Lex Luthor himself. Why didn't he think of it months ago? Not that he could've sold it to the powers-that-be. Hell, he doubted he could have sold it to himself, even if he had thought of it. Come to think of it, maybe he had. So incredible, he didn't remember. Come to think of it . . .

Time to forget it. Work to do. He retraced his steps, climbing up the bank of a wadi to scope out the area where he had left the Force Recon team standing. His night vision monocular told the story. Gone.

He studied the ghostly, ghastly images of Al Qaeda fighters, bodies lying scattered. The most dangerous spot on Earth, a battlefield littered with wounded. Dying, dazed, fear-crazed men who might shoot at a whisper.

He picked a spot near the crater. He would start there. With the dismembered corpses. Even if they survived the initial blast, they would have bled out by now.

A minute later he stood by half a man, the top half. Less the guts, less the glory. Just half the man he used to be, reeking

and leaking gas and fluid at a cold simmer. He began with the
Al Qaeda fighter's backpack. It peeled easily from his shoulders, because the man had no arms. *I bitched that I had no
shoes.*

He dumped out the pack's contents, some packets of food,
a plastic water bottle, a blanket, jacket, personal papers. He
started with the bag of Swiss chocolates, milky, cloying, sensual. To fortify himself for the night's work before his hands
wore gloves of gore. Perhaps even a greater risk than the
wounded man in a stupor sitting up and emptying an AK-47
clip in his direction. How many of these heroes had AIDS, he
could not know. Not that it mattered. He was going through
with this no matter what the risk. For the reward.

He tossed aside everything but personal papers. Those he
put back into the bag. Then he began patting down the pockets. A nice find, a German passport—no, two passports. A
British one as well. A gold mine.

Carnes looked around for the man's bottom half. His wallet might yield even more treasure. But he could not find the
bottom half. So he went to the next man. And the next. Here
an engraved, bejeweled watch. Here a book of Islamic scrip-
ture. There a lovely family picture. An even more lovely .32
caliber pistol with mother-of-pearl handles. Lots of cash—
Yen, pounds, and dollars, U.S. and Euro. And, of course, currency from all the Arab and other countries in the region. He
threw the cash into the air, letting it scatter. One thing the
Agency had was cash, real and counterfeit. When the Al
Qaeda troops came to police the battlefield, all that money lying around might cause a stampede of collectors before they
harvested this body farm. That would be a good thing. To
wipe out the evidence of his intel harvest. At least until they
had too many men to ID and no papers to help them.

When the backpack bulged with his treasure trove, he began filling another. He could carry two backpacks. If he didn't
bother with carrying food and water. The day was not going to
be a total loss, after all.

Now. If he could just find a way to get some use from the
stuff.

Spangler finished his briefing.

Hands went up. Not because these people gave him respect. But because, when they tried to blurt questions about details in the middle of the briefing, the woman in the red coat told them to stifle. "Wait till he's finished," she said. She didn't raise her voice. She didn't allow a single note of *please* or *if you don't mind* or *why don't we discuss it* creep into her command. Just the command. *Without even raising her voice!* Nobody interrupted again until a vice admiral, the highest-ranking messenger Spangler had ever seen, stepped into the room and dropped a folded note on the table before the woman from the White House.

And now that he had finished, the hands went up. Her simple command still had its effect. These men of crime and combat and international intrigue. Like schoolboys, they dared not blurt. They knew who was in charge.

So did Spangler. He looked to her. She raised one eyebrow: *Well, it's your briefing.*

"I'll go around the table. First question here." He pointed to the CIA man.

"Ever heard of Executive Order 12333?" Next to the woman, Spangler feared this man the most. He had a lethal look about the eyes, like the serial killers on Court TV.

"Yes, sir. I mean, yes. President Reagan signed it. It prohibits assassinations."

"Meaning it prohibits commando groups going into foreign countries, say, Afghanistan, to assassinate Taliban and Al Qaeda leaders and operators. Meaning it prohibits the type of operations that *Swift Sword* envisions."

This from CI? The original James Bond licensees? Spangler shrugged. "*Swift Sword* assumes a new executive order."

"How are you going to sell that to the president and the American people?"

"He's not," said the woman from the White House. "That's already been done. Today. By the enemy. The fundamental assumption of *Swift Sword* is no longer an assumption. It is a reality." *Any questions?*

The man from State flapped a hand on the table. "Our allies would argue that assassination is counterproductive. Once you begin killing a country's leaders, that country feels a freedom to assassinate our own leaders."

Spangler did not even try to field that question. He knew the answer, but he also knew that it was not for him to speak just now. He knew she would handle it. And she did.

She shook her head. A look of: *Have you all got amnesia?* "One suspects that ship has already sailed." She flashed the note handed to her by the naval three-star. "At 10:06 a.m., a fourth airliner crashed in Pennsylvania. Early reports are that American Flight 93 was taken over by terrorists. That it was headed back toward Washington. Perhaps the White House. Perhaps the Capitol. One can only assume the worst. One can only assume the terrorists felt free to assassinate our leaders. Without said provocation."

Spangler wanted to chip in his two-cents' worth. Like the other men in this room, though, he dared not blurt.

She crumpled the note in her hand. "I'm sorry to say there's even more bad news than that."

The room went breathless. "Two more are rumored to be hijacked."

Spangler glanced around. He saw narrowed eyes, gray faces, rapid breathing. He saw fear. A thrill ran through him. *Swift Sword* was a lock.

"I think it's safe to say, the United States will respond in kind to the awful events of today," the woman in the red coat said, from Spangler's mind to her mouth. "If not with *Swift Sword,* something very like it." She looked at Spangler, unfazed by his wounds.

"Major, I have a question." Spangler noticed Four-Star didn't object to her using his tank.

The woman in the red coat narrowed her eyes at him. "Assuming you have approval for them, how long to launch these attack teams, these PT—what do you call them?"

"PTTs. Preemptive Terrorist Teams.

"How long, battle-ready?"

"Six weeks, tops, I should think."

"We can do it in four," said Four-Star. Spangler opened his mouth. A look from the four-star shut it for him.

The woman in the red coat shrugged. "Four weeks, six weeks. How about two weeks?" Her eyes drilling Spangler. "Just to war-game it."

"We could do that," the four-star said.

She never even glanced Four-Star's way, but just kept staring at Spangler, who needed every ounce of sedative in his blood to deaden a smile. That was so beautiful. A put-down for all time. It settled everything for him. Definitely retirement. Definitely today. Life didn't get any better than this.

"Two weeks?" Spangler shook his head. "I suppose if we cut the testing to bare bones. And if we had high-pri on resources."

"I need to know for sure."

"I need time to study it."

"Take all the time you need. But get back to me on it tomorrow. Assume minimum testing, maximum resources."

"Yes." The four-star again.

The woman in red spoke in a low voice to Spangler. "Would you mind stepping outside? Perhaps take a short walk down the hallway?"

0729 Hours PDT, September 11, 2001—Las Vegas

When the North Tower of the World Trade Center collapsed, so did Amy Tyler. It had begun as any other day. Up with Brendan at 5:30. Nursing. A wrong number. The first tower burning on the tube not a movie. The second plane striking the second tower as she watched. Trying to call her husband's cell. No answer. Checking his messages. Hearing the voice of a frantic woman, his lover. Calling her husband *darling*? Telling him she loved him? *She calls him Connie?*

Calling that major at the Pentagon. Not getting through. Checking the TV. Seeing the Pentagon in flames and seeing why not.

Calling Connor's phone again and again. Getting no answer again and again.

The first tower crumbling. Her marriage crumbling. The second tower crumbling. Her hopes crumbling. All in only two hours?

She lay on the floor, gazing into the face of her bawling infant son. "Oh, Connor," she said. Then, as if the baby had touched a nerve at her core, she began to bawl as well.

1020 Hours EST, September 11, 2001—The Bat Cave

Spangler walked as far away from the conference room as he could. Even so, he was not far away enough.

The doors of the room rattled with the shouting that went on inside. He tried not to listen, but he could not help hearing the snatches of conversation shouted back and forth.

"He's a major, for chrissake, a major . . ." So much for no mention of rank. The four-star wasn't going to give up ragging on that.

"Requires an executive order . . ." State Department guy. He didn't get it that a carrot wasn't going to cut it in response to today's acts. Unless it came in the shape of a big stick.

"Adequate commando forces already . . ." Defense guy.

"Redundant, duplicate, superfluous . . ." CIA guy.

"Loser, a goddamned loser . . ."

Loser? For the second time this day, a black cloud swept over Spangler, this one cold. Not even Bowers had called him a loser. At least not within earshot.

The shouting in the conference room stopped at last, and at last, the door opened, and the four-star beckoned him. Spangler saw that they had turned on the wall television while he was out. He didn't give it more than a glance.

At the table Spangler rested his hands on the thick *Swift Sword* document and looked down, keeping his eyes away from the four-star. So he would not piss off the four-star. Or Defense Guy. Or for that matter, anybody.

Only the woman in the red coat spoke.

"I've got good news and I've got bad news."

"Ma'am?"

"The good news is I want you back here in a week to brief this staff on your progress in testing these teams of shock troops, these Preemptive Terrorist Teams, as you call them."

Spangler went numb. A briefing? She wanted a briefing instead of a deployment? Shit.

He tried to look her in the eyes, but she wasn't having any of it. "While you're preparing to brief, the various departments will test the waters, send out feelers. We'll convene to put together a consensus."

"Consensus." A week of behind-the-scenes maneuvering? While he was out west in America's own Bumfuck, Egypt? One word for that: *Shit!*

"Ma'am?" One last-ditch effort, then back to oblivion. "You can't win a war by consensus. You need a remedy." He held up *Swift Sword*.

"Cancer," she said.

"Beg pardon?"

"You're paraphrasing Churchill again. The exact quote is 'You cannot cure cancer by a majority. What is needed is a remedy.'" She let it lie. At the far end of the table, Four-Star snorted. If his OPLAN really were a sword, he'd pick it up and use it on himself. Shit. Might as well go back to the 'Gon and toss *Swift Sword* into the fire. It was that dead. Give a guy like Four-Star a week to stack the deck and . . . *Sheee-it!*

"Shit!"

Spangler looked up to be sure it wasn't he who spoke the word aloud, but, no, it was Defense Guy. He pointed at the television set anchored to the wall. "Turn up the volume."

Four-Star already had the remote control at hand. He grabbed it and jabbed at the surreal image on the screen. An image that sucked all the hostility from the room. An image that filled the vacuum with a full range of emotions from alarm to dismay.

Four-Star's hand, the one that held the remote control, dropped to the table. The plastic cover to the battery compartment went spinning away. Two AAA batteries rolled down the table.

Away from Four-Star, who cursed under his breath.

Past the FBI man, who let out a barely audible groan. "We've got people in there. I've got friends—"

The batteries rolled past the assistant SecDef, who finally raised his head, but not his chin, leaving his mouth agape.

One battery rolled to a stop against the splayed fingers of the guy from State, who picked it up in one hand and squeezed it in his fist.

The other battery continued to roll. Past the CIA man, who paled.

The woman in red did not pay any notice to the battery, even when it rolled off the edge of the table and tumbled into her lap. She was transfixed like everyone else by the enormity taking place on screen, not in real-time, but a replay the announcer said, barely two minutes old.

Spangler looked at his watch: 1029 hours.

And watched a replay of the last of the South Tower of the World Trade Center collapsing on itself, concrete and steel folding like a pillar of cards, a movie stunt, a demolition demonstration on the believe-it-or-not cable channel of voyeurism and degradation.

Armageddon. All in one day. All before a decent coffee break.

"My God," said the woman in red. "What else?"

They sent Spangler from the room again. When Four-Star summoned him back, Spangler knew at a glance that *Swift Sword* was a go. He sat down and kept his eyes on the table so he would not betray his delirium. Forget consensus. *Swift Sword* had won the day.

"General, we want the first team ready to deploy within two weeks," said the woman in red. "Both feet on the ground in Afghanistan or anyplace else the commander in chief commands. Am I making myself clear?"

Four-Star did not answer. Spangler looked up. To see the four-star, his color crimson, his jaw knotted, his neck swollen like a buck deer in rut, the collar of his powder blue shirt cutting him like a noose, staring at a blank television screen hung on the wall.

Spangler took in the others in a glance around the room. Defense guy glared at him from beneath his knotted brow, for some reason more angry at him than before.

The woman in the red coat tried to smile at him. It came off as more the mask of a smile than the actual thing.

"Ma'am? Are you talking to me?"

"The whole time."

"I don't get it."

"Yes, you do," she said. "You get the whole ball of wax. You get the job of putting *Swift Sword* into action, and you get the horsepower to go with it. If you fall on your face, you get the blame, too. You know how it works, soldier. So, if I were you, Brevet General Spangler, I'd get busy."

"I beg your pardon."

Defense guy spoke up. "It's only temporary, Spangler. You get promoted to full-bird, but you get the one star, as I say, temporarily, to help you get your job done Brevet general at bird-colonel pay. I'll clear it with the SecDef, detach you to Central Command as a technical adviser, that kind of thing. But you have the reins for this one. CentCom won't be taking the fall for your screwups."

Spangler's numbness had turned to paralysis. His lips tingled. "I don't know what to say."

"Don't say anything," Defense guy said. "Go back to your office and wait until you hear from me. Start putting the pieces together, the people and resources. A budget. A timetable. And for granny's sake, get a medic to tend to your wounds. Next time I see you, you'd better be in a uniform that's not covered with blood."

Spangler stood up and locked his knees into place, fearful that they would buckle on him. He picked up *Swift Sword* and gave a thought to how he should leave. Maybe salute? That was the automatic reaction, but no, a salute wasn't proper. Try to execute a proper military about-face? On this carpet, he would topple onto his face. No, in his state, no *probably* to it.

"Leave the document," the woman told him.

Out of habit, he hesitated. *"Swift Sword?"*

His turn to get one of her glares full in the face. *Is there any other?*

Spangler tossed it down like a hot rock.

"I need to have copies made," she said. "You can trust me, General."

"Of course." Did she just call him *general* again?

Spangler needn't have worried about how to get out of the room. He simply floated.

The euphoria didn't last long. He had work to do. Phone calls to make. That damned Tyler; why hadn't he called back yet?

He need a staff—it occurred to him that all of Bowers's people might have been killed in the attack. From a human point of view, a terrible loss. For what he had in mind, no loss at all. Those people mocked him. To his back and to his face. Even with his new rank, they would mock him. How could they work for him? This morning he was a toad in a tunnel. Not even a jump in three ranks, not even the star of a brigadier general would turn him into a prince. Not in their eyes.

He had the terrorist attack on the Pentagon to thank. Awful as it was, it had cleared the decks for Major Mushroom to blossom into Brevet General Roscoe G. Spangler, a temporary brigadier general. Better yet, the new C-3PO, United States Army, United States of America.

1058 Hours EDT, September 11, 2001—Charlotte, North Carolina

Tyler's cell rang at him the second he turned it on. Again and again. Urgent messages left for him.

The first from Amy. "Shit, Connor, call home as soon as you get this message. I need to talk to you."

The second, also from Amy, began: "Conn, honey, I'm fine . . ." and ended with, "I love you."

His stomach flip-flopped. Was it only this morning, no, just a couple hours ago, that the big worry in his world was how to tell her they needed some time apart?

The third from Amy: "Connor, damn you, call me."

The skin at the back of his head went to gooseflesh as he punched up the fourth message, from Spangler: "Tyler, Spangler, for the second time this morning, get in touch. ASAP." Spangler left him a number, but before Tyler could copy it down, the telephone rang in a new tone, a real-time call. But Tyler's mind was on the last word from Spangler.

The second time? Spangler had called a second time? Where was the first message the old pink-eyed troll had left? And why was Amy pissed? What had gone on between call two and three?

He answered his cell on the sixth ring.

"Tyler, this is Spangler, where the hell have you been? Are you in the air? Are you in a secure place? Can you talk?"

"Slow down, Major." Tyler looked at the suit sitting at the desk in the tiny office next to him. The suit listening in on the call there. "I can talk, but maybe not for long." The suit nodded at the squawk box. *You got that right, buster.*

Spangler, back in his office in the Pentagon now, bristled. Not because Tyler had called him a major. The kid could not know all that had happened to the staff weenie who woke up as a major this morning but would go to bed as a one-star. No, make that *the* one-star. The main man in charge of striking back at the bastards who had hit the U.S.

"Okay, sorry. One thing at a time." As he talked, Spangler kept his eyes glued to the TV, as the smoke poured out of the North Tower of the World Trade Center. He checked his watch. 1059 hours. "Are you in the air?"

"No, sir, my flight was sent to Charlotte. I'm on the ground. In the airport." Looking at the same pictures on TV as the rest of America. Watching the tower without a twin, watching it burn.

"That's lucky as hell. Get over to Fort Bragg and get back in touch on a secure line."

"Major, I can't."

"Like hell. The things we talked about in our meeting yesterday, the things that Bowers gave a thumbs-down to?

They're on again. And this time, I'm in charge. I need to talk to you."

Tyler's mind searched for a euphemism. He found none. So he came right out with it. "No other way to put this, Major. I've been arrested."

"Arrested? Not funny, Tyler. Don't mess with me, pal. Today of all days. Not a good day to joke around."

"I'm not joking, Major."

"What? D&D at a bar? DUI? We can get you out of that but—"

"I beat up a guy on my flight. An Arab-looking guy. I thought he was a terrorist."

"Just an Arab?"

"Sort of."

"So what? A simple mistake. Anybody could—"

"He was one of ours."

"Ours? What you talking about, ours? An army guy?"

"More. A guy just like me. Same career field."

Two beats. "Tell me it wasn't . . . You didn't beat up one of ours?"

"I did."

"You saw his card?" Not a normal ID, of course. A lost card could not point a finger at a Delta man: *The bearer of this card is a trained Delta Force killer*. No. A Delta fighter carried a photo credit card, carte blanche with a special twist, good for cash anywhere in the world. Tyler's limit was a hundred grand, and he was a measly captain.

Spangler cleared his throat. "Um . . . you saw his—"

"Yes, I saw the holograph." The second, rainbow-colored photo that winked in and out of focus from beneath the surface of the credit card, the bearer's photo on top of a fluttering flag, the twist that IDed a soldier as a member of Delta Force.

"Shit. You get a name on this guy?"

"Baker. Ramsey Baker." Tyler sighed. "I might have killed him."

"Shit. I know Ramsey—well not *know* him, exactly, but I know he's a . . . was a good man. You killed him? Killed him how?"

"Hit him in the head with an ax."

"An ax? On a plane? How the hell do you sneak an ax onto a plane? *Why* the hell—?"

"It was a crash ax, all right? The pilot's. I got it from the pilot. He gave it to me. It's one huge comedy of errors, one screw-up after another. But now they think *I'm* the terrorist."

Spangler sank into a chair, his eyes still on the television. "They can't do this to me, Tyler. I need you, man. For my plan. I need you to take the point on going after these terrorists. The things we've been talking about? They've all come to pass. And then some. We have to act. I need you. I need you here."

Tyler sighed. "Major, I think it's going to take somebody with juice to get me out of this one."

"Who's in charge down there? Let me talk to him. Tell him I'm a brigadier general."

Spangler shot to his feet as the door to his office opened, and the four-star general from the X-Staff, Antonio Caranto, threw a plastic box of general's stars at him. He tried to catch it with his stiff and bandaged left arm. The box hit Spangler's chest, landed on the edge of his desk, and fell into the trash can.

"Consider that your promotion ceremony," Caranto said, dropping *Swift Sword* and a fresh copy of it on the desk. He stepped up to Spangler's ear, the one not covered by the phone.

In the phone, Tyler was saying, "Nice try, Major. The guy in charge is a U.S. marshal. He's been listening to us talk. He isn't going to buy the general thing—Oh, Lord."

The U.S. marshal forgot himself and spoke up into the squawk box. "Not again?" he said, adding a string of curses. "I can't believe it."

"Who is that?" Spangler asked.

At the same time, General Caranto, his back to the TV, spoke into the other side of Spangler's face. "Temporary promotion," the four-star said. "Very temporary. They pulled Bowers out of the fire. He's in ICU. He's going to live. As soon as he's on his feet, he's back in charge, and you're Major Mushroom again."

Spangler flopped into his chair.

"What the Christ?" said the four-star, turning to the TV.

In Charlotte, the air marshal cursed under his breath. Tyler's jaw fell to his chest.

All four men, as sick to their stomachs as any of the millions across the country, watched the North Tower fold into its own dust and the black smoke of its own fuel fire.

Nobody in America more ill than Brigadier General Roscoe G. Spangler. *They pulled Bowers out of the fire? He's going to live?*

2046 Hours Local, September 11, 2001—Kandahar, Afghanistan

Outside the rambling, walled compound carved into the belly of a modest neighborhood, a six-vehicle convoy stopped at an intersection. From an apartment building doorway, Nabil Abdulah Aziz watched as four rough men slouched out of the first four of the sport-utility vehicles and bunched up curbside next to the fifth vehicle. The door opened, and a trim, tall figure joined the others. Together the five swept toward the apartment building as the convoy sped off.

If anybody on the street paid any attention, they did not betray that they had seen so many weapons bristling from the windows of the convoy, carried by the four rough men, and the half dozen others in the shadows at the entrance of the apartment building.

Inside, the group burst into a stairwell, its door marked by the sign in Arabic: *Area Under Construction, Entrance Forbidden.*

At first glance, it did look like a construction area. The stairwell above was blocked off entirely with a mountain of sandbags. In fact, all the interior walls were lined with sandbags and the door double-lined with steel plates.

The men were met by a gangly six-foot-five sixteen-year-old. Aziz greeted the group, speaking over the head of one of the escorts, trying to see the tall figure behind. "Welcome, Sheik Osama bin Muhammad bin Laden, your glorious, your worship." As many times as he had practiced speaking like a man, his voice sounded shrill, like a child, no, like a girl.

"Praise be to God, not to me," bin Laden said from behind his guard.

The words were a wasp sting to Aziz's heart. His worship reprimanding him?

"And peace be upon our prophet Muhammad," bin Laden said, a gentle reprimand, to be sure, spoken in his soft singsong voice, but a reprimand nonetheless. "For the prophet was sent with the sword to ensure that no one but God is worshiped."

The guard's left hand shot out, grabbing Aziz by the ear, twisting and pulling to add a literal sting to that in his chest. "Did you hear, little ass? No one but God is worshiped. Now get out of the way." The guard used the boy's ear as a handle to throw him aside. "Where is our clarion?"

"Here."

"Where?"

"I am the clarion," Aziz said, pressing his ear against his head with one hand, to cool it and flatten out the new wrinkles in it. He glared at the guard, reflecting the evil eye. "And no ass." As he said it, he stepped out of range of that left hand. And a good thing, too. The hand shot out again, to grab him, but it closed only on a yellow scarf, a scrap of silk.

Aziz took off running, waving his own square of yellow silk ahead of him.

Ahead of the group of five tramping down two flights of stairs behind him, past a pair of guards and through double doors, and into a long corridor.

Aziz had won this job of clarion, running ahead of bin Laden, his worship, letting the compound guards know the signal for the prince's approach. Only he carried the signal cloths, a pair of blue squares in one pocket of his tunic, red in another, green in another, and the yellow. Only he would decide what color could pass. Nobody could fake a radio call and invade the compound through the passageway. Nobody would know the color of the true signal until Aziz ran by, waving it in his left hand. The escort of bodyguards must carry the same color, in the same hand, within moments. And his worship, so announced and cleared by Aziz and only Aziz, would pass through half a dozen guard stations along the way without delay.

Past four more guards Aziz ran, through a single door and an even longer corridor, this one much more narrow. At the far end, at the last guard station, he waved his yellow flag of victory and stood aside to watch back along his path.

Two of the rough men led the group, shoulder to shoulder, their outside shoulders touching the unfinished brick walls. Two more brought up the rear. The corridor, lit by naked twenty-five-watt bulbs spaced so far apart that his worship vanished into the darkness between them, was cold, and its floor uneven. The ceiling, perspiring with its underground dew, pressed down on the group, most of all his worship, boxed in by his bodyguards.

Aziz felt a twinge of disappointment as the group came close to this, the last post before the compound. Upstairs his worship had walked with grace, with deliberation, with the regal air of the prince he was. In the corridor he walked bent at the knees, leaning forward at the waist, long beard thrust forward of his narrow handsome face, his head cocked to keep his headpiece from brushing the ceiling, his full lips pursed like a woman's, an old, oddly pretty, bearded woman.

Aziz stood at attention. He braced himself, as the escort tossed the yellow silk at him. He felt a moment of pride as the prince walked into the light, the area with a full ceiling and stood up to his full height, once again his worship.

His heart stopped as bin Laden turned to him and smiled, forgiving him his mistake. Then, against all odds and even Aziz's most ambitious daydream, his worship focused those soft, friendly eyes on him and spoke to him.

"What is your name?"

"Aziz, your—your grace. Nabil Abdulah Aziz."

"A fine job as clarion, Aziz. Have you heard the news today? About our great victory over the infidel?"

"On the radio, Prince. Praise Allah, it was a great victory. Truly. I danced with my family in the street."

Bin Laden smiled. "You played a part in it. As clarion. And what part do you seek against the infidel, after you become a man?"

Aziz bristled. "I am a man already," he said, hoping he did not sound disrespectful to the prince but eager. "And I want his job." He pointed at the bodyguard who had twisted his ear and shot him a look of as much disrespect as he could muster. "To serve you, my prince."

Bin Laden laughed. "Better watch yourself then, Ahmed Ali Kamel." The guards in the stairwell beneath the compound joined bin Laden in laughter. Except for Kamel, who gave only a wisp of a smile on his bleak February face. Aziz felt its chill.

"Would you like to see this victory, then?" bin Laden asked.

Aziz was confused. "Yes, Lord, I wish I was there to see the infidel die, to give my own life, if possible."

"I suppose. But for now, would you like to see the images? On the television?" Aziz was too stunned to answer. He didn't have to, though. One of the sentries pushed him toward bin Laden, who captured him by the shoulder. "They are holding a video showing for us. Let us go."

All the way upstairs, bin Laden rested his hand on Aziz's shoulder, patting him like a pet hare. Aziz looked up into bin Laden's face, but his hero was thinking of far more important things than him. He kept patting his shoulder, but otherwise paid him no mind.

That didn't matter to Aziz. The hand of God had touched him. No matter that the thought might be blasphemy. His worship was as close as he ever expected to get to God. Until he died, in the fight against America and the others.

As the group strode into an anteroom upstairs, they were met with applause. The men there bowed in deference to his worship. To Aziz, it felt as if they were applauding him too.

The prince smiled. He nodded his head in humility. He gestured to the crowd, as if bestowing a blessing on them.

Aziz thought he should be bowing, too, to the prince. But he could not overcome his curiosity. His study of the man's every gesture, every expression. If he were to someday pick up the mantle of the prince, he would have to know how to act. He needed this study. He might never see the man again after tonight.

Only when the prince sat on cushions did the applause stop.

Bin Laden said a prayer, thanking Allah for the victory, praising his soldiers who had taken the battle to the unbelieving Americans. It was a long prayer, a boring prayer, but Aziz did not squirm as he sat at his worship's feet. He supposed that long, boring prayers were part of the job, if he were ever to follow in the prince's footsteps. He could endure it.

With a twirl of his fingers, his worship ordered the pictures to run.

Aziz looked around the room, packed tight with perhaps a hundred men, no women, of course, and he was proud to see, nobody as young as him. They were quiet, in awe of his worship, as they should be.

A murmur rose up, and he looked at the television. At the building burning with black smoke. "Praise Allah," he said, and the men in the room dared to echo his call.

The reaction surprised Aziz. Grown men following his lead.

As an airliner struck the second building, the South Tower of the World Trade Center, he remembered from the Al Jazeera radio reports, a cheer rose up from the crowd, the way the crowd cheered at the football game when the home team scored a surprise goal, say, from thirty meters out.

"Death to the infidel!" he shouted.

"Death to the infidel!" a hundred men shouted.

Aziz smiled. He liked the feeling of power it gave him to lead grown men at a time like this. The feeling was short-lived, though. A boot lashed out at him, striking him in the kneecap, paralyzing his leg down to his toes. He looked up through tears welling in his eyes. The bodyguard that he had insulted, Kamel. Aziz could not hear through the cheers of the crowd, but he could read lips well enough. The man called him an ass again.

Which he surely was, if he had offended his worship. He looked over his shoulder to see if bin Laden had noticed him. He had, in fact. His smile wondrous, his eyes damp.

Certainly the wonder was from the fire, the crash, the deaths of their enemy. His worship had called all these things. But, no, the prince had bestowed the look on him. Aziz melted in the warmth of it, and felt in that instant as if he and his worship were alone together in that room of rowdy celebrants.

It was too much for him to bear, as if looking into the face of divinity itself. He turned back to the television. The screen went dark. When it flickered back to life, one of the smoldering towers began to crumble. As if his worship had struck it by his own hand.

Aziz could not contain himself. He jumped to his feet and began cheering, "Death to the infidels! Death to America!"

The crowd picked up on it, and the noise grew so great that it penetrated to his core, not just through his ears, but through Aziz's skin, echoing in his chest.

"Death to the infidels! Death to America!"

He did not care if the bodyguard would hit him again. He would not feel that.

"Death to the infidels! Death to America!"

The video image flickered again, and when it came to life, the second tower, also struck by the hand of his worship, began to fold in upon itself, settling into the gray cloud of the first tower, until it, too, collapsed into its own heap of dust and smoke, the pointed antenna on its top the last image to vanish into a cloud the color of the desert.

Aziz began to scream.

"Death to the infidels! Death to America!"

He turned to throw himself at the feet of his worship.

But the prince and his contingent of rough men had vanished. He looked around and caught just a fleeting glimpse of the group as the door shut them into an adjacent room, the four guards, a man with a video recorder, and his worship.

He knew where they were going. To dine in celebration with other dignitaries. A place in the compound that he could not go. Not unless his worship had again placed a hand on his shoulder. To guide him there.

Which he had not.

One hundred men in the room danced and sang and prayed as if at a wedding on the day their national football team had won the World Cup. A celebration of his worship's victory. A miracle of America's defeat. A frenzy of joy. Aziz felt the joy as surely as he heard the roar of the crowd passing through his body. He felt like singing the praise of the prince who had changed the course of the world in a morning.

But he could not bring himself to dance, because the source of his joy had left the room with not so much as a wave to acknowledge his existence. The tears of joy in Aziz's eyes began to boil in bitter disappointment.

"Do you remember where you were?"

The question, from another clarion older than himself, puzzled Aziz. "What are you talking about?"

"Do you remember where you where when you heard the news of the strike of our heroic brothers against America?"

"Of course," Aziz said with a sneer. "How could I forget?"

II

Four Days

Ramsey Baker came awake all at once, ejected from a black hole. One second he's lying dormant in a deep, dark, fuzzy, state of nothing. The next second, he is thrust into too much light. One moment he is an empty shell of a spirit, no body, no thinking, no feeling, no nothing. The next second, he is wracked with pain and dazzle.

The light is the sun itself boring red and loud through his eyelids. He would put up a hand to shield his eyes, but his arms can't move the throbbing weights that pin him down. He would call out, but all that issues from his throat is a hiss. He would turn his head away from the light, but somebody has driven a spear through his forehead, tacking him to the pillow like a moth on—

The hatchet! Not a spear, but a hatchet. Buried in his skull.

He senses a shadow at his left. He begs the figure, "Don't hit me again." His mouth cannot form the words. His lips and tongue too fat. He can hear, and that's the best of it. All he can do is hear his own gargling that passes for words. Hear and gargle.

"He's awake," says the figure to his left, a woman. She's not going to hurt him. Her voice is too gentle for that. A cool, damp cloth wipes at his eyes, loosening the crust and rolling it like spikes across his skin. Maybe if it weren't so bright, he could open his eyes now, open his eyes and let out the tears.

"I need to talk to him," says a man near his feet. "Is he aware enough?" A man whose voice alleges he will not hurt. He could, if he has to. But he will not. For now.

The woman cares about Ramsey and protests. "I don't know, General. How can I know? This is inhuman, using drugs to bring a man out of a coma after such an extensive trauma. It's a wonder he hasn't coded already. It's happened. The injury to his head—he could toss a clot and stroke out. The stress on the heart—"

True enough to Ramsey, his heart ready to burst. He sounds a warning. "The terrorist," he calls out. "He tried to kill me with a hatchet." No words. Just grunts and groans, whistles and whines. He'd have better luck farting in Morse code. But he has to ask: "Did the plane crash?"

"He's aware of his surroundings," the woman says. "For heaven's sake, let us close his skull, suture the wounds, set the broken bones, bring in an orthodontist, a plastic surgeon. In two weeks he'll be back on limited duty. In six months you could have him debating UN resolutions. But this—"

"I'll ask him if he wants limited duty. Or a post at the UN."

"You think that's funny?"

"I have to talk to him."

"Fair warning, General Spangler, I have to report this."

"Don't waste your time."

"I'm obliged. By regulation."

"Of course you are. Now if you don't mind."

"All right. Go ahead. Talk to him."

"You can't be in here, Major."

"Call me doctor."

"You must leave, Doctor Major. Top secret."

Baker feels the swirl of a cool breeze as she goes. He smells a thin wisp of her antiseptic fragrance leaking into his swollen nose.

"Oh, Doctor? Oh, Major?" the man calls after. *Oh, Bitch?*
"General?" *Asshole?*

"In time, if you do get a plastic surgeon to work on this man?"

"Yes?"

"See if he can do something about these ears, while he's at it."

Baker heard a whisper of a curse word and couldn't tell whether it was hers or his own. The bastard adding insult to his injuries?

A shadow filled the left corner of his vision, the place the major had left vacant. He felt a hand, too soft for a working man, slide under the little finger of his left hand. A spike pierced his left forearm. He felt the grinding of bone ends inside his arm swollen fat and hard, but he did not cry out. Beneath all this damage, he was still a Delta Force officer. And this was a senior officer.

"Captain Baker, I'm General Spangler. If you roger that, press on the back of my hand."

Baker winced at the pain of trying. He lifted his good right hand into the air and pulled his trigger finger three times.

"Hey, General, you goddamned moron, that arm is broken. Move your ass around to the other side of the bed, shit-for-brains." Baker nearly fainted with the effort of his gargling.

"For chrissakes, I must have shit for brains. This is the broken arm, isn't it?"

Baker felt the hand slide away and kept a cry of pain inside. Had the general heard the *shit-for-brains* remark? No, no way. He couldn't even make out his own words. He felt a touch at his right hand and closed his fist around three fingers, trying to reassure the man he didn't mean to call him such names as shit-for-brains.

"Once again, I'm General Spangler. Do you roger?"

Baker squeezed the hand, not only soft but weak. For now, he set aside his pain—did not forget it, just set it aside. The Delta operator in him willed the hurt to the back of his head. So he could work in the front, where he had so many questions.

"Any idea what happened to you? Who did this? How?"

Baker forced his eyes open, breaking the glue. He saw stars first, then the bandages on the general's face, and the seeping blisters. The thick, dark lenses. And beneath the lenses he could see a slice of . . . *pink eyes? What happened to me? What the hell happened to you?* He couldn't get over it—this wart on an albino toad's ass was a general? *Guy looked like he was the one in a hatchet fight without a hatchet. This guy was making remarks about* his *ears? With a mug like Freddy Krueger?*

Baker opened his fist, palm up, splaying his fingers and flopping the back of his hand on the mattress

"Okay, okay. Roger that. I have to ask *yes* or *no* questions, right?"

Baker gave a thumbs-up. And one at a time. Seeing the lenses in those glasses were so thick. If the guy stood in the light just right the focused glare might fry him like an ant under a kid's magnifying glass.

"Okay, I've got it. You know about the terrorists?"

Baker snapped his fingers twice, like gunshots. *The turd had to be a cousin of the chairman of one of the joint chieves. No other way could he get stars. Come on, general, get with the program.* He held his thumb and first two fingers together and scribbled in the air just above his sheets.

"Write? You think you can write?"

Thumb up.

After the general thrashed about for a minute, bashing the lid of a briefcase against his throbbing right knee, Baker felt a legal pad slid under his arm. He closed his fingers around the barrel of a ballpoint pen and wrote: *Terr on my plane? Crash?*

Spangler smiled before starting the grim fairy tale of 9-11. This Baker, what a pro he was. And Delta Force. What a bunch. Cut off an operator's head but stay clear of the dismembered mouth so the man doesn't rip out your throat in his teeth. Baker. He just met the man. Already his hero.

A hero he could barely look at for the oozing split in the skull, the lips of the wound left gaping on his own orders. And his ears. What the hell had Tyler done to the guy's ears?

Spangler averted his eyes to the wall as he recounted the events of 9-11. Saying the words out loud were incredible enough, even to him, although he had watched a hundred replays of the two towers falling in on themselves. And he'd lived through the one blast. There was that image of Bowers lurking at the near side of his mind's eye, hair on fire, lips blistered like overcooked hot dogs on the grill, one side of his face hit with double-ought buckshot, black scabs of heat-dried blood pools in the ears, fire-crusted ooze—

He shook his head free of the vision. Man. Bowers used to think his pet major looked bad. Guy'd better beg his stars to die, so he wouldn't have to live out a life looking worse than Spangler.

Since the face of Bowers took over the wall, he told the rest of his story to the ceiling. After he'd finished, Baker lay inert. Spangler took his hand and squeezed it to comfort him.

"I know, Ramsey. It was a horrid thing. I saw it, some of it in person, and I don't believe it yet."

Baker shook his hand free, scribbled, and tapped on the legal pad.

"Terrorists aboard your plane?" Spangler sighed. "No. No terrorist." He shook his head. "Worse." He filled his lungs with air and told the truth about Connor Tyler, Baker's fellow officer, a Delta guy nearly killing him. How the man reacted would tell Spangler whether he could propose his own harebrained purpose for coming here.

Baker scribbled: *I got call on cell re wtc crash—Saw guy coming w/hatchet—thought hes terr*

"I understand. He thought you were a terrorist, too."

Bc Im Arab?

"Yes, because you looked like an Arab terrorist and because the captain called him forward to tell him about the second airliner crash."

My plane crash? Baker tapped the pen on the pad for emphasis.

"No, Tyler beat you up. Some passengers got in a few kicks when you were down and out. I'm sorry. Tyler is sorry."

Id do the same to him

Spangler laughed. God, even a sense of humor. "Just to
bring you up to date. The president says we will strike back at
terrorists and any nation that supports them. The airlines still
aren't flying. Some Ārabs in the Middle East are dancing in
the streets. The air force is flying AirCap over Washington,
D.C., and New York City. The navy—"

Baker tapped rapidly on the legal pad. He had written
something while Spangler was talking, trying to ease into the
reason he'd come.

U want—what?

"Well, it's a long story, but—what?"

Talk fast—Im tired

With no more setup needed, Spangler did as Baker wanted.
As he spoke, he cringed. Said aloud, it was truly a bonehead
plan, a pipe dream, an absurdity wrapped in a fantasy locked in
a delusion. When he finished, Baker stabbed at the legal pad
as if he were carving his response in stone.

For christ sake—who fricking dreamed this up?

"I did," Spangler said. "Crazy, huh?"

F—ing insane!!!!

Spangler smiled that the man didn't write out the obscenity. At a time like this, when he could take all kinds of liberties, he still kept to a code of respect. Still. "I guess you don't
want to play. I don't blame you."

Screw that

"I understand."

No U don't

"What do you mean?"

Ill do it

"Are you sure? It probably won't work. It'll probably get
you killed. Nobody would blame you for saying no."

Baker grasped the pen in his fist, like a chisel.

Do it, he carved. *ASAP!!! B4 Ichange—mind*

Spangler would have hugged the man. Except he was
afraid of doing more damage to his body. That he could not
do. Not when his country needed that broken body and titanium spirit in the worst way.

"Couple things and I'll let you sleep," Spangler said.

Baker flashed his palm. *What?*

"Are you a Christian?"

No. Y?

"Muslim?"

Thumb down.

"Any religion?"

Scribble. *Army—DF Army*

"Fine. Just drop the references to Christ, okay?"

????

"You wrote *christ's sake*. You can't do that if you're trying to pass as a Muslim."

Thumb up and fist clenched.

"Second, we change your name. You're now Ramsay al Bakr." Spangler spelled it.

Thumb up.

"Third, I see in your file you speak Arabic. It says like a native speaker. Is that so?"

Thumb up.

"Scale of 1 to 10?"

One angry hand flapped at him twice.

"Right. I have a meeting to get to—you'll be happy to hear this—we're going to a new team concept to hit back at these bastards, hit them where they live. Literally."

Open palm. *So what?*

"Right, if you can't be a part of it, what do you care, huh? Okay, here, I'm sliding a form under your hand. Sign your name right . . . there, where your pen is touching. That's a release form. It gives us your permission to take you into military care and custody. You'd be leaving all your medical decisions to us—the army—me." In truth, the CIA, but Spangler wasn't about to spring *that* on the kid. Not on top of all the other pains in the ass.

Baker scrawled his name. Then found the pad and scribbled: *Now outta here! For Muhammed's sake!!!*

"Funny. Get some sleep. When you wake up, you'll be in the custody of a CIA man. Carnes is his name. You'll be his prisoner, a POW."

Thumb up, finger pointed at the door. *Out!!*

"Captain Baker, I—" Spangler's voice broke with emotion.
Palm up, Baker fluttered four fingers. *C'mon, c'mon, out with it.*

"You understand, they might take one look at you and kill you on the spot."

Open hand, palm up. *So?* He patted around for the pen, found it, gripped it like a javelin and scribbled, *ThatdBworsen this???????*

"Yeah, it'd probably be a relief with what you're going through now. But . . . you say the word, and I'll have them take you right down to surgery, close that head wound, set the broken bones, stitch up the cuts. Fix the ears. You don't have to do this. Nobody would blame you if—"

Baker stabbed the pad. *Get the F—out————before I change my mind—————SIR!!!*

"Good, that was good, the way you didn't use *Christ* there."

Baker groaned with an involuntary smile that contorted his fattened face. Spangler squeezed the fist that clamped the pen and stepped away. He took the legal pad with him. Just in case it fell into the wrong hands, say, some righteous, bleeding heart-doctor-major-bitch with pals in the media.

In the hallway outside Baker's room, he came face to smiling face with the CIA man.

"I heard every word," Carnes said. "You're good, Roscoe, very damned good. Ever thought about a career in CI?"

"I've got a sudden new talent for lying, I guess," Spangler said, letting a sneer play at his mouth. "Twenty-four years of playing straight arrow, and I make it all the way to pissant major. One day of lying out my ass, and they bump me three grades to One-Star."

"What's 'at tell you?"

"That I should have been in the CIA all along?" Spangler shook his head as he held out the release form with Baker's signature, scrawled like a kid his first week in penmanship. "Carnes, take care of this guy."

"Course. Kid's got balls. I gotta love that."

"Balls?" Spangler turned his head to dry-spit. "Brain damage is more like it. A hatchet in the head? Practically a lobotomy? He's not the same guy he was. And never will be."

"We didn't put the ax in his head, Roscoe."

"Maybe not. But we're the ones not letting him have full medical. We're the ones throwing him to the wolves."

Carnes held up the signed release, one finger pinching the paper at the scrawl of a signature, a look of: *See here? He signed it, didn't he?*

Spangler shook his head. "It's us doing this, all right. He doesn't know what the hell he's doing."

"Take it back if you're getting a sudden case of the scrupes. Take it back and tear it up." Carnes held out the release.

Spangler pooched his lips. "Okay, I get what you're saying. It's not the CIA to blame. If they string him up by his gut, I'm the guy with his nuts stewing on a hot rock."

"No," Carnes said, shaking his head, flapping the paper. "If you'da reached for it, I'da pulled it away and run like hell. Guy like this? Plan with this kinda balls? Chance to infiltrate the A-Q? It comes along once in maybe two dozen lifetimes. We gotta play it. We gotta play it out just cause it's there. It's like, from that movie. We're on a mission from God."

"Yeah. We're the Blues Brothers, all right. More like the Lose Brothers."

The irony was wasted on Carnes. The CIA man was half a corridor away, walking at lope, getting clear before anybody else in the hall could have that attack of scruples.

"Take care of that kid," Spangler shouted.

Carnes turned and called back, "You gotta plane to catch, Roscoe." He waved the release sheet one last time as he turned the corner beneath a sign and arrow, leaving one last glimpse of himself for Spangler, his free hand pointing toward the sign: Patient Discharge.

Spangler went to find Major Doctor Bitch. She'd gladly give Baker a cocktail that would put him to sleep for half a day.

Tyler said an awkward thanks to the air force VIP driver assigned to take him to home, sweet hell, from Nellis Air Force Base.

"You're welcome, sir," the woman said. Already a tech sergeant at twenty and proud enough to say so on the drive into suburban Las Vegas. Just making small talk, but revealing so much more. A young life of driving generals and looking drop-dead pretty had boosted her self-assurance into an orbit right up there with the actresses on the *JAG* TV show. Smile right out of the tooth-whitener ads, legs out of *Cosmo*, air force-issue skirt out of regulation specs, its hem cut a full four inches too high. Tyler could see that—hell, any man could see what she wanted him to see. But Tyler? Women went out of their way to *make* him see. And he was too weak not to notice. Which was why he was in the fix he was in.

He stepped from the sedan, wincing at the cramp in his back, a leftover from the assault on Ramsey Baker. When he stuck his left hand into his pocket, the scabs on his knuckles reminded him again. He leaned down, his hair cascading into his eyes as if telling him not to look. He tried not to, *damn,* he tried. He averted his gaze from her bent right leg, the knee cocked up on the front seat, skirt riding far higher than four inches, much too Sharon Stone high to be an accident. *Pink.*

"I guess that's all," he said, not-noticing as hard as he could but seeing against his will. Pink panties.

"For a second there, I thought you were going for your money clip to give me a tip." Her teal-tinted eyes circumnavigated his face, eyes, hair, eyes, mouth, eyes, nose, eyes. "Like as if I was a cab driver."

"Yeah. I guess I've spent too much time in New York." He let his gaze lock to hers. Not a come-on. But to not notice her panties. And to notice . . . *what*? What was it about this young woman? Something—

"Yes, sir. Will you be needing me for anything else?" Perfect smile. Perfect contact-colored-blue-green and sharp, wide-eyed look of the hawk. Perfect innocence. Perfect danger. Perfect package on a fast track to master sergeant before she could buy a legal drink. He didn't want her looking into his eyes, but where else, not pink, could he look?

"No, thank you." Fighting to keep that eye contact, fighting the pink, fighting, fighting.

She took his gaze as *his* come-on. "I could wait here for you?" *Inside, if you like?*

"Be back here in thirty minutes."

"Sure, sir." A wry smirk. *Screw you, sir.*

He shut the door between them. Too much time in New York, indeed. Too much time spent toying with women. Always walking that wire. Look where it got him.

He limped up to the front door of the ranch rambler, far too rambling for an army captain's salary—Amy's money, not his. Careful to use knuckles not sore from the beating he'd given them on Baker's face, he rapped four times, then twice, then once. So she would know him by the paranoia he'd forced on Amy. And knocked the sequence in reverse when she did not come right away. Had she had already walked out? Yes.

Good.

No. A *rap-a-tap* tapping of her heels sounded from inside.

She yanked the door open, her hawk eyes glittering the cold green of emeralds, square jaw set, full mouth turned down, a suitcase in one hand, the rest of their luggage on the floor behind her. Any day but this, it would have been funny. Him coming back from a trip without bags, her answering the door amid mountains of Gucci, hers.

"You're packing." *Jesus, you're beautiful when you hate me.*

She raised one thin eyebrow, looking him level in the eye, as tall as him in flat, beaded five-hundred-dollars-of-her-own-money shantung thong sandals: *And you're a genius.*

"For you or me?"

"I'm taking Brendan to live with my parents until we can get a place of our own." *We don't need you; we never needed you all that much, in case you've forgotten who wears the purse in this family, Mister-army-officer-salary-no-good-low-rent-shit.*

"No need. I have to catch a plane in an hour. I don't know when I'll be back." *Or if I will* in the tone of it. He surveyed the bags in the hallway. "Mind if I take the duffel? Marshals confiscated my stuff. They said they lost it. Probably send it in by a week."

She stood stiff and brittle as an icicle, the duffel grip locked in her hand, leaning atilt under its weight. He leaned in and pried it from her white-knuckled fingers, catching a glimpse of her breasts, full and free behind the silk of her Versace blouse, catching the scent of her own musk mixed with that of some damned French fragrance designer whose name he could never remember or even want to, feeling a moment of dizziness to go along with his shame and regret. It was her eyes. Falling in love again, for the second time today already. With a woman who hated him. Chrissake, falling in love with his own wife. How sick was that?

"Aren't you going to ask how I know about her? Laren?" She shook her head. "How I know her name?"

He locked eyes with her. *No need, Ice Queen.* He patted the cell in his breast pocket. *Beautiful. Angry. She hated him. He hated her. He wanted to throw her on the floor and screw her.* "I checked my messages. All of them. Even the saved ones. You know, the ones you checked for me." He should tell her. He and Laren had talked some serious things. Things that didn't involve Amy. *Screw her first, then tell her.*

"So I'm the guilty party here?" She didn't try to hide her fury, but she didn't shout, either. "I catch you cheating on me, and you're the victim?"

"How long have you been snooping?" Staring still.

"Not until after she called here, this Laren." Wielding her name like a cudgel, barely making a sound as it crashed against his skull.

"What?" Laren wouldn't do that. Call his home number. He was the one who was to broach the topic of a separation. A trial. He did not blink. He stared into those hawk eyes. She stared into his. Her magic was working on him. His was not. She was pissed.

"She called here first, Laren did, before she left that . . . that filthy voice mail about you two spending the night." Amy looked as if she might puke, remembering it. He had to wince himself at the replay in his head: *I love you, Connie. I love you, I love you, I love you.*

He shook his head, feeling truly ill that Amy had heard those words on the message, still not breaking the stare, but— "She wouldn't do that—call here."

"So you say, but she did. A wrong number. She was shook up. Maybe she called by mistake, but she called all right—Laren did. I'd never forget that voice."

"Fine. She called here. What does it matter? That's beside the point, isn't it? The point is—"

"Don't tell me what the point is, you son of a bitch." She had this way of enunciating every word, even the curse words, clipping and cutting them in that flat tone. A way of shouting at him without ever raising her voice. "The point is, you slept with Laren. You spent the night with Laren. You committed adultery with Laren. You—" She ran out of clean words to throw at him. "You fucked her, damn you."

"Okay, enough. I get it, Amy, I get it. I'm—"

She stabbed at his face with a finger. "Don't you dare say you're sorry. Don't you dare." She shook her head, flustered in her fury, though still not shouting. "Forget you." She could not use the other word again so soon.

Leaving them both to stand fidgeting, locked in the grip of each other's eyes.

He. Falling into the green. The deepest sea green of a roller before it thrashes itself to foam. Sheeny, shiny green, rising, curling, uplifting green in the instant before it curls, posing, hanging, backlit by a low sun, giving the barest glimpse of the deepest reaches of the sea floor, promising in days past the warmth of a velvet embrace, but now little more than the warmth of an emerald, all hard and faceted and impersonal, tipping, toppling, wrapping into a pipeline, eager to grind him to bloody pulp against the salty coral bottom. Only the brave dared to be drawn into that curl, only the foolhardy risked its agitation, its crumple, its crush. There in those eyes be dragons, a rough sleep, a drowning, an infinite, restless exile, an eternity spent floating facedown bobbing in the surf.

Still he tried to see into her. *Don't blink,* he pleaded. *Let me see past the green this once and into your soul. Let me love you.*

She. Dulled by the steely gray that gave her back her own reflection. Afraid to see behind the buffed titanium doors to his vault.

Let me soak here in your eyes, forever. Let me stay here

until you learn to love me in full. I will wait for you to come to me. For as long as it takes, if you but give me the smallest sign, the faintest of hopes. Tell me that you will come to me in time. And I will be here. But . . .

I will only wait alone. Not with her. I will not share you with her. Laren. And I will not be shared. Say it's me. Me, me, me, and not Laren.

Until the crying of their six-month-old son broke the wooden silence. They both blinked as one and stopped staring.

"Brendan," he said. "You'd better see to him. I have to catch a helicopter in an hour."

She grasped a fistful of her hair, chopped above her ears, reckless and rough-cut in the way only the beautiful dared wear it. "That's it? You walk in, pack your bags, turn around, and walk out?"

He shrugged, the duffel swaying. "Ten minutes and you would have left."

"How come you never called me?"

"Isn't it obvious? I checked my messages. Two of them had already been listened to, Spangler's and Laren's. What was I going to tell you? 'Hey, babe, that message from the other woman? Ignore it because it's not what you think it is? She really doesn't—'" He couldn't bring the rest of the lie to hearing: *She really doesn't love me; she really doesn't mean a thing to me.* Because Laren had already told Amy she did love him—what the hell was Laren thinking, anyhow? Was that on purpose? And Amy could fill in the rest, that he'd told Laren he loved her, too. So he went another way. "Besides, I was in jail. Chrissake. I had to deal with that first."

Now she had two fistfuls of hair, and her face screwed up with questions. "You were in jail? You said marshals before. You said marshals had your luggage? What's going on?" She threw a worried glance over her shoulder as Brendan's crying rose an octave and refitted her frown over her mother's face again when she turned back to Tyler.

He felt his stomach lurch. "It's a long story." He didn't have time to get into who loved whom, and he damned well wasn't going to get into his assault on another Delta Force operator, an assault that might yet turn into a homicide. Not right now. Maybe later, when he had a month or two to explain, or never. He should do the decent thing, at least. At least tell her he was sorry. For cheating, for lying, for wanting out of the marriage. He owed her that much. *I'm sorry, Amy. Truly. I was wrong to treat you like that. But I've made a decision. I'm leaving you. For Laren. She loves me. I love her.*

"We're at war," he said, lame as it felt from his mouth. And what a relief war was. Not to have to talk about infidelity and separation and divorce at the time of war. "I have a job to do, and I can't talk to you about it now." Goddamned terrorists. If he ever had a chance at bin Laden, he'd kill the sonofabitch for personal reasons above all else. He could not hold the stare.

He looked down, unzipped the duffel and tried to step around her.

She let go of her hair, folded her arms, and stepped in front of him. "Did you call her?"

"What?"

"Don't play games with me. You didn't call me, and I want to know. Did you call her? Laren? The home-wrecker? Did you return her voice mail? Did you tell her I know? Did you call her? Laren?"

She wanted the eye contact now. He looked past her. She stepped into his line of sight, her hair wild as bed-head. Brendan shrieked anew.

"Come on, Amy, let me by."

"Did? You? Call? Laren?"

"No." He looked her in the eye. *Okay, bitch*—And it struck him. For the first time. That look of the hawk. She and Laren had it. For that matter, RuthAnn and that VIP driver—yes, that was the something he saw in the driver's eyes. Not just green eyes, but—the look of the hawk. They all had it. Maybe that's what drew him to them. *No harm, no foul, dear, I only went for them because they look like you.* Right. That'd go over. *You see, the reason I'm leaving you? I found a woman who looks just like you, only more. One good idea after another, Conn, one good idea after another.*

She glared into his face. He didn't dare let his silence give its own wrong answer.

"No," he said. "Whatever else I lied about, I can tell you this now, the one true thing. No, I did not call her back. I did not talk to her. I wanted to—" It sounded so out of tune to his inner ear, but he said it anyhow. "I wanted to talk to you first. I figure I owe you that much."

"Ha!" She raised her chin and squinted one hawk eye. "Are you going to leave us? For her? For Laren?" Upstairs, Brendan cried out as if he, too, wanted to know.

"I already told you I have to go. It's a war. I'm a soldier." *And a gutless husband.*

"Damn you," she said in that infernal flat tone. "You know what I mean. Do you want a divorce? So you can be with Laren instead of us?"

And there it was. Out in the open. All he had to say was: *Yes, I want a divorce.* Or he could simply say, *No, I don't want a divorce. I'm sorry. I want to save our marriage.*

"Yes. No. I don't . . . I don't have time to get into all of this. I've got"—he glanced at his watch—"I've got to lift off from Nellis in an hour. I'm in charge of a strike force—forget I said that."

"Screw you and your top secret secrets. I don't care about them."

"Fine." He tried to step past her.

She stepped in his way. "Call her."

"What?"

"Laren. Call Laren now."

"What the hell for?" He wished she'd stop saying *Laren.* But that was her point, wasn't it? And he dared not let her know how it pricked him each time she said it.

"Okay, so you don't have time for all the other, but you do have time to call her. Call her this very second. Go on. Tell Laren what you just told me. 'Laren, I don't want a divorce. Laren, I don't want to be with you. Laren, I want to fix my marriage.' Tell her that. You say you owe me? Before you leave. Give me that, that one true thing."

"Amy. This is nuts." If only she knew how nuts.

A tiny smile creased her face. "No, this is nut-crunch time, buster. Fixing a marriage will take time, maybe years, if it can be done at all. Breaking it off with Laren will take you ten seconds, tops. 'Laren, we're history.' If you want to. If you don't—" She left the rest to hang in the air. The house was quiet, except for the unrelenting cries of their child.

He felt the knots in his jaw. She had him, and he knew it, right where she said, by the nuts. She was right. He was a shit. He wanted it all, both of them, Amy and Laren, plus all the other hawk-eyed women on the side. She was telling him, *No deal; choose me, or choose the rest of them.*

"Connor?" The smile had evaporated. Her voice was small and reedy, Lady Disdain melting into a puddle of herself. "If you don't call her, Laren is all you'll have. I won't be here— Brendan won't be here—when you come back. I swear it. I'll hire the best lawyer in the state . . . in the world, to keep you from him." She had the bucks to do it, too. And the grace not to say so.

Brendan. He wanted to stall, to look at his watch, to pack, to make some space in his head to think about it, but he dared not stall. She was right again; this was crunch time. Whatever else lay ahead of him lost in the fog of war and marriage, one thing was clear. When she told him to choose, a single beam of light in his head shone on a single truth. He chose. He might lose his wife or even his lover, maybe both. He could not lose his son. Not for all the hawk-eyed women in the world. He chose Brendan. Maybe he could keep up the stopovers with Laren. Maybe she would get over that biological clock thing she was always bitching about lately.

He plucked the digital phone from his shirt pocket and flicked it open. Shame prickled his skin. He'd preset Laren's number. Which was no better nor worse than knowing it from memory, which he did. Another topic for later. He touched the preset and found a spot on the ceiling to study so he could avoid meeting his wife's accusing hawk eyes. Upstairs, Brendan's cries went from howling to sudden sobbing. Laren's voice spoke to him in flat, tired tones.

He closed the phone. "I got her machine." He knew the

greeting and did not listen to it. No way would he leave a message, not now, in Amy's hearing. "She's not home."

"Call her at work."

Again the prickles. He chose the second preset for Laren.
Her desk. *Be there, Laren.* He didn't want to call one more
preset, the cell phone.

"EveningTimes-MirrorFran," a husky smoker's voice said,
as one word. A woman in the tone of, *And-this'd-better-be-
good.*

"Connor Tyler for Laren Hodges."

Amy watched with a look of calm. She kept up the image of a
resolute hard-ass. Inside she was a wreck, her heart beating
fast as a sparrow's. Even if he told Laren the news, even if he
wasn't calling a pizza joint and faking it, she knew she might
yet lose him. All that staring. It made her want to take him,
right here in the doorway, on the stairs. What was it about
those eyes of his? Oh, dear heavens, what was she thinking?
He had a kept woman. At least one, maybe more. How long
had he kept up these things after the wedding? Did he ever
stop? Oh . . .

Would he ever stop? No matter what he said now, an hour
from now he could call Laren back and undo it all. She saw
the cuts on his hands. From marshals? Or a bar fight? What
new lie—?

His face grew hard. "I'm a friend of hers is why. I flew out
of town Tuesday and wanted to let her know I'm safe . . .
Tyler . . . right, that guy."

His face went slack. She was coming on the line to talk to
him? Why else would he look so sick? Would he back out
now? Ditch his wife instead? Dammit, he had to go through
with this or—Or what? She wasn't sure.

"Yes, Tuesday, 9-11 . . . yes . . . yes, the army guy."

He dropped the duffel.

"What? Are you sure? . . . Well, yes, of course you are.
I'm—Sorry to bother—So sorry."

He shut his cell and looked into her eyes. He was ill. But no, she'd come this far. Now was not the time to go soft on him. Make him tell her, even if he was faking it. "Call her cell."

"No."

"What?"

"Hell no."

"Are you telling me you don't have that preset, too?"

"No."

"Then call her."

"No."

"Bastard." She heard her voice crack. "Call her, Connor, call Laren on her cell, or I swear to you—"

"Shut up, Amy."

"What?"

"She's dead."

"What?"

"Laren. She's dead. They pulled her body out of the rubble at Ground Zero this morning. She died in the collapse"—his throat clicked shut—"of the towers, one of the towers." He shook his head. "The second tower. The South Tower."

Amy put a hand to her face.

He shoved by her. "Happy now?" He took the stairs two at a time, tossing clothes from the duffel on the way up, leaving a bra-and-panty trail of clutter. Brendan howled, the sound in her ears pounding in tune with her heart.

She dropped her hand from her face. In the entry mirror she saw an ugly trace smile. "No," she said to herself, for she was the only one who could hear her flat, hushed tone. "I'm not happy." Well, maybe a little, God forgive her, that Laren that woman that mistress that bitch home-wrecker was dead. That part gave her a rush of relief. But Amy was not so happy at the other part, what Tyler's face told her: that he'd just lost the love of his life in the rubble at Ground Zero.

Atin-hut!

Tyler stood erect. Like the other forty-five men in the tiny briefing room at the back of a hangar in Tonopah, Nevada. His leg still throbbed where Ramsey Baker had kicked him twice in the same spot, just below the knee. His fists ached, and a strained pec muscle needled him in the chest. Nothing like the pain on the inside, though. The pain of Laren. He'd kept her voice mail. She said she loved him, and she meant it. He'd started to play it back on the HC-130 ride out, but felt tears welling up and dared not try in front of others who—

A door opened at the back of the stage. What the hell was he doing? Thinking like that? At a time like this? This time of war.

He forced his body rigid, shoulders square, thumb-knuckles touching the outside seams of his trousers. He held his chin erect and locked his mouth shut, putting his body into the regulation posture. Except for his eyes. Instead of staring straight ahead, he watched the ranking officer take the stage.

All that effort. Wasted on the twerp now dragging ass out of the shadows. General Roscoe Spangler, with all the military bearing of a bum picking cans out of the gutter. A couple of groans rose up from the crowd, and Tyler felt sorry for the general. Short, fat, lumpy body shifting in his uniform like a sack of rats. Wearing a mask of day-old roadkill. Thick, smoked glasses, prisms in the harsh light, sending reflections all over the room like a mirror ball at the prom. *Chrissake, Spangler, shape up.* Pigeon-toed and knock-kneed, he didn't belong in this room full of the best fighting men the army could muster. Spangler needed a few weeks on the Atkins diet. Make that a few months. Hell, he'd never shape up, not in two army careers. And Tyler was not the only one to think it. Hushed curse words hissed up from the crowd. Feet shuffled.

Jesus. The country at war, and this bent-dick-freak-Halloween-mask-sack-of-shit in charge of its most deadly fighting force? What the hell was the Pentazoo thinking? That they might show this guy to Al Qaeda and get bin Laden to laugh himself to death?

Spangler found the spotlight. He stood in the glare at the center of the half oval stage, a frog on a lily pad. Ambient scars, fresh blisters, fat lips. *Christ.* He found every face and stared at it in turn. Until every noise petered out, until even the breathing shut down.

Spangler spoke in a tired mild voice. "At ease, take seats."
The murmurs drifted up again.

"I said sit your asses down, goddammit."

Forty-six sets of knees buckled on Spangler's shout. Forty-six spring-loaded seats slapped open as one.

"Standing there at a half-ass position of attention." The stage lights caught the glitter of his spit-spray. "Moping and grab-assing like a bunch of snot-nose recruits." Spangler pointed his finger into the crowd and jabbed at the faces out there in front of him so each man could take each insult to heart. "You. And you, and you, and you." He shook his head. "Call yourself soldiers. You make me sick."

He let it lay for a full half minute of aching silence, then took a deep, weary breath. *Now that I have your interest . . .*

"Try not to think of me as just a fat-ass midget with stars." A couple of stifled laughs turned into pig snorts. "Think of me as the fat-ass midget with stars who gets to handpick the roster of the teams that go after the Al Qaéda somebitches that killed so many of our people two days ago. They killed our brother- and sister-Americans, and I'm gonna pick the men to make the payback calls. That. Is all. I am. To you."

With that, he had them. A gush of curse words came from forty-six gut reactions.

"Let's get the obvious out of the way," Spangler said. "I ain't never been in special ops." A death-mask smile sparkled in the spotlight. "I ain't got the body for what you do. I'm too short, too fat, too crippled, too weak in the back, the bowel, and the bladder." Letting the tension out of the room like air from a bike tire. "I can't see to shoot straight. Only time I ever jumped out of an airplane, it was on fire." Open laughter now. Tyler gave an uneasy grin. As the audience eased into Spangler, the wall between a general and everybody else went flat. Spangler no longer the midget, but the cat trainer. No longer the toad, but the owl. No longer the one-star, but the good old boy riding the rap of the grunt.

"Only time I ever low-crawled was to the latrine so I could puke in the shitter." That got a few amens, as he began to click with the men. "I got crooked feet, crooked legs, a crooked back, one crooked arm, and a bent dick." Laughter. "Which the ladies dearly love." Roars.

"Only thing we have in common, me and you, is we are both of the same mind. We both want to kill Al Qaeda bastards in the worst way, maybe string up that somebitching Osama bin Asshole by the balls." The men leaped to their feet to clap. Tyler got up, not to cheer but to stand with the rest. "A little rat poison in their tea and a red-hot poker up the ass, so they can fry at both ends." More roars and woofs.

Until Spangler spread his arms over the crowd as if he were the Christ figure. "At ease. Take seats." The men sat ramrod straight and silent. As he grew solemn. "We share the same mind. And I have only one thing that makes me superior to you—and it sure as shit ain't these stars." He tore one of them from his collar and sent it skittering across the stage. "Hell, last week I was nothing but a pissant major shoveling darkness out of the basement of the Pentagon, singing my one-note song to nobody because only nobody would listen. That's right, that's all I got, a one-note song: how to kill terrorists that strike at us in America. The goddamned powers-that-be didn't think we needed it day before yesterday." Clapping. "But goddammit we need it today." Roaring. "So we can put it into play tomorrow." Standing ovation.

But Spangler wasn't showboating now. He flapped a hand for quiet and got it as the men sank into their chairs again.

"I got this plan." He jabbed a finger into the side of his skull. "I'm the man with the plan. I wrote the plan. I called you here so I could give you the plan, so you could have the plan, so you could take the plan, so you could wrap it around a smart bomb, so you could shove it up Osama bin Laden's ass."

Again, Tyler stood up with the rest. Chrissake. So this is how Hitler started a world war.

Spangler let the room settle into quiet.

"You're not volunteers. You're handpicked because we need a mix of skills—language, weapons, electronics, medical, demolitions, and so on. More than that, we need a frame of mind. Smart people willing to meet the enemy on his terms and kick his ass. We think you've got what it takes. That's why you're here. We could fill this room ten times over with volunteers. But we don't have time to sort them out. I don't want volunteers." He posed like the poster: "I want you. And you, and you and you. Many called, only a few chosen. And in the end, that few will be owed by the many, by the people, by the country."

When the room went quiet, he went on. "In a little bit, I'm going to call a break. Just a few minutes. At the end of that time, either you put your ass in one of these chairs again, or you climb into one of those buses outside that door. It will take you home. Back to your units." He held up a hand like a traffic cop to quiet the protests.

"Yes, you do, too, need a break. I'm ordering it. But I want to make one thing clear. There is no shame in it, if you go. Every man in Delta is going to get a piece of the action in this war. The people who come back to this room are going to try out for the first team is all. These people will fight a new kind of war. You will not be under the control of CentCom. You'll deal with me, and I will be your liaison between Central Command and the higher ups. You will—" He shook his head.

"No. No more. That's all you get. I've already said too much. But what I have said here is top secret. Even the meeting is top secret. You can't talk about it, if you decide to go back and join your unit. Nobody can know you were here. This flat didn't happen. If you're idiot enough to come back in here after the break, nobody can know you were here. Any questions?"

Tyler knew the man who stood up in the front row, Travis Beauregard Barret, a sergeant first-class and made for this kind of duty if anyone was. They'd served on special ops faculty together at Fort Bragg. Barret was a genius at killing, an expert in demolitions, hand-to-hand combat, survival, and a fluent speaker of Arabic besides.

"All due respect, General, what the hell you gotta test us on?" Barret said. "We already been through every test any nose-picking, college-educated sadistic bastard can dream up in training. Speakinawhich, how can we afford to waste time training? The quicker we hit them raghead bastards, the better."

Spangler had begun nodding even before Barret finished his question. "Mind, good fellow, I didn't say training. I said testing. You'll spend a week, tops, taking the test. Then you'll need a week of recovery. R and R. Personal time. Kiss the girls goodbye. We launch in two weeks."

"I got one more question, general. Who—?"

"Save it. Break time." The restive men turned to each other and began their soldier's trade in curse words of awe and rumors of war. Spangler glanced at his watch and spoke into the hive before the buzz grew too loud. "It's now 2217 hours . . . mark. If you're going to come back, I'll see you here at 2230 hours. Dismissed. Get out of here you idiots." Spangler called over the roar to the back of the room, "Captain Tyler?"

"Here, sir."

"Front and center."

Tyler vaulted up onto the stage and into the spotlight. "Sir."

Spangler's teeth gleamed behind the wet lips of his Komodo dragon smile, and his watery eyes sparkled behind his thick spectacles. Looking into the empty seats.

Tyler turned. No, one man still stood there. Barret.

"You're dismissed," Spangler said.

"No, sir."

"What?"

Barret gave a sly grin. "You dismissed the idiots." He looked around him. "There sure were a lot of them, huh?"

Spangler, already juiced in his own enthusiasm, broke up. "Get out of here, sergeant."

Barret clicked his heels and right-turn-marched out of the hangar.

Spangler turned to Tyler. "Funny guy." He did a take. "You cut your locks."

Tyler shrugged. He had a fresh haircut. Not much of one, either. Barely enough hair remained to cover his ears. *So what?*

"How did I do? How many do you think will come back?" He saw Tyler's stiff posture. "At ease. Well?"

"Honestly?"

"Of course *honestly*. You're not going pissy on me?" Spangler grabbed Tyler by the elbow. "Are you?"

"No, sir."

"*Sir?* I know that game, pal. Why the hell is your nose out of joint?"

"Sorry, Ros—General—I thought we agreed about how to sell this."

"Apology accepted. Connor, for shit's sake, you been my right-hand man on this for months. You have a test in place to ID the kind of man we want on this team. You built the test sites—hell, all I had to do was dust them off. I owe you. Now how did I sell it so wrong?"

"You can handle the truth then?"

Spangler laughed, but in his throat. "Damn you. Give it up."

"The truth is, you sold it too well, General. You came off too Knute Rockne—Let's win one for the Gipper." Tyler pried his elbow out of Spangler's grip. "You should have kept to the asshole pitch, the way you opened, chewing ass and taking names. So we could cull the ones who hate officers and those who hate taking orders from their officers, the one-man-army types."

"Like that smart-ass asking all the questions? With the idiot thing?"

Tyler snorted. "Barret? Guy bleeds green. We'll be lucky to get a crew as good as Barret." Tyler shook his head. "We agreed. You weren't even going to use bin Laden's name."

Spangler couldn't contain a smile. "I know, I know. I lost my head. You realize how long it's been since anybody actually listened to me when I talked? Let alone a room full of kick-ass fighting men?"

Tyler let it drop. "You said you owe me?" In his heart, he cringed—those were Amy's words, when she told him to break it off with Laren. "I want to—"

"Go in on the first wave. No way. You said we agreed? We agreed on that, too. I need you here in Nevada. If we lose every man on the first wave, who's going to test the second one? Maybe train a third? You can't go. And that's final."

"You said—"

"Captain Tyler?" Spangler poked a scabbed finger into the six inches between their noses.

Tyler backed off.

Spangler closed the space again and kept his finger in it. "What does *final* mean to you? I was a one-star for an hour—hell, not even that. Not even a single lousy hour before I had to bust your ass out of jail. I hadn't even pinned on my stars before I had to spend all my goodwill chips. That little get-out-of-jail-free card with the FBI shot my whole wad. And you want to tell me I owe you?" He took out a hanky to daub his weeping face dry.

"I—"

"Ouch!" One of Spangler's bandages pulled free, stuck to the hanky. Tyler looked away from the ooze.

The wound topped off Spangler's mood. "Forget it, Connor, we're square. I don't owe you shit. Look at the risk I'd be taking. Putting a felon at the point of *Swift Sword*?"

"Chrissake, Ros, a *felon*?"

"Alleged felon, then. A small point in the circles where I run. All they see is a guy that just tried to kill one of our own. How's that gonna play if the press gets hold of it?"

Spangler blinked as if sending Morse code. A trickle of clear liquid ran down his face. One day he might thank Connor Tyler for handing him a wounded Arab-Delta-guy like Baker. One day, if Baker survived, he and Tyler might marvel at the pure-dee balls of the plan he and Carnes had hatched, Rube Goldberg-style, out of the broken bones of Ramsey Baker. Courtesy of Tyler, said alleged felon. Technically, Tyler was right. Spangler did owe him. Of all things, for giving him a broken, battered Ramsey Baker.

But he could not repay him yet. Now he needed a humble Tyler. And Tyler, head hung, at last looked properly whipped.

Spangler shook his head in genuine pity. Not for Tyler, a good officer and tough. He really did deserve to go in on the first wave. A shame it was, too, that he had all the personal baggage, the wife, the dead lover, the other girls on the side. A real mess, that. Not even Tyler knew how bad a mess he'd made. When Spangler had spent his chips with his man in the FBI who took custody of Tyler from the Marshals, he learned how Tyler's name had come up in the odd, unrelated case of leaks of state secrets to the press. A source inside the *Times-Mirror* put the names of Tyler and Laren in the same bed. No proof. Yet. But this was a bed of Tyler's own making and a waste of shame to pity him for it.

Spangler did feel a bit of pity for Randall Bowers: pity the poor bastard didn't die. Somebitch ever lived to tell the tale of how Major Mushroom walked over his body and left him to fry in his own fat . . .

Yeesh, he couldn't even bear to think of it. So his only true pity was for Ramsey Baker nee Ramsay al Bakr. Tyler had beaten the man to within an inch of his life. Poor Baker. Talk about living in the pull of a black star. One of the good guys tries to kill him on the first day of the only war he'd ever see.

But Connor Tyler? Screw the pretty boy, the Mister Perfect who suddenly was just another somebitch. Baker was the guy gonna get to the king rat bastard bin Laden.

Thursday, September 13, 2001—Over Central Pakistan

Ramsey Baker awakened to find himself strapped to a gurney, fixed to the deck of an aircraft. A SC-130, from the sound and vibration of it. He'd ridden into combat on this bird. He'd jumped, high and low, from the 130. One had snatched him from the ground, trailing a grappling hook that snagged a low-impact rigging and harness. He'd flown on one into deep, dark Africa to rescue a pair of Mormon missionaries. He never dreamed he'd travel on one as an invalid.

His body throbbed in time with the buzz of the jet-props. It hurt, yes, but at least the pain had settled on a new vibe.

He felt the SC-130 level off, then begin a nap-of-the-earth flight, keeping to the contours of the terrain, flying up, then down at a hundred feet. *Why?* He opened his eyes and found he was no longer an invalid. He sat in the cockpit. The aircraft was flying at a mosque in the distance. Except that was no mosque, but the Taj Mahal. *The Taj Mahal?*

He looked to the pilot. *What the hell?* The pilot handed over the controls. *No prob.* He took the controls and began a turn away from the Taj. There! A speck on top of the minaret. A man, dressed in flowing robes. A thin will-o'-the-wisp figure with a beard. Osama bin Laden.

Baker leaned into a turn, pointing the SC-130 at bin Laden. He did not know how to fly, but the craft answered his input. He pushed forward on the flight controls, to drop some altitude and gain airspeed. He banked left, then right to line up for a final, dead-on approach. Bin Laden came up with a rifle. An AK-47. He took aim. He fired. He looked as unfamiliar with the AK as he did in his recruiting vid. Baker laughed. A waste of bullets, a waste of effort. The man would have better luck jumping off the Taj Mahal. Maybe he should try for a soft landing in the reflecting pool.

And, as Baker thought it, bin Laden leaped, arcing out in a huge, fluttering swan dive, belly-splashing into the pool. He surfaced and looked up, smiling his girlie-girl smile, smug, confident that he had fooled the Americans.

Baker laughed. He had seen it coming. Hell, he'd willed it. He pushed his chest into the controls. The aircraft stood on its nose.

He dived right at the bastard, aiming for his blubber-lipped face.

Bin Laden looked up, his girlie eyes going wide in alarm. He looked left. He looked right. There was no escape. He looked down, seeking a place of safety under the water, but he was too late. Baker caught the terrorist leader wide-eyed, wide-mouthed, full in the girlie-face, splattering him on the windshield, yellow, like a bee.

Tyler lay cross-wise across the deck of the Blackhawk special operations helicopter, propped up by the 150 pounds of weapons, ammo, rations, and gear strapped to his back. Four other men filled the rest of the floor space, alternating head to toe, reclining on their packs as well. Like any other combat soldier, Tyler knew how to grab a few winks on the fly.

Except every time he closed his eyes he saw them. Amy and Laren and that army officer. Baker, a Delta Force officer, for chrissake. He put them out of his head. Put his mind on the rest of Spangler's brief.

He was right. Not a man got on a bus during the break. To a man, they wanted a piece of bin Laden. Spangler. He just couldn't stop himself from putting it in brass-ball terms. Now Tyler would have to do the dirty-dirty himself, sorting out those who did not dare sort themselves out for fear of looking weak. He and Gunnery Sergeant Robert Night Runner.

Night Runner. He was the question that Barret wanted to ask Spangler after the break.

"Who is this guy?" he said, jerking his thumb at the marine noncom. "What's a jarhead doing in an army Delta meeting?"

"He's just back from Afghanistan," Spangler said. "Combat. A shooting fight. End result? The body count of Taliban and Al Qaeda of more than two hundred. Killed by a marine Force Recon team of four." He held up the fingers of one hand. "Count them, four marines taking out two hundred of the enemy. On September 11. And that one of the dead guys was a key Osama bin Laden lieutenant. One of the guys in on the planning for the attacks on America." Spangler stabbed a finger at the crowd. "Like to see you do as well as this marine." He put a finger to the side of his head. "Let me cipher here—put down the two, carry the one—that's more than nine thousand dead Al Qaeda. If, I say *if*, you do as well as this jarhead." He looked at Barret. "Any more questions?"

Barret shrugged. *So what?* "He gonna be taking the same test as the Delta men in the room?"

"Nope. He's not here to be tested. He's a made man. He's here to test you. See if you men are worthy to go on the mission he just came back from. So don't mess with him, okay?"

Barret sank into his chair. The room was quiet.

"I suppose you all want to know the mission?" Spangler

said. A general murmur answered that they did. "Tough. It goes beyond top secret. You have to have a need to know. And that comes only with passing the test."

He looked out over the crowd. "And I suppose you want to know when the test begins." This time the crowd didn't take the bait.

"That I'll tell you," Spangler said. "The test began when that first jet bored into the World Trade Center. That put all of you on a course for war. Ever since you walked into this room we've been testing you." Spangler put his hands on his hips and stood like a poor imitation of George C. Scott doing his imitation of George S. Patton. The only thing missing was a wall-sized flag "Any more questions?"

There were none. Emphatically none. Even from a distance, Tyler could see Barret's ears going red, thinking his fat mouth had got him cut right out of the gate.

The briefing broke up, and forty-six men had hustled out to draw combat gear.

And now eight Blackhawks, flying in flights of two, taking five to six men apiece and one evaluator per helicopter, were en route to the four test areas. Four groups going to four starting points on a course more than two hundred miles long.

The pilots had covered the faces of their instruments. The men had no maps, compasses, or GPSs, except for the tiny passive devices strapped to wrists and ankles. The PGPS didn't help the wearer, only Tyler's cadre. An AWACS at 20,000 feet could pinpoint a lost man to within a meter. The Delta men would have to rely on the stars to navigate tonight, the sun tomorrow.

No big deal. These guys knew hardship, a given for special ops. Mind games? They'd been through the best tests the best army sadist could dream up. To a man, they put on an air of confidence, even arrogance, ready for anything he could throw at them. Some of these men had been in battle. And a few had killed the enemy du jour. They were the most cocky in the crowd. They were the ones Tyler most wanted to test. If he could throw a new wrinkle at them, he'd have done something. If they got by his wrinkles, they'd have done something.

The hum of the helicopter lulled Tyler toward sleep. He dared to close his eyes.

To see the woman that lurked there, behind his eyelids. Laren. The night of 9-10. Smiling that wicked smile. Giving him that evil, tempting hawk eye. Leaping upon him in a savage sexual assault that last night, the night before she died.

Died. The word numbed him to the core. He wiped a sleeve across the dampness in the slit of his eyelids. Laren. Dead.

Amy. He loved her, yes. Just not enough. He tried to call up an image of her face. Nothing. He called to Laren and saw her again. Even dead she could arouse him. How sick was that? Only a woman that looked like his wife could do that to him? Including his dead lover? But not his wife.

Amy. Divorce a done deal. He tried to imagine her gone. Nothing. Brendan. Gone. *Unh* . . . he felt gut-shot.

Yesterday he had a perfect wife, a perfect son, and a perfect lover. Now there is no yesterday, no wife, no son, no lover.

He tried another, even more sadistic mind game on himself. Suppose she *didn't* want to leave him. What then?

Forget that. Too much for him to know. Too much to deal with.

He let a flicker of mental video replay on the insides of his eyelids. The plane slashing into the North Tower of the World Trade Center. He'd seen it real time. Add to that the endless replays on the news. And the collapses of the towers. He could deal with those pictures. For they gave him and the country the green light for the OPLAN he had to set in motion from here in the Nevada desert.

Never mind that he'd war-gamed these scenarios long before 9-11. Forget he'd invented the test before the trigger of a terrorist strike. At Spangler's urging, to be sure, but he did it willingly. In his head, he'd eviscerated women, strangled kids, set charges in safe houses where children played, head-shot men sitting tied up in chairs, and bayoneted men in their sleep. Now here he was. On a quest to handpick a couple dozen men willing to do the same things, not in made-up war games and not in the mind's eye, but in reality. Looking for a few good men willing to kill people in their sleep.

He opened his eyes. Too scary in there.

When Baker awakened again, the giant noise of the C-130 in flight had gone silent, leaving his body to throb in the old wavelength. He wanted drugs to ease the pain, to put him to sleep. Without dreaming, if you don't mind. He'd fly a plane into bin Laden's face, all right, but did he have to dream about it to no result?

Still, that last look on bin Laden's face.

"Where am I?" he said into the quiet.

"Sir, Tech Sergeant Andy Lee." A young, broad Asian face stepped into his line of view. "You're aboard an air force SC-130. I'm the crew chief."

"Hello, Andy. And where we parked?"

"Sir, I'm not allowed to say."

"Dammit, Andy, I'm the reason we are where we are. You tell me, or I'll get up off this gurney and—"

The tech sergeant smiled at the improbability of the threat. Baker felt a stirring of the air above his head, and a new face came into view, looking at him upside down.

"Captain Baker. My name is Brian Carnes. I work with General Spangler."

"You were at the hospital back there—wherever I was."

Carnes's upside-down eyebrows wrinkled like furry inch-worms.

"I heard your voice in the hall."

"Oh? Are you sure it was me?"

"You said I had balls?"

"Right." The eyebrows went flatline, a look of relief.

"I heard the rest, too."

"Oh?"

"Spangler said I was brain-damaged."

"Well, he—"

"Where am I?"

"You're in Pakistan, Captain Baker. By special arrange-ment of the American government. And it is a sensitive situa-tion, so you can't blame the sergeant."

"Of course not." Baker looked around to apologize, but the sergeant was not there.

"I sent him off," Carnes said. "So we could talk."

"I need a drink. Water, please." Baker had never felt so helpless. "Or maybe a frozen margarita."

"Use your powers of imagination." Carnes put a straw to his lips and held a designer water bottle.

After he vacuumed the last of the icy water, Baker asked, "Where do we go from here?"

"Literally? Afghanistan," Carnes said. "By helicopter. At night. With luck, we won't be spotted."

"Figuratively?"

"We meet up with some friends and sometimes enemies of mine. They're going to *capture* you, quote-unquote—after a battle that took place on 9-11 ironically enough. They'll take care of you."

"But? I heard a *but* in there."

"But first I have a medical team coming in here to do some work on you."

"Surgery?"

"Right. Work that you already consented to."

"When?"

"When you signed this, Baker-man." Carnes held up the consent form Baker had scribbled on back in the hospital.

"What kind of surgery?"

"You don't want to know."

"What if I change my mind?"

Carnes smiled the weakest of smiles. He lowered his eyes to the gurney. "Is that what you want?"

Baker felt what the CIA man was looking and smiling at. The restraints. He would have smiled himself, if his swollen face could form a smile. "Leave me alone. I want to get some sleep in peace."

"You're gonna need it, pal."

"I've got a feeling."

A dozen men sprinted in four groups of three from the two Blackhawks and sprawled, their weapons at the ready. After the craft climbed out in eerie near-silence, leaving behind the gentle eddies of their furious rotor blast, the men cleared the LZ and took new positions.

So far so good. So far Tyler could identify only one man not playing the game. One stolid, slope-shouldered, tombstone shape against the night sky. Tyler zoomed close in his night vision goggles, close enough to see the face in detail. Powczuk. Who else?

Stanley Powczuk used the butt of his rifle to lower himself to the ground, careful not to sit on a cactus or sharp stone. "Are we tactical yet?"

Each man had a radio receiver plugged into one ear and boom mike within kissing distance of his lips. Everybody on the ground here was tuned to the same tactical radio channel. No need to shout into the night. But this was only a test, and that was Powczuk. Above all rules.

Tyler's night vision goggles gave him a full-color, 3-D picture of Stan Powczuk, Alberto Solis, and Edgar Poole. He knew both Powczuk, a corporal, and Solis, a first lieutenant. Poole, another first lieutenant, he did not know except from his dossier picture. Tall and black, his skin the color of a well-oiled saddle, Poole could have been an NBA small forward. Or an Olympic decathlete, well-muscled as Leonardo's David, graceful as Nureyev. Movie-star good looks with a strong jaw, straight nose, high cheeks. Or maybe the junior congressman from the new Alabama. Tyler didn't know him except from his personnel jacket.

But the junior man, Powczuk, he knew too well. He had a rep in Delta. You didn't make corporal in the army on the way up in rank. You only got busted down to corporal. Rank, either his own or somebody else's, never mattered much to Powczuk. Give him a gun and a mission and keep the officers the hell out of the way. If the military ever formed a million one-man armies, Powczuk would be first in line for his own.

Strike one against Powczuk.

Powczuk found a spot for his elbow and lay back as if he were on a picnic in the park. He had to know Tyler might be watching him. He also had to make sure that Tyler knew he didn't care.

Strike two.

Tyler kept quiet. Just to say the test was on was to identify it as a test. Any second now, they'd know.

He heard it first, because he was listening for it, the pitiful voice. A woman's plea. "Help! Over here. Help!"

Tyler switched his tiny radio pack to a discrete control frequency. "Stand by," he said to a specialist sitting at a remote control keyboard at 30,000 feet in an AWACS plane.

In the next second, murmurs and curses filled his ears—and the ears of everybody else on the ground and in the monitoring stations for the test. The noise tapered off as the men got the point.

"What the hell is going on?" Powczuk again. Over the radio. And again, loud enough to be heard without the radio.

"At ease." A quiet voice, but one of authority. "You got a hot mike." Pause. "We're all hot, so don't say nothing if you don't have nothing to say."

"ID, please," Tyler asked the AWACS on a discrete frequency the others could not overhear.

The operator in the AWACS told Tyler the name of the man who spoke up to establish order: "First Lieutenant Edgar Poole." Every radio on the team had a distinctive electronic marker so the radio traffic could be sorted and reported in the after-action brief. The man's name and rank appeared on-screen next to his electronic voice transcription. A voice-to-speech program made a text record of each man's words as he spoke them.

"What do we do? Go get her?"

"ID?" Tyler murmured.

"Lieutenant Soiree Ward."

Tyler knew the man's history. Another first lieutenant, Ward was fluent in Arabic, electronics, and signal communications in everything from World War II-vintage radios to digital satellite to classical music.

"I'll go find out." Powczuk. Tyler didn't need to ask for an ID.

"Negative," said Poole. "Hold what you got." And in a tone that did not invite debate.

Tyler liked it.

"Listen up, Delta soldiers," said Poole into his mike, and Tyler knew that he was about to take charge. "A-Group was on the lead bird. B-Group on Number Deuce. Both put out one man for security. The rest of y'all rally your asses on me."

Tyler saw Poole raise his right arm and give a circle-the-wagons signal. The men went to him at once. Hell, he even felt compelled to follow the man, and he was evaluating him.

Tyler turned to the pair with him, Night Runner and Barret, both part of A-Group. He saw their NVGs on him and pointed to Night Runner with one finger, then put two fingers to his own goggles. Night Runner was to remain on watch. He gave a thumbs-up. Tyler nodded, lowering his gaze in the NVGs for a second. When he looked up, Night Runner had vanished. Tyler looked around him. Nothing. He checked the footprints. Yes, Night Runner had been there. And beyond the sand dune, a puff of dust wafted up, then drifted away in the night breeze.

He looked to Barret, who was shaking his head. He had seen even less of the man.

Barret put a hand over his mike. "I've known farts more conspicuous than that guy," he said in a whisper.

Tyler didn't want to encourage Barret, but he couldn't help shaking his head in wonder.

After they'd formed up on Poole, the man didn't waste words.

"Get your butts into your separate three-man teams and stay there," Poole said. "So's I can tell y'all apart." A few seconds of shuffling. "Anybody put anybody in command of this outfit?" He looked to Tyler for an answer. Tyler looked away, avoiding NVG-to-NVG contact. Nobody else spoke up.

"I'm it then," Poole said. "Until we check out the chick. Anybody got a problem with that?" There were none. "We can do the date of rank thing later. For now, stay in three-man teams and six-man groups. Y'all pick a leader for each team. Since we all got hot mikes, only the leader better be talking. But I don't even want to hear the leaders except for a damnt good tactical reason."

Tyler liked it. It was good, a quick plan and simple. Organized in seconds.

Poole pointed to himself than the others in turn. "Team one, two, three, four." He knelt and scratched a finger in the sand. "Yonder is where the sound of the woman come from." He pointed into the night, and, as if on cue, she cried out for help.

Poole worked fast. "One move here and Two move this way." He drew two curving arcs and two hash marks. "Three and Four take up covering fire. Don't expose yourself to direct fire. When y'all get close enough to her, don't go out lessen you can snatch her. Call her forward. Make her keep her hands up. Check her over for booby traps before you let her get close."

Powczuk snickered. "I wanna check her for boobs. Let me."

Poole stared at him. "Shut the fuck up, soldier." Even the night vision goggles seemed to glare in anger. Powczuk's mouth slammed shut. He had heard the words often enough.

Tyler shuffled his list in his head, putting Poole at the top.

Poole flapped a hand at the men. "Y'all get on outta here and do your thing."

Powczuk aside, Tyler liked what was going on. Not only that Poole would step up to take command—he had expected somebody to do that because this was Delta for chrissake—but also that the other men would accept his command so readily.

The woman cried out a third time as the four teams crept up the back side of a gentle ridge of gravel toward her. They saw a woman dressed in a thin housedress and bare feet, her hair in tangles, about a hundred meters off. She staggered toward them. With no fanfare, Teams One and Two moved out to intercept her.

Tyler had invented the scenario, so he knew there were no enemy players nearby. This was just a setup so he could watch the team organize and deploy at night. A simple test, but one that could turn into disaster, even for experienced troops. So far, so good. In just minutes, the two teams had swept along their arcs of travel, as if Poole had drawn his lines onto the actual ground instead of making a sand map.

Poole only spoke up once, warning Team Two not to get so far ahead they might get into a crossfire situation with Team One. No casual concern. Each man was armed with a 9 mm pistol and the M4 assault rifle, a version of the 5.56 mm M16, except with a shorter barrel and a shoulder stock that could telescope inward, turning the gun into a submachine gun. Each man knew that each weapon was hot, loaded with live rounds.

Tyler knew everybody in the maneuver group. Master Sergeant Simon Ballard took charge because he was the senior noncom and an old hand at Delta ops. His men knew him—hell, everybody in Delta Force knew him—so he was a given.

Tyler turned his NVGs to 20X power to watch Ballard work. Ballard pointed at Blue Dolan. A good choice. "Blue, she ain't got no booby traps there. Hell, she ain't even got no underwear on. Take our damsel in distress."

Dolan handed his rifle off to his teammate and crept toward the woman.

Tyler had to smile. Sylvia Diller was no damsel and sure as hell not in distress. She was a warrant officer, an instructor pilot, and an expert in survival skills. Her shift, hiked over her knees, revealed trim but calloused knees. She staggered through the sand like a drunk. Fake-staggered, to be sure, for she was as graceful as any dancer, as athletic as any Olympic gymnast, and tough as venison jerky. She was to put up a fight. Two or three normal men might handle her. One Delta Force operator, maybe.

Dolan wasn't taking any chances. As he moved out, he slipped on a pair of leather gloves. A wise move.

Tyler watched closely to see if she would spot Dolan first. Not until the last second, when he lunged from behind a juniper bush and tackled her from the side, did she react. She tried to spin away, throwing a heel his way, and an elbow. The elbow hit the night vision goggles and spun them off into the night, but Dolan had the weight and strength. And he had her in his grip. Dolan drove her into the ground, face-first and held her there without risking even gloved fingers over her mouth.

Dolan's mike picked up her muffled screaming. And his voice growling into her ear. "Quiet," he said, both in English and Arabic, covering all his bases. "You scream again, and I'm going to punch you."

She yelped into the sand.

He shoved harder on her neck. "Quiet, I said."

She moaned. He released her neck. "Not a sound, now."

She spat sand and gasped for air. Once she could breathe at all, she went at Dolan in English, "You sonofabitch. You didn't hear me calling for help? I already have a dozen terrorist bastards trying to kill me. I don't need you to do it."

"Does that mean you want a knuckle sub?"

"Okay, okay," she said, lowering her voice, her hands held in front of her. "I'm sorry. I lost my head. Thank you for saving my life."

"You said terrorists. What about them?"

That got him extra points with Tyler. His first concern, once he had her under control, was for intel on the bad guys. Dolan shuffled his way up Tyler's mental list, right up there beneath Poole.

As the ad hoc Delta Force squad began to collect around Sylvia Diller, she started talking nonstop, part of Tyler's scheme again. She brushed a layer of sand from her face to expose a thick set of eyebrows, blond hair, penetrating eyes, full lips. Drop-dead gorgeous, even in the unnatural lighting of the NVGs. At the first sight of those eyes, his own focus failed. Hawk eyes. Chrissake, another one. Amy, and Laren, flashed through his head. He replayed Laren, feeling a stab in the heart . . .

Until Sylvia said, "I was raped. Taliban militia. Six of them. There. No, over there." She pointed into one sector of the darkness, wavered, and swept her arm ninety degrees left. "Or maybe there."

"You're all over the map," Powczuk said. "Stupid bitch."

"Last time, soldier," Poole said.

"Excuse us, Miss." First Sergeant Marcus Garner took Poole out of Sylvia's hearing, covered both mikes, and suggested the lieutenant put out security again. Tyler, standing close by, heard the suggestion.

Poole shook his head. "Thanks, Top. Scouts out." Each team sent a man out for security.

"What's the point of this drill?" Powczuk asked. "We res-

cue the lady? That's a mission for Delta Force? What? We a
buncha Cub Scouts?"

This time Poole didn't tell him to shut up. Powczuk had
asked a good question. What *was* the point? Poole looked to
Tyler: "Anybody got a clue? Y'all know—?"

"Stand by for orders." A voice from the sky—literally, from
the AWACS—answered his question before he finished asking
it. "Delta Task Force Alpha, this is Delta command, over."

Poole answered, "Delta Task Force Alpha, over."

"Mission order follows. Stand by."

Poole rogered, and dug out a pocket notebook and stub of a
pencil. "Ready to copy."

Tyler's man in the AWACS gave a quick briefing and ordered the team into a night attack against the Taliban force
that Sylvia had described. A terrorist camp. Six buildings.
One Taliban militia man per building. Armed and dangerous.

The final words of the order: "Execute Zero Option."

Poole looked to Tyler. "Zero Option?"

Tyler handed over a code book. Poole flipped into the
pages. Powczuk smirked. Several men were shaking their
heads, trading *hoo-boy* glances. It didn't sound like much of
an operation to send a dozen Delta operators against six lousy
Taliban bananas.

About the way Tyler had scripted it. A little too Hollywood, a little too simple. Still, the voice from the AWACS left
no wiggle-room in the mission order. Poole read the entry at
the back of the code book, shook his head, and read it again.
He looked into Tyler's face. Tyler turned away, leaving Poole
on his own.

Tyler and Spangler had written the Zero Option. In military language it said: Attack the objective. Get in and out in
thirty seconds. No prisoners, no wounded, no human rights issues, no trials, no press, no mess.

"Wilco, Zero Option," Poole said. "Request eval of G2 on
this mission."

Tyler liked the question. A good officer would ask for the
validity of the intel report.

"Alpha-one, corroborated," the booming voice of the god

in the AWACS said, meaning an impeccable source and a dead solid perfect report from at least two intelligence sources, an unheard of level of reliability. Meaning no wiggle-room. "Delta Command out." Silence.

Every member of Delta Force team had gotten such a mission in the course of training. Every one of them had been part of a kick-the-door assault. Every one of them had burst in, high and low, alternating directions, taking out pop-up silhouettes of unshaven terrorists with beady eyes, the likeness of Yasser Arafat.

Still. No admin briefing yet. No safety lecture. The voice in their headsets had just thrown them into a situation and told them to kill their way through it. This didn't feel like any test they'd been in.

In mere seconds, though, the men began to ease their way out of the dilemma. As they reminded each other this was a test, only a test. And not much of a war crime to kill a gap-toothed silhouette with a picnic tablecloth wrapped around its head.

Poole didn't waste any time. He called for his three team leaders. Sylvia had begun babbling again, telling her background as a Red Cross aid worker kidnapped on a relief mission. Powczuk was eager to help calm her. Really getting into it, getting close enough to touch her. Tyler hoped that he would. Sylvia'd put him on his ass so fast—

"Y'all still down with me in command?" Poole said. "I didn't ask for this. I don't mind. But if you got a better idea—?" He left the question hanging. Nobody said a word. These men knew leadership when they saw it.

"Fine, then I'll be it until higher tells me to stand down." He looked Sylvia's way. She'd begun chattering like a squirrel. "Somebody put a sock in that. You, soldier, you got a name?"

"Stanley Powczuk, Corporal, United States Army. Be glad to take the gash under my wing, L-T. Put a sock in her. Or something."

"Corporal Stanley?"

"Yeah?"

"Y'all take a post off yonder, soldier, to the west, and take that aggro shit with you. Stay away from the lady, and I'm not gonna tell you one more time to stay off my net."

Powczuk didn't even lean westward, just stood staring at Poole.

"What're you beaming at, soldier?" Poole asked.

Now he leaned. Toward Poole. *Wanna settle this right here, right now?*

"Corporal, you want me to call you a taxi home?"

Powczuk blinked once, then slouched toward the skyline.

Poole gave a quick brief. Tyler shook his head. Poole was so damned good. Too damned good. Thirty minutes into the exercise and he had already learned enough in the dark to put Powczuk into a spot where he could do no harm. If the lieutenant kept it up, Tyler might never get the chance to take command—

Poole went silent. Tyler realized he was looking at him. *You paying attention, soldier?*

"Y'all an evaluator, right?"

"Affirm. Captain Tyler."

"Cap, you got anything to add, anything I need to know?"

"Nothing to add."

"Tell me this, Cap. Y'all put a tracker on this team?"

"Affirm." *Did the man miss anything?*

"I want him sniffing on the woman's trail. Backtrack to where she exscaped."

Tyler wondered for one ridiculous second whether he could count a mangled word against Poole.

"I want him to scout ahead of us," Poole said. "Find the camp. Give us a report before we get there. Mind if I ask you his name, Cap?"

"He's the marine, Night Runner."

Night Runner spoke up. "Here, sir."

"Gunny, you copy what I just said?"

"Affirm, sir. On the way."

Poole tried a second tack. "We got us an interrogator?"

The interrogator spoke for himself. "Sergeant First-Class Gabriel Foucault, sir."

Poole grinned at Tyler, proud of himself at how well he

was doing. "Foucault, you and me. What say we go gobble at the girl, see what's she's got in the way of intel."

Tyler tried not to look as crestfallen as he felt.

Sylvia didn't yield much intel. By Tyler's scenario, she wasn't supposed to. She repeated that six men raped her in turn. They left her alone. She ran away. Simple as that. She wanted to talk about her role as a Red Cross worker, the good she was doing for the people of the desert.

After only three minutes, Foucault turned to Poole. "There's nothing else here. L-T. She's afraid. Signs of traumatic stress. It'd take too long to get anything else out of her."

Poole nodded. "Take her off yonder a ways and calm her down."

Poole ordered a simple march on the terrorist camp, attack plan to follow after the team hooked up with Night Runner.

On the word, go, Tyler took Barret on their line of march, going as fast as he could and still stay tactical. He needed the speed to burn off his anger.

Spangler didn't want him on the first wave. But Tyler had a few ideas to get around that. Such as going to Spangler with a long face: *Sorry, General, I'll have to lead the team. I found a good bunch of men but no officer worthy of the name. I tested them all and I didn't find a one.*

Except for Poole, the bastard.

The next time Baker came to, he still lay on the gurney, at the focus of hot lights again. A surgical team stood around him, working on him, no concern that he had awakened and was aware of them. Not far away, muffled diesel engines raced at a high rpm. Generators for the light stands? And beyond the lights, he could see beams and braces sketched into the darkness above. A hangar?

"What's going on? Where am I?"

"Well, hello, little darling?" A woman with sassy hazel eyes and a wide, wrinkle-free forehead over her surgical mask stood into his line of sight. "We're prepping you for a long chopper ride," she said in a lilting Southern accent. Georgia, if he heard it right. "We're just now finishing up cleaning up your wounds and such. You ain't in the Land of Oz yet, honey, but you sure as hell ain't in Kansas anymore, either."

Baker lifted his right arm, the uninjured one. It was filthy.

"How did I get so dirty?"

"We did that," sassy-eyes said. "Not too shabby, huh?"

"This is cleaning me up?"

"Why, yes, darling. We're using antiseptic makeup to make you look dirty without actually infecting you with any bugs and such. Ain't it a miracle?"

She giggled. Talk about infectious. Baker wanted to laugh with her, but that would hurt too much. Besides, he was a moron. What did every recruit learn in boot camp? Never volunteer for anything but airborne? He deserved what they were doing to him.

"You're clean as a shot of vodka," a new-old voice said. "Not that it matters, once you get into the desert."

"Carnes. Is this going to work?"

Carnes came into view beneath his bare toes. "Who knows? We never tried anything this far out. Clean dirt? It's like black magic, no pun. Except that, after twenty-four hours, you'll be dirty with actual dirt, and not sterilized, either."

Baker asked the woman, "What's going on with my broken arm?"

"It's set internally with screws and surgical plastic. We're fixing to resplint the exterior now. You know. For show."

"Resplinting how?"

"Actual materials from inside Afghanistan." The woman held up a square of rough-cut cardboard with odd writing on it, her eyes on high-beam green.

"From a case of Soviet rations," Carnes said. "I picked that up myself. Along with your new ID, pocket change, family photos—shit like that. You can even have a library card if you want."

The woman brandished a fistful of black bands. "Cut from the inner tube of a Taliban military truck." She tossed her head at Carnes.

"One of our boys found a wreck in the desert. Or caused it."

"What about the hatchet wound?"

"Fixed."

"Fixed how? If you put stitches in, won't that—?"

"Surgical glue that looks like green pus. Practically undetectable, except that it stinks to high heaven." She flashed a roll of silver at him. "We'll wrap you up tight as a tick. We got the universal fix-it, duct tape. We see it all the time in the Taliban ERs."

Baker winced as she moved his broken arm.

"Sorry." Sassy-eyes glanced at Carnes. "Anybody mention to him that we implanted one of these in the arm wound?" She held up a black speck the size of a dime.

"What's that?"

"PGPS. Passive GPS node. Know what it does?"

"Yeah. Never saw one that small."

"We got all the modern marvels, huh?"

"We, huh? You're with him?" Baker looked from the one to the other.

The green eyes looked away. Carnes just smirked. "You never know, huh?"

"Speaking of marvels." Baker clenched his eyes shut. "Got drugs?"

"Certainly, little darling."

He opened his eyes as a soft, fuzzy darkness settled over his body, replacing the aches. To catch a last glimpse of those sassy eyes. A CIA surgeon. What a waste of beguiling eyes. What next?

On second thought, as sassy-eyes said, he didn't want to know.

Night Runner closed on the camp by shadowing Sylvia's track, keeping to its downwind side. He found it first with his nose. A fire, of pungent desert wood. Roasted meat, camp coffee, cigarette smoke. So he knew regular troops were playing the Taliban—most Delta types did not smoke.

He turned full-face into the wind and crept up and over a ridge. He knelt among a pile of boulders. He kept to the shadows, the stones at his back, leaving no outline against the sky.

He saw just what Tyler's script said he would see. Six men sitting around the fire, smoking and joking. Fully at ease because they knew they would have plenty of warning.

He turned on his radio and popped his teeth in front of his mike, a signal more natural in the desert than words.

"Roger," Poole's voice said into the speaker in his ear. "Got vid?"

Night Runner turned on the camera in his NVGs. He did not have to make a radio report. Did not have to say how many men were at the camp or what they were doing. Digital images spoke for him. His headset sent a video stream to a KY spy satellite, which downlinked it in real-time to the Delta team and the AWACS aircraft. Through his night vision goggles, each man on the team could see the camp in a heads-up area of the screen, just as Night Runner saw it.

The six play-terrorists stood up and drifted toward the line of shacks, one to a hut. They poured out their cups of coffee, butted their smokes, and spat. Three of them stopped to urinate on the sides of their huts. Night Runner focused his eyes on each hut in turn as the plank doors went shut.

Poole gave the order to move out.

Night Runner circled the line of cinder block shacks, keeping an eye on them so the team leaders would get a clear picture of the ground before the attack. Each hut was about ten by ten. Only the one door, no windows. A solid, flat roof. Without explosives—and they had none—there was only one way to take down these terrorists. Through the front door, guns blazing.

With men inside? Runner shook his head. Until he realized his men might get dizzy at his unsteady heads-up video. He heard men breathing nearby and steps in the sand. He saw Tyler and Barret and turned off his feed. *With men inside?*

Tyler inched his head up next to a shrub on the ridge so he could look down over the camp. He knew it in detail already, down to the floor plans. He'd designed the setup a year ago and watched it go up, stick by stick, brick by brick.

Night Runner's video blinked off as an image of Barret, then himself came into view. Tyler looked around, trying to look back at Night Runner looking at him. He saw nothing. He heard nothing. He sensed nothing until Night Runner touched him on the shoulder.

"Shit," he said. "Don't do that!"

Barret cursed. "Man you're spooky."

"Hot mikes, hot mikes," Poole said. "Y'all stay off the radio net."

Tyler and Barret looked at each other and shook their heads.

As the rest of the team closed on the site, Sylvia began to act up, on cue, on script. She balked at going back to the scene of her rape.

Poole didn't waste a moment. "Foucault, take her to the rear, calm her down, shut her up, make got-damned sure she doesn't freak and undo this mission. Then haul ass back here."

"Wilco."

Tyler bit his lip as Foucault led Sylvia away. Give Poole a grudging mark in the plus column. Sylvia was a pain, but a life to save, if for no other reason than getting some intel later. Poole had handled her at no cost to the mission, damn him.

"Circle up," Poole said. After the huddle formed on him he said. "Six shacks, twelve of us. Don't take a Einstein to figure two men per." He took out a roster and went down the list, forming the six teams.

"Teams, put your heads together," Poole said. "Pick the kicker and the point. Check weapons hot." He gave Tyler a look. "Travel weapons hot. And don't be shooting for the French Heart."

Tyler shared Poole's unease about going hot, moving on the camp with a live round in the chamber, safety off. Many Delta training injuries and nearly all the fatalities came with the French Purple Heart. When men got shot in the back, most often the butt, in the chaos of a quick-action, high-energy assault.

But nobody in training had ever burst into a building with live men. *Shooting back? Nah.* Tyler sensed the anxiety in the group. He knew what they were thinking. It had to be a trick. Beneath those buildings was an escape tunnel, right? Maybe this was a good training exercise, but, at the end of the day, still an exercise. They'd bust the doors and shoot the shit out of Yasser's shit-eating grin, end of drill. *Right?*

Foucault rejoined the force, and Poole briefed the rest of his hasty plan in the form of the five-paragraph field order: "Situation. Night Runner's circled the camp. Y'all eyeballed it on the vid, one man per hut. No sentries and no escape tunnels that we could see on his little recon jog. And no support forces in sight. Mission. Close with and destroy the enemy. Kickum and stickum. Questions?" He got none.

"Execution. One team of two per building, left to right, teams one to six. On my rifle shot. Shoot the locks, kick the doors. Go in hot. Anything moves? Kick it and stick it. In an out. Pass through the objective area. Assemble and count heads a hundred meters yonder. Next rally two klicks yonder of that. Play it by ear from there."

"Command and Signal. I'm Team Four, center of formation with Foucault, this net. No chatter, no body count, no nothing. I hear anybody be talking it better be me."

He looked at Tyler. "Admin-Log?" waiting for an admin briefing, a word on safety. An explanation of any kind. Tyler shook his head.

With that, Tyler could see the anxiety rise, each man looking for a clue to the trick play. A basement? That escape tunnel? Maybe they'd find mannequins, like crash dummies, full of electronic devices capable of reading hits to tell whether the shots would be fatal? Yeah, that was it, crash dummies. *Right?*

Poole gave the rest of the order, the only administrative and logistical aspect left.

"Night Runner."

"Sir."

"After we taker down, you haul ass back and pick up the woman. You be rear guard to the rally point. On my go."

"Wilco."

"Questions?"

There were none.

They walked down the hill on line, twelve abreast, in six pairs, each pair homing on a door.

The ranks broke only once, to sidestep the campfire's dying embers. Tyler saw all the focus on the building. It wouldn't have hurt for Poole to assign two men to watch the flanks and another pair to check to the rear now and then. So far, not very much to bitch about in the post-mission brief. Not that it mattered. This wasn't a test of tactics. This was a test of will. The will to kill.

Night Runner was impressed as they closed on the shacks. All in all, a quiet group for a bunch of non-Indians. His partner, Barret, was a fireplug of a man who walked with a swagger. Barret had a way of flashing his teeth, less a smile than a sign of aggression. Night Runner had seen that look at the zoo, among the baboons. And in men from the city streets, where body language meant more in day-to-day life than in rural areas. Unlike most men he had known from the city, other than to flash his teeth, Barret kept his mouth shut.

After the attack brief, Tyler had pulled Night Runner aside to tell him to kick the door and let Barret go in first. To test him. That was fine with Barret, who was only too happy to take on the shooting duty. As they formed on the ridge, Barret, a hand over his hot mike, leaned in close to Runner's ear.

"Whaddya think we gonna find in there? What kinda surprise, you reckon?"

Night Runner wagged his head. He didn't know. It was Tyler's test and Tyler's terms.

Night Runner at first had thought it a goofy scenario. The fake camp looked too fake. He had killed real terrorists himself, but never had he seen a setup like this. He thought it too staged. Until he saw the men. Until the men went inside and shut the doors. Then he knew. This was not a demo of how to set up a terrorist camp. This was a mind game. Every pair of eyes had seen those men go inside. Every mind wondered how it would play out. The game kept every mind off-balance. Tyler's wicked little head game.

Soon enough six teams stood in front of six doors, six men ready to kick, six shooters ready to go inside and kill. But kill what? Or whom?

He glanced to the right and saw Poole shift his weight and brace himself behind his M4, ready for the recoil, ready to step through it and kick the door.

Night Runner braced himself. The door looked flimsy.

On the quick blast from Poole, five other guns shot into five other doors.

Night Runner's burst of six hit the lock and stitched across the door. He shot at an angle, firing blind into the left half of the hut. He leaned into the recoil to start his weight forward. When he shut off the firing, he was already in motion for the kick. All he had to do was lift his right foot and strike like a rattler, smashing the door, sending it sailing off its hinges.

Barret busted past. Going in low. Shooting to the right. Stepping to the left, where Night Runner's bullets had gone to clear his way.

Night Runner stepped inside to the right and went down on one knee, sweeping his rifle from the corner to the center of the room, taking it all in. Two rooms. A doorway. A hallway, dimly lit.

A figure. Moving. No silhouette. No dummy. No mannequin. A man. Swinging a rifle their way.

Night Runner swept his rifle left.

Barret was a tick ahead. Shooting on auto, the muzzle blast lighting up the figure of the terrorist. Not a piece of fiber board. Not a paper target. *But a man!* A flesh-and-blood man.

A loud white flash and its deafening bang came from the left, the flash washing out his NVGs. A flash-bang grenade.

"Shit!" Barret yelped. The cries of other men came from the other teams. Men getting hit? A test where they killed people? What the hell kind of exercise was this? In America? No way. *No way, right?*

"Let's go, let's go, let's go. In and out." Poole kept his head. He barked the commands loud but with no hint of hysteria. His level tone put his men back on the plan.

Night Runner checked the room for intel. Nothing.

He checked the ceiling and tried to blink away the optical illusion of—*of bullet holes in the roof?*

He heard noise outside the shack, and more shooting. He kept his focus in the room. They had not yet cleared the back room. They—

"Barret, down!"

Night Runner saw another figure at the back of the hut. Standing. With a rifle. In motion. Rushing them.

He and Barret both cut loose with a second burst of fire.

The building rattled. The blasts hammered in Runner's ears. He felt a wet spray. The figure sprawled in the hallway, on his back, just three feet away.

"Get out, get out, get out." Poole again.

Night Runner backed out the door before he turned to give Barret security as he came out. He pressed close to the building, his pulse crashing like a boom box in his ears. He had seen men excited in combat before, men who would shoot at a shadow. One of his own men in a Force Recon team, in fact. The raw marine had tried to kill him as he ran back to the team's position one night in rainy Kosovo. He never took chances after that.

Barret came out of the door low, his swagger gone. He flashed his teeth, one side of his mouth drawn down. He looked shaken, blood spatter dotted his face. Runner knew what was on his mind: *A test where men tried to kill you? A test where you killed other men?*

"It's real blood," Barret yelled. "I can taste it." He spat. "Shit, man, am I gonna get AIDS?"

"Get off the net." Poole.

Night Runner put a hand over his mike. "Did you finish him?"

"Am I gonna get AIDS, you think?"

"Stop shouting." Night Runner knew the score. Barret thought he had to yell over the ringing in his ears from all the shooting in close quarters. "Did you finish him?"

"Am I gonna get—What?"

"Two-tap? Did you do the two-tap?"

Night Runner asked it over an open mike. The question raised the anxiety level from one end of the Delta Force team to the other. Men bumped into each other, trying to get back into their huts. In the riot of emotions, more than one had forgotten the double-tap.

Barret cursed and pulled his 9 mm pistol. He ducked back inside. Two quick shots. The double-tap: *Two slugs to the head make Osama double-dead.* Barret came out of the hut, the spatter pattern thicker and dripping, as if he'd taken a shotgun blast to the face.

"Warm," he said. "The fucking body is warm."

Night Runner shook his head. "One body? Why not two? We shot two, didn't we?"

"At ease." Poole. "Cut the chatter. Rally, rally, rally."

Night Runner, flat against the wall, waited until the men cleared the huts before sprinting to the rear. Too many men too frenzied, running around, weapons hot. They might forget that Poole had ordered Night Runner to backtrack to get the woman. He didn't want to be seen running off the wrong way. Not in the middle of a blood frenzy like this.

Blood frenzy. He'd felt the spray blowing back from that second man. He'd seen it dripping down the lenses of his NVGs. Killing men in a training exercise? Was that the best way to train? He had heard of life-and-death reality. How the army ever got people to volunteer to get shot down and double-tapped, he would never know.

He took off at an angle, shifting course every few steps, so nobody could draw a bead on him. As soon as he could, he found some low ground and dropped below line of sight. When he stood up again, he was a hundred meters from where he had vanished. Only then did he begin to feel safe. Only then did he make his way back to Sylvia.

He had to hand it to the army. The Marine Corps could learn a trick or two from Delta Force. He had been in firefights no more realistic than that, that . . . whatever it was back there.

After the headcount, Tyler thought Poole had lost one. Until he remembered Night Runner. Poole had sent him back for Sylvia.

He could not believe how his pulse still raced. He'd built the test. He knew its every angle. And yet the realism sucked him in, too.

When they reformed on Poole, the rest of the Delta men weren't much better off. They were jittery, even giddy, picking flecks of dry blood off themselves and each other, wondering aloud what the trick was to the test, cursing, bantering, near-silent yelping—until Poole barked into their headsets.

"Y'all settle down. Put out security. Team leaders, front and center." It was a good show of good sense. But even Poole's voice warbled with an excess of energy.

Once Night Runner brought Sylvia up, Poole picked a new rally point more than a mile away, a place to take stock. That included first aid for the wounded. Staff Sergeant Porter Seger limped from a mild sprain, an ankle turned as he fell inside the shack. Three men had splinters in their shoulders from bashing into a door where a bullet had struck. Each man made it a point to say he'd accept first aid. *If* he could go on to the next part of the test.

Tyler took Poole and Night Runner aside. "So we can talk in private."

"Let me shut a pack of yaps first," Poole said, his hand over his mike.

Tyler shook his head. When they had changed to a clear channel, he said, "It's part of the test. To see whose emotions go off the charts. See who stays tactical, who lets down."

Poole nodded. "Y'all plan that drill back there?"

Tyler's turn to nod.

"Offing men in training? Couldn't be. Right?"

"I can't say," Tyler said. He kept his smile to himself—he didn't want to like the man. He wanted his job, but he didn't want to take it from a friend.

"Helluva head-fuck," Poole said. "Come on, Cap, give it up. How'd you pull it off?"

"Get over it. I need your help."

Poole lifted his chin.

"This was a first cut. I have video to study, but I want your input. Suppose I pick you to lead one of the teams on the combat mission. Anybody you'd rather do without?"

"Powczuk." Not even a tick to think about it. "He's a cowboy, a idiot, a got-damned fool. I can't lead a dozen men when one of them is dissing me. Even if it is only with his heatseekers and his bad-ass looks."

"Then Powczuk is out," Tyler said. End of story. "Anybody else?"

"I'd have to view the vid."

"Later. If I pick you. Don't read too much into that." Tyler flipped up his NVGs so Poole could look him in the eyes. "You're not a lock. You still have to pass the same tests as them. Only edge the lead-dog gets is he doesn't have to be looking up another dog's ass. You don't get an inside track. It only makes it all the harder for you. Worry about that."

"One thing, Cap?"

"Yeah?"

"Can I ask y'all for a man? Somebody I want on the team?" He shrugged. "You know, if I be lead-dog at the start line?"

"What did I just say? Wait and see. See how you're doing a few days from now. Then we'll talk about it."

"Look, I see what you're saying. This thing I'm asking about? It could take some time to work out the wrinkles. Better we get started on it ASAP. Even tonight. You know, if—"

"Wrinkles?"

"The Gunny." Tyler pointed at Night Runner. "I want his ass be on my side. If I have to go into the shit, this is the dude I want with me. Y'all think you could set it up with the corps?"

"He's already on loan for this test."

"So the general said. All the more reason I should have

him on my team, Cap." Poole lifted his hands, palms to the sky. "You know, if I go."

"I'll work on it." Tyler didn't try to soften the edge in his voice.

He might get Spangler to ask the Marine Corps. Hell, he'd even beg, if that's what the one-star, four-eyed bastard needed to hear. But not for Poole. For himself, once he took over one of the PTTs.

"What's up?"

Carnes. Baker's voice croaked with the first few words. "The pain. The drugs've worn off. I feel alert, too alert. I-hurt-alert. I'm cold, and it's dark."

"Forget I asked."

"When is the helicopter coming?"

"Helicopter?"

"To take us into Afghanistan?"

"Come and gone. You're here. Waiting for my peeps."

"Oh? Too late to get out of this?"

"We're in Northern Alliance country now. You're in the shit, pal. Right where you wanted to be. Might as well quit your bitching. Ain't no getting out now."

Baker smacked his dry mouth. "What the hell was I thinking?"

"I don't know. I helped dream up this cracked plan, and I think you're crazy, too."

They left it at that for the rest of the night. Except once, when Baker lay shuddering beneath his wool blanket. Carnes draped his own blanket over him. "Better?" he said before Baker could protest. "Take it. I have to take a turn around our position."

After only twenty minutes into the morning, Baker began wishing for the chill of nightfall again. In those few moments, the sun warmed him, comforted him, and let him nap, even re-dream the C-130 strike against Osama bin Laden's face.

But soon the insects were warmed as well, and they began to swarm him. Carnes didn't seem surprised, and not in the least concerned.

"It's that stuff they put on you. The fake dirt. For some reason, it attracts the bugs. Who'da thunk it, huh?"

"The putrid smell." Baker groaned. "Another CIA miracle."

"Yeah, but you should see the effect. You got the look of that Pigpen kid in the Charlie Brown comics. Dusty. Dirty. Fly-infested. It's a good look for where you are. You know, for what you're trying to do."

Baker raised his one good hand and gave the CIA man the finger. If only his left arm wasn't throbbing to the near side of paralysis. He would have given him both barrels.

Tyler called for a Blackhawk to send Powczuk back ASAP, to get him out of the area along with his insolent eye and smart mouth. Before he could poison the air for the rest of the team.

He tried to be nice about it. "Look, Stanley, this isn't—"

"Corporal Powczuk." Tyler could read the anger in the florid face. The man knew what was up—other officers had fired him before.

"Fine, Corporal Powczuk. You're not making this easy."

"Why should I make it easy?"

"Why should I make it easy, Captain Tyler."

"Right." Powczuk gave him a wink. "What you said."

Tyler didn't let him off the hook. He stared until Powczuk gave in and said it himself, "Why should I make anything easy, Captain Tyler? Sir."

"I'm bouncing you from the test."

"Big surprise. You had a hard-on for me from the start." Powczuk turned his head to spit. "The gingerbread man in on this, too?"

"What'd you say?"

"The gingerbread L-T."

"Lieutenant Poole?"

"What you said."

"Think, Powczuk. If you piss me off? What if I don't send you back to your Delta unit? What if I send you off to a regular army post? Maybe Fort Irwin. So you can hang around there pulling detail NCO while your Article 32 investigation goes forward. While some officer like me, maybe even a personal friend of mine, sees if he ought to bring you up on court-martial charges for insubordination, for racial slurs. With your record—"

Powczuk threw up his hands. "Okay, I get it. Sir. Captain Tyler, sir," turning military courtesy into curse words. "Pep talk over? Sir? Captain?" A threat running through it. *What about it? You and me? What say we step off? Settle this right now?*

Tyler got it. Every unspoken word. He was tempted. Except after Baker, if he sent another Delta man to the medics, Spangler would have his head. He choked down his anger. "What is going to be, Powczuk?" He kept his voice level low. "Fort Irwin? Or Fort Bragg? So you can rejoin your unit, maybe ship over with them? Pick. Before I pick for you."

Powczuk went stiff and lifted a crisp salute. "I pick Fort Bragg, sir."

Tyler returned the salute. "Get your gear, soldier. I hear your ride coming."

He watched the Blackhawk take off with Powczuk belted in. Just to be sure he was shed of the man.

Leaving him alone in the desert. Tyler had already sent Poole's team—as much as he hated to admit it was now Poole's team—on the next leg of its mission hours ago. A simple endurance test. Simple because it required the team to travel from a simple Point A, to simple Point B. Not so simple because the distance between A and B was more than fifty miles. Across the desert, over a rugged black range of basalt, down into a soda lake bed into more desert, and finally, more desert. No weapons, no matches or compass or first aid kit. Besides their clothing and boots, the only thing they would wear were their passive GPS devices. The only thing they could carry was a fanny pack with bottles of water.

Tyler wanted to go along. And would have. Except now, he had to look over videos from last night. Not only from Poole's group at the terrorist camp, but also for the other three teams working at different stages of the test. In the morning, before joining up with Poole's team, he had one nasty task to take care of.

Tyler waited for his own Blackhawk to take off, a hand over his eyes to deflect the rotor blast. Once the sand devils settled, he took in the terrorist camp Poole's team attacked last night. By day it was innocuous enough, no more than a dirty line of shacks. Until he drew near and saw the place in gory detail. He saw his NCO directing men as they dragged full body bags from the six huts and lined them up at the cargo door of a huge tandem-blade helicopter, a CH-47 Chinook.

He stepped up and returned the NCO's salute. "First Sergeant Wainwright."

"Sir." Wainwright waved at the line of bodies.

Tyler set his jaw. "How did the cadre do, Top? Anybody hurt? Anybody want to put in for a transfer out of this detail?"

"Anybody?" Wainwright mimicked a laugh. "They all want out, sir. Even me. But nobody is quitting." He handed over a stack of Polaroid pictures. Tyler didn't look at them. They were for later. For now, he had the real thing just a few meters away.

Tyler stared at the line of fresh bodies the detail was taking off the Chinook. Civilians, mostly, mostly dead veterans. A few dead soldiers, victims of cancer, disease, suicides, training accidents, and auto crashes. Men who'd checked the boxes on the backs of their drivers' licenses. Donating their bodies to medical science. Soon as the Chinook lifted off with last night's bodies inside insulated stainless steel coolers, frozen by nitrogen liquid, they would wing their ways to labs and trauma centers around the country. Forensics experts would go over the bodies. In return for specimens, they would send their detailed autopsy reports to the Pentagon.

"Any survivors?" He shrugged. "So to speak?"

Wainwright shook his head. "All dead. Most center of mass, at least three fatal hits each. Four of them double-tapped besides. One single-tapped."

Tyler raised his eyebrows.

Wainwright shrugged. "Number Five: One tap fatal, one tap not. Nicked an ear. A twitch shot is all."

"Do we know who it was?"

"Foucault. Caught on tape."

"The sixth guy?"

"Eight shots to the groin and belly. He would've died."

"Eventually."

"Eventually."

Tyler shook his head. "I don't like that one. Well, I suppose I'd better look. God, I hate this."

"It's almost as spooky as being in them cracker boxes when your boys kick the doors."

Swayne did a take. "You? You were inside one of the huts? Are we that shorthanded, Top Sergeant?"

"No, sir."

"You know you don't have to do it."

"Yes, sir. I do. What kind of leader would I be if I didn't do what I ask my men to do?" Wainwright barked at one of his men. "Let's have a look." A soldier unzipped the body bags, exposing the wounds on the six cadavers.

Tyler didn't waste time on the first five cadavers, all dead, all head-shot at least once. He had to study the last one, though. It was his job.

"This guy?" he said. "Building six?"

"That's the one."

Tyler checked his roster. "Blue Dolan and Simon Ballard?"

"I know, it don't figure," Wainwright said. "They might shoot low. Hell, they might even miss. Any man could miss. But leave without being sure? That ain't like Blue."

Tyler agreed. Neither Dolan nor Ballard would make that mistake. He knelt beside a young man and consulted his history, a few brief remarks on a five-by-eight card tucked into a transparent plastic sleeve on the outside of the body bag. Harvey (NMI) Denis, thirty-three. A shriveled caucasian army sergeant. Suicide by crack cocaine overdose. Reeking of nicotine. Re-killed by Delta Force.

"Harv," Tyler said to the body. "Sorry about this." The morning sun warmed the body's gases escaping through the torn and shattered lower abdomen of Harvey Denis. The low body shots didn't matter. They would have been fatal, but maybe not right away. The man might have lived for up to half an hour. Time enough for a terrorist to give up what he knew—that Americans had attacked him.

Tyler looked at the head, bald, the scalp translucent. Denis was giving him a gaunt, open-mouth, gap-tooth smile. Tyler saw a glitter beneath Denis's thin eyebrows. Up close, he could see the holes beneath the brows. One each. He took a deep breath, put his fingers one on each eyelid and pressed. His fingers slid into Denis's head on the twin paths that two projectiles had taken, until a frozen chunk stopped his fingertips. Two bullet holes.

"Nine mill," he said. "Dolan got the two-tap, after all, one in each eye. You got a towel, Top?"

"Dammit," Wainwright threw up his hands and ran off a string of curses, ending with, "Anderson, get your ass over here with a pair of gloves and those damned wet towels." He walked a tight circle in the sand. "Holy shit, I'm sorry, Captain, what with the AIDS and all. You shouldn't of had to do that. That kinda shit is our job."

"Not your fault," Tyler said, shaking his head in disgust. "For some reason, Harvey didn't thaw. His brain is still like a block of ice. No blood, no apparent bullet holes."

"Still," Wainwright said, and he turned his head and shouted, "Anderson, you better get your ass moving." Wainwright bit his lip. "Jeez, I'm sorry, Captain. I mean we should of given you a pair of gloves. We shouldn't of missed this one. We—"

"Forget it."

"This is so damned sick."

Tyler tried to work up some moisture in his dry mouth. "My fault. I could have waited. But I had to know if two good men would get the ax."

"I'm sorry, sir. I know Blue Dolan. He's a good man. Like you say. If he knew I ever doubted him—"

"He won't know." Tyler wiped his fingers with antiseptic towels long after they were clean. "Have you changed over the buildings? Set them up for the next group?"

"Done, sir." Wainwright was only too happy to change the subject.

"Let's take a look."

Wainwright led the way.

Two men, combat engineers, had pulled the shattered door to Building 1 free of its hinges. They set the bullet-riddled planks aside, stacking them with the remains of five other doors. A new door, on new hinges, leaned against each of the six buildings. Ready to install for tonight's test of a second team. The men stepped aside, and Tyler lowered his head to clear the door jamb. Inside, his eyes adjusted to the light. A wooden cot to his right, draped by a blanket. A foam pillow. He lifted the blanket, saw the bullet holes in the wooden slats.

Wainwright spoke up. "I didn't see any need to replace those things," he said. "The blankets and the slats. What do you think, sir?"

"Fine." That didn't matter so much. What mattered was the setup for the optical illusion of two live, armed terrorists inside the shack.

Tyler stepped toward his reflection, backlit in the doorway. Even in the light of day, it was a good illusion. Just like in a fun house at the carnival, a shiny sheet of metal stood in the center of the room, swung from hinges on the ceiling. In fact, the sheets did come from a factory that supplied carnivals with metal mirrors. When the Delta Force soldier burst in, he saw movement and caught a glimpse of an armed man—himself.

Once he started firing, and his night vision goggles washed out from the muzzle blasts, a hidden member of Tyler's training cadre pulled a rip cord that ran from inside his hiding compartment in a false wall. The cord fed into the ceiling. The cord first set off a flash-bang device on the left wall, then released a catch on the mirror's hinges. The cadre reeled in the cord until the mirror went flush to the ceiling, its backing plywood, a match to the rest of the ceiling.

If the Delta men looked up, they would see nothing but the bullet holes shot through the mirror, splintering the plywood.

But most of them would not look up. Because at the rear of the room, no longer hidden by the mirror, a freshly thawed corpse stood propped up, dressed in the robes of an Arab and carrying an AK-47. Once released by a second rip cord, the corpse would slide toward the men on pulleys, then crumple to the floor, completing the illusion.

The man behind the false wall, lined with a steel plate for extra safety, could triple-lock the door to his hidey-hole and secure it with a steel drop-bar besides.

Tyler stepped aside as two of his men carried in a new corpse, frozen stiff in the nitrogen chamber, finishing the swap-out for the old, shot-up corpse.

As they began to stand the corpse into position and hook up a cable to the harness beneath the robes, Tyler inspected the hidey-hole as he had a dozen times before. He swung the door open and closed to be sure it traveled freely. He stepped inside and pulled it in on himself. He shut all three deadbolts and set the drop bar. Except for the glow of light from above, no cracks. As long as a man didn't light up a smoke, he would have plenty of air.

Tyler threw a shoulder against the door from the inside. Nothing. It did not budge. Solid, hard, cold.

Too cold. He slid open the bolts and lifted the bar. The door stayed shut until he leaned against it with a shoulder. He had to shove hard, and that was good—the door would not come open unless the man inside wanted it to. God help him if he stepped out of his hidey-hole before getting the all clear.

His men were finishing up on the cadaver, strapping the AK-47 across its chest. It was a young man, shaved bald, with a haggard, blue face, thin and sallow as a famine victim. One of his men wrapped a strip of terrycloth around the head, making a turban of it. When the two men had finished, they flapped their hands, trying to warm them after contact with the body, frozen to minus ten.

They didn't say a word to Tyler, but their looks spoke for them: *Good enough? Please say it's good enough.*

Tyler gave them a thumbs-up.

The men were only too happy to get back outside into the heat of day. The corpse would thaw by evening. Then, transfused with thick, red, and warmed cow's blood, and pressurized with bulbs of CO_2, blood would spatter when it was shot. More than realistic enough.

Spangler had insisted on using cadavers. Tyler didn't fight it. To get the realism, to test the Delta fighters, to see if they would put killing shots into a body lying helpless and bloody on the floor. Neither Spangler nor Tyler really doubted they would. They'd already trained to kill. But against paper targets. The test was just a precaution, really. To see if a squeamish soul had slipped through the process.

And to set them up for tougher tests to come.

Carnes left Baker to sleep until well into the morning, although it wasn't much of a rest. "Make a note, Baker-man. A hundred-fifteen degrees Fahrenheit at zero-niner-zero-five hours."

"Don't be giving me the goddamned temperature," Baker said. "I know how miserable I am. I don't need you to put a number on it."

Carnes laughed. "Don't be stupid, man. I'm not telling you the numbers for your sake. I'm doing it for my own enjoyment. I love to watch your face tighten up every time it climbs a couple degrees."

Baker had to join him in the laugh, but not for long. His face ached, his head wound throbbed, and his sore ribs jabbed shooters of pain at him from the inside out.

Toward evening, Carnes leaned in close to him, a finger to his lips.

"You sadistic bas—What is it? What's out there?"

"Somebody."

"You guys always so precise?"

Carnes grunted. He studied the landscape through his binoculars, looking over Baker's body.

"It's okay," he said finally. "It's one of ours. Mine."

"Too bad."

"Huh?"

"I was hoping for a suicide bomber. Put me out of my misery."

Carnes shook his head. "I'm serious, Ramsey."

"About what?" The CIA man had never used his first name.

"I don't know how you've lasted so far without killing yourself. I'd have offed myself shaving by now already."

"It's nothing." Baker studied Carnes's face. He wasn't kidding. It awed him that the man would show so much respect. "All I did was get beat up."

Carnes exhaled in admiration, puffing up his cheeks. He stood up and waved at the horizon. "I'm going to meet him. Back in an hour."

Friday, September 14, 2001—The Nevada Desert

Poole's task force finished its march two hours before sunset. The scenario called for them to meet up with a band of Tyler's so-called Northern Alliance militia. Walking scout, Night Runner spotted the three men first, sitting in the shade at the base of a cliff half a mile away. He flashed a mirror at them, the letters O-B-L in Morse code. One of the men walked out into the sun and flashed back the proper reply, R-I-P. Poole and Night Runner went down to parlay with the trio. The rest of the men stayed out of sight until Poole waved them in.

Night Runner expected a break, perhaps a drink of water, a boxed Meal-Ready-to-Eat ration, maybe the overcooked pasta in a bag. After two nights of hardship and a day of laying up out of the sun, he did not expect the drinks to include designer bottled water on ice, sodas, milk, and beer. He didn't expect the ration to include fresh cheeses, rich and stinky. What was this? A roasted carcass, a goat from the look of it? Pasta in a garlic-olive oil-butter sauce? French bread with whipped honey-butter? Ice cream for dessert? Incredible.

The men went at it with gusto, no restrictions but a hand-lettered sign on a five-feet-long cooler, Limit 2 Beers.

Night Runner held back. Too incredible. He had fasted before. Often in combat, but most often in self-discipline. He knew what could happen if he tucked into a heavy meal, alcohol and ice cream on the side. First the carb high, then the carb crash.

So he found a tanker pup parked deep in the gully, 500 gallons of fresh water, set up for a shower station.

Showers, too? The better this rest break got, the less Night Runner liked it. Tyler was up to something, surely. He admired the man's drive. He had never seen a test like this, a test as tough as combat. Maybe tougher. More than a test of the body's ability to endure pain and hardship. More than a mind screw. But a test of ethics, too?

The testing ground Tyler had carved out wasn't the desert. He had chosen the darkest landscape of all, the remote reaches of each man's head, heart, and soul. What kind of times were these that made men like Tyler?

Night Runner, refreshed after a splash bath, did try some of the meat—it was goat, strong and peppered. He flavored it with melted butter and tore a chunk of bread from a loaf. He chewed each bite a long time, washing it down with bottled water only. He kept ragging at the problem like a terrier at a long-dead rat. What the hell was Tyler up to?

Around the fire, men drank sodas, nursed beers, and pounded down bottles of water. The mystery of the killings at the camp, still far from solved, was no longer a topic the men relished. They had new adventures now, less troubling tales to tell. So they took to re-marching the march across the desert, the encounters with snakes and scorpions, the hawk swooping in for its kill of a quail. They laughed at the mishaps, the man whose leg plunged into a badger hole and came free with a pair of rattlesnake fangs stuck in the sole of his boot, a thick five-pound reptile still attached. They roared at the name of the dance, coined on the spot, the rapping-rattlesnake-two-step-hip-hop-stomp. That was Barret's dance. Until Night Runner stepped up and plucked the snake from the boot.

A day later, they still marveled that the Blackfeet warrior held the animal by the head, its body wrapped around his left arm, and used his right hand to crack one basalt stone against another, knocking off a shard the size of a meat cleaver. They *oooh*ed as he used the scalpel-sharp flake to first take off the snake's head, then field-dress it, and *aahhh*ed at the retelling of it. They cursed sharply yesterday at his ability to strike sparks into a puff of tinder and have a fire going within thirty seconds. And they cursed softly at the flavor of rattlesnake cooked over an open fire, seasoned with pungent herbs from the desert. They cursed again today, this time in whispers, at the memory of that taste.

Night Runner felt good about this Delta Team. These were men as good as marines. This was a time of good feelings, good feelings that did not recall a bloody test at the terrorist camp, at least not aloud. That was then. This was a now filled with food, drink, a couple brews. These Delta men, like all fighting men, knew when to savor a moment. Things to come and things in the past, unpleasant things all, had no place in this moment, in their memories.

Except for Night Runner. He could not relax in his head.

He tried to give Tyler one last benefit of a doubt. Maybe the captain had set up this feast as a way to let men bond after a simple bit of travel. Maybe they would get a night's sleep before taking on the next part of the test. Maybe he was wrong about Tyler. Maybe he wasn't a fiend, after all. Maybe—

In the distance, over the laughter around the fire, now in the long shadows of afternoon, Night Runner heard a helicopter. A minute later, so did everybody else. A Blackhawk came into view and set down inside the faded blossom of its own sandstorm. Night Runner saw the figure of Tyler, running bent below the blades of the Blackhawk. He couldn't help feeling that he was wrong about being wrong.

"The party's over," Tyler told the group. "I hope you've had time to fill your bellies and clean up. In five minutes, you're on the march again. I have a new mission for you, an urgent combat mission."

When Carnes came back with his companion, Baker said, "You got that temperature shit down. Now maybe we could teach you something about telling time. You call that an hour? I call it three."

Carnes's smile sparkled pink in the fiery sunset as he spoke to the new arrival. "There he is, Robin, your captive—you might have to knock him around a little bit to correct his bad manners. Ramsay al Bakr, I'd like you to meet your captor, Robin Roberts. He's a friend of mine."

"Like that's a good thing," Roberts said.

The two figures stepped into Baker's line of sight. All he could see were their outlines dark against the bright sky.

"Pleasure, I'm sure," Baker said.

Roberts turned a beam of light onto Baker's face and uttered soft curses.

"Damn, Carnes. It's worse'n you said. Somebody try and scalp him? How bad is that bone broken?"

"Radius and ulna both," Carnes said.

"Jesus, what the hell'd they do to his ears."

Carnes cleared his throat at the top of his voice.

"It's a birth defect," Baker said. "A set of boxer's ears but without the boxing."

"Jeez, I'm sorry, man."

"Forget it." Baker lifted his dirty blouse to show the purple and green bruises all over his chest. "I used to cringe about the ears all the time. I hardly think about them anymore. Unless—"

Carnes butted in. "Done chatting, girls? Let's go over the cover story." He met Baker's weary expression head-on. "Yes, again."

Baker sighed deeply. "I got separated from my unit in a battle against a commando unit in the west of the country. Near Uzbekistan."

"The agency snatched him up wandering around in the desert," Roberts said, picking up on his part of the story. "Probably a deserter. They should have killed you straight up but decided to turn you over to me so I could give you to our friends in the Northern Alliance. Maybe get some intelligence out of you. Maybe some entertainment value."

Lying on his back on the sand, Baker saw the pair of CIA agents gawking at him, shaking their heads. He couldn't read their faces, but their body language said plenty. Once a man put the scheme to words and spoke it aloud, he couldn't believe his own ears.

Carnes shook his head. "Let's go over it again."

"Jesus, Brian," Baker said, "this roadkill isn't going to get any better with age."

Carnes threw up his hands. "You see that, Ramsay, you see that? How many times I gotta tell you? If you gotta take the name of the Lord in vain, the Lord's gotta be Allah."

"Jesus, sorry."

"What'd I just say?" He caught Ramsey's eye and saw that Baker was joking. In Pashto this time."

Tyler gave the men just five minutes, and they were ready in four. Delta men knew how to shift gears. Trouble was, most of them were going to regret that they had shifted into too low a gear at the end of their desert march. In combat, self-discipline counted for more than the ability to take orders. A man could not assume their enemy, either Tyler here or Al Qaeda over there, might give them the night off just because they put in a full day's work.

Already he had watched a live video feed of the stand-down, pictures fed from support crew at the test site. Tyler had focused on pictures of Staff Sergeant Porter Seger, pictures that would cost the man his place on the team. Seger was a good soldier, a crack shot, and an expert at survival. Even with an ankle sprained at the terrorist camp, Seger had gutted out the desert trip. But around the campfire, he pounded down his ration of beer, two cans without a pause. After a few bites of pasta, he had gone back to the ice barrel to take two more, as if they were his first ration. He didn't drink any water, just the four beers. Then, after gulping the fresh pair, he went back for another pair. A six-pack in thirty minutes. Seger looked stone sober which meant he was a practiced drunk.

Tyler called him out before Poole formed the men into march formation. He didn't ask Poole's opinion. This one was his own call.

"Staff Sergeant Seger, get on the Blackhawk. You're being pulled out on a medical. The ankle. You'll be shifted to another team."

Seger cocked his head. He looked down at his right boot, laced fatter than his left. "I just did fifty miles on a bent wheel." Except for a trace film that glazed his eyes, he looked sober enough. He sniffed and spat. "And you're cutting me?"

"I'm putting you on a new team."

"No you're not. You're cutting me."

"It's a medical." Tyler knew the lie was a no-go, even as he said it.

"It's because I had a few extra brews."

Tyler kept a flat affect.

Seger's left eyebrow went crooked, forming the shape of a question mark. The right eyebrow crooked the opposite way, in anger. His thin mustache twitched into the curve of a smirk.

"Don't say it," Tyler said.

"Don't say what? Sir?"

"Just get on the aircraft."

"What? Why?"

"If you leave now, without a word, nothing happened here. If you say one smart-ass-Powczuk-type thing, I'll have you arrested."

Seger's mustache went flat. *Oh yeah?*

"And thrown out of Delta Force and into a program."

The eyes narrowed.

"For drunks." He pointed a finger at the sky. "One. Word."

Tyler waited to see whether he'd get his answer from Seger or from the beer. Seger won out. He saluted, turned about awkwardly in the sand, and slumped toward the Blackhawk. Tyler drew a deep breath of relief. Ten minutes—or two beers—later, the beers would have trumped Seger's good sense.

Tyler held a brief powwow with Poole and sent off two more to the Blackhawk to join Seger. Alberto Solis and Marcus Garner got the hook, both on true medicals. Solis for a swelling in his lower leg, from a bite or sting. Garner because for treatment of a cough that developed into full-blown pneumonia. Both would get a second shot, if they wanted it, on the next cycle.

As the men stood lounging in formation, seven strong, a
Humvee pulled up with a loaded trailer. An NCO issued one
set of high-tech binoculars to each of the Delta men.

Tyler pulled Night Runner aside and gave him a sketch map.
"You're not in this test."

"Sir?"

"Your commandant would have a cow." Tyler pointed to
the sketch map. "When I give you the word, lead my six-pack
on this short march."

Tyler then turned to the team. "We suspect an Al Qaeda
vill, a second camp." A surge of tension swept through the
group. For the low-tech types, stubby pencils hovered over
pocket notebooks. For the tekkies, styluses no longer poked at
PDAs. *Another camp?* As he handed out photos of a dozen
Arab men, Tyler saw the edge on each Delta soldier's face.
The memory of that first night attack, set aside on the desert
march, had crept back raw. Each man knew he'd have to kill
again. Each took inventory of his will.

Fair enough. A soldier couldn't afford to wait to decide to
kill until the moment he lifted a rifle and saw his target over
the front post of the sights. A soldier didn't have time for self-
talk and moralizing with his thumbs poised over the buttons
of a remote detonator set to blow a fuel dump with a dozen
Filipino terrorists—four of them women—sleeping hard by.
He made that call early on. Long before he picked up the
rifle. Before he set the charges. Before he went into special
ops. *Will I kill?*

You asked; you answered. And long ago. Or else you let
your finger freeze on the trigger. Better you stayed home and
pumped gas, unloaded beer kegs, crunched numbers, sold
Volvos to soccer moms.

Now Tyler was forcing them to ask and answer again. *Will
I kill?* Or, more to the point, *Will I kill Tyler's way?*

"Refer to the mug shots," Tyler said. "Try to ID key A-Q
men. On order, you'll light up targets for smart bombs. Don't
kill innocents unless you have to. But at all costs . . . at *all*
costs, kill any or all of these men." *My way or the highway.*
"Questions?"

There were none.

Night Runner led the men on a march of less than a mile to high ground above a deep wadi. The men took positions from which to observe a cluster of rough houses on the near, steep bank of the dry wash.

"That's the vill," Tyler said. "Skin your eyes and get at it."

The edge softened on each face as the men worked. Learning the new, high-tech binos as they used them. Marking GPS locations, recording sightings with their onboard video cams, taking notes on the numbers of people in the village. The activity eased the tension.

They saw children playing in the dirt. Women in head-to-toe burqas drew water from a common well and carried clay vases back to the huts. Smoke rose from chimneys. One or two men lounged around in the shade a quarter mile away. None of the Delta Force scouts connected them to the pictures of Al Qaeda suspects. Before long an air of hopeful relief settled over the group.

Until a yellow pickup raised a rooster tail of dust from the far edge of the wadi. Tyler's men grew alert as it closed on the oasis and dipped over the steep far bank. In turn, Tyler crept up behind each of the Delta Force men as he took notes. The edge was back on each face.

Toyota.

Three men in front.

Four in back.

3 AK-47s, 2 SKS.

One by one, the scouts circled mug shots that matched men in the back of the pickup. When the Toyota nosed up and over the near bank and stopped beside the well, children ran indoors, herded by mothers. The Al Qaeda suspects drank water and smoked around the well, giving the Delta scouts a full two minutes to circle more pictures.

Tyler checked each scout twice. Except for Poole, who circled five terrorists from the photos, everybody else picked either three, or four, the correct number. Of Poole's five selections, only two were correct. Tyler kept a smug smile to himself. So, Poole was not all that perfect, after all.

Not that it mattered. Recon was beside the point. Intel was simply the flourish that distracted the eye from Tyler's sleight of hand.

The Al Qaeda men moved in a mob and went into the largest of the buildings in the village. Tyler took to the radio to give a new order.

"HQ has fragged a stealth bomber to us," he told them over the radio net. "Ordnance is two 2,000-pound bombs. The aircraft is on call to you for an immediate strike against enemy suspects. Each man paint the dwelling where the suspects went to meet." He sniffed. "I hope to hell you kept track at which hut is which.

Delta men had used the J-DAM system in training. A scout could identify his own position by GPS, then range by laser to a target and send the data to the heavens. Spy satellites could calculate the range and bearing to get target coordinates. That data could be relayed to an in-flight bomber and keyed by the crew into a bomb. Once released within a so-called capture distance, the bomb would home on the target. A spotter could paint-and-skate, making his escape hours before an air attack. In much the same way a pilot could fire-and-forget, drop his bomb, and head back to the barn, his smart bomb smart enough to fly its own way to dusty death.

But Tyler didn't want these men to rely on J-DAMS. Each was to paint the target the old-fashioned way. The smart bomb would capture the laser beam and fly down to its end.

Tyler finished his order. "Strike ETA in two minutes, twenty seconds . . . mark."

"Got a tick for a question?" Poole asked.

"Roger," said a second man. "I got a couple questions."

Tyler gave them dead air. He knew their questions. He and Spangler had war-gamed questions on every aspect of this test months ago: *U.S. soldiers bomb a hut full of children? Is this just a head game? Will a live bomb actually strike the vill?* Let them answer for themselves, in their hearts and in their heads.

They'd try to psych out the test, of course. So they could go to Afghanistan. To flinch now would put them on that washout-bird back to base to join Powczuk, Seger, Solis, and Garner.

Each man would paint the house, each man on his own laser wavelength, each man thinking Tyler was trying to find out if any of them would lose his nerve. And, this being a test, after all, they wouldn't. No test would risk killing a bunch of kids. Not in America. *Shit, man. Bomb a bunch of kids?* No way. *What the hell was I thinking? It's a test. It's only a test.*

Exactly the mind-set Tyler had to erase in those six minds—he checked his watch—in the next forty-five seconds.

He slipped away to a van to study six video screens. Six monitors showed the picture each man saw in his binos. Six screens showed a laser spot playing on the terrorist hut with kids inside, more kids nearby in the second hut. Two of the spots were not all that steady. Tyler's techs had scribbled names on the monitor glass in felt-tip pen. Edgar Poole and Soiree Ward, the two officers. Their laser dots drifted. At least Poole tried to keep his steady, pointing it at the base of the near wall, so in case he missed, the bomb would strike low. Ward aimed too high, near the peak of the roof. His bomb, if it missed, might overfly the target and go off in the wadi beyond. Ward's aim was a blink in a stare down. He hadn't exactly lost his nerve. Yet. Poole's aim betrayed the jitters, but at least he was willing to err in favor of the mission.

Barret was spot-on the line where the near wall met the roof. Gabriel Foucault, ditto. Blue Dolan had laid his spot on a doorjamb. Simon Ballard at a window sill.

Tyler checked his watch. *Three . . . two—*

Six screens flared into white, then the village erupted. The screen came back to a pair of dirty black clouds.

As the view in the six screens refocused, Tyler watched to see who stayed on target and put down his binoculars to see over them. About half and half. Not a big deal. What happened next was the big deal.

Tyler spoke into the radio, calling the scouts off the hill.

Tyler met a sober group at the camp. He could see them dealing with it, each in his own way trying to pick the test apart, each trying to identify which was smoke and which was mirrors in the trick.

Tyler gave them each a sheet of paper and one instruction: "BDA."

Each found a place to sit and write an assessment of bomb damage. Tyler didn't care what they wrote. He just wanted to buy some time.

In less than a minute, Tyler pushed them again, "Thirty seconds. Come on, finish it up. Hand in your papers to me and stand by for—" a series of explosions from beyond the ridge-line cut him off. He shrugged. "Secondaries. As I was saying, stand by the next mission."

As he took each BDA, Tyler looked into six sets of eyes. What would give away a weakness? Ward, a black man, had paled to the color of gray ash on a charcoal fire. Remorse? Gabriel Foucault's mustache dripped with sweat. Revulsion? Barret, Dolan, and Ballard showed nothing but a cool reserve. Poole's tell, an acrid stare, was a hot rebuke: *You one sick sonofabitch.*

Tyler gave it back. Poole was not a fellow officer, not even a fellow American. He was a competitor for the job of leading the Delta task force into Afghanistan. He raised one eyebrow at Poole in rebuff: *You think that was sick? Tell me what you think ten minutes from now.*

A truck rolled into the Delta camp. Tyler's NCO issued 9 mm pistols, holsters, and a clip of ammunition to each man. "Lock and load," the NCO said. "Safeties on, hammers down."

Tyler watched each man jack a round into the chamber and set the weapon to safe. He waited until each snapped his pistol into his holster.

"All set?"

"Cap, y'all mind if we test-fire the pistols first?"

Tyler cleared his throat. He saw the double-dare look in Poole's face, the man trying to throw his own wrinkle into the test.

Poole smirked. "You know, so we be sure there's no misfire down below? You know. Once we make a sweep of the battle-field?"

Tyler's eyes flicked left and right. "I don't . . . I don't suppose it would do any harm."

Poole's smirk turned into a *gotcha* smile. He pointed toward the campfire. "The trash barrel? That be fine?"

"I don't know." Tyler gave a weak smile, looking abashed but watching the faces all the while.

The smug among the Delta operators, Dolan, Barrett, and Poole, withdrew their pistols and released the safety levers, expecting to fire blanks toward the barrel. Or to have Tyler try to tap-dance his way out of his bluff. So willing to believe this was no live-fire exercise, after all.

"One thing," Tyler said.

"What's that, Cap?"

"You can test-fire, if you want. But just two rounds. No more, no less."

Poole's turn to flinch.

"To conserve ammo," Tyler said. "Lieutenant Poole, since this is your idea, you make sure that each man's weapon will fire."

"Yessir."

"Police up the brass and count it."

"Yessir."

Tyler turned away so he might hide his own smug smile.

As Poole directed each man to fire two rounds in turn. Every round spanged into the trash barrel, sending up sprays of dust, beer, and water.

"Saddle up," Poole said.

Tyler caught the lack of passion in Poole's voice and the lack of conviction in the troops. Each man hauled himself up into the truck. No man gave a hand up to another man, the bright spirits that had prevailed during the meal, gone dim.

Tyler rode shotgun in a Humvee. He told his driver to stay well behind the truck. He didn't want give up any tells of his own, didn't want the men to know he was just as sick about what came next as any normal person should be. Almost.

They homed on the column of roiling black smoke from the burning Toyota. A pair of steaming craters had displaced the main terrorist hut. Lazy fires nibbled at the remains of two other buildings.

Now and then, one of the Delta men would look back toward Tyler, their lips moving. Calling him names, perhaps. Perhaps wondering whether an army officer could do this, or whether a country could allow it. Perhaps one or two wondering whether they should stick with the program. Good that they should ask now. Good that they should answer.

As they closed in on the site, the answers lay about in stark detail. First came the body parts, an arm and a leg. Then smoldering weapons. The smell of roasted flesh. Tempting for one brief second, as if a neighbor had tossed a T-bone on the grill. Then the visual recall of those flashes that made the stomach lurch. Even for Tyler.

The diesel's engine coughed and went silent. Letting the men hear the tiny, distant screams of children.

Ward and Foucault draped the upper half of their bodies over the railing of the truck to decorate the desert floor with vomit.

Tyler shook his head. Dumb bastards. Next time, they wouldn't gorge on hot, rich food and cold, heavy beer. Next time they sat down to a meal in the middle of a mission they would remember this day, those smells, the screams, the body parts that made them un-eat.

Tyler bit his lip. He got no satisfaction from their sickness. He simply had to know about them. Would they fight through it? Or fold up and lie at its feet?

Tyler waited for the group to form up. Neither Ward nor Foucault jumped from the truck like the others. They sat on the edge, rolled over onto their bellies, and slid their feet to the ground. Ward's knees gave way, and he had to squat to steady himself. Only to see the truck had stopped beside half the corpse of a child. Ward shied and fell. He made it to the formation on his knees, where Poole helped him to his feet.

Tyler surveyed the faces. Foucault and Ward swallowing

their vomit. Poole shooting lasers of hatred. Ballard chewing first one lip, then the other. He avoided looking at the corpses. He was a father to two children. He needed the bodies to be a trick.

Barret and Dolan not caring. They had a mission: *But at all costs, kill any or all of these men. At all costs.* So they had killed. The children? The women? The men not on the list? Collateral damage. If you lived by the terrorist, you died by the terrorist.

A second deuce-and-a-half roared up the road toward the group. "Enemy?" Poole asked. His hand went to his pistol.

"No," Tyler said. "Those are Northern Alliance soldiers. Our allies."

"What up?" Poole didn't trouble to hide his disdain.

"BDA. Close recon. You're going to go over the ground with a fine-tooth comb and pick up any bit of intel you can. Count bodies . . . and body parts."

The very idea was too much for Foucault. He could not choke down his vomit any longer.

Night Runner was glad he did not get a BDA sheet. He could see what Tyler was up to. Another test. Make the man record it on paper. Tally the body parts. Look the beast in the eye. Now, before he had to confront it in combat. Was that a very good idea? Or a very bad one?

He sauntered around the camp. He knew it had to be a trick. *But how, dammit, how?*

As he circled to the far edge of the crater, he began to see the picture, written in the dirt. Beyond the sweep of the blast, he saw prints take shape. The tracks led him from the back of the hut—the crater. Small prints—of children and women. They led him to the edge of the bank and down into the wadi. He looked back toward the ridge where the Delta men had laser-painted the hut. Before the impact, the women and kids went out the back door. Of course.

He followed the bank to a flat spot behind a huge pile of

boulders and debris. A parking lot scraped clean by dozers. He traced the tracks to a bunker, concrete, square, big enough to hide a bus. Two buses, in fact, by the tread marks.

Beyond the parking lot the ground fell away. On the far side of the wadi, and he saw a road. Beyond that, at the next range of peaks, a cloud of dust rose like red smoke. So. That was how—

He felt a touch on his shoulder and wheeled, ready to throw a punch.

"Whoa!" Tyler raised his hands in front of him. "You shouldn't be here. I want the Northern Alliance guys to lead the team back here. Part of the test."

Night Runner nodded. "The test." He looked toward the distant cloud or red. "You took the children away."

Tyler smirked. *What else?* "In buses. The men were in bunkers when we touched off the main explosion."

"No bombs?"

"No bombs. A small blast at first, mostly smoke and dust. We brought in the main charges after—"

"After you called us off the ridge. They were the second-aries."

"Roger."

"The body parts?"

"Cadavers," Tyler said. "You might want to think twice about checking that donor box on the back of your driver's license."

"The screams?"

"Taped. A screaming contest. The kids had a riot doing it."

Night Runner turned away from the hills and looked at Tyler closely, as if seeing him for the first time in this new and awful light.

Tyler shook his head. "Army brats. They had no idea what went on here. To them, it was just a field trip, a game, a trip to an Arab village to see how people live in another culture. They were long gone before the explosions and the fire." He pointed his chin at the far mountains. "They're eating Dove Bars on the bus."

Night Runner saw that the man's facade had eroded a bit.

"They didn't see a thing," Tyler insisted. *What do you think I am?*

"What about the men, Captain? Combat takes a toll. Every time you get into a fight, you pay a price. After a few times, men are not the same as when they began. I'm thinking—"

"Why take a slice out of a man's spirit? Why take a normal man and turn him into an animal? Why shorten his value? Why spend too many of a man's chips before he even gets into actual combat? Is that what you're asking?"

"That's what I'm asking. Sir."

"Asked and answered already, Gunny." Tyler looked past Night Runner to a band of soldiers in ragged garb and worn military gear jogging their way. "My Northern Alliance guys. But this mission? It's not for normal men to do. I can't find what I need in normal. You get what I'm saying?"

"I do. You start with a type not quite as crazy as Powczuk. Then you push him to the brink. And hope it's not too far."

Tyler shrugged his face. "Close enough. It'll have to do. You can't talk about it. Not now, not later."

"Ever?"

"Not ever."

Night Runner took a deep breath. "I've seen such a thing as this. In Kosovo. And this is it. This is the real thing."

Tyler watched Night Runner walk away, back toward the rest of the Delta team. *This is the real thing.* That was no compliment. He felt sick at the truth in it.

The Northern Alliance players surrounded the bunker. Inside, in the dim light, Tyler could see wounded terrorist players sitting up, adjusting their torn clothing, freshening their wounds with blood sprayed from plastic squeeze bottles. "Stay in character," he ordered. The players flopped to the ground and began moaning again.

The Northern Alliance leader said, "Sir, are we off schedule?"

Tyler looked to the horizon and shook his head. "No, not if we hurry and get set up."

Tyler rounded up his Delta team. He briefed them quickly, telling them that the Northern Alliance soldiers had found a number of wounded Al Qaeda in a bunker. "The bastards wouldn't let the women and kids in after the strike." He shook his head. "Women and kids. They were outside for the secondaries."

He studied the faces. No smirks this time. He had them where he wanted them, ready for finals.

"The Northern Alliance people want to interrogate the suspects. Some of them are dazed. Others have intel."

"What kind of intel?" Blue Dolan wanted to know.

"Possibly about more terrorist attacks against the United States. The rumor of a chemical attack in Los Angeles." Tyler knew that Dolan had come from Los Angeles, had attended UCLA for one year, in fact, on a soccer scholarship.

"Let me."

"You'll each get a turn."

"Then I want to be first."

"That's a neg. Foucault is the interrogator. We'll start with him. Sergeant?"

Foucault edged out of the formation, more than a little eager to get away from the body count, less than keen about getting a first look at perhaps an even worse evil. "Here, sir."

"Check your pistol. Safety on but locked and loaded."

Foucault looked as if he might step back, maybe pull his hat down over his eyes, try to hide. Tyler held him with his gaze as he spoke to the others.

"Everybody else mount up on the deuce-and-a-half." Nobody moved. "We're going to make a sweep—several sweeps, in fact. See if we can pick up any stragglers."

"With pig iron?" Poole said, slapping his holstered pistol.

Tyler was ready for him. "No, rifles. You'll find gear in the back of the truck. Mount up."

After the truck had roared off with the men, Tyler led Foucault toward the bunker, running his checklist through his head one last time. Spangler had sent him back to the drawing boards three times to write this test. Each time with darker requirements. In the end, Spangler had clapped a shoulder a hand on his shoulder and laughed. "Looks good on paper," the four-eyed toad said.

On paper. If only the little bastard could see it on the ground. Spangler didn't have to smell the smells Tyler had invented. Spangler didn't have to hear the desert scavengers, magpies and vultures above, and packs of coyotes below, closing in on a feed trough of body parts. Spangler didn't have to see arms scattered, chunks that would elude the search, no matter how hard his cleanup team worked to gather and cremate them.

Spangler didn't have to see the crater that the bomb had made, thirty feet across and half as deep in the sand. He didn't have to supervise Tyler's men throwing limbs and torsos in a heap, pumping diesel fuel, setting it on fire, letting it burn. Covering the residue with bulldozers. Marking off the territory with a chain-link fence, pour concrete on top. Putting up a sign, already made: Keep Off—Toxic Waste. To keep away the curious.

Toxic wasteland. Nice name for a mass grave. What would Stalin call it? And where would a family go to mourn?

Foucault stood in the interrogation area as if ready to flee. Just an open space in the waning sun, with a sand dune as a backdrop. A single bench, four feet long. Two men on the bench.

One man stepped forward from the clutch of Northern Alliance soldiers. He held out a rough brown hand. A genuine Arab, a Lebanese. Tyler took the hand and let it shake his briskly. "Sergeant First-Class Foucault, meet General Adnin Abdul al Nidal. He's in charge of this force of Northern Alliance soldiers. He's also in command of this interrogation. He is in command of you, as well. You will take your orders from him."

Al Nidal hand-wrestled Foucault into submission. "Sergeant, pleasure to introduce me who speaks good English, no?"

Foucault gazed into Tyler's eyes, giving him a look of, *Don't make me do this.* Tyler would not meet his gaze and turned to al Nidal.

"He's all yours, General."

Al Nidal laughed. "All mine? I am marry already." The general's men laughed along with him.

Tyler took a last look at Foucault and began to worry. The sergeant rocked from side to side, like a palm tree in a hurricane. His complexion had turned the color of brushed stainless steel to match his mustache and sideburns.

"Foucault, are you all right?"

"I'm fine." Even without his distress, Foucault had a long face. A mule, Powczuk had called him before Tyler cut him from the team. But Powczuk was right. Foucault had sad eyes, big as a mule's, his lower eyelids drooping.

Tyler narrowed his own eyes. "Sergeant, you don't have to do this. You can opt out. You can go back to your unit. I understand it hasn't left Fort Bragg yet. You could still make the flight."

Foucault bit his lip. "I could be a big help to this team," he said.

"I know. But first, you have to do this." Tyler started counting in his head. If Foucault hadn't decided it by ten, that was his decision.

As the seconds ticked away, Tyler realized he had lost a sense of real time. Only three days ago, the men were trying to think of ways to explain the kick-the-door exercise away as a sleight of hand, as something not as serious as it looked. And now, here in broad daylight, where a man could see all that was going on and the mission seemed much more straightforward, Foucault was wondering how much worse the day was going to get, how much worse was possible. He was afraid of what they would they ask him to do. His mind had come—had fallen—a long way. This was no more an exercise. This was a new, fearful reality.

At Tyler's silent count of nine, Foucault lifted his chin and thrust it forward. He had decided. His eyes looked out from under his unruly eyebrows. "I'll do it, sir."

"Are you sure? Are you willing to put yourself under the command of General al Nidal?"

Foucault stiffened. "I said—I'll do it. Sir."

"No matter what he asks?"

"Dammit, sir, can we just do it?"

"That's settled up, then," al Nidal said. "Let's get working on these terror whore sonbitch." He gave a boisterous laugh. Just another day at the office.

Tyler eased away as al Nidal drew a long-barreled pistol from his belt, a stainless steel Colt 44 revolver. A nice touch. Something to make Dirty Harry proud.

Not so nice a touch as he smashed one of the prisoners on the head. Foucault flinched. He could not know that the head-piece contained a sculpted gel packet that took the force of the blow. He could not know that the cry of pain was fake. He could not know that the blood that ran from beneath the turban was real blood, but from a cow and thinned with anticoagulants.

Al Nidal fired off a list of questions in Arabic. "Who are you? Where you come from? Who sent you? Where is bin Laden? You are a Taliban? You helped those bastards fly an airplane into the World Trade Center? The Pentagon? Where else?"

Foucault turned and tried to make eye contact with Tyler. Tyler wasn't having it. This wasn't his exercise anymore. It was al Nidal's. And Foucault's.

The general pistol-whipped the man once more, then stepped in front of the second man, a corpse propped upright, and smashed him over the head as well, asking the same set of questions. When the man did not reply, he smashed him again, setting off another flow of cow's blood from a cellophane packet.

Al Nidal shrugged. He turned to Foucault. "You try. With him." He pointed the long-barreled revolver at the first man, the live man, an army Ranger who wanted to become a Delta Force officer himself.

Foucault stepped up and began speaking softly in Arabic. "What's your name, please?" The good cop to al Nidal's bad cop.

Al Nidal wasn't having good cop–bad cop. "Ask him where to find bin Laden," he said in Arabic. "Where is Al Qaeda? Tell him I want to know these things. Tell him I am serious."

Foucault looked around again, but Tyler had stepped out of

sight into the bunker. He wanted to leave Foucault on his own. He would review the video later, from the camera carried by one of the Northern Alliance soldiers, disguised as a Soviet rocket-propelled grenade launcher. Tyler could hear well enough.

"Ask him," al Nidal commanded in Arabic. Al Nidal had a rough voice, laden with threat and more than enough realism. Tyler had to smile. He was a finance corps officer, A numbers cruncher. But he had that voice, and a mastery of the Pashto dialect. Not to mention a background in community theater.

Foucault began asking the right questions, but still in that timid voice. Foucault was spent. The endurance test that began on 9-11, when every military professional went on a kind of personal alert in advance of his unit's military alerts. Spangler's briefing. The night attack. The two-day march. The beer. Followed by the bombing mission. The assault on the senses, and now this. Physically, mentally, spiritually spent. Spangler had worried that four days might not be enough of a test. Now Tyler wondered. Was it too much?

He should cut short the script, let Foucault and the others off the hook. Chalk it up to sensory overload. Admit that his test had already done enough damage. Let the man go. Let him save face, mind, soul. Let them all go.

Tyler would have, except for one thing. Why was it his job to save souls? The man wanted to quit, all he had to do was say so.

Al Nidal pressed on. Tyler could picture it without seeing it, just by hearing. They had rehearsed how the general, his breath reeking with garlic and cigarettes would get into each operator's face to demand in English, "Mr. Foucault, ask the sonbitch again. Not nice like before."

Foucault shouted the questions in Arabic. This time he got a response.

"I don't know anything," the prisoner said. "Dear Allah, I know nothing."

Two quick shots from al Nidal's revolver, shots that echoed through the bunker, shots that pierced Tyler's ears. Shots that pierced the head of the corpse, tearing off chunks of scalp, throwing the cadaver backward off the bench. Letting loose a quart of blood stored in a rubber bladder inside the man's blindfold.

Foucault choked on a curse word, then called out in English, "Tyler. Captain Tyler, where the hell are you?"

Tyler stayed put inside the bunker, waiting for the words. Waiting for the surrender. Waiting for *I quit*.

Al Nidal shouted at the second prisoner in Arabic. "Where is bin Laden?"

"Kabul," the man screamed. "He's in Kabul."

"The address."

The man shouted an address.

"Where is that?"

"It's at the edge of the central market, south of the market. I swear by Allah." He repeated the street address.

Al Nidal growled in English, "You sonbitch," then continued in Arabic. "I'm going to use my radio. I'm going to send somebody to check. If he's not there, you die. If he's out for coffee, you die."

"He's there, I swear it."

Al Nidal, in a softer voice but determined, "Foucault?"

"Yes."

"I will call this in. Good work, my friend."

"But I didn't do anything."

"Indeed. But you will."

"I beg your pardon?"

In English. "Killing him."

"What? Why?"

"Killing him. Because he kill your people in Pentagon and New Yorks, in the D.C., in Pennsvania. Killing him dead."

"How can I—?"

In Arabic. "With your pistol, the bastard. Kill him. Kill him now. Two shots to the head like this other Al Qaeda bastard. Kill him." In the pause that followed, Tyler knew what was happening as well as if he could see it. Al Nidal raising the barrel of the 44, the size of a cannon when Foucault looked into the bore. "Or I am no-shit killing you," he said in English.

Tyler edged close to the door of the bunker. He needed to see what came next. Al Nidal was good. He played his role to the hilt. Tyler himself believed his real name was al Nidal, his position was a general in the National Alliance, that he was a killer. That he would kill an American soldier if Tyler let him.

He peeked around the doorway of the bunker and glimpsed Foucault. Standing in the sun, sweating through his clothing, holding his pistol in front of him, pointed toward the ground one hand on the slide. Looking into the eye of the Colt 44.

The final test. The bar exam. Foucault did not have many choices. But he did have them. He could raise the gun and kill the man on the bench. Now that al Nidal had ordered him to kill, now that he had a loaded pistol in his hand, this was not a play exercise, a game of pretend. This was the real thing. He had seen dead bodies, real blood, murdered children.

He could kill the man on the bench. He could try to kill al Nidal. He could throw down his pistol and walk away, looking for Tyler, maybe to throw a punch. If he did throw a punch, Tyler wouldn't even press charges. But. If Foucault wanted to go to Afghanistan on the Preemptive Terrorist Team, if he wanted to stay in the game and kill terrorists, he had to raise the pistol and kill the man sitting on the bench in front of him.

Foucault raised the pistol and looked down his right arm, pointing arm, hand, finger, and pistol into the face of the terrified prisoner. Not knowing the man was an army officer waiting to get into special operations training himself, having passed all the tests and ready to go. Except that he sprained his knee two weeks ago. He was available when Tyler called for training support. He was willing. He was playing his role to the hilt, and Foucault now saw him, not as a man—certainly not as an army officer—but as a captive Al Qaeda terrorist.

"Don't kill me," he pleaded in Arabic. He did not close his eyes. He stared right into Foucault's face. "Please don't kill me. In the name of—"

Foucault's hand trembled, but he pulled the trigger. Asked and answered, the hammer fell on a dummy round. Foucault, trembling, went into automatic mode to clear the pistol. He jacked the slide on the 9 mm and tried to fire another round. And another. All of them dummy rounds. Again and again until thirteen brass nine-mill bullets, copper-jacketed heads gleaming in the sun, lay at Foucault's feet. As he continued to work the slide, point it, pull the trigger, even after the clip was empty, and the slide stayed to the rear.

Tyler came out of the bunker. He stepped up to Foucault and put an arm around him. "That's enough, sergeant. That's enough."

Foucault turned his head to stare into Tyler's eyes. "I have to kill him."

"No you don't."

"Or else the general will kill me."

Tyler bit his lip. "No he won't. He's one of us. An American. Sergeant, this is a test. It's only a test. You passed it. If you want to, you can go into Afghanistan on the first wave. If you don't, you can still go home to your unit. Nobody will say a thing. You took the best we had. You passed. Now it's your call."

Foucault blinked. He looked around him. "I passed?"

Tyler took away the pistol and beckoned to one of his Northern Alliance pretend soldiers who came forward to lead Foucault away.

"It's over?" he called back. "No more of this shit?"

Beyond the dunes, a tent was set up, the walls rolled up to let a breeze through. There were iced drinks there, including alcoholic drinks, and comfortable chairs. Foucault would be left alone, to sit quietly and think.

Just think. Reflect. Eventually all of them would decide for themselves. If this was just training, what would the real mission be like? Would they want to do it? Would it be worse? Could it be? It was their choice. Whatever they chose, Tyler doubted that he would overeat. Or get drunk. Not until he got away from the sadistic bastard running this test, far, far away and into the privacy of his own home.

The deuce-and-a-half came back around and dropped off the next man to be tested. Barret. Sergeant First-Class Travis Barret was an expert in demolitions. He also spoke Arabic. And he had a mean streak. Yet he could control himself in ways that Powczuk never did. He never had signed onto Powczuk's private war against the officer corps, never felt the need to use a superior skill to put down another man. He saw any excellence in skill as a contribution to the team rather than proof of his personal superiority.

Barret went through the same drill as Foucault. When al Nidal ordered him to shoot the prisoner, Barret said in Arabic, "Let me get this straight. General al Nidal, you're giving me an order to shoot this terrorist, is that right?"

"Kill him."

Barret lifted the pistol into the man's face. Before the man could even beg for his life, Barret pulled the trigger. He ejected the dummy and tried again. Then he turned to al Nidal reversed the pistol, and handed it, grip-first, to the Arab chief. "Is this the test?"

Tyler stepped out of the bunker. "Yes."

"Well then, Captain," Barret called out, "is it over?"

Tyler answered from the bunker. "Yes."

"Am I on the team?"

"If you want it, you can have it."

"I want it."

"You don't want to think about it?"

"I already have, ever since 9-11. Count me in."

"Welcome aboard." Tyler held out a hand. He couldn't help feeling the slightest bit of disappointment that Barret had seen through the order to kill. After watching Foucault unravel, Tyler had thought it too hard a test. Now he wondered whether it was too easy.

Until Barret said, "Helluva mind screw, Captain. You had me going there, right up until the second misfire. I thought I was really going to have to kill somebody to get onto this team." He gave his Barret smile, the mask of a predator in the attack. "I would have, too." He gazed into Tyler's eyes. "If the general here had ordered me to, I would have killed you." He shrugged. "Nothing personal." Wide smile. "Just business."

Tyler's own smile froze on his face. Barret was exactly the kind of man he was looking for. Then why did it give him such a chill down his spine?

Dolan and Ballard were next. After al Nidal gave his order, Dolan said, "Look here, General. It's against the law to kill a POW. We have a right—a duty—to disobey such orders."

Al Nidal spat in the sand. "I spit on your law. That nice guy *boolsheet* was for last war. You ever hear 9-11? This is new war. New law now." He got into Dolan's face, nose-to-nose. "You want law? I am law. You are an Afghan now. Under my law. I say killing him." He shrugged. "Or maybe law says I killing you."

Dolan, faced with murder or suicide, chose murder. He clicked on only two dummy rounds before he caught on. Then he sighed in relief, threw down the pistol, and walked away.

Tyler called to his back. "Are you in or out?"

"No more tests?"

"No more tests."

Dolan squeegeed the beads of sweat off his face with one hand. He stared at the ground awhile. Then looked at Tyler as if he wished he still had a 9 mm in his hand, no blanks, no dummies. "I'll do it. As long as I don't have to take any more of your goddamned tests. I'll do it."

Ballard was so wired, he broke into tears at the idea of either his own death and that of a helpless man. In the end, his hand trembling, he pulled the trigger. At the vacant sound of the hammer hitting the firing pin, he convulsed, as if the gun had recoiled. He tried to eject the first round, but the second round jammed in the chamber. When he could not clear it, Ballard swung the pistol. He hit the helpless man on the head. The blow broke a second bladder of blood, sending a stream of red down the Ranger's face.

"Hey, you stupid bastard, you're suppose to shoot me, not beat me to death."

Ballard cursed him back and swung again.

Tyler ran from the bunker as al Nidal grabbed Ballard. "Calm down, man," he said in English. "It's just a test. It's only a test. It's over."

For a second, Tyler relaxed. Then he saw it. In the eyes of Ballard. A wild and rabid look. The man wasn't here. He was in the Afghan desert. On a mission. With an order to obey.

Tyler cried out, "Stop him!"

Al Nidal did a take. He gawked at Tyler. *From what?*

Tyler tried to leap but he was too far away, and the sand gave way beneath his boots. He went to one knee.

Al Nidal whirled to get away from his captain gone mad.

Ballard grabbed at al Nidal's Colt 44.

"Stop him!" The man on the bench, his hands tied and helpless, saw it coming, too.

Ballard wrenched the gun free of the war lord's hand, in one motion, kicking the bigger man's feet from under him.

Tyler froze, as the pistol came his way.

Al Nidal, scrambling like a crab, backed off on all fours. "Hey, man, I'm a finance corps officer, not a general. You don't have to kill anybody."

Tyler eased to his feet and called out, "Master Sergeant Ballard. Cease-fire."

Ballard pointed the gun at him. Tyler flinched.

"The test is over, Ballard. Don't shoot."

"This shit is too much," al Nidal said. He'd lost his accent. Now on his feet, he backed away, holding his palms toward the gun. "Man, I didn't sign on to take a bullet."

"Come on, Ballard, put the gun down."

Ballard continued to point the huge pistol. In turn, at Tyler, al Nidal, the prisoner, and the guards. The pretend players from the National Alliance of Afghanistan cringed in horror.

As one American soldier put a pistol to the head of another and executed the army Ranger sitting on the bench.

"Jesus, mister, I'm not an Al Qaeda, I'm a goddamned Ranger—"

A double-tap. Two rounds broke open the skull like a watermelon. Every man but the victim cried out in agony, as a fine, red mist blew up and floated away, settling over the sandscape. The blood pulsing into the desert was not cow's blood.

Baker decided the CIA men had drilled him long enough. "No more," He said. "Help me up. I have to stretch my legs, get my balance. You sure I have to ride a damned horse? You don't have a truck to take me to this guy, this warlord, what's-his-name? Mansour?"

"Ahmed Abdullah Mansour." Carnes looked doubtful as Baker struggled to his feet and staggered around in the sand, bent in half and dragging one foot. "He isn't going to make a horse ride, Rob. Look at him. Two days ago he was on his deathbed."

Baker stood up straight and gave a wincing grin as he took a few almost-normal steps. "Relax, I'm busting your balls."

"Very funny," Carnes said.

"I got a question," Roberts said.

Baker tried to work the stiffness out of his limp. "Shoot."

"Powczuk? Ever meet an operator name of Stanley Pow-czuk?"

Baker shook his head and winced at the pain of doing it. "Why?"

"He's new in country but he's been here before on Delta missions. During the Soviet incursion. He's already the right-hand man of the tribal leader Mansour, the guy we're going to deliver you to."

"And?"

"Powczuk's a loose cannon, a freelancer, a cowboy."

Carnes groaned. "A cowboy? But he is on our side, right?"

"Very funny," Roberts said. "Of course he's one of ours. Just a little wack sometimes. I don't think it will be a problem. As long as Ramsey doesn't know him."

"Come on, Rob."

"Seriously, it's not a problem." He shook his head and looked to Baker. "But if he did know you, he'd find a way to screw up this little operation to suit his own ego. Try to talk to

you. Give you away. Bring Mansour into it? Hell, I don't
know. Like I said, he's a cowboy—"

Carnes bolted erect and grabbed the front of Roberts's
shirt.

"What?"

Carnes let go and threw up his arms as he paced a tight circle. "Why didn't you tell me, Rob? I could have moved him."
He stopped pacing and waved toward Baker. "I could have
placed him with another chief."

Roberts shook his head. "No, Mansour is the best place for
our guy to be. He's a swinger"—Roberts looked to Baker—.
"He plays on both sides of the war. He started out the side of
the Soviets a dozen years ago. Then went with the resistance.
Supported the interim government. Then was part of the Taliban lynch mob that stole the country. Now he's playing both
sides again. So he can end up on the winning side, if you know
what I mean?"

Carnes said, "Two flakes in one camp? I'm starting to get
cold feet for our guy."

"Mansour won't hurt him. Hell, he's like an Afghan Uncle
Remus or something, all full of shit and folksy wisdom. He
avoids fighting when he can, steps up when the fighting's
done. To be in the winner's camp. The guy'll be fine."

"You bastards stop talking about me as if I'm not around,"
Baker said. "If you're nervous about this, I'm shaking in my
boots."

"It'll be all right," Roberts said to Carnes. "What'd you expect, the president of the chamber of commerce?" To Baker:
"If things get too dicey, I'll clue in Powczuk, so he can keep
an eye on you. I'd rather blow the mission than lose you."

Baker winced. "Look at me. Do I look like I have a huge
margin for error left in my body?"

The CIA men laughed uneasily.

"This Powczuk," Baker said, narrowing his eyes. "You said
ego. I've run across a few men that are adrenaline junkies,
guys that get their thrills from combat. But ego? That's for
generals, the George C. Scotts and Douglas MacArthurs of
the world."

"He's a New Age Rambo," Roberts said. "Very anti-officer. Now he's out on his own. He's supposed to be the liaison between the United States Army and Mansour's tribal army, but we don't expect to get many reports back from him. He's too busy looking for an in to bin Laden, know what I mean? Wants to collect the big scalp, get a little fame within the Delta community, maybe pick up a medal of the top secret variety, right from the prez. Get it now?"

"Ten-by."

"I can't believe I'm saying this," Carnes said. "But you can opt out if you want. It's a cracked idea, I admit it."

Roberts gave Carnes a long stare. "You ain't the Brian Carnes I know. Okay, what'd you do with the real Brian, you damned imposter?"

Carnes shrugged Baker's way. *I mean it. You don't have to do this.*

"After all this stage makeup?" Baker lifted his hair, showing off the duct tape butterfly stitches in his head. He waved his cardboard cast. "No way. I'm going in." He hoped his words sounded braver than they tasted.

Once Tyler tackled Ballard and took away the revolver, Ballard stopped struggling, Tyler threw him to the ground. He put a knee to the madman's throat.

Ballard went into a spasm, and his eyes went wide. Then, as if he had come up from a nightmare, he looked left and right. He gasped for breath, hissing a prayer. He looked toward the dead body. He confirmed that what he had just seen was real. He went limp, knowing that he caused it. His eyes went shut and stayed shut.

Al Nidal called for two of his Northern Alliance players. They took their nylon flex-cuffs, for the pretend POWs, and linked them over Ballard's wrists. They led him away. A staff sergeant called for a pair of medics. They churned up the sand as they ran onto the scene and knelt beside the new, still-warm corpse.

Tyler shook his head. "Forget it." A Colt 44 double-tap to

the head? No way a man could survive it. No way would he want to.

The senior medic, a sergeant, stood up. "What should we do, sir? Bring up a litter? Prep him for air evac?"

Tyler heard the approach of the deuce-and-a-half truck. Two more men to test. Nobody had made a move to reset the stage for a new test interrogation. Two Northern Alliance men stood with a corpse between them at the door of the bunker. Time had stopped on this spot in the desert. As every man waited on Tyler.

He looked around, felt the stare of the men and of the sun, burning into him like a spot focused through a magnifying less.

"Leave him lay," he said to the senior medic.

"Say again, sir?"

"You're dismissed, sergeant." He turned to the two men propping up the new, cold corpse. "Bring him over and set him up. Then go get another one."

"You're going to keep on going?" The finance corps officer-Afghan general al Nidal asked.

"I have two more men to test and I don't suppose you or any of your soldiers are going to volunteer to take this guy's place." He held out his hand toward the dead man, the army Ranger who had given his life for his country in a way that his family could never know. "It's a training accident. Can't be helped now. We're going to finish up."

Finish up they did, in short order. The scene lacked punch because although al Nidal still growled at two cadavers propped up on the bench, he'd lost his vigor. Every face was pale beneath its tan. Tyler's Afghans just went through the motions.

It didn't matter to First Lieutenant Soiree Ward. After al Nidal shot his corpse and before he could even order Ward to shoot the other corpse, Ward threw down his own pistol. "You sick bastard."

Tyler walked out of the bunker, and Ward gave it to him, too. "All due respect, you, too, sir, I ain't signing on for this kind of shit. Get me out of here. I want to get back to my unit so I can go in with men and not you crazy mother—" He saw Tyler lift his chin and cut off the obscenity.

Tyler didn't care to make an issue of the disrespect. He signaled for a guide. "Stand by. I'll have a Blackhawk for you before the sun goes down."

Next came Poole. He went through the motions by the numbers. This was just a drill, now that there was no live prisoner to deal with. He tried to shoot the corpse, disgusted, but without pause. He laid the pistol on the bench and turned to Tyler at the bunker door, with a look of *Is this all you got?*

Tyler took a deep breath. It was, truly, all he had left for one day. "Your choice," he said. "Are you in or out?"

"This the kind of shit-mission we be pulling in Afghanistan?" Poole said.

Tyler shook his head. "I can't say. Not until you decide. In or out?"

"Got-damn, I don't want any part of this."

Tyler could not suppress a tiny look of relief. Maybe now Spangler would—

"But I'm signing on anyhow. Better that I take it on than leave it to y'all. The army shouldn't be having a psycho in charge of a combat unit." Poole looked him in the face, waiting for the captain to dress down the lieutenant, daring him to do it.

Tyler felt a twinge of shame. Poole had read him through and through. He knew Tyler wanted the PTT, so he was snatching it away. Was he that transparent?

"Join the others," he said. He waved for a guide. "I have some reports to make."

Poole looked to the dead man lying behind the bench, the last of his blood barely seeping from the massive wounds. It might have been another illusion. Or it might have been real. Didn't matter to the guy on the ground. Or to Poole. He shook his head and walked away, following his guide to the tent.

Tyler called for a pair of helicopters. One for the Delta operators, the other for himself and the dead Ranger. Except for the corpse and the crew, he rode alone, the doors open on the

way back to the airfield, his briefcase full of cards that held all
the images and reports he would need to form the first team.
At the outset, he and Spangler thought they might get twenty-
four men, enough for two teams of twelve from the first set of
candidates, slightly better than a 50-percent success rate. Now
he wasn't so sure.

Ask Delta operators to do the impossible in the sense of
physical hardship, and they would leap to it. Even if it meant
risking their lives. Ask them to get into a shooting fight, at
close range or far; they would take it on. But put a loaded
gun into his hand and ask a Delta Force soldier to execute a
man tied to a bench, and everything changed. Even their
years of training could not undo a lifetime of the idealism in-
grained into Americans. What was it? The war-as-glory image from the movies? Hell, John Wayne never killed a POW,
did he?

Religious upbringing? Lack of poverty and desperation?
The rules of war? Ethical training in the military? Who knew?
Whatever it was, it took a hell of a drill to undo it.

He felt another prickle of shame. He didn't care how. He
only cared that he had done it. At the cost of only one life.
He'd found the kind of man he wanted to go up against Al
Qaeda. He'd served his country.

The bigger question was: How could he get Spangler to
give him a spot on the team? Tyler spoke Arabic, two dialects,
but on Poole's group alone he had plenty of Arabic speakers.
Hell, in any case this wasn't a UN mission anyhow. The team
had a good mix of combat skills. A healthy cross section of
rank. Every man had proven himself able to fit into a team.
Every man had shown his ability to kill on his own, when ordered. Each of them had shown the willingness to direct a
2,000-pound bomb onto a terrorist camp, even if there might
be innocent women and children in it. Each of them, some of
them reluctantly, had tried to execute a POW.

One of them had even succeeded. He'd served his country,
too. Even as the man vibrating on the deck of the Blackhawk
had paid the ultimate price. Thanks to Ballard.

Ballard. Poor bastard. Before he left, Tyler put his own

needs aside and told the master sergeant of his decision to cut him from the team.

"Why?" Ballard wanted to know.

"You killed a man."

"You told me to—the general did. That was the test. I was supposed to kill him, wasn't I?"

Tyler bulled past his own astonishment that Ballard could be so cold about it. "But you snapped."

"I did what you wanted me to do. Captain, wake up. What did you expect? That it wouldn't bother me to kill a man? It wasn't easy. But I did it. You have to put me on the team now."

Tyler was stunned. Not because of the truth in what Ballard said. But because the man had come to his senses so quickly. He held up his nylon flex-cuffs to Tyler.

"So I can get a drink, Captain. And so the others stop staring like I was a criminal or something."

Tyler directed the medics to examine him, and they declared there was no reason to keep him cuffed. Ballard had a couple of drinks—water only—and started up a conversation with the other Delta Force soldiers. Spattered by the backblast of his murder, he stood drinking water and eating cold chicken wings. Any old Fourth of July picnic.

Tyler suspected the man was nuts. But he agreed to let him stay on the team if he passed a mental eval. Which he probably would. Besides, Tyler needed a body, somebody in fact, with Ballard's state of mind. Ironic. When they said that 9-11 had changed everything, they didn't know the half of it.

Now, aboard the Blackhawk, Tyler noticed the Ranger's hands, still bound with nylon ties. He felt sick about that. He took out his Case knife and cut him free. The least he could do, the only decent thing. Christ. He didn't even remember the man's name.

He closed his eyes and kept them closed until he felt his gut lift as the Blackhawk began its descent. Then he saw that the open hand of the Ranger had vibrated across the floor to cup its fingers across Tyler's boot. A gesture of comfort from a dead man. *It's all right, buddy, I forgive you. What was your name again?*

Tyler felt his gut lurch. He could not move his foot away from the dead man's grip. All he could do was look to his clipboard. He flipped pages until he found what he wanted.

Owens. The man's name was Paul Owens.

Saturday, September 15, 2001—Near Khost, Afghanistan

"Don't forget about your amnesia," Roberts said, his voice low.

"You're a regular comedian," Baker said.

They had traveled for hours, bouncing aboard their small Asian horses. Every jogging step of the animals sent sparklers of pain shooting through Baker's body. Even if he didn't have his injuries, this would have been a terrible ride. All night, the animals, not so sure-footed as Roberts had sworn, slouched their way across the desert. How did the Mongols ever conquer Europe on these plodders?

"Are we getting close?" Baker asked.

"Very. Once this wadi joins up with another dry streambed, we'll turn for the mountains. Then the ride gets rough for another couple of hours. We'll be there by daylight."

"The ride gets rough? For a couple hours? That's close? You CIA types ought to start selling used cars."

"Quit your whimpering."

"Whimpering is all I have." Baker said.

"At least do your whimpering in Arabic. We can't let anybody hear us speaking English."

"Fine," Baker said in the Pashto dialect. "Satisfied?"

"Perfectly. Want to go over your story one more time?" the CIA man asked.

"No. It's already beginning to sound rehearsed. I just want to sit here and bitch."

"You think it's bad now, wait until I have to tighten the ties that bind you to the saddle."

When they turned their little horses toward the mountains, Roberts called a halt and pulled the slack out of Baker's bonds. True to Roberts's word, the going got tougher. Baker allowed himself the luxury of burrowing into his own head. He let his mind wander. Better that he act the captive. Better he remain oblivious. Time enough to meet his new enemy, the Northern Alliance. Oh, and the Delta cowboy name of Powczuk.

"Did I tell you that once we get to the camp—"

"You told me," Baker said. "You're going to turn me over to the tribal chief and turn your back on me. You have to act as if you don't care. I'm on my own. That's what you told me, maybe five times. This is six."

"No need to get testy about it."

"Why the hell not? I'm supposed to like you?"

"Fine with me, you Al Qaeda bastard."

"That's more like it, you American son of a whore."

The laugh they shared was their last exchange. An hour later, just as the first light of day began to streak the sky, Baker's mind was in the seat of his filthy pantaloons, stained with blood and grease, part of the authentic wardrobe they'd issued him along with the cardboard splint. He had already shifted every possible way in the saddle of the little horse. There was no spot on his ass that did not hurt. To top it off, a wedge had worked its way into the cleavage of his butt, trying to invade his body. His aching knees would not bend around the fat pony's middle. So he let his mind settle into his broken arm, which also throbbed. A different kind of pain, but a relief in a way, a distraction that—

He saw his horse's ears prick forward. The animal tensed, rumbling in its chest, loosing an eager, tiny nicker. The sound turned into a horse scream as the boulders on the uphill side of them came alive. Men stood up, shooting their rifles on automatic. An ambush? No, he saw the bursts rake the sky. Arab fireworks.

Baker's horse didn't know the difference between an ambush and a greeting. The wiry animal bucked and thrashed like a trout, throwing him over the saddle, across the horse's neck.

He hung there, still tied to the saddle horn, and the shaggy yellow pony kept bucking, pulling away to the left, trying to get free of the man, the man trying to get free of it, the man screaming in pain louder than the horse screaming in fright. No play-acting here.

In minutes, four of the men closed in on his horse, holding it steady by the reins. Although Baker's feet touched the ground, his legs were too weak to stand, his knees too numb. A black, fuzzy border formed a tunnel of his vision.

The men around him spoke dark threats, their body odor laced by the smell of their spiced diet.

As hard as he wished for it, Baker did not pass out from the pain.

His arm, if it had healed in the slightest, was re-broken inside the splint. He could feel it, the bone ends grating against each other, piercing the muscle inside the arm, the damage not likely to be undone out here. And he could see it, too. The wrinkle in the cardboard bent to a ten-degree angle, as if it were his elbow in there, instead of his forearm. Waves of nausea swept through him. Already undone. And he still hadn't even met—

A booming, gruff voice from perhaps twenty meters away shouted in Pashto, "Is this a prisoner you bring me?"

"Mansour," Roberts hollered. "Yes, an Al Qaeda fighter. My people found him wandering in the desert like a lost Jew."

Laughter all around.

Baker saw that Roberts looked sick and would not meet his gaze.

Somebody drove the butt of a rifle into Baker's lower back, cracking it against the spine, shooting a numbness down his left leg. He felt closer to fainting and prayed to both his Christian God in his head and to Allah aloud, cursing Roberts for comparing him to a Jew. In this company, of all things.

"Infidel. Don't you dare pray to our God," another voice said. Another rifle butt to the kidneys.

This time Baker blacked out, giving thanks in his head to all the gods of all the faiths.

Spangler had promised to keep his hand out of Tyler's test. But. The killing of an army officer, a bullet to the head as he sat with his hands tied behind his back in the Nevada desert in a training exercise? No way to see past that. He called Tyler to Washington.

"Bring all the records, all the video, all the results," he ordered Tyler over the secure phone to Tonopah. "I'm sending over a plane from Travis. And for God's sake, put it all under a classified cover. Top secret."

They met at 0337 of a Saturday morning, in Spangler's office, the cave in the basement. The destruction by the terrorist plane had caused a wholesale shuffling of offices. Temporary digs were set up on the Pentagon grounds, trailers and prefab offices. For security reasons, an operation with the secrecy of Spangler's had to be kept deep inside the walls.

Spangler didn't mind. In fact he wore the office, cramped and cluttered, like a badge. A general with humility. Unlike Bowers, who always went for the perks. Bowers, so fond of telling him, *Roscoe, you have so much to be humble about.*

Spangler had to smile about that. Bowers on his deathbed. Bowers scarred by fire, his stars so hot they'd melted into his flesh. The surgeons had to dig two inches into—

Tyler cleared his throat.

"I read your report," Spangler shook his head as if coming up from a deep thought. "Lotta typos."

Tyler cocked his head. *Typos? A dead Ranger, and you want to talk typos?*

"Forget it, I'm pulling your chain," Spangler said. "You look like hell. Didn't you get any sleep?"

"On the plane, sir. Maybe an hour or two." Tyler drywashed his face in his hands. He needed to shave. But first he needed to know, "What's the verdict?"

Spangler shrugged. "Training accident, what else?"

Tyler slumped into a chair. He looked relieved. And hopeful.

"Forget the accident," Spangler said. "I'm more concerned about putting in a viable combat team. We thought we might get twenty-four men, we end up with seventeen from all four cycles?"

Tyler's cadre had to drop four men for drinking beer alone. Another half dozen fell out because of snake and scorpion bites, sprains, and injuries, including one man with a broken back and ribs. If they wanted, most of the men could retest later. The thirteen who failed the final test would not.

Tyler shrugged. "We wanted cold-blooded killers. We got them. Three officers, fourteen men."

"How do we organize them? The marines do it with Force Recon teams, only four men. Too light, don't you think?"

"I have an idea."

Spangler shook his head. "You're not going."

"But, sir."

"No buts. First you bury a hatchet in the head of one of our own aboard a jetliner. Then you let another one get half of his head taken off by a 44, for chrissakes. What were you thinking? Letting that guy use a 44 in a training exercise?"

"Forget the 44, all right? Two shots to the head with a 22 would have killed the sonofabitch."

"Coleman."

Tyler shook his head. "Coleman?"

"Coleman. Captain Theodore Coleman. The name of the somebitch you're referring to."

"I'm sorry." Tyler hung his head. *Shit.* Aboard the Blackhawk, he'd looked up the wrong name. *Then who the hell was Owen?* He saw the glint in the red eyes behind Spangler's glasses. "I only meant—"

"I know what you meant. Look, Connor, this is going to be a visible mission. Not in the sense that it's going to be open to the press. In the sense that all eyes with a top secret and need-to-know are going to be watching. I'm going to brief on this thing every day, twice a day. You get that, don't you?"

"Look, General, you said it yourself. A training accident. Your words."

Spangler wagged his head during the whole speech. "An accident, I can handle. Even two of them. What I can't handle is a disaster inside Afghanistan with this operation. Anything goes wrong, I'll be in shit up to my neck anyhow. But if it has your name on it besides? After two screw-ups like that? Somebody'll push my head under, and I'll die in the shit."

"So that's it? Your career? Your second star?" Tyler had both of his hands pressed down on the desk as if he were going to leap across at Spangler. "You're no better than Bowers."

Spangler laughed. The words stung him, but he laughed. He had had better men than an accident-prone army captain give him this kind of crap. "That was a cheap shot. A captain to a major, it's an out-of-order cheap shot. A captain to a brigadier general, it's a court-martial-offense cheap shot." Amazing how much of Bowers's voice he heard in his own words.

"I'm sorry. General." Tyler didn't hide the sarcasm in his voice.

And Spangler didn't either. "Forgiven. Asshole." He threw up his hands. "Look, I haven't been a general long enough to find offense in the words of every other man I meet. But I been inside this building long enough to know what is politic. Shit, I've kept my ear so close to the ground it's a goddamned ant farm. Connor, you're not going to Afghanistan with the first wave. And if the first wave falls on its ass, you're not going in with the second either. Do I have to say it's an order?"

"No, sir." Tyler's eyes widened a little. "Did I just hear right?"

Spangler began nodding. "Yes, you did. I'm sending you back to Nevada. Train a second wave. I'm going to need somebody to lead that group, because it's a second-tier outfit, by definition. By then, we will have proved our work with this kind of operation inside Afghanistan. Or not. By then I can risk sending you into the grist mill." He shook his head. "Unless the first team screws up. You better pray you did your job well out there at Tonopah."

Tyler took a deep breath. "I don't know how to thank you, sir."

"Yes you do. Get back to Nevada and give me a second wave. Screen the names, get the bugs out of the tests. Improvise. Get it done, get it done, get it done. *Hoo-ah,* and all that shit."

Tyler stood up and saluted.

Spangler made a motion of pushing the captain back into his seat. "We're not through yet." Tyler sank into the chair. "The next week is crucial for Poole. I assume he's the one."

Tyler held back. He hadn't wanted to endorse Poole. Thinking that maybe if the man didn't get the job—

"You're not going on the first wave," Spangler said. "And that's my final word on the matter. Now give me the truth. I saw the tapes. I read the reports. Poole worked wonders. He stepped up and took charge. Nobody had to push him into it. The men respect him. He never went over the edge. Do I have all that right?"

Tyler flinched.

Spangler cut off any reproach. "Any hitch in his performance was a minor one. Am I right?"

Tyler bit his lip. "Affirm."

"That's it, then. The first thing we do, you and I, is organize the team. I have an idea or two. You help me do this. I'll relay the info to Poole. He can use the training facilities to work his men, get them into shape, give them a couple days off to get laid, then deploy."

Tyler got over his defeat and became the pro. He sat up straight in his chair and scribbled notes on the legal pad before him. "I'm thinking two teams of eight, with Poole in overall command of both. That gives them some flexibility. We could set up the commo—What's wrong?"

"We'll get to Poole in a sec." He cleared his throat. "One more thing you have to do." The frog in his throat grew into a cough. "Let's get it out of the way right now."

Tyler, on guard, leaned back in his chair, ready to fight or flee. *What?*

"Amy."

"Amy what?"

"Forgetting Coleman I can halfway see. But Amy? You do remember Amy Tyler, right? Your wife?"

"What about her?"

"She called me."

Tyler sprang to his feet. "She called you?"

"She told me the whole story."

"The whole story?"

"Everything. The girl? Laura?"

"Laren."

"Laura, Laren. Your mistress. A reporter? You were messing with a newspaper reporter? The talk about divorce. The works."

"Son of a—"

"Don't get going on that. That stuff isn't what's on my mind. What's done is done. What matters is what you're going to do."

"What?" Tyler sank into his chair. "What I'm going to do?"

"While Poole is training his team for the next week or so, I want you to go home. Take a rest. Get yourself together." Spangler doodled on his legal pad. "Get your marriage together."

"With all due respect, sir, what does my marriage have to do with anything?"

"It's part of your problem. Either fix your marriage or get out of it. I can't have you trying to pull off this mission with that kind of distraction going on like background noise."

"It's my personal life, Roscoe."

"General Roscoe, in fact. If your personal life gets in the way of your professional life it becomes part of my professional life. And I don't want my life screwed up by your marital problems. Fix it. Now that, if you'll forgive the Hollywood, is an order. Do it and give me a full report."

"Sir—"

"That's my agenda," Spangler said. "Speaking of which, I didn't give you one, did I?" He opened up a classified document folder and slid a sheet of paper with six items listed.

1. Training accident
2. T's personal affairs in order
3. N. Rnr
4. Organize PTT
5. Assign PTT missions
6. Set final briefing and deployment

He crossed out two items. "That takes care of 1 and 2."

Tyler put a fingertip to his copy of the agenda and ran it down the list, pausing at 2, thinking better about arguing over that again, and stopping at 3. "Night Runner? What about him?"

"What to do with him?"

"He's a marine." Tyler shrugged. "Send him back to the marines."

"Poole asked to have him detailed to the army for the mission."

Tyler tried a bluff. "He went behind my back?"

"Actually, he went right to your face and asked you to ask me. You didn't pass the request along."

Tyler had nothing to say. He sat in his chair, turning a bright shade of pink beneath his harsh desert tan.

"I got the okay from the Marine Corps. I'm going to detail him to Poole. Send him to Afghanistan on the first wave. As a guide and a fighter. He's the ultimate warrior. I watched him on the video. On satellite and the stuff you shot. He's amazing." Spangler shook his head. "It'd be a waste of his talent to keep him in Nevada."

Tyler blanched. Spangler never even winced, the insult unmistakable.

Night Runner surprised himself by accepting an open-ended tour of duty with the army in the combat zone. He missed his own captain, his own Force Recon team. He liked working in a small group. But something in this larger group fascinated him. Not just that these were able men, and willing fighters. Maybe he just needed a change of pace.

He didn't know everybody on the PTT in person—some of them had trained in the other three test groups. But he knew what they had been through in the last four days. They had tested on the same issues. Except for the assassination drill, he had lived in the head of every man who had to go through Tyler's hell.

He liked Poole. He was a good officer. Instead of meeting inside the auditorium at Tonopah, he gathered his men around a fire outside a little after midnight. These men belonged outdoors. The darkness pushed them closer together, and the fire drew them to each other and its warmth. Poole stood on one side of the blaze and talked to his men across the flames in that even tone of his. He struck the same level note he used to keep the men calm under the stress of the past few days. Night Runner noticed Poole sometimes forgot to talk the street talk, dropping into the more formal address of a high-dollar education. He asked Poole straight out. "I went to school at West Point," Poole said, almost abashed to admit it. "Not a quota thing. I earned my way in on merit and grades." He shrugged. "My father teaches Lit at Brown. I had a classical upbringing." He shook his head. "I had to work my ass off to learn to speak street. As you can see, I still haven't mastered it." He lifted an eyebrow. "Y'all be hanging in there wit me, an we be fine. Word? Just don't be axing me the wrong questions." He pronounced it *quershuns*.

Night Runner smiled.

Poole shrugged. "When I get nervous, I talk the street shit. In a hot situation, it goes over better with the men than the Ivy League shit."

Later, Poole struck a middle tone for his fireside chat. "You can still opt out," he said. "If y'all don't like the team. Or if you're not down with your leadership." The men gave him their vote of confidence with a group snicker at the last suggestion.

He gave them a quick outline of several new twists that Spangler had thrown at him in a brief phone call from the Pentagon. The new weapons and gadgets they'd be using for the first time in combat. The one that raised the most stink was the PGPS implants. Each PTT man would get a tiny computer chip, complete with transmitter, surgically placed under his skin.

"They gonna keep track of me like a fricking shark on the Discovery Channel?" Barret wanted to know.

"Just like a shark. Only the chip is smaller."

The device was passive, responding only when queried by a signal from a satellite or AWACS.

"Take about ten seconds to implant," Poole said, parroting Spangler's pitch.

"Install where?"

"Under the skin. Scalp. Shoulder. Hand. Your call." Poole let a grin creep across his lips. "Foreskin of Mr. Peeper, if you want."

Barret got a charge out of that. "So the Pentagon can know every time I unzip my zucchini? No thanks."

"I shouldn't worry about that, Barret," Foucault said, with no hint of a grin on his long, sad face. "Them spy cameras are good, but they can't see a thingie as small as your midget-digit."

Even Barret broke up. Poole waited for the laughter to subside. "Look here. Y'all passed the test, but you don't have to take the trip with this group. And you don't have to decide today. You can sleep on it. Get with me in the morning. You can talk with each other, but you cannot call home or discuss it with anybody outside the team. Not your wife, of course. Not a mentor you may have, not a senior officer. Don't call back to your units and find out where or when they might be deployed just so you can draw to the best hand. Decide on your own, from what you know. Then, after you decide, live with it."

A hand went up across the fire. Poole gave a nod to First Lieutenant Moss Knapp, a slow-talker and a Texan. "Lot of us figure what's going on by what was on the test. About time somebody come out and told us what this mission is for sure. Help us decide."

Poole pooched his mouth. "Straight up?"

"Straight up."

"We're going in to kill got-damnt ban, ban, Ta-Taliban and Al Qaeda leaders. Were going to throw down on the highest levels we can find, all the way up to bin Laden his own damnt self."

"So. We gonna be assassins."

It wasn't a question, and Poole didn't address the remark, except by a twitch of one eyebrow.

Another voice spoke up. "Staff Sergeant Wendell Yosarian, sir. Isn't there a law against that kind of thing?"

"An executive order. I'm told it's due for a change. Does anybody doubt it?"

"Does anybody care?" said a voice at the margin of the night.

Yet another voice that Night Runner recognized. "Sergeant First-Class Foucault, sir. From the tone of this training, sir. From your words, sir. We're going to be America's terrorists, aren't we?"

Poole bit his lip. "Y'all didn't get that from me."

"I ain't doing no fricking suicide bombings." Barret got a few laughs, but Foucault wasn't through.

"Who told you we wouldn't have to kill innocent people? That lying Tyler?"

"Y'all can refer to him as Captain Tyler."

"And you believe him?"

"I did. It makes no sense to kill innocent people. Not on purpose. Think about it," Poole said, bouncing a fingertip off his forehead. "If they just wanted to off civilians, all they'd have to do is lob a hundred Tomahawks, drop a few dozen cluster bombs on every city in Afghanistan. Taliban'd be farting terror for weeks."

It answered that concern. The crackling of burning oak pallets filled in the silence and kept back the cold. Nobody had any more questions until Blue Dolan spoke up. "Do you have a deployment date? And a first target?"

"No, I'll get that later. General Spangler's inbound from the Pentagon. Later today he's gonna tell us what up and send us off."

A groan rose up from the crowd. Yosarian wanted to know, "At least we don't have to put up with Tyler again, right?"

"Captain Tyler put this team together. Looking around this fire, I'd have to say he did a got-damnt good job." The night grew quiet, except for the snap of oak embers. "Give it a rest about the captain. That's my last word on dissing the cap."

There it was. Done. Night Runner admired that about Poole, too. Tyler had done a good job of testing these soldiers, and Poole gave him credit. Poole himself was proof that Tyler had done a good job. Picking the best officer on the ground, as far as he could see, when it was clear that Tyler himself wanted to lead the group.

"Tonight we kick back. A few beers—and I mean only a few. I don't want to catch any of y'all out yonder barking at the ants. Fall in at zero six. For PT. We have to keep in shape. Rifle range later in the morning. We're gonna train ourselves the rest of the way for this op. No more head games from higher."

A few murmurs of appreciation at that.

"That doesn't mean I'm going to make it easy on y'all. I'm going to make myself familiar with each of your skills. I'm going to see what you do best. I'm going to find out how you can cross-train others in this group. We'll see how the leadership works out, how the skills split out. Speaking Pashto to each other. Like that."

Blue Dolan still wanted to know, "When do we launch?"

"Rest of the week in light training here. Five or six days travel time to Fort Bragg. Y'all be on your own. Four or five of those days to pay a visit to mama. If you want, time enough to visit all the little mamas."

From the look of things in the security lights, the weeds in the landscaping gravel and the random array of yellowing newspapers, he knew she must have left. If only. Hoping against hope, he did not either try the bell or knock. He just used his key and walked in.

To find it a letdown that she was there, after all. In the very air, her fresh fragrance, the pheromone that turned on all his sensual switches. He supposed that the smell of her was probably what attracted him in the first place. After the hawk eyes that hooked him like talons.

He called out so he would not alarm her by clattering around. No answer. He wondered. What she gone, after all? Or was she upstairs, waiting with the pistol? *I heard a noise, officer. Somebody breaking in. I shot without thinking. And killed him. Yes, he was an unfaithful husband. But I still loved him. The shooting? Well, the shooting. Yes, the shooting. An accident, pure and simple, and, oh, so terrible.*

No, he heard a shuffling of bare feet on the floor. Maybe she had fallen into depression. Let herself go. That might make it easier for him. If she wanted him to go, he would not argue. Spangler had given him permission to leave her for good, if he wanted. Imagine that. A general giving him permission to walk out on his wife. To save his career. Tyler shook his head. Talk about cognitive dissonance. Even if Spangler was a toad, that was one hell of an idea. Turn that one into a DoD OPLAN, Roscoe.

Amy wasn't playing along. She came down the stairs, freshly showered, toweling her hair. The rich musk. The lack of makeup. The nightgown that clung to the damp spots on her body, her flanks, her buttocks, her midthighs. And those eyes. He steadied himself by putting a hand to the banister of the stairwell.

"Connor?" Although she could see it was him. "You're back." Too bad.

He flapped his hands, then dropped his arms to his sides. "A week's leave." He flapped again. "If you want me to be back." He looked toward the door still opened a crack. His escape hatch if he needed it. "I can leave, get a room."

"And so eagerly." She stood at the bottom of the steps now, putting the towel to the center of her chest, pulling the silk gown across her breasts, her nipples hard, her thighs prickled by gooseflesh, her tone oh so flat and level.

He looked down at the floor between them. "After the way I left. After the phone call. After you saw that I had her numbers on speed-dial." He looked up and saw tears in her eyes. "I don't know what you want."

"And you?"

He shrugged.

"Can we talk? Maybe tell each other?"

He closed the door, giving her his answer.

She came to him. "Will you love me first?"

"Funny," he said. "Well, not funny, but I never stopped loving you, ever. Even when I was . . . at my worst, I loved you. I still love you."

"That's not what I mean."

"Now?" With an effort, he shut his mouth. "What about Brendan?"

"He's with my mother." The robe fell from her shoulders.

Ramsey Baker nee Ramsay al-Bakr awoke to find himself on his knees, naked, bent at the waist, face to a slab of stone, arms splayed, nearly the way his father prayed at the mosque. And, indeed, he did pray. He prayed for death. Ropes pulled at him in six places. Knots bit into both wrists, putting traction on his broken arm. If the bastards only knew that it gave him the first real relief from that pain in days.

Ropes at his ankles tried to pull him in the opposite way, but ropes around his knees kept him in place, stretching to the sides, straining at his groin. After that pony ride—

He heard a sound effect from the movies, that of a sword cutting through the air. Next he heard a snap across his back. And then a shriek. His shriek. Not just in his ears but in his head like the roar of the surf.

Again and again, he wailed. He could not stop the shrieks, no matter how he willed himself to get it under control. The pain was just too much. More pain than the hatchet to the head. More than the broken arm, even re-broken.

"Lift up your head, you bastard." In Pashto, but with an American accent.

Baker's mind snapped to. He tensed himself for another blow, trying his best not to bring on another lash, trying to obey. Sobbing because he could not.

All he got for his troubles were twin cramps in his neck.

Another lash.

More screams. Was that him? *Oh, God of Islam*—

He tried to make words, shrieking the Arabic words. "I can't raise my head. Release the ropes and—"

Three more quick lashes shut off his words, his curses, his shrieking, his breathing.

In a moment of panic, he could neither inhale nor exhale. This was the end of the Apple Dumpling Gang's brilliant plan, of Spangler's wet dream of infiltrating Al Qaeda, of Carnes's scheme of turning him over to this sadist. To die.

Soon, Baker hoped.

No such luck.

A man untied the ropes around his knees and ankles. They pulled his legs straight. A new fire streaked across his buttocks. They had hit him there, too? While he was out? What the hell was the point of that?

Any relief he got from the cramping in his knees and back was soon canceled out. As they rolled him over onto his back, twisting his broken arm again inside the splint. He caught a watery glimpse of his fingers, swollen fat. That was why the arm hurt less than his back—it had swollen tight and numb against the cast.

For a second, his military instincts kicked in, and he tried to gather some intel. He lay on a table, he could see that. In a cave. With perhaps forty men around him. Few paid mind to him or his misery. They sat around small cook fires, stuffing their faces with greasy, stinking food.

He saw a huge Arab. Mansour, the chief, as ugly as he was big. And an American with a radio antenna in his right hand. The American was whipping him? Jesus. The guy was smiling. Powczuk, the guy Roberts thought a bit squirrelly, the guy—

"How does it go with you, you Al Qaeda bastard?" Mansour asked.

He rolled his head from side to side. "Not well."

The pair guffawed.

As he had promised, Roberts had put some distance between himself and Baker. He wasn't in the cave. Baker didn't blame him. He wouldn't want to see this, either.

More than that he didn't want to say anything to piss off the tribal chief. Not if Mansour was going to have him whipped some more. Baker lost his resolve to gather intel. He felt his eyes begin to leak anew. Nothing fake about it. He was afraid and on his last reserves of will. Much more of this, and he would scream out his true identity to the American holding the antenna high, waiting to deliver another lash. Screw Spangler. Screw Carnes. Screw this. If the bastard hit him across his genitals—

"I have questions," Mansour said.

Through his tears, Baker could see an angry, unforgiving glint. In that look Baker saw how his life had gone in the last few days. An American had buried the hatchet in his head. Another American was now eager to beat him. Both Delta Force. That one with the antenna in his hand, that Powczuk. His look was more savage than even the chieftain's. Powczuk raised the antenna.

Baker gasped in Pashto, "I will tell you what you want. Ask any question you want."

"Your name."

"Ramsay al Bakr." He spelled it. *Don't beat me.*

"Your unit."

"I don't know. I'll try to remem—"

The whip came down, striking his thighs, slashing his genitals.

Delta Force. I'm a Delta Force officer. A captain in the army. He did not have time to scream it. For the sheer, vicious, sudden audacity of the pain knocked him out.

But too soon he came back. Electrified again. This time by a splash of cold water. His body convulsed against the ropes. He felt a torrent of sensations, chaotic and tumbling, like silverware falling off the table. The broken bone, the sting, the heat, the anger, the fear. Water up his nose, drizzling into his throat. He coughed, then gasped. He tried to raise his head to see whether his penis had been cut off. He could not raise his head high enough to see. And this time, when he tried to scream into the uproar of his own body, nothing came of it. So damaged was his voice, so overloaded his ears and nerves and head.

"Your unit." This time it was the American.

Baker could only manage a squeak. "I don't remember. Dear Allah, I don't."

"He's telling the truth," Powczuk said in English. "He doesn't remember. Amnesia. He would give us his own mother now. Or else he would make up really big lies to get us to stop whipping him."

Delta Force. I'm Delta Force. It was just a whisper away.

Powczuk switched to Arabic. "If we suspect a lie, you will suffer even more." Powczuk moved around so he could look into Baker's face.

"Do you dig it, you son of a pig?" He said it in English.

Baker kept his head, crying out to Mansour. "What is he saying? Don't let him hit me because I don't speak his tongue."

Powczuk asked in Arabic.

"Yes," Baker said. "Anything. Ask me anything. I will tell the truth." Any man would. Amnesia was supposed to be the perfect cover for him. He could say he didn't know anything. Because he didn't. No matter how much they beat him. But how much would they beat him? How much could he stand before screaming his identity in English?

"Where did you hide out with Osama bin Laden before?"

"Bin Laden?"

"You don't know him?" Powczuk raised the whip.

"I know this name, but not who he is. I never met—"

"Liar." The antenna whooped, cutting him across one nipple, sending yet another jolt of his own body's electricity through him, pain so fiery it might have been molten, and flowing through his veins.

"I swear," he screamed. "I ran away from the fight. Before that I do not know. My head. I was struck on the head. A bomb, I think a bomb. I forgot my own name at first. Give me time, and I will tell you about this bin Laden. Believe me, dear Allah, you must believe me."

Mansour leaned down into his face, breathing his bad breath on Baker. He grabbed a shock of Baker's hair and pulled.

Baker heard the rip of his healing scar tear open as the surgical glue failed. He felt a blast of air cooling a spot under his scalp. If the man pulled any harder, he would not have a scalp left to pull.

This he thought as screams so thin and plaintive escaped his chest through his throat, hurting his larynx so terribly that the screams might not even have been his own, so little did he know them. He might even be screaming, *Delta Force, Delta Force,* but not even he could make out a word of it.

"Bin Laden," Powczuk said. "We know you've been with him these last months. Where?"

"Bin Laden? Yes, I know this bin Laden? Give me a map—"

"Liar." Powczuk again. "One minute you don't know him, and the next minute you do."

"Yes, no." Baker began sobbing. "I don't know; I don't know; I will tell you all I know, just stop whipping me."

"No!" Mansour.

Baker heard a sound of metal whistling through the air again, but in a different pitch this time, higher, lighter, smoother, cleaner, quieter.

He heard and felt it strike his arm, the sound first, then a sudden release of the tension on the broken arm. Powczuk had cut the rope? He lifted his arm. Mansour recoiled from the lawn sprinkler spray of . . . *blood?*

Yes, blood. Baker knew blood. He did not realize it was his own, until he moved the stump of his left arm into view, showering his own body warmly. Only then, when he saw that the arm was cut off, did he feel the pain. Odd. That he could still feel the bones grating at the break and the swelling in his fingers. So odd he did not cry out.

He craned his neck to look up. The cardboard cast—with the arm from just below the elbow still in it—lay on the table leaking, still tied at the wrist. And Powczuk stood above him, a bloody hatchet—dear God, another hatchet—in his hand.

A fresh scream rose in his throat. *You stupid son-of-a-bitch. His thoughts in English, using the man's name. You bastard, you just cut off my arm. I'm one of you, I'm an American. An army officer. Delta Force, you stupid bastard prick. You just cut off the arm of one of your own.*

But he could not get out the scream, let alone the words, before he blacked out yet again.

Mansour grabbed the arm and waved it at Powczuk like a fat, bloody wand. "Are you stupid?"

"What?" Powczuk said, raising the hatchet to dry it on Baker's filthy clothes. He glared back at Mansour. "You talking to me?"

"How much will we get out of him now?"

"What good was he? The liar." Powczuk shrugged, the hatchet still in his hand. "Trying to tell us he doesn't know bin Laden. Everybody knows bin Laden. Hell, every moron in my country knows him now."

"You and your obsession with bin Laden." Mansour turned his head and spat on the dirt floor of the cave. "My enemy is not just bin Laden. My enemy is the Taliban. And the Al Qaeda army."

"An army led by bin Laden. Don't forget that."

"You don't care about the army of Al Qaeda. Or the Taliban. You only want bin Laden. For your own glory. Perhaps you can find a way to get the cash reward offered by your CIA."

"What? Are you accusing me—?"

"Take him out and shoot him."

Powczuk stepped back, at first raising his hatchet in earnest, then realizing it was a feeble weapon. He dropped it and pulled at his 9 mm. Mansour's soldiers stepped back from him.

Mansour shook his head. "Fools, I'm surrounded by fools." He pointed at Powczuk. "Not him." He pointed at Baker. "Him. Take him out—for the sake of Allah, nobody around here can do a thing right. Bring him along, and I'll shoot him myself." He drew a snub-nosed matte black pistol, a 357, a gift from the CIA man, Roberts. From the president of the United States, Roberts had said. Another stupid American. Stupid enough to believe that Mansour was stupid enough to swallow that.

Mansour grabbed Baker's bloody stump and clenched it.

He turned to shout over his shoulder. "Don't forget to bring a shovel." One of the three men carrying Baker dropped a leg and ran back inside the cave.

Roberts monitored as much of it as he could from his vantage point above the cave entrance. The CIA man heard shouting from inside the cave, but could not make out any words. Then, he saw three men carry out Baker's naked body. He could see the blood, lots of blood, and his heart stopped. At the sight of

the man running back inside and coming out with a shovel, his
pulse started up again, like a jackrabbit taking off. Then the
two quick gunshots from afar. Mansour killing the man. Goddamned warlords. Just when you thought they were going to
stay in character and betray you, they did just the opposite.

Roberts lay back in the shade, exhausted and disgusted. He
felt sad about Baker and offered up a prayer for his soul. He
closed his eyes and shaped the words of his report to Carnes.
Poor Carnes. Couldn't catch a break anymore. First the disaster of not getting the 9-11 intel back in time to stop the strikes
on the World Trade Center. Now this.

Two hours later he awoke, hot. The sun had pushed the
shade away. He tried to remember Baker's face, but could not.
He was glad of that. He went down to the cave.

At the entrance, he saw one of Mansour's men, carrying
the shovel again, walking toward the gully, complaining under
his breath, carrying a piece of cardboard—no, the cardboard
splint with fat, blue fingers sticking out one end, a bloody
shank cut at the other. He steadied himself at the mouth of the
cave for a full ten seconds, getting his stomach under control.
He was getting too old for this kind of work, and too sensitive.
Both were weaknesses. After this operation, he was going to
have to give it up.

Poor Baker. He should've stuck to the regular army. This
spook stuff. It was the death of him. Hell, it'd be the death of
them all. He started formulating a report in his head. This one
was going to break a lot of hearts. Their best chance for infiltrating Al Qaeda with one of America's own. Shot down in the
desert. And his arm cut off for good measure.

Just inside the cave, he came face-to-face with Mansour.
He tossed his head the way of the man carrying the arm. "The
man didn't have any word on bin Laden? No information of
value at all?"

Mansour shook his head. "That Powczuk. He's insane, you
know."

Roberts shrugged. *Who wasn't insane in this place?*

"The arm?"

"Powczuk cut it off."

"For no reason?"

"He had plenty of reason."

"Oh?"

"Pain gives him pleasure."

Roberts tipped his head to the side. *So what?* Thinking: *Funny. Mansour upset at Baker's death? One more body in the never-ending count?* He was upset at losing the man. A good man and a valuable asset. But at least he knew Baker for a few hours. Traded jokes and insults with the man on the pony ride out. But Mansour? Why did he care?

Spangler again stood before his men. This time to address just the seventeen. He had sat the way they did now, while some blowhard general gave a mission briefing as if he were some damned glorified platoon leader who'd been watching too many John Wayne flicks. He vowed to do better than what he had seen.

The emotions he would not have to fake. They had lost Ramsey Baker, the poor somebitch. Beaten, battered, broken, and thrown to the enemy as bait. He'd read the CIA report before flying out. A firsthand A-1 intel source. His arm chopped off. Then double-tapped by one of those goddamned Afghan warlord barbarians, a cretin name of Mansour. A KY2001A2 satellite aimed at the last spot where the signal had faded away. In a dry ravine near the tunnel complex of the warlord bastard. A hasty grave. Spangler wanted to send a brace of Tomahawks up the warlord's ass. The CIA wouldn't allow it. They needed all the Northern Alliance help they could muster, even the sunshine patriots.

He couldn't wait to send these men in to kill Afghans. Maybe he could frag a mission at Mansour. Maybe Tyler. Yes, Tyler, a genius at creating accidents. Let him lead the next PTT into Afghanistan so he could accident Mansour right straight to hell. Bring back his head on a platter of shit and—

His audience came down with a group cough.

"Men," he said, "I have given a set of sealed orders to Lieutenant Poole. After this briefing, I will turn you over to him. He will put his touches on your orders and give you a full mission brief."

Routine stuff. Spangler could see it in their faces: *Here it comes, the blowhard general stuff.*

He threw them a curve. "I'm staying out of every aspect of the mission briefing. My job is to make sure that you get every form of support—high-tech toys, hard currency, conventional forces, air support, all the refinements of science wired with the cruelties of the Stone Age—anything. You ask for it, and you get it. No questions from the Pentagon back at you. Not from nobody. I'll see to it. As long as you keep doing your job, nobody will second-guess you. Nobody."

He could not tell them that he had gotten this guidance from the mouth a top presidential aide. He did not relay the source of the assurances from the woman in the red coat. Nobody could trace this back to the oval office. But he could give them his word. In public. He might as well. If anything went wrong with this operation, he was going to be the fall guy for it. He was the Ollie North of America's terrorist war in Afghanistan. So he gave it to them straight. It got their attention.

"I don't have a long speech, and you don't need a pep rally. All I want to do is tell you the name of your mission. It comes from a secret OPLAN, and it's called *Operation Michael's Sword.* Here is the last known image of Michael Woodrow, age six. Taken by a security camera. Video recovered from the rubble at ground zero at the World Trade Center."

The room, already silent, went black. A grainy video image came to life. People running, people screaming, in time-lapse. And in one corner of the frame, as the adults ran by, a child.

Spangler moved to the side of the stage, and found the door handle. He would like to have stayed around to see their faces, to feel their reactions, to read their eyes.

As Michael Woodrow cowered in that corner of a stairwell. As the adults in full panic ran by him, nobody noticing.

Until a firefighter in a black coat moved into the frame from the bottom right, fighting his way upstream against the torrent of fearful men and women. Hauling on the banister to take himself up to the landing against the current. To lean over the child. To pick him up. To toss him over one broad shoulder.

Michael Woodrow. Staring into the camera, the faceless people flooding by in black and white, every eye in the room on the face of that boy. Huge eyes anyhow, but eyes made so much wider by the panic that infected him from the adults in the stairwell. And simply not knowing. He took no comfort in being picked up by a stranger in a black coat.

So Michael began screaming.

Spangler had his copy of the tape doctored. So the video could zoom in on the face, the screaming face, beautiful eyes, even in fright. White skin. Even, dazzling teeth showing through a wide mouth, a mouth made wider by his terror.

Michael screaming. Michael tilting. A crack splitting the concrete in the background. The first tile blocks from the stairwell peeling away behind his head. The dust settling like a monsoon's downpour. The image of the screaming mouth going to first, full-frame, then freeze-frame. The audio, dubbed in, shrieking still.

Fading to black, sudden, utter silence. Then a still from Ground Zero, the rubble of the World Trade Center.

"Gentlemen, this is *Operation Michael's Sword*," Spangler said into the dark quiet. "It's not about simply doing violence to Osama bin Laden or Al Qaeda or Hamas or Yasser Arafat. It's about Michael. This child is the reason you are fighting. He is your reason to be."

Spangler would have liked to add Ramsey Baker's name to the reasons they should go out into the world and kill. But that might mean owning up to a debacle he had helped create. So he left it at Michael.

In the first few seconds, as the lights came up, Spangler saw something out there in front of him, a bit of a glitter. On the bared teeth of an audience of killers. And in the eyes of a few, tears.

Spangler had nothing to say that could surpass what was in their heads. That last frame of Michael's frozen scream, burned like a tattoo into their minds, had said it well enough.

Spangler pushed through the stage door and out into the hot glare. He let the door slam shut behind him before he pulled his hanky, lifted his glasses, and dried his own eyes more weepy than normal.

III   Four Weeks

Week One: September 18, 2001—Near Khost, Afghanistan

Ramsey Baker was both surprised and disappointed when he awoke from his nightmare. Surprised to be alive. Disappointed because it was no nightmare, after all. He lay in bed, hot, itchy, stinky, at the edge of a scream. He kept his shrieks in because his throat felt torn. And because he heard so many men. Singing, shouting, taunting each other in Arabic. Like any other barracks he'd lived in. A military camp. He had no idea where he was, or who had brought him here. He felt a throb in his broken arm. Then he remembered. He had no arm.

A figure came out of the dark, floating his way.

"Are you awake?" A woman's voice. Surely a woman was not going to torture him or cut off any more of his parts. Her shadow moved across his body. "Yes, you are awake, Ramsay al-Bakr."

"Sadly." Not the word, really, just a hiss of air.

The woman let out a sigh of relief. "They brought you here at the very edge of life. I thought you might die for the loss of blood."

"I wished for it." Baker could only whisper. "Even now—"
Even his whisper broke. He could not stop the welling of
tears. *Dammit*, a Delta officer weeping.

"You are going to live."

"Water? Please?"

She turned her back and lit a candle.

Baker tried to wipe his eyes while she could not see. He used
the wrong arm, no arm, and a sob escaped his chest. *Dammit*.

Forget about bin Laden. He'd lost an arm. He was useless
now. To himself, to his country, to his cause. When she turned
back to him, he was disappointed at what the flicker of flame
revealed. He had hoped for an almond-eyed Arabic woman of
twenty to materialize from the darkness at his bedside. At
least a girl to hold his one good hand and comfort him until he
died. Not this woman. She was beautiful, but mature, twice
twenty, probably the mother of six terrorists-to-be. He drank
the water in long gulps and hissed for more. He watched her
eyes. Not many people could look at him and keep their gaze
from drifting to and from his disfigured ears.

He found his voice. "What is your name?"

"You can call me Mother."

Perfect. "Why am I still alive? Mother."

"Mansour. He took you away from that one, that American.
He kept you from bleeding to death. He buried your arm in
your grave, but he brought the rest of you to me for healing."

"Mansour?" The chieftain who'd let him be tortured?

"The same."

"How long ago?"

"Two days. You were delirious. That first night I thought
you had died. Twice." She reached out a hand to his head and
traced her fingers through the rumpled cartilage of one ear. "A
birthmark," she said. "I have seen this affliction before."

Birthmark. One way of putting it. Better than defect, which
was how he knew it. "You saved my life, Mother. Thank you."
I think.

"I merely brought you to health. As I say, Mansour saved
your life."

"But why?"

She smiled at him. "You are a respected man among our people. You remained loyal to our prince. Even at the cost of your arm."

Baker's pulse quickened. "What about the prince?"

"Mansour said you have met the prince, that you served by his side. He will be grateful to you."

That goddamned Roberts. Is that what he told Mansour and Powczuk? That he knew bin Laden? That he'd been in the terrorist's inner circle? No wonder Mansour saved him. No wonder Powczuk was willing to cut off his arm if that would make him talk. Trouble was, the same bullshit story that had saved his life would just as certainly get him killed if—

"You will be taken to him at a secret meeting place. And there the prince will give you your just reward."

"Wonderful," Baker said to her. His just reward. Just fucking wonderful.

Tyler spent his entire week of leave at home, never leaving the house, except briefly, in the mornings, to track down the paper among the gravel, boulders, and cactus landscaping of his arid front yard.

Amy never left at all.

Except for his brief forays outside, neither one of them even dressed. And then only Tyler, in his robe.

On the seventh day, he came out of the bathroom after his shower, in his underwear. The first time he had had clothing on inside the house. He went to his walk-in closet and slid hangers from side to side.

"It's over, isn't it?" she said from her lanky, untidy sprawl on the bed.

"I have to go." He spoke softer than normal from inside the closet, and she could barely hear him.

"That's not what I mean."

He came to the door of the closet and looked at her, lying on the bed, her hair wild, her body limp, the bed tousled and stained. She had won. They had lost.

"Then what do you mean?" Although he knew. *Say it. Aloud.*

"I mean," she said. "Us. We're over."

He sagged, leaning against the doorway. There. Aloud. *Are you happy now?*

And that was that. Not another word. He packed and left, knowing he would never come back as her husband, leaving a brief note.

> Amy, I'm sorry. This is my fault. When I get back from Afghanistan, I'll have a lawyer get in touch with you.
> Connor.

He thought about it on the way to Nellis. The sex could not restore their marriage. Especially not that kind of sex. They had strained and worked at it. They had had true orgasms. They had gone through the motions only. They had not talked. They had not addressed his betrayal of her. And she had driven a stake in his heart, using Laren's name and asking to be touched like the other woman.

He had thought about it as he lay there sleeping fitfully. Cruel as it was, he could use her words to broach the topic. He could turn over and face her. He could apologize. He could tell her the entire story of how he met Laren, how he fell into an affair, the only serious affair in his entire marriage. He could lie, too. Say Laren never meant anything to him. Betray Laren's memory. Forget what was dead and gone, and hold on to what he had, wounded, but alive.

But he did not. He walked out the door. Left that note. The end.

His heart ached. Not for Amy and the damage he did to their marriage, but for Laren.

He had cried in those seven days, to himself, briefly, on those few trips to the bathroom when she did not follow him. Not for Amy. Not for him. Not for Brendan. Not for their marriage, or their family. But for Laren.

He could not lie. And he could not tell Amy. Somehow, impossible as it seemed, although he only saw her two, three times a year, tops, he had fallen in love with Laren Hodges.

Not in the way he fell in love with every other woman who

had the hawkeye look. But seriously, inescapably, emphatically, obsessively in love. Not even Amy, the original hawkeyed woman, had done that to him.

Laren was gone. He had seen Spangler's security film from inside the World Trade Center. When the building began to crumble, it was not Michael's face that he saw in his mind's eye, but Laren's. Her beautiful eyes terrified. Her lovely mouth distorted in that silent scream.

He took out his handkerchief and blew his nose. He wiped his forehead, checking to see the taxi driver wasn't watching before he daubed at his eyes. He could not allow anybody in the world, not even a taxi driver, but especially not Amy, to know how much he missed the love of his life.

Amy Tyler found the note and sank, naked, into a chair. She knew her husband well enough. She knew his weakness for other women—had known it all along. But she had always been positive him that she could overcome his weakness by her own sense of style in fashion, good looks, and refined behavior. As a last resort, she thought her wealth could hold him. And Brendan, certainly.

Until this other woman, this Laren, came along. She had talked to Laren—well, not really talked to her. But she had listened. She had heard the urgency in her voice, both when she called the wrong number here at home and in the explicit telephone message she had left for another woman's husband. That woman, that Laren, had been so in love with Connor, so desperately in love, so worried that he might have died in one of those airplane crashes. On that day, that day of infamy in their marriage. Amy herself, as much as she loved Connor, felt a little guilty. She had not been quite so desperate about whether she had lost Connor to one of the airplane crashes. No, she had worried that she had lost her husband to another woman. Was that all there was to her love for him? The selfish part? No wonder he had found his true love in another woman. It wasn't there in his marriage. Ever.

She couldn't get him back from Laren, even in death. Because she never really held him that deeply in the first place.

She had seen the look on his face when she hurt him. *I*

want you to take me like you took Laren. Emphasis on the past tense. The words hit him hard. In the heart. And it showed.

That made her saddest of all. That look of love in Connor's face was still far more intense for Laren than ever was for her.

Week Two: September 25, 2001—Near Kandahar, Afghanistan

Poole had to marvel. Spangler lived up to his promise of infinite support. And DoD didn't pull any punches, either. The team had satellite priority, even ahead of the CIA, on tonight's mission: a government ministry in downtown Kandahar.

Poole formed three teams of his men. He and Night Runner plus five made up a heavy team. An officer and an NCO each in two other light teams of five.

Poole met with a pair of Afghan rebel contacts. The pair came up with a taxi company, a fleet of sixty cabs, if he wanted. He took six.

The navy's vaunted Special Ops pilots had landed Poole's group from three Blackhawk helicopters off the carrier *Enterprise* in the Indian Ocean two at-night-in-flight refueling nightmares away. An hour's march put the team into the foothills above the city, ten miles distant.

After a mere hour's wait, a convoy of six sets of headlights snaked along the dirt road toward them. Poole waited for the taxis to reach the rendezvous spot, a hairpin curve in the road. The convoy bunched up, and each set of lights went dark. Poole called out from cover, in Pashto, ordering the drivers out. He told each one to open every door of his cab, and to pop open the trunk lid.

Poole then ordered the Afghan leader to have each driver stand on top of his vehicle.

"No way," the Afghan said in near-perfect English. "These are brand-new hacks. I don't want no damned footprints on them."

"How about bullet holes?" Poole said. "Y'all want them got-damnt hacks filled with bullet holes?" *Trust nobody,* he'd told his men. Trust was a commodity, bought and sold between tribes, and traded even-up among enemies in this part of the world.

"Fine and dandy," the man said in his Midwestern accent, "but I want cold cash to fix them damned footprints."

"Fine and dandy."

The man gave his order in Arabic, and his squad of drivers climbed up on top of their vehicles gingerly. Poole was glad to hear each of them bitching about the cost of pulling out dents and painting. They cared about the cars. Meaning they weren't about to blow them. Maybe. He refused even to trust his own instincts on that.

Poole sent Blue Dolan and Travis Barret out to make sure there were no Taliban soldiers lying in wait in the trunk or in the backseats. Once they gave him the all clear, Poole sent his two expert mechanics out to inspect in detail.

Tony Michelotti had passed Tyler's terror test in a group other than Poole's. The buck sergeant was a semi-reformed cat burglar and a chop shop artist out of Boston. George Epps, a spec-four, was the junior member on the team and a true grease monkey, trained in GM's Mr. Goodwrench school. Neither spoke Arabic. Both proved their worth on the team within the first five minutes.

Michelotti stepped up to the leader of the Afghans. "Who are you, pal?"

"I am Yussef bin Laden, I am a leader of this group," the Afghan on top of the first vehicle said. "Top dog, alpha male, big kahuna leader."

"Tell your men to get down and lift the hood on each car," Michelotti said. "Then have each of them go back and take out the spare."

"Spare?"

"Tire." Michelotti bitched into the mike at his lips. "They know *kahuna* but not *spare*? Buncha phonies here, boss."

"Roger," Poole said. "Keep the chatter to a minimum."

Michelotti and Epps went to work. They checked air filters, oil caps, and washer fluid for explosives and flammables. They let a hiss of air from each tire and sniffed the sample to make sure it was air only. They crawled beneath each vehicle looking for bombs and beacons. In two minutes, Michelotti gave his report. "All clear. Unless we go to blades."

"Blades it is."

To the howls of the Afghans, Michelotti and Epps shredded the headliners, visor, and seats of the taxis. In five minutes more, Michelotti called all clear again.

"Unless we get out the wrenches," he said. "In ten minutes per, we could have six piles of parts."

"No time. Mount up." As his men took their spots inside the six vehicles Poole spoke to Yussef bin Laden for the first time.

"Too bad about the name, bin Laden." Poole smirked.

"Not so bad. It brings me lots of business. Don't forget. This is not New York."

"Oh-h-kay. Too bad about the cabs then."

"I bring you the best I have, and you turn them into a pile of shit."

"We'll pay."

"Through the ears you will pay."

"Nose."

"What nose?"

"Forget it."

Two hours later, the convoy eased into the margins of Kandahar. Poole called for a stop. He ordered five of the Afghan drivers out of their vehicles, and put five of the Delta men behind the wheels.

"This is outrage," Yussef said, his English flagging as his anger grew. "My people be in famous danger out here. They have no way home."

"Relax." Poole said, "I'll leave them a ride."

"Your men will get lost in the city."

"My men know this city as well as you."

"How can they?"

"Before the Soviets," Poole said. "Many of my men be living here." He left it a simple lie. He didn't want to get into computers, GPS, and live overhead video that would keep watch as well as direct them better than any Northstar operator. He didn't want to reveal that three Afghans on the payroll of the CIA, natives of Kandahar, sat at computer screens and watched from a secret station inside Saudi Arabia. They would guide the taxi drivers, while other sets of eyes watched for Taliban troops and cops. American ears owned the air waves. American hands had the controls of Stealth Bombers at the edge of sky above.

A reaction force of Delta fighters stood off less than ten miles away, waiting on alert inside a flight of Blackhawks. Medical teams stood by. Contingency upon contingency. Poole had more options than any combat leader dared dream about. Too many even to sort in his head. Against the rules, he had to keep a three-by-five card in his flak vest. He'd have to eat it before he died. Or before Spangler could catch him with it.

The team took only seconds to take over the five taxis.

Poole handed Yussef the keys to the sixth vehicle. He chose his words carefully, no street jive, no idiom that Yussef might get wrong. He didn't want to kill men who simply didn't follow his instructions because he used language off the street. "Tell them it's locked. Tell them not to open the door or get into the vehicle for an hour." Poole showed him his wrist. "By my watch. Tell them." Yussef did as he was told.

"Now tell them that my men are going to search them, taking all phones, radios, and other shit. No Game Boys, no BICs, no flashlights, no nothing." More protests as Poole's men came up with three cell phones, one of them a digital job. Poole made no comment about that. Technology had made it around the world into both friendly and enemy hands. You couldn't tell the players apart by their cell phones. If he had time, he might check out the preset numbers. But he did not have time. But he would take the phones back and let analysts harvest what intelligence they could.

"Tell your men to stop bitching," he said to Yussef. "I'll leave the cells with you. You can give them back after we're gone." Seeing the things that Tyler had trained them to do, a bit of lying didn't amount to shit. Once bin Laden passed along the lie, the drivers calmed down.

Poole pointed a finger into Yussef's face. "And remind them to stay away from the taxi. Tell them to not even put their forks on the taxi."

"Forks? What forks?"

"Fingers, I mean fingers. Tell them not to touch the damn taxi. For an hour."

"I told them."

"Y'all best tell them again. It's like . . . a matter of life and death."

Yussef spoke to the men, and the gripes started up again.

Poole told Yussef. "Again."

"You speak my language. You tell them."

"They should hear it from you. Tell them I mean business."

Yussef pointed to the wrecked taxis, bits of seat stuffing cluttering the road like dumplings. "What you think? That they are stupid?"

"We'll see." Poole ordered his own men into the five taxis, and three Delta teams scattered into the city, splitting away to take separate routes.

The eye in the sky was a remote-controlled drone similar to the Predator but smaller and quieter. Called the *dirty bird,* it flew low enough to give an oblique view of the sixth taxi under the trees and the five men standing in a huddle, arguing. Within hearing of a transmitter draped over a branch in the trees, a mike that one of Poole's men left.

Two of the men voted to leave. One of them held up the keys, pointed to the taxi, and tried to reassure the others that they could get away. He said he wanted to go home, to sleep with his wife. Or the wife of any man too scared to go.

He broke away from the group. He told them that it was safe, that the Americans were only bluffing. "They're up to no good. Think how bad it will look for us if we are found out at night after they set off a bomb in the city." He shouted to his own men, but men inside Saudi Arabia heard him. Michelotti had planted a second mike in the base of a wiper arm.

An air force intel specialist inside the bunker in Saudi Arabia kept Poole up to date in real-time minus the three-second delay. Poole could have watched vid for himself on his palm-size screen, if he had a mind to. But he didn't want Yussef to know the kind of toys in play tonight.

The pair who wanted to be home before the Americans roused the Taliban police finally won out. The man with the keys unlocked the door gingerly. When nothing happened be raised his arms and looked over his shoulder at the others, still fifty meters off. He opened the car door and jumped back, as if that would keep him safe from a blast. A snap of the electric locks made him flinch, but he turned to the others and beckoned them toward the car.

They waved back and hollered for him to start it up. He slapped a hand at them in a pooh-pooh motion and slid behind the wheel. He looked at them and smiled, all the while cursing them as cowards under his breath. "Hurry up, you sons of whores," he muttered. "I must get to a phone."

Six seconds later, a voice repeated the exact words, in English, to Poole.

"Stand by. Keep me posted," he said.

"What?" Yussef wanted to know.

"Nothing, I was talking to one of my men. He wants to stop and use the latrine."

"He has to keep you posted when he needs to piss?"

"I told him to go before we left."

Four of the men crouched low when the fifth leaned over the steering wheel and turned the ignition. The taxi roared to life. The driver pulled the door shut, lowered the electric window, and shouted, "Hurry up, you sons of whores." He threw up his hands. "See how safe? You cowards."

The four ran to the taxi. Four doors chunked shut. A voice spoke in Poole's ear. He grunted into his radio mike and said, "Barret, let there be light." He covered his mike and mugged at Yussef. *Too bad.*

"You can't stop and let the guy take a piss?"

Barret spoke into his ear. "Wilco." One word, short for *will comply,* one word that both acknowledged Poole's "let there be light" code and set off the first act of terror in country. As Barret pushed a pair of buttons as one on his remote detonator.

Nobody in Afghanistan even saw the light, not even the five Afghans vaporized by the set of charges beneath the seats of the taxi. One more car bomb in a region of car bombs.

Poole shrugged at Yussef. "Some people gotta learn the hard way."

A voice in the sky directed Poole's Delta teams into attack positions across the city. Poole asked to make a splash. Spangler was only too happy to go for it. They mapped out a bold and noisy plan. Put the Taliban on notice, light a fire under Al Qaeda. Give them get a taste of their own fire. Forget timid strikes with standoff weapons fired from afar. Make some noise, let there be light—of explosions and of gunfire. Send them a message: Americans kicking ass on the ground up close and personal.

Poole's team of Night Runner, Barret, Foucault, Dolan, Ballard, and Michelotti drove to the Taliban's Ministry of Agriculture. The name so innocuous. No Western nation would strike a farming entity. The West was slave to public opinion and the media. The U.S. had to play fair. Strike the enemy military, but don't even give the finger to poor, innocent farmers.

Poole, Night Runner, and Barret stepped out of their taxi and melted into the shadows. They found the front door guard post empty. A chain looped through brass door handles, and a two-pound padlock secured it. SatIntel said that a handful of security guards stayed inside nights. A former guard, a spy for the Northern Alliance, confirmed the satellite report.

While Poole's trio set up security, Foucault, Dolan, Ballard, and Michelotti lugged hundred-pound backpacks up the steps. Michelotti produced a set of picks.

"I thought you had an electronic pick," Foucault said.

"This is faster."

"Y'all puta sock in it." Poole said. They looked at him, wounded.

The padlock snapped open, lighting up Michelotti's smile. "Fast enough?"

Night Runner removed the chain and held the door with

one hand, his rifle with the other. Inside, they worked in teams. One pair to keep watch on things, including the taxi driver, Yussef, the other two teams carrying the team's preset charges. They fanned out and worked their way around the second floor, hoping to bring down the five-story building by taking out all the lower supports. A World Trade Center maneuver. The building might not fall into its basement, but there was enough incendiary in the explosives to set fires that could not be put out for hours, if ever.

Working with Blue Dolan, Night Runner found the lounge where the security guards had laid up in the dark. He cracked the door and saw them through his night vision goggles, sleeping on couches, cots, and bunks. He counted six, just as the intel said. Now that he had a fix on his known enemy, he could look for the inevitable surprises, the unknowns that a satellite could never predict with certainty.

As Dolan placed his charges, Night Runner set a charge of his own on the door to the guards' dorm. He used a concussion grenade hinged in two halves, with a magnetic backing to hold it in place on an iron hinge. Before he armed it, a thought struck him. He left the grenade stuck to the door and crept into the lounge.

Odd. Six guards napping in one room? Did they feel so secure? So soon after 9-11? Or were they just lazy?

The room had two bunks and two cots for six men. Did the Taliban set up the room this way? Three shifts of guards? Four guards off duty, two on? Where was the guard post? Certainly not outside. Somebody had locked these men inside with the chain and padlock. Was this the post? Inside this room?

Night Runner marked each guard on the map of his mind and crossed the center of the room, silent as his shadow. As he went, he ID'd light switches and bulbs, in case he had to shoot them out. At the back of the room hung a Persian rug, not high on the wall like the other tapestry. But from halfway down the wall, its fringed bottom trailed the floor, polishing a dust-free arc on the tiles. He could see that the edge was dirty, frayed. He looked behind without touching it, fearful of booby traps. He saw the reason for six guards—a vault door.

He tugged on the rug. Its hanger was hinged, and it swung open, itself a door.

The Taliban clerics might call this the Ministry of Agriculture, but it held more than farming secrets. Night Runner drifted back outside the room and made a report.

Foucault gave a time hack. They had been inside the building three minutes. Poole had set a limit of five.

"I gotta love a vault," Poole said to Runner. "Stand by until we lay the last charges. Then let's checker out."

In minutes Poole met with the team outside the guard room. He nodded at Night Runner, who came up with a plan, quick and simple. Poole gave it a second nod. Foucault looked dubious. Poole stared him down. "Let's go."

As a group, the team walked into the room, all keeping watch through their night vision goggles until they all stood in the center of the chamber, their weapons pointing outward, covering their enemy. An enemy would expect an attack from the windows, or the door. The team would gain a second by standing in their midst. Except for Foucault and Ballard, who stayed out in the stairwell, well out of danger of taking a stray. They were to keep an eye on Delta's new sidekick, Yussef.

Night Runner led Michelotti to the vault door. Michelotti dropped to one knee and studied the lock. He turned back to the center of the room and beamed a smile bright enough to flash in every set of night vision goggles. Everything about Michelotti was a smile, his flippant eyebrows, the crow's feet that radiated from his eyes to his ears, the double set of parentheses on his cheeks, the single quote marks at the corners of his mouth. And those teeth, keys on a baby grand.

Michelotti removed his radio earpiece and replaced it with a tiny headset of his own design. He attached a suction cup to the door, near the lock, and began spinning the dial, tentatively at first, then faster to clear the tumblers. In ten seconds, he grew serious. His fingers worked steadily, slowly. Ten seconds later, he removed the headset, replaced his radio receiver and boom mike, and stood up. He put his handle on the door lock and looked toward the center of the room and tapped the side of his NVGs.

Poole gave him a sharp nod of the head and tapped his own NVGs. Michelotti leaned into the handle, shielding its noise with his body. He leaned away from the door, pulling it open wide enough to look inside the vault.

Night Runner marveled at the kid. More than a cat burglar, he was a cat. Michelotti turned on the video recorder in his binoculars. When he looked into the safe, every man on the team with his heads-up view on could see what Michelotti saw.

Night Runner left his heads-up video off. In case something dazzled Michelotti's NVGs. He kept an eye on the sleeping soldiers, moving his eyes left and right, covering each man in each sweep. Like the elk he hunted in Montana, he did not check every detail of the landscape each time he looked. He merely imprinted the image once, then kept track of any tiny change or movement.

Michelotti gazed into the safe. A second later, his head recoiled, like a bird's. He saw the same reaction of the other members of the team who had turned on their heads-up display.

Poole saw caskets on his heads-up display. Stainless steel caskets lining the walls, floor-to-ceiling inside the safe. No way. The Taliban could hide bodies, even valuable bodies, in a million ways. Or grind them. Or burn them. Drag them into caves and blow down a rock slide.

Besides, these caskets weren't long enough for bodies. The huge safe ran deeper than the ambient light that Michelotti let in through the cracked safe door. *What the hell would the Taliban find so important that—*?

Oh, shitsake not that. He tapped Simon Ballard on the shoulder. When Ballard turned to him, Poole tapped the black case hooked to the front of Ballard's web gear. The NBC detection kit, a handheld unit called the Sniffer that could pick up radiation, biological agents, and the common chemical weapons agents in ten seconds and classify them by type within thirty seconds. *WMDs.* Those you'd hide in a vault.

Ballard soft-shoed across the room to the safe. Poole didn't

like it that only two men would go inside the safe, leaving
only three in the room. But WMDs? He couldn't blow a building full of WMDs. He had to know—

"Five minutes," Foucault said into their ears from his post
at the stairwell outside. Poole clicked his teeth twice. He
dared not talk now. He felt a rising anxiety. The five minutes
was a deadline of his own making. He could change it. He
could ignore it. Assuming an alarm on the vault door, the
clock didn't start until a minute ago, two tops, when Michelotti cracked it. If he kept to the five-minute rule, they still had
three to four minutes, worst-case.

He watched Michelotti's video. Ballard, in close-up,
helped Michelotti lift down one of the buffed boxes. Michelotti used a stepladder he found in the vault. He climbed it to
take one of top boxes, about two feet wide and three feet long.
Not bodies. The two men struggled with the heavy case. Ballard's face, in a bird's-eye view, twisted like a dishrag in
close-up, as he took its weight. Poole cringed as the NBC de-
tector, swinging from its lanyard on Ballard's chest, rapped
the metal. The NVGs showed Michelotti's toes working down
ladder steps. Ballard swept the NBC device around the seams
of the box. He looked up into Michelotti's video camera and
gave a thumbs-up sign near his own mouth. Michelotti's
hands came into view on the case. He snapped open the
latches and stepped back. Ballard tested again, at the crack.
Again, thumbs-up. Michelotti's hands lifted the lid free of the
case. As the stainless steel blur slid to the side, the contents of
the box came into view like a close-up camera shot in every
heist movie he'd ever seen.

Money. Cash money. Bundled American greenbacks.

The camera panned back as Michelotti recoiled in shock,
then swept around the room. To show the entire room-size
safe. Filled with cash boxes, floor to roof.

The images brought a smile to Poole's lips. Michelotti, in
his wildest dreams as a cat burglar, had never seen a score like
this, bigger than even his biggest dream score. Michelotti began walking toward the darkness at the back of the room. The
ambient light wasn't strong enough to show more than twenty

feet ahead of him. He kept walking and felt secure enough to talk from deep inside.

"Holy shit! This safe goes on forever. Sergeant Ballard, open up the safe door all the way so we can get some light in here." The NVGs showed Ballard's silhouette reach for the door, put a shoulder to it, and let in a little more ambient light from inside the guard room.

Even that light did not reveal the back wall of the safe. Michelotti picked up his pace, and his quick tour revealed a room bigger than most small town libraries, stacks after stacks of the stainless steel cases. Michelotti, a small man anyhow, barely had space to clear the aisles with his shoulders as he strode deeper into the darkness.

"Gotta be millions in here," Michelotti said, his voice going giddy. "Make that billions." He giggled. "Shit, fifty-eleven kazillions. Score the Taliban treasury. The Fort Knox of Omar Capone. Shit-fire, boss, we—"

Poole cleared his throat, bringing Michelotti's guided tour to a halt. He had seen enough. He had found a gold mine, all right. Nothing struck at the heart of a government like a strike at its wealth. The face of American terror now had a new look, three faces in fact: Jackson, Franklin, Grant.

Poole tugged on Barret's sleeve and signaled to Dolan. They followed him to the door of the safe and took up the two spots on either side of the vault, standing guard. Poole stepped into the safe and pulled the door toward him. Before its could shut, he signaled to Ballard to hand him a stack of currency. He propped the cash, a brick of $10,000 in hundreds, into the seam of the vault door so that the safe could not be shut from outside. Talk about a fiasco. He and his safecracker locked inside a branch of the Taliban's treasury. They'd have to change the dictionaries, put Poole's mug shot beside the definition of *military dumbass,* bumping Gomer Pyle.

He felt a touch of the giddy-bones that Michelotti had shown. Both at his plan and at that image of himself locked inside the safe when the Taliban militia broke in to do the day's business. A deep breath. Pause. *Don't let the money mess witcher head. Whodaman? Youdaman.* Poole walked deep into the vault. He let out his breath. Gathered himself. Gave the team a brief on his new twist on terror.

Night Runner heard the plan leak into his ear from the vault. He liked it. Bold. Splashy. It even had a dark shade of humor to it. Poole didn't say a word about killing, and he didn't joke about it. But men would die. No joke in that. Men. Would. Die.

The team went to the center of the room, pistols at the ready. Poole strode to the door. With a slap, he turned on every bank of lights in the room. Each Delta man hinged his NVGs off his eyes.

Poole yelled in Arabic. Then he said in English, flat and mild as you please, so the non-Arabic speakers would know what was going on. "On your feet! Get up, you lazy bastards. Stand by your bunks."

Night Runner knew the drill. This was the funny part. Sergeants in armies big and small all over the world had pulled this drop-your-cocks-and-grab-your-socks wake-up call on recruits for as long as men armed armies. The soldiers acted on instinct. All six sprang up beside their cots, bunks, and chairs, packing their privates into position in their shorts, rubbing their eyes, trying to peer out into the dazzle from beneath their fingers. And bitching, yes, of course. Night Runner could guess: *You see what time it is? What the hell is going on? What now? Abu? Abu, this better not be one of your pranks.*

Poole spoke up again, again in Arabic, then English: "Shut up. You are now prisoners of the United States. Do not move. We will kill you."

They froze. People had threatened to kill them before. In this job, maybe twice a day, three times on Ramadan.

Their eyes came into focus. Jaws fell. Curse words seeped from their open mouths. Five men in black gear, five pistols pointed at them. *Americans? How?*

A look of group fear crept across the faces of the guards. If these men did not kill them, their clerics would. Taken without a fight. They would die hard and slow, and they knew it.

To keep a lid on their panic, Poole spoke again. He told them first, then the Delta men, "We need to keep you alive unless you resist. We're going to take you as prisoners of war. We will take you away to Pakistan where we will question you. Then we will release you to the Pakistanis."

He let them have a second. Night Runner saw it sink in. A tiny sag in the faces. Relief. They had to believe the fiction. Or else they had to try to break free now. They chose to believe.

Night Runner gave a nod. Smart. Very smart.

Poole ordered the guards into the safe. He found a set of switches inside the vault and turned on the lights. He barked a series of orders, giving the men no time to think or scheme or flee in panic.

They set up a chain gang and began ferrying the metal cases out of the safe, sliding them along the floor. Two men at the end of the chain opened the boxes and dumped the cash. Two Delta men went out to recover some of the demo packs they had placed. Ballard stood guard inside the safe, Poole outside. Night Runner took up enemy weapons and cleared them.

It didn't take long for the pile of cash to become a mountain. Night Runner had to move to the side because he could not see over it to keep tabs on the men.

"Ten minutes," Foucault said from the stairwell, antsy now.

Already? Night Runner worried, too, that they had taken so long. Too long, if there was a silent alarm in the vault door.

Michelotti set the charges as Poole wanted them.

So far, so good. Now if only—

"We got company. A convoy." Foucault, the rich bass of his voice gone thin and reedy.

"What up? Maybe a changing of the guard?"

"That's a neg. Looks like the cavalry."

"Bring it in."

"Yussef?"

"Especially Benedict Yussef bin Laden."

So much for *so far, so good.* Poole shouted in Arabic to his captives. He said to his own men. "I told them to hide in the vault. We're going to shut the door. So they'll be safe in case the shooting starts."

Night Runner heard tires squeal on the street below. And urgent shouts of the reaction force.

The guards were only too eager to run for cover inside the vault. Foucault burst into the room with Yussef, Ballard in trail watching their six.

Poole pointed Yussef at the vault. "Do you want to go in there? With them? Or stay out here with us?"

Yussef's eyes looked left, then right. He kept his voice low. "Do they have guns in there?"

"No."

"No offenses, please," he said, his English again flagging under stress. "I'll please to wait in there behind them." He ran toward the vault door. Night Runner hauled it open. Inside, the security force stood in a huddle, confused. Yussef walked in, his hands over his head, looking over his shoulder. "Don't shoot me," he hollered at the Americans. "Don't shoot me, you American Satan bastards," he gave Poole a secret wink.

Already Night Runner could hear steps pounding up the stairs. Still, he had to grin. One hell of a bad actor, that Yussef.

"Turn out the lights in the vault?" Night Runner asked.

"No." Poole hollered in Arabic to the men inside the safe.

"I told them to get back to work," he said in English. "Pull down the boxes and empty the cash onto the floor. Keep them busy. Make some noise."

Night Runner pushed the vault door against the bundle of cash, leaving it open a foot.

Poole gave a few quick orders. The men took up spots in the room, some with their backs against the same wall as the doorway. Others to the left, behind bunks.

Night Runner gave it the once-over. A classic L-shaped ambush. Indoors. One for the tactics books.

Poole gave him a hand signal, and one hand wiped out the lights as the steps clopped into the hallway at the top of the stairs.

Night Runner moved so the open door would shield him from view when the lights came back. The bootsteps stopped in the hall. A second of confusion. One man gave an order under

his breath. The group bunched up and came at the room three
mobs of four.

Night Runner looked at it from the POV of the Taliban soldiers as the first mob came into the room. The glow of the
light from inside the vault. The sounds of the steel cases clattering on each other, metallic snaps, grunts of men. Every set
of eyes on the vault. Every ear tuned in.

One of the Taliban soldiers turned on the lights.

Runner saw as the reaction force seeing the pile of money
in the center of the room between them and the vault. Next to
gold, nothing could seduce a man like the sight of cash. More
money then most of these men would dream of seeing in the
afterlife when they settled down to their one-a-day allotment
of virgins.

Four men trained their weapons on the cash. And their
eyes—the money was all they saw. A pair pushed in from outside. The men spoke in hushed tones as they began flitting
across the room toward the sound from inside the safe. More
footsteps outside, and six more men rushed in. Like the others
they put on the brakes to stare at the pile of money.

Night Runner heard new steps in the hall, and another
detail—no, two—checking out the building. A call from up
top. They'd found a pack of explosives? A group pounded up
the stairs, three, maybe four men. Another set of boots ran in
the hall. Coming this way. Night Runner crouched behind the
open door to see. Through the crack, five more men ran at
them, mouths wide in panic, yelling. He didn't know the
words, but guessed they were trying to warn the others about a
bomb. He made eye contact with Poole and held up one
splayed hand. Poole nodded, drawing a finger across his
throat.

Night Runner stepped around the door. He tossed a concussion grenade into the hall. Boots and sandals skidded as
the grenade hit the floor, bounced off the wall, and spun at the
Taliban soldiers. More yells.

Inside the room one set of Taliban focused on the cash.
Another, seeing no reason to fear, on the first set. They turned

toward the racket in the hall as the boomer took out a third set, and the ambush was on.

A blast of light. A slap of air. It stung his face, but Poole kept his focus. And held down on his trigger. M-4 carbine set to auto. He hosed down the Taliban men in one long burst. He sprayed the men, the room, the men, the cash, the men. The slugs belted them like body blows. They jerked away from him.

The rest of the Delta men had opened fire, too. Other body blows from the side impacts. Slugs tossing the men to and fro. Throwing them against each other. And onto the cash. They barely had space to fall. Back and forth. Dying. Spattering. Splattering. Strings of blood, chunks of meat. Ricochets taking out the lights, flashes and glass splashing the scene.

Poole called out, then called out again to call a stop. The Taliban man far more than dead. Dead, flayed, splayed, and silent. Not a groan. Not a cry. Not a sound but the reports of the Delta guns. Not a shot fired in return. Not a man of his flinched. And, as he looked around, he saw his men in the eerie dim of the vault lights, grim, yes, but not shaken. Mouths set with bile at their task fresh done.

In what? Ten seconds? Christ.

On this point, he had to give Tyler credit. He had done his job well. Just the act of terror Tyler and Spangler wanted. More a mob kill than an act of war. No smart remarks. No call for surrender. No quarter. Just ten men dead in ten seconds, each man killed ten times over. The pile of cash took many of the bullets, and much of the blood.

But even Tyler's drill not as real as this, not as warm. They didn't tell you about the smell of a fresh kill zone. Ever. About the gases released. About the muggy fragrance of blood, the contents of the stomach and the gut. The chunks of the lush organs, the brain and the liver. Heavy, congealed, sticky, a smell richer and thicker and more sickening than shit because shit was a familiar odor while the freshly ruptured liver was exotic, repulsive and attractive in the same breath.

Foucault turned away to vomit. "Sorry," he said. "The stink got to me there."

"No prob," Poole said, wincing from the new rancid stink himself.

"I got a problem." Ballard. "No biggie." The safe door. Delta bullets had spanged off it and sang around the room. One, a tumbling, spent slug had struck Ballard in the shin. It knocked him off his feet without breaking the skin.

At first the only sound was silence. Then Ballard cursing in pain, as he tried to walk off the sting in his leg. Then the others cursing in awe. As each one saw himself as a cold killer in the mirror of their deed.

And finally the sound of a gurgling brook. Blood trickling from bodies lying about like Lincoln Logs, a harmless noise in the fog of death, like the first melt of snow in spring.

Night Runner turned from the scene, his body low, to survey the hall. There was danger there, one tentative set of footsteps.

One faltering voice called out, one word, into the darkness—the boomer had killed the lights as well as the men in the hall.

Night Runner saw him through the peep sight and over the post sight of his rifle. Standing. At the end of the hall, bathed in the glow from the stairwell. Crouching toward the unknown, but fearful of taking one step into it. Night Runner knew. The Taliban man did not know whether his own kind had shot or been shot.

One more word. Maybe *Hello*. Maybe the name of a friend. One more word, and the Taliban man had his answer.

Night Runner shot him in the face, in the crease below the right eyebrow and above the eye. He dropped like any head-shot man, as if taken down by a ball bat.

Night Runner took Michelotti to check the dead and finish the undead. As he went by the last Taliban to die here to check the rest of the building, he saw there was no need for a double-tap, and he was glad of it.

The two taxis raced through the streets of Kandahar, toward
the city limits on the northeast side of town. They took separate routes, as Poole had briefed. Even with the diversion at
the Ministry of Money, MoM, as Michelotti had dubbed it,
they were just twenty minutes off plan.

Behind the team, the trail of terror would fester on its own
energy, building to a critical mass until it finally exploded
with true terrorist intensity. First was the calling card he'd left
behind. Spangler's idea. The joker from a deck of playing
cards. Printed with Osama bin Laden's likeness. Overlaid
with the crosshairs of a sniper scope, offering a million-dollar
reward for information leading to the killing or capture of the
bastard. The back of the card a greeting from America. In
time, leaflets with the same image and message would flutter
all over Afghanistan, as the psyops types ramped up their part
of the war.

Little chance any Afghan would risk giving up bin Laden.
No big deal that. This little gem, the joker showing up at
scenes of destruction, would speak for itself. The Americans
have landed. We're after bin Laden. The prince might not be
dead, but he'd better go to ground.

And what a rich destruction they'd sown at the MoM. Barret and Michelotti hauled two of the cases of cash to the roof.
They had propped up the cases at opposite corners of the building, opened them, and with those fabulous boomer grenades
beneath each case, set them to blow remote.

Poole then let the original security force go. Not to be kind
or merciful, but to serve a new wrinkle in his plan. He told
each dazed man that he could leave the vault. And that he
could keep as much cash as he could carry.

Amazing the strength a man could muster when he had a
world of wealth in his hands. Five of the guards were able to
carry or drag two stainless steel cases of money apiece. One
giant of a man tied three of the cases in a string and dragged
them like dog sleds into the dark. They left swaths of dead
men's blood in the hall, the stairs, and even the street.

Those soldiers would not raise an alarm. Not now, after they had stolen their country's money. If the Taliban clerics found any of them with no more than a twenty-dollar bill, they would die.

Trying to spend a twenty-dollar bill on the open market would get them killed. Trying to pass off two hundred pounds of American greenbacks, would get them shredded alive, with every member of their family, three-times removed, likewise filleted.

But that didn't stop them from taking the risk—and the money.

Yussef dragged two boxes of cash down the stairs to each of his taxis. At the cost of some shoe scratches and one blown taxi, he'd made millions.

The team set incendiary devices all over the inside of the vault. They buried the fire-bomb grenades inside the mountain of bloody money, these, too, set to remote. Lack of oxygen would contain the damage, but still would make it tough to fight the fire. Especially after all that money blew in the guard room. Poole doubted a firefighter could walk through an ankle-deep swamp of cash to risk his life inside that flaming vault anyhow. More likely, the fire department's finest would stuff their pants and boots with torn and bloody bills and run. The blast on top of the building would scatter cash to the four winds. Normal citizens could pick up enough money before sunrise to equal a life's income in Afghanistan for ten men.

And, as they sped down the streets, a casket of cash in the backseat of each taxi, Poole handed out bundles of currency. Each Delta fighter broke the paper strap and held out the stacks, letting the wind take the bills and scatter them through the city, psyops leaflets of their own kind. Poole noticed that Yussef could not let go of a single bill.

Once he was satisfied that they'd scattered enough money to cause an uproar in the provincial capital, he ordered the last of the money dumped. Again, Yussef held back. Poole reminded him of the two cases in the trunk of each taxi. "Don't get greedy," he said. "Don't let the small change betray you. What if they see a single bill in your cab? They will torture you, they will kill you, you will tell on us, you will die—all without being able to spend a dollar."

"Of course, of course. Money. It is nothing to me," he told Poole. But his eyes betrayed him. Yussef would backtrack and try to pick up as much loose cash as he could before the masses found it.

Poole shook his head. What the hell did he care? He ordered a change of direction so the cash and rioting would not lead the Taliban to his team like a trail of bread crumbs. They still had work to do, in another part of the city.

But first. . . .

He slid back the cover of his PDA, and pulled the antenna to its full six inches. To blow the Ministry of Money. He pushed the star and the pound sign at the same time.

The second floor erupted in a brilliant orange glow, taking out the windows, blowing embers in every direction. At first people outside, as they gathered to gawk at the fire, would dodge the flaming paper drifting down from the roof. Then one person would notice that it was an odd kind of paper. Money. A cry would go up. People would riot. Joy would turn to terror as people fought each other, as armed militia of the clerics shot down citizens. Money, the love of it the root of all evil. *Yo, Ta-Taliban, you want terror? Get down wit dis ta-terror.*

After more than a week in the care of his new mother, Baker found he had his legs under him again. Both on the ground and in his head.

His wounds healed quickly at the hands of the Arab woman. She would not tell him her name, yet she treated him like an adult son, minus the affection. She changed his dressings, hourly at first. She brought him thin, spiced broths at first. Later she dipped nan into the broth, and he devoured the sesame-sprinkled bread of the Afghans. Later he ate hearty soups, and graduated to rancid-smelling goat cheeses with his bread. He filled up on *aashak*, scallion-stuffed dumplings drenched in a thin gravy and garnished with mint. He knew authentic Arab food from his own home. He knew what to look for, how to eat it, and how to appreciate it. Once every three days or so, she found a way to serve *qabuli palow*, spiced rice with chicken, and *mantu*, a red-meat eggroll. What kind of meat, he did not ask. Beef was a scarce commodity in Afghan cooking since the scorched-earth days of the Soviet occupation.

By the end of the first week, he had begun his rebound in his body. He had stopped pissing blood, and he could walk in circles in his room for an hour, resting only five minutes—whereas the first day he tried it, he could only walk for five minutes and needed an hour's rest. He tried to walk without tilting, but could not help compensating for the off-balance gait. The loss of his left forearm meant less weight and a shorter arm swing besides.

For the first time since his captivity, the wound in his scalp began to heal, and he felt he might survive gangrene of the head. He had lain still on his second day of consciousness as his new Mother lifted up the flap of his scalp and cleaned his head wound with a solution she made by dissolving a yellow powder in boiled water. She stitched his hide closed with a curved canvas needle she sterilized by passing its tip through a candle flame. He saw her use the same needle and black, waxed thread to repair a torn boot upper two days after she fixed his head.

She saw him staring at her as she worked and shrugged. "A torn boot, a torn head. It is all the same."

"Mine was not the first head you cobbled."

"I treated thousands of wounds and hundreds of fighters in the war to drive out the Soviets." And by her failed attempt to keep her smile modest, she was proud of it. The smile soon faded. "Now we fight against other tribes of our own people. And soon, against Americans." She gave him a long look.

It took all his will to stay in the capture of her gaze and not flinch at the accusation, real or imagined.

"Were you a nurse?" Asking the question was his way of blinking first.

"No. A doctor, trained before the Taliban outlawed women in the professions." Her words crackled with bitterness. "I am forced into the Al Qaeda and only to practice medicine in emergencies. When they need a hand to reach into their guts to clamp off a bleeder, they don't care so much if it is a woman's hand."

"Yes."

"And you?"

"Yes?"

"You are an educated man, by your speech and manner."

"Am I?"

"Yes, but I suppose you don't remember that? What, with your amnesia?"

"No." He answered her irony with a wide, forced smile. "I wish I knew."

She let it go at that.

His tongue limbered up as he immersed himself in Arabic conversations with her, speaking in Pashto, the language of the Afghan majority. The woman told him of rabid radio reports telling of increasing threats by America to invade Afghanistan. Already bombings and scattered fighting had taken place across the country. This news gave Baker hope that he had to conceal as disgust and bravado.

"Let them come," he said. "We will gladly give them the same fate as the Russians."

"Yes," she said, giving him half a smile, "gladly," not at all sincere.

Poole's team arrived at the rally point with Team Three. The two taxis spun into the GPS point less than a minute apart. Near the edge of the city, between the bright lights and the mountains, the Taliban army had taken over a sprawling Soviet base. After the Soviets slouched home and with no armies to fight, it morphed into a concentration camp, a Taliban heavy industry. The clerics kept prisoners in tents and shacks with no sanitary facilities, no fresh water, and little food. Taliban soldiers didn't fare much better. Satellite video showed troops moving out of the barracks in streams after 9-11. The Taliban, no matter how much it claimed it was not a part of Al Qaeda, feared the Great Satan's Tomahawk missiles. The soldiers moved into bunkers and caves dug into the sides of sandstone bluffs around the area. Taliban generals didn't want to stay too near the troops. So they moved their command center five miles farther away. They took over the granite caves carved into the faces of cliffs by the early tribes before they were Afghans.

After the explosions and fires in Kandahar, Spangler had guessed that a military reaction force would barrel into the center of the city. They couldn't afford the loss of face of hiding out once they learned that only a small force had struck. They had to react.

And, Poole figured, now that he had looted their treasury, they would call out the National Guard, the militia, their version of the minutemen, Al Qaeda and anybody else.

He surveyed his new position quickly. Team Three had prepped the area for them already; they had taken up the best ambush spot. Atop the tallest building along a main route into the heart of the city, the only road a reaction force would take. An inferno of money would be just the emergency that called for a quick response.

Poole's own building was only two stories tall. Barret threw a grappling hook to the roof. Night Runner climbed hand over hand to the top, with Barret close behind, a duffel slung across his back. Once on top, Barret unrolled a rope ladder from the duffel. Foucault, Ballard, and Michelotti came up.

Poole hung back and put a finger under Yussef's nose. "You wait here for us."

"Of course."

"Don't leave."

"Of course not."

"I mean it. Don't even step off yonder to take a piss."

"Do I look like a fool?"

Poole bit down on his answer. *Straight up? That's affirm.* The guy did look like a fool. Now that he had all that cash in his hack, he might well be the fool, too.

He looked over the situation through his night vision binoculars. Already a convoy of military vehicles, perhaps

thirty strong—more a Chinese fire drill than a convoy—had
formed inside the compound. In the distance, Poole could see
a smaller convoy, perhaps half a dozen vehicles. The leadership. He checked his watch. Choices, choices. Ambush or remote strikes. He wanted something in-your-face personal.
Remote strikes would not have the same psywar effect. Still,
they had a third mission on their plate. If these goons didn't
start moving soon—

A voice came across the command channel. SigInt analysts
flying in an AWACS reported that the leadership ordered a
convoy into play.

"The orders are getting more urgent," said the analyst in
the sky. "They're making threats to get people to move."

Poole smiled. The money. Follow the money.

"I've got movement on the ground," said a second voice.
Van Exeter, the first lieutenant in charge of Team Three on
site. Van Exeter and his five men had taken over the roof of a
six-story office building a bit deeper into the city.

Poole saw the convoy get underway, if only seven vehicles
strong. Then a gap of perhaps half a mile, then eight more vehicles, then a cluster of twenty.

The gaps between convoy segments would complicate
matters. Still. Not that big a deal.

The strategy here was to strike hard and fast, then get away.
It made no sense to get into a prolonged fight. The point was
not to inflict casualties, not to win a fight, not to take prisoners
or ground or glory. The point was to inflict terror. A new concept for Poole. A tactic beyond the army that he knew. A strategy his country would never learn to love.

The Taliban must know in the morning that a force of
armed men, exaggerated perhaps a hundred times over, had
invaded one of their provincial capitals and the home of the
central government. The Taliban must spend their days waiting for the next fearful blow. They had to learn terrorism from
the other end of the terrible swift sword of Michael.

Poole took Foucault aside and said, "I want y'all to put
your NVGs on that command team moving down from the
mountains yonder. Keep your eyes skinned. If they don't catch

up soon, I want you to direct a separate airstrike at them, your call. Keep me posted. If you decide to hit them, don't leave the roof until you see the flash-bang on their convoy. I want BDA on the leadership."

"Ordnance?"

"Cluster bombs. Fry they terrorist asses."

Foucault saluted and walked away, talking into his radio on a preset frequency. Poole permitted himself a grin. So much for the Taliban's officers thinking that they could hang back and guarantee safety for themselves. Show them the business end of U.S. resolve.

Poole checked out the fighting position of each of his men on the rooftop. Plenty of hand grenades. Plenty of magazines loaded with ammo for a thirty-second spray of auto-fire. Nothing to do now but wait for the Taliban military to start killing themselves.

Oh, yeah, a military suicide on tap for the night. Poole had seen the films of Desert Storm. He knew how armed convoys reacted under fire. Men in panic always did the same things when they were hit. That was his edge.

The Taliban convoy, now rolling through the gate of the military compound just a half mile away, was about to relearn the lesson that the Iraqi Republican Guards failed to grasp nearly ten years ago. And, perhaps for the first time, they were to learn the true meaning of terror.

Night Runner watched the attack from the roof. The first seven trucks of the broken convoy raced by. At first the drivers held back, reluctant to move at all. Once in motion, they came on like rally drivers at full speed. Thinking, maybe, if they went fast enough, nothing could hurt them. Night Runner shook his head. Sad.

If they'd kept to a safe speed, they might have seen the cars and trucks that Van Exeter's team had hot-wired and parked crossways on the side streets. Too late now. The trucks roared into the kill zone, no way out but the way they came.

Exeter blew down four utility poles ahead of the seven. The

first driver stood on his brakes. Smoke. Howling tires. As each driver stood on his brakes, too. Shouts. Curses. Men in a crush in the backs of the trucks. Trucks slammed into each other in a chain crash.

Each truck had a 12.7 mm machine gun on a ring on the roof of the cab. The gunners found their feet and stood on the seats, their heads poking through the canvas. They could spin around to shoot 360 degrees. So they did. All seven gunners at once.

The panic spread to the men in the backs of the trucks. They fired their rifles and pistols out to the sides, shooting up the street with small arms. While the drivers began to jockey back and forth, trying to turn around. None of the shooters had a target. They shot in the blind. And the moving trucks jerked their wild fire wilder.

No Delta man fired a shot. No need. The ambush began to rack up a dozen casualties on its own.

The lagging half of the split convoy came racing up to the first. All but one driver stopped in time to avoid more crashes. The one driver turned too sharply to miss the rear of a truck. The wheels on the left side lifted, hovered, and went over. The truck dumped its load of men. It skidded on its side, grinding three soldiers into the asphalt. When the convoy came to a stop, a dozen trucks were jumbled over both lanes of traffic like boxcars in a train wreck. But not for long. They saw a battle going on ahead of them. Drivers in panic wanted no part of that. At least ten more gunners added to the lethal fire in the street. Men thrown to the ground lay too hurt to move, or too scared. Until drivers trying to get the vehicles free began backing over the injured lying in the streets.

The street was wide enough for trucks to turn around. If every Taliban driver stayed calm. None did. *Ambush. Kill zone.* Every soldier in the world knows the words. Even a raw recruit knows how to react to them. *In an ambush, keep your head and get out of the kill zone.* Except for the part: *keep your head.* So the men in the street panicked. They shot at sparkling ricochets on the walls. They shot at muzzle flashes up and down the street. Caught in an ambush, they turned the street into a kill zone of their own making.

A third group of trucks roared toward the carnage. The first driver to see the mess let up on the gas and began to coast. Then he hit the brakes, showing his taillights, but he was too late. The six following vehicles bunched up one at a time in an accordion effect. Then drivers and soldiers saw the shooting from ahead of them. Even more gunfire erupted as the Taliban soldiers began to fire blindly at imagined enemies outside their trucks. They, too, shot down the street at the fire in the intersection. They shot high for the most part, as men in panic tend to do. But they also shot into their own men, the first ones into the kill zone.

Night Runner kept his head low. Let them kill each other.

Poole saw the first driver in the convoy show the first sign of good sense. The man tried to drive out the front of the kill zone. Not a bad idea. *If, if, if. If* the truck could climb the four utility poles. *If* his men did not kill him with a wild shot. *If* the Delta men let him.

The truck hit one pole with its left front tire. The pole skidded but did not yield much. Poole could not hear the grinding of gears over the racket. But he could see the driver cram the truck into all-wheel drive. He went at the pole again. This time the left tire took hold. The truck bucked into the air, turning, driving forward still. Plenty of power. Poole raised his rifle— no *if* about it.

But the truck lost its grip on the pole. The front end leaned left, bucked higher, leaned right. The right rear duals caught all too well. The truck pitched hard left and fell over onto its side. A second load of men landed in a heap on the asphalt. Several just lay in the street, their bodies tucked in pain. The driver sitting in the cab perhaps stunned, perhaps still in panic, kept the gas pedal floored. The truck tried to pinwheel on the street. One set of duals snatched at an injured man's arm, caught his shirt, pulled him into the fender well, and shot him out limp as a pile of wet rags.

Poole saw that some of the Taliban fighters tried to keep their heads. They snaked over the poles to the front of the ambush site. They tried to crawl to the side street. They used the pole as a shield from the convoy's fire. To no avail. A second driver tried his luck at the poles. He plowed into three of the wounded, roared over them, and hit the poles. Unlike the first driver, he took the poles squarely. Both tire treads chattered and spun and finally caught a grip on the wooden pole, lifting up the truck's front end. The cab went over. The front wheels found the other side. The truck dropped onto the thick end of the pole, high-centering the vehicle. That didn't stop the driver. He hit the gas as hard as he could. Eight driving wheels shoved the truck forward, pushing the telephone pole like a rolling pin over three more soldiers. The only three soldiers who had kept their heads. They died like ducks in a steam roller cartoon.

The Taliban fighters still in their trucks saw it. They dared not dismount to fight now. Their own drivers might run over them.

Men already on the ground who could run ran only far enough to get away from their trucks—their worst enemy their own drivers. They sought cover at the base of the buildings on both sides of the street, lying in the rubbish. Poole shook his head. Bad choice. He felt a twinge of pity for them.

The last two trucks in the kill zone finally got turned around. The cargoes of men still shot wild. Sparks lit up like sparklers on the walls on both sides of the streets, shattering windows. Bullets spanked other trucks. The two drivers drove hell-bent, back the way they'd come.

The men in the backs of trucks in the second part of the convoy lay down in heaps to escape the fire from the front. Each tried to get beneath the other. They writhed like worms on the decks of their cargo trucks. The drivers ground gears, pushing and shoving to create space until they had enough room to turn. They looked as if they might turn and run back to their camp.

Poole shook his head. No more *ifs*. He could not let it happen. He flicked on his radio and spoke two words as one.

"Take-um." Night Runner ducked.

As the team leaders set off charges in the trash piles on the sidewalks of the city. The men burrowing into the litter died outright when the boomers went. Those in the trucks with their heads up were blinded. Night Runner had bored his fingers into his head. Still his ears ached. On the street, the blast blew eardrums to shreds. Men could not hear anything but a tinny static in their heads, and they felt the concussion of every shot hammered like a stake into every ear.

Next came the rain of death from above. Each man among the Delta Force teams had two boomers. Each looked up from cover, picked a target, and dropped or tossed the grenades over the side. They'd set the boomers to go off in 2.5 seconds. Some Delta killers tossed theirs into the air, sending the camo egg shapes arcing upward, then outward. These went off as air bursts above the trucks. Others bounced on the ground. At least four went off under trucks, lifting them off the street. Two trucks caught fire after their fuel tanks blew.

Night Runner did not see any of it. He crouched below the parapets of the roof. Like the other Delta men, he kept his eyes shut. Even with ear plugs, he clapped his hands to his head. He pushed the cartilage tabs in front of his ears.

The boomers went off in a string. They lit up the streets in strobe-bright light. Even with his head down and lids shut tight, Night Runner's eyes felt the dazzle.

He looked up. It was eerie. Every Taliban fighter in the street was out of action. In another world. Either stunned or taken to his terrorist heaven. Only driverless trucks moved. The pair barreling back from the first kill zone were still going, out of control, smashing into the sides of trucks in the second group. Other vehicles, left in gear, idled forward—or backward. They drove over the curbs and ran into brick walls. Their engines growled, great beasts at the edge of their own deaths. Their driving tires churned against the walk, grinding rubber dust into piles.

Poole saw his men flick away the joker cards to flutter over the street. A rain of litter to prove the point: *How ya likin' yer terrorism now, Osama?*

Foucault had no part in the ambush on the street. Poole gave the order to rally and moved to Foucault's shoulder. "Got time for a SITREP?"

"Negative," Foucault said. "Impact on the command group in five—four—three . . ."

Poole picked out the headlights, maybe three miles away. The lights were bright enough. But they soon got lost in the glitter of a thousand other, brighter flashes, as a cloud of bomblets settled over the vehicles and went off.

The cluster bomb fell like any dumb bomb, sticking to the laws of gravity. Then, at a preset altitude, the bomb's casing flew open. The drag scattered two-pound bomblets. The ordnance exploded like firecrackers near the ground, covering a large area, some of the charges floating to earth on helicopter-like wings in their tails. A carpet of cluster bombs would destroy everything, including tanks. The bomblet casing held the charge into the shape of a funnel. When it went off the shaped charge sent out a stream of fire. It could melt through two inches of armor. Taliban tanks had less than half that armor on top. When the device went off, it scattered the shrapnel of its casing in every direction. It could kill a man at ten meters. And the bomb had a rep. It left bomblet duds behind, scattered, still armed to kill at the slightest touch. An unreliable ordnance, the media reported. Not so. American technology had improved the device to make it explode at better than a 99 percent rate to appease humanitarians across the globe. But Poole knew full well that for this mission of terror, technicians had dialed back the burst rate to 75 percent. Hundreds of duds lay in wait. For a man's step, a bird's peck, the wind's gust.

Rescue teams and medics would not go to the aid of the officers Foucault struck. Unless they were brave or stupid or ordered to go at the point of a gun. The cluster bomb—terrorism squared.

"What else you got?"

"Watch the gates of the compound," Foucault said.

Whether because of a radio call or because of what they had seen happening on the boulevard ahead of them, the remainder of the Afghan convoy, twenty vehicles, remained bunched up at the gates. As if they thought it safe to remain behind the wire.

Foucault kept his binoculars trained on the spot, Poole standing by his shoulder, until they heard a new voice in their headsets. "Impact in five—"

Poole and Foucault lowered themselves behind the knee-high wall atop the building for the rest of the countdown. The compound was a mile away, so they saw the light first, and clenched their eyes shut against it, holding their ears again. The sound was that of a muffled cannon, not all that powerful from this distance. Any one of the grenades on the street below stung them more with its concussive blast wave. Still, the twenty trucks vanished in a sudden black, flickering fog.

"End of mission." Foucault chose the grappling rope over the ladder, walk-hopping over the side, the rope draped over his shoulders, running down the face of the building in the expedient, short-drop rappel.

Poole vaulted over the side, grasping the rope in his gloved right hand, sliding down in a near free fall, his rifle slung across his chest. He recovered the grappling rope but left the ladder dangling, so the Taliban would see. And so they would know, he dropped one of his jokers, making sure bin Laden lay flat on his back, his face looking up from the ground with that feeble, cheesy smile.

As the four taxis sped to the city toward their third target of the night, Poole kept a rein on his nerves. He felt jazzed. Two missions down. Both with huge results. No return fire, no serious injuries, except for the minor French Heart for Ballard, no danger—the Taliban army convoy had been destroyed, almost to a man, as much by themselves as anything else. Delta's men hadn't fired a shot from the roofs.

But Poole wouldn't allow himself to rejoice. He needed to pull off the next trick, the one that counted. Big enough for all three teams. If they could pull off this one . . .

Poole's teams staked out the compound. The entire force was to take on the third target of the night. An Al Qaeda compound, the CIA, NSA, and DIA had said.

More than three years ago the Taliban cleared a city block in a slum to build a fortress. The walls were more than four meters high and a meter thick. Trucks hauled off a mountain of dirt. Giant earth-eaters gnawed more than fifteen meters deep. Ton after ton of concrete went into the floors and walls, at least two meters thick, the intel said. Then workers laid almost as much wet tonnage over the top and left it thirty days to set. Finally they built offices and residences above ground, also concrete, but covered in brick and made to look plain. Meaning only important people trying to look ordinary would stay behind the walls.

They added a mosque, yet no Taliban cleric took up residence. Families, yes. Women and children moved in and out freely. Past a heavy guard, too heavy a security force for plain wives and kids.

No Taliban visited, not even for short stays. Conclusion? Osama bin Laden, the Al Qaeda chief, owned the joint. By keeping out the Taliban, bin Laden meant to keep his place off a target list. By filling it with women and children, he could ensure the always-fight-fair Americans would not strike it.

Tyler and Spangler hoped the night's first two missions might do more than rattle the Taliban. Could they prod Al Qaeda into action behind those walls? They might not net the big fish himself, but they'd get his attention. Strike at the heart of his private life. Crash his home, kill his guards, terrorize his kids. Bin Laden had many—two hundred and mounting—and was the seventeenth of fifty-one children himself.

A simple plan.

And all in place. Moss Knapp's Team Two had moved in quietly, hours ago, as Poole's team was striking the ministry. Knapp's team scouted for intel, secured the perimeter, and reconned escape routes.

He told Poole what he'd seen. People stirred inside after

the ruckus at the MoM. Some house lights went on. Others went out, as figures moved from room to room. Shadows crossed in front of partly shaded windows. Armed men hustled along covered walkways between buildings.

Minutes after the ambush on the convoy, the place came alive. Fifty men streamed from a single outdoor gazebo in a garden oasis, running to surround the house's exterior, keeping to the bushes. Bomb curtains inside the house were pulled, blocking all lights. Out of a rooftop patio floor came an anti-aircraft gun, Russian, 23 mm. A double-barrel weapon that could take a bite out of a helicopter landing inside the walls.

Overhead, the AWACS sucked a flurry of cell phone calls out of the ether. Seconds later, the AWACS and chain of spy satellites triangulated the source of the signals. A smile crossed Poole's face as he took in the IntSum. Both men and women inside the walls cried for help. In fear. The terrorists, terrified.

Analysts pinpointed the source of most of the phone signals. The mosque inside the walls. The tip of the tallest onion-bulb-shaped parapet was a radio tower. The Delta men outside focused their infrared binos there. Troops, more than a hundred, milled about inside the mosque in the dark. Poole smiled. The Al Qaeda soldiers gave new meaning to seeking refuge in God.

More reports came from Knapp's scouts. More soldiers. From the huge greenhouses at the back of the compound: barracks. Poole crammed all the intel into his head. He gave it a taste and made his decision.

"Take-um."

He called the AWACS and fragged a pair of bunker-busting bombs for the residence, two for the barracks, and two for the mosque. One cluster bomb for the grounds, set to 99 percent detonation. Give or take a percent, that left a margin of safety for his men. And the Al Qaeda would not know that. Plan A.

"That leaves the gazebo clear for us," he said.

Spangler, halfway around the world in the Pentagon, heard the plan unfolding, and chipped in only on a technical point. "For the record, that isn't a mosque."

"Say again?"

"It's a bunker. Any structure we bomb with a hundred troops in it is a bunker. Do you roger?"

"Roger." Just like a staff officer. Uptight about bad press in the middle of a strike. "Any intel on bin Laden?" Poole asked. "Anywhere in country?"

"Negative," Spangler said. "Maybe we'll get lucky."

"Right," Poole said. Fat chance. He felt a twinge of regret. Spangler had just trivialized the mission. Didn't he think it'd succeed without nailing bin Laden's hide? Generals. For chrissake.

He reminded his men to stay low, beneath the level of the tops of the building, as they waited for the strikes. Poole had left them to Team Two, which had arrived in plenty of time to flash J-DAM coordinates and double-check them. From here on, electronic circuits and machines would direct the bombing, a true fire-and-forget system. Ironic. Again. The actual was easier than Tyler's test in the desert.

Fire-and-forget. Fire the weapon and forget about guiding it. Fire and forget any human touch in guiding the weapons of pinpoint destruction. Fire and forget the consequences, too. Just as Tyler had trained him.

Not that Poole cared. Scruples be damned. Tyler had done his job. He was out of the equation now, no more blame nor credit due. This was his deal now, his blame, his credit, his consequences to forget, without a scruple of a scruple.

Plan A. Take the gazebo. Exeter's team would hit the gazebo. Knapp's team, longest in the area and most familiar with the layout and dangers, was stay in the position as the eyes and ears outside the walls. Poole's team was to secure the gazebo after Exeter's team went in. So nobody else could follow.

Poole began his countdown. At ten seconds, he told his scouts once more: "Get your hat racks down: ten, nine . . ." His men huddled to the far edges of their rooftops. Those on the grounds lay well clear of the compound walls.

It came like a quake, the shock as soon as the sound. The roof lifted beneath his body, a violent and sudden shove, the tiles bucking and heaving beneath him, like being tossed by a trampoline. He separated from the ground, and when he hit it again, it lifted him again. And again. A third time, as he was falling back toward the roof, a secondary blast sent the roof back up toward him, and he met it hard, losing his wind. Then all went silent.

He peeled his earplugs. Odd. He found it quieter than when they were in.

He eased up to look. The parapet of the mosque had vanished. Two breaks in the walls. Beyond that, he saw little wreckage. No surprise there—bin Laden had an engineering background. If he were going to stay in the building it had better be bomb-proof, by Allah.

At least by conventional standards. But the bunker-busters were of an even newer technology than bin Laden's education.

A bunker-buster would burrow through roofs and ordinary floors just by using its weight and mass. When it struck real resistance, its titanium nose-bit and momentum could drill into ten feet of soil or two feet of hardened concrete before going off. Then it continued boring with fiery, explosive gases capable of melting concrete and even asbestos and following up with a concussive blast. The shaped charge again. True, part of the explosion would be directed straight up, along the path the bomb had taken in going into the building. That was by design of the most evil arts. To incinerate anybody still alive in rooms behind the bomb. The back-blast would start fires, too, fires that would rage through a building. Below, if the bomb did not get through the concrete in its direct shaped charge, it could still spall the ceilings inside the rooms below, flaking off half boulders the size of Volkswagens and blasting them into chunks of deadly aggregate shrapnel, flinging molten iron rebar like some medieval arsenal used to defend the walls of cities.

That was the first of paired, tandem bombs. Ten seconds later, the second bomb would strike in the same hole, already cleared of ordinary obstructions. The second bomb guided by GPS precise to an inch or two in a mile's fall, three inches in a drop of three miles, could punch through another three to four feet of now weakened reinforced concrete. It would detonate, sending a second fire-hydrant-sized stream of gases hotter than the sun along the same path, vaporizing anything not yet melted.

After the second trio, he waited. Then came the rattle and glitter of the CBU cluster bombs. Wiping out anybody exposed on the ground.

Poole didn't give a damn about any of that. He took radio reports from each leader, in turn. No lasting casualties. One man who'd lost an earplug would be deaf in one ear for a while, but that was the worst of it. Poole had seen worse injuries at a stag party.

He gave the order to go, while the dust and smoke hung in the air for cover. Forget the first two bouts with the Taliban. This one was for real. Aimed at Al Qaeda, hitting them close to home, bombing Osama's home and bursting in uninvited.

The last thing Poole had said to Yussef, his Afghan taxi driver with the trunk packed full of U.S. currency, was to stay put in an alley three blocks away from the new ground zero. The first thing the driver did after the bombs strikes was take off. Careening down the city streets without headlights.

"Your stagecoach driver, boss." Poole got the report from Moss Knapp. The eyes and ears had seen and heard.

"What about him?"

"He's booking."

"You know what to do," Poole said.

"Roger." The sound of a three-pound charge of space-age explosives going off inside the trunk of the taxi arrived a heartbeat later.

Poole sighed. The money. Definitely the money. Next to sex, money made men do the most stupid things. The story was the same all over the world. Nasty people—hell, even decent people—thinking that Americans would be held to the high ideals the press always spouted and politicians always waved in one hand, the flag in the other. But acting with honor made the world think Americans were weak. The home press howled that the U.S. was stupid to act with honor but went livid when they didn't. Yussef had all that running through his head. And a trunk full of money besides? How was the guy going to resist? *Shitsakes.*

One moment's reflection. That's all Poole could afford to give it. He had a live enemy now. Forget honor. Now gunfire, fear, anger, cowardice, heroism—all those things dictated the direction of the battle. The best a combat leader could do was try to keep track of things, stay flexible in his mind and in his battle plan. The enemy zigs, you zag. He punches, you jab. He counterpunches, you answer with a ferocious attack, hooks and upper cuts—to the body, then to the head. Wait for him to throw one wild punch and in the split second that he's vulnerable, put him to the canvas with a killing, crushing blow.

Now that the bombs had hit the compound, the Al Qaeda fighters inside were dazed, trying to get up from the mat. There was no neutral corner, no mandatory eight-count. Get inside, follow those bombs into the bunker for the final blow. Rush in for the kill, man to man, hand to hand.

First Lieutenant Van Exeter came through a break in the compound wall first, near the barracks, with his four men. Poole's team had to scale the wall from the outside, but the rubble of the mosque inside lay against the wall and gave them a rough ramp to walk down, to hide on, and to fight from, if need be. Poole lay behind a pillar and watched the action unfold in his NVGs. He saw Exeter's men, working in two elements, maneuver across the yard toward the gazebo. While a trio rushed forward, the pair stayed in place, ready to spot danger and support by fire. So far, nobody had seen them. Through the heads-up vid display, he watched through Exeter's eyes, seeing what he saw. So far, no danger.

The Afghans knew bombs had struck them, of course. And they knew Americans had done the deed. What else? He heard the cries of the injured and the panicked. He could guess at their intent. They cursed George Bush. They cursed all the Satans. For now. Soon, their officers would collect them. They would come like army ants to get revenge on those who stirred up the nest.

Poole's team kept to the wall, keeping to the height and cover they gained from the rubble. From there they could watch over their own.

Two of Exeter's men reached the gazebo and waved the

trio in. The money shot, the danger zone. The team at the trap-door in the gazebo, exposed to gunfire from outside, at risk to ambush from inside.

Poole listened in as Exeter gave his orders. Boomer grenades at the ready, two men stood back. Two others held the hatch open. The boomers would go in, the explosions would go off, the blasts served up to anybody lurking inside, blinding them with flash, collapsing eardrums, smashing organs. After the dust settled, the fighters would pile in, and Poole's team would take up spots near the gazebo, posting security, acting as a reserve force. So far, so good.

The doors flapped open, releasing a red glow from inside the entry. A smoldering fire. Poole could see it from where he sat, and he could watch through Exeter's eyes. But only briefly. As two boomer grenades sailed into the glow and before Exeter duked hit the ground beside the gazebo. Poole's only view was a patch of grass and soles of two combat boots. Before—

A blast. A blast far too large huge. Not from the grenades. Too loud. As the patch of grass and gazebo itself erupted beneath the toes of the boots he had in his view an instant before the IR light went out.

The blast knocked Poole off his pile of rubble and threw him back against the wall. *Shitsakes!* He gasped for wind. The night went from green to black as a sudden, violent gust sheared his NVGs from his face.

Blinded, Poole felt around for his NVGs. Grasping with his mind as well as his hands. What the hell? A dud bunker-buster from the strike? No, he'd counted. A late drop, a tardy strike? No way.

A booby trap. Yes. Al Qaeda had set charges around the gazebo. Either bin Laden's people had set off the charge or else the boomers had blown it.

No difference to Exeter and his men at the base of the gazebo. Nobody could have survived that. A voice called to him. Night Runner. He caught a snatch of the report: *man down*. He reset his earpiece.

"Say again."

"Six, this is four, we have a man down. Alpha five. Both legs trapped in the debris when the rubble shifted."

One of his. Ballard. "Roger, is he conscious?"

"Six-by," Ballard spoke for himself, straining the words through his teeth. "Much as I hate to say."

Poole had to ask. "Can we get you free?"

"Negative," Night Runner said. No hesitation, no doubt.

"Five, can you fight from where you are?"

"Roger."

"Roger, then hold your position and watch our six."

"Wilco," Ballard said, biting down on the word.

Poole felt a sudden sickness. Already six of the twelve who'd gone into the compound were down. Fifty percent casualties without a shot fired. Bad as the Taliban ambushing themselves. When that crossed his mind, he flinched. *Call it off?* He could bring in a Blackhawk. The bombs had taken out the 23 mm AA gun on the roof. He could sound retreat.

Retreat? At the very verge of breaching a bin Laden stronghold? No.

Shitsakes, what the hell was he thinking?

Now was not the time to go gutless. Leave that to the U.S. press and the inevitable antiwar crowd. Let them second-guess the soldiers, crucify the commander, sift the battlefield for mistakes weeks and months later, first shoot the wounded, then the leaders, then the soldiers.

But, for God's sake, leave it to the press. Don't let him start second-guessing *himself*.

Poole gathered himself. How much time had he spent in self-doubt? He found his night vision goggles. He fit them to his head and reset his mike in front of his lips.

"Let's go," he said. "Back on plan." He corrected himself. "Plan Bravo." His men didn't need to be told twice, and Poole had to sprint to catch up with them. Running felt good. Running toward the enemy. Not a retreat but an attack. Running toward the gaping hole in the earth where the gazebo had stood. *Goddammit! Six men at a stroke!*

All that remained was a crater. He saw no evidence of bodies, and probably would not, unless he turned on the infrared, heat-sensing feature in his night vision binoculars. Then he might see the warm bodies scattered around the perimeter of the crater. Or perhaps warm spots where blood and body parts had splattered against buildings and trees. That he would not do. Anybody who lived could not help him, and he could not stop to help them. Why put an image of their damaged bodies into his head?

Instead he caught up to Night Runner, who led the rest of the team across the yard. Poole looked into the smoking crater. The charge had not done its intended job; it had not closed the hole. He could see an opening below, three meters down the crater, a dark, jagged hole rimmed with broken chunks of cement and rebar.

Not many things could raise a cold sweat from Poole's body. Not a firefight, not the head games that Tyler had played. Not women, not reptiles, not street gangs, not bugs, not gays, not even gay white people. He was not even afraid of people in mobs dressed in white sheets. He wasn't afraid of motorcycles, helicopters, planes, trains, or automobiles.

Just the one thing. Even the thought of being trapped, barely able to breathe, as the sides of a tunnel collapsed on him, pressing in. Dying a claustrophobia-induced death less merciful than drowning. That was the one thing, the one thing down below his feet right now, that scared him. Hell, he couldn't even take an MRI.

Maybe Night Runner saw it. Or maybe the Indian just didn't like standing out in the open at the focus of the latest flash-bang inside the walls. Such things drew enemy eyes.

Night Runner slid into the funnel of rubble until he got to the hole. He looked inside, ducked back, looked again, then stepped into the opening and dropped out of sight.

Poole shuddered. Was he a coward because he had hoped that Night Runner would find the hole closed? Would he be able to make himself crawl through that narrow space on his belly, maybe have the ceiling collapse? Or would he rather call off the mission? Did he need an excuse to—?

"All clear," Night Runner said. "The blast put out the fires."

Poole went in at once. So he could face his fear like the

Taliban drivers racing into the ambush. So that his men might not see his mind balk, his body blink. He still had that urge to get up and run, though. Scramble out of the hole. Run away. The difference between courage and cowardice only the direction a man runs. The difference—

He felt an arm close around the knees.

"Let yourself down," Night Runner said. The floor is uneven, but you're tall enough to stand."

Poole did as Night Runner said, and found himself standing on a landing in a concrete stairwell, his face hot. Bullets of sweat prickled his face. He looked below and saw two soldiers crouched against the walls. He recoiled, but Night Runner spoke up. "They're sleeping with the virgins."

Poole saw the puddle of ooze on the floor. A second look at the men. Not men, after all. But their final images outlined against the wall where they'd been blown by one concussion or other. They had literally melted down the wall and lay like smoking pools of protoplasm. The men had been the fuel for the fires. Instant cremation in the works, their flesh turned to black jelly, the ash their combat uniforms airbrushed against the wall. And he was worried about a little claustrophobia. Christ.

Below the two dead man, perhaps twenty feet below them, the landing turned to the right. Poole thought he could hear voices, tiny in the distance, coming from below.

"Do you hear?" He asked Night Runner.

"I've heard several men, moving by in groups. Probably a tunnel that comes up in the city."

Intel assumed it. Bin Laden would never allow himself to be trapped inside walls. Like the killer monster gopher bastard he was, he would always keep a safe way out.

Night Runner spoke up. "Maybe we can cut them off. Or tag along, follow them out, drive them out so the team up above can get a bead on them."

Poole saw the hint in Night Runner's posture: *Not safe here, boss.* "Let's go," he said.

"Single file. Me first. I'll make the least amount of noise."

Poole followed the marine down the stairs, amazed at how

the man could walk without seeming to disturb even the dust
in the stairwell. He stepped over rubble and bodies and nego-
tiated tangles of wire hanging from the ceiling, moving
through them as if they did not exist. Poole himself got tan-
gled up in the wires, as if they were a spider's web. The men
behind him knocked chunks of rubble down the stairs. Poole
decided that silence was more important then speed. He
turned back toward his men and patted the air in front of his
face, urging them to take it easy. When he turned back to look
down the stairs, Night Runner had vanished around the corner,
gone without a sound. Getting ahead of them to stay ahead of
their noise.

When they finally did catch up to him, it was because
Night Runner had reached a sprung door and was waiting for
them. The stairwell had swung back upon itself twice, creating a baffle for an explosion's concussion. Still the blast had
knocked a pair of steel double doors askew on their hinges. A
diagonal stripe of yellow light leaked into the space where
Night Runner peeked out. Poole stopped clear of the doorway
with the three other men. There was no need for them to
crowd forward. They could see in their heads-up displays
what Night Runner looked at, what he transmitted to them in
line-of-sight video.

A view left, then right, of an empty hallway lit by emergency spots. A view of the floor, scuffs in the dust.

"Six, maybe seven men, going left to right," Night Runner
said.

Poole tensed for a fight until he saw Night Runner's view
scanning the hallway again. The empty hallway. "No joy on
the enemy?"

"They've already passed by. Maybe a minute ago."

"How do you—?"

"Footsteps. The blast put down a layer of dust before the
men walked by," Night Runner murmured.

But how could he tell the age of footsteps in dust? Poole
told himself to stop wondering how the man knew such
things. He told himself to trust the Blackfeet warrior. "Let's
go in," he ordered. "Night Runner, take out the lights first,

then follow the tracks." Everybody else knew their jobs from the chalk talks below deck of the carrier off Afghanistan. Poole would follow Night Runner once he took the point. That way he could stay close to the front, keep up with the action as it developed, deploying his four other men. Make that three. He had forgotten. No Ballard. They had left the man sitting in a pile of rubble, his legs nearly pinched off below the knees. He'd forgotten about Ballard. Is that what Tyler and his series of God-awful tests had proved about himself? That he could forget leaving one of his men, practically a double amputee, sitting exposed to danger?

Ballard sweated like a racehorse. His heart beat like a racehorse's too, in the homestretch, trying to hammer its way out of his chest. It wasn't so much the pain. At least not in the legs. He could barely feel the legs, except as a pressure below the knees. When he tried to lean forward to look at the damage, to see if he might find a way to slip free, he did feel a twinge, but in the knees, above the spot where the rubble held his legs. Torn cartilage, probably. Or maybe tendons and ligaments ripped free of the bone. His mind's eye worked like moving X-ray pictures, letting him see beneath the clothing, beneath the skin and through the concrete into the interior of his legs.

The way he saw it, his leg bones had been snapped clean in two, the major veins and arteries pinched shut, the muscles severed like torn rags. Still, it wasn't the pain or lack of pain or even the intellectualizing about the extent of damage to his legs. It was a picture of one of the street people back home in Cleveland, the guy with the perpetually dirty face and black fingernails, not just underneath the tips but all over, as if every single fingertip had been smashed by a hammer. Knots in his pants legs where his knees should've been. Sitting on the sidewalk, propped against the building. Scratching his nuts. Holding out those dirty hands with the black fingernails. Begging. As a kid he couldn't stand the sight of the sonofabitch. As an old man he would take the sonofabitch's spot on the walk.

He felt around the concrete and stone edges with his hands, trying to assess to damage by touch. He could get a fingertip into the crack. But only a fingertip. Shit. That pretty much said it all. Bones, arteries, veins, muscle. Everything crushed, just as he pictured it. Nerves, too. That's why he felt more pressure than pain.

Damn. Not even lucky enough to get a clean amputation. That he might have been able to deal with, even a double amputation. Apply a couple tourniquets. Stop the bleeding. Cut the trousers. Wait for somebody to haul him down the pile of rubble and into the helicopter.

They could save his life. If only the legs were off. If he was ready to go when the helicopter got here. That gave him a moment of reflection. Did he want his life saved so he could live it out to the end as a double amputee? He'd have to rag on the question awhile. Be a good way to occupy his mind until the team got back for him. He tried out his face, dirty and unshaven, on the picture of the homeless man, scratching his nuts back in the hood.

Not a pretty picture. But plenty of motivation. Ballard shook his head to erase it.

He dialed up his nerve. Better he not sit here on his useless ass. He could do something. He could act as a rear guard, of course, stay alert to sound the alarm, maybe ambush any raghead trying to approach the tunnel entrance. And he could get ready for extraction. Make it easy for his team to pull him out, save them a couple minutes' work and spare them a lifetime's nightmare.

Reluctantly, he put his mind to work on the central issue, getting his legs free of the concrete pincers.

His knife? He didn't have the stomach for it and knew it. One leg maybe. But by the time the first stump of a leg came free, he might well faint and bleed out. No, he needed something quick. He fumbled in his fanny pack.

He brought out a cord, dark green, almost black, about the thickness of clothesline. He figured one wrap for each leg, below the knee. He debated using two wraps, decided two would be too much, then re-decided. He'd use three. He had figured charges before. For trees, fences, bridge struts, and steel railroad tracks. He'd never considered blowing off legs before. Least of all his own. Two. He'd use two wraps. No, one. One wrap of det-cord, since the bone was already broken.

Unable to decide, he set the cord aside. He could come back to it.

Into the pack again. He found a pair of nylon slip-ties, heavy ones. Like drywall screws and duct tape, the nylon ties, of several lengths and thicknesses, were indispensable to special ops. If a Delta team did not have flex-cuffs, a pair of ties, one on each wrist and hooked like chain links, could serve as expedient handcuffs. A man could even use one to commit suicide. He'd given that idea the once-over more than once before.

Then again, he had his rifle and pistol, which were much quicker. Maybe the det-cord around his own neck. Four wraps.

He laid out a pair of ties. Nothing inventive about how he would use them here. SOP to apply them as tourniquets. One by one he slipped them around his legs, above each knee. He threaded the tips, dried his hands, then yanked each of them as tightly as he could, hopeful that he could cut off the blood flow.

Finally he went with two wraps of det-cord. Tickling beads of sweat jostling down his face, he wound a length twice below each knee twice and cut the cord, leaving ends long enough to tie an elaborate knot between them. Enough for a solid contact between the legs.

Into his pack again, to get a blasting cap. He fit the one-way cap over a loose end of the det-cord. A wire antenna no larger than a piece of fishing line coiled away from the cap. He didn't bother trying to straighten it out. At this distance, there would be no trouble with reception. He packed all the loose ends of the cord and the antenna, including the knot, into the crack between his knees.

He checked his tourniquets. They seemed tight enough.

Of course he needn't worry about bleeding to death. The heat of the blast would cauterize the wound or collapse the blood vessels or both. More likely, the blast would shoot a massive surge of blood pressure up through his veins and arteries, the pressure in both sides of his circulatory system more than enough to stop his heart and blow out half the capillaries in his brain. Moment of dark laughter for the self-induced power stroke.

Night Runner squeezed through the sprung doors. Once in the passage, three quick steps took him down the hall to the lights. He poked the barrel of his M-4 carbine into the bulbs, putting out the light and giving the team the edge in visibility. Beyond either end of the passage, other lights burned, too dimly for the naked eye, but plenty for their NVGs.

Night Runner jogged fifty feet after the footsteps in the dust, to the first bend in the passage "Six, request you hang back until I call for you."

"What up?" Poole said. "Don't like being followed by a herd of rutting rhinos?"

"Roger."

"We'll keep posted on the heads-up vid."

Night Runner was gone without a sound. No rattle of gear, no scuffing of a footstep. He moved swiftly. By his pace count, he was soon below the west compound wall. The passages were a gopher's maze of tunnels like those back on the prairies of Montana. When the badger dug down one tunnel, the gopher would escape a rear door of another.

The light ahead of him grew bright, until he could flip up his night vision goggles and see with the naked eye. Twenty meters away, the passage took another turn, to the right. He poked his rifle around the corner, activating the cordless video night sight. In his television eyepiece, he could see nothing of the enemy. Just the lights, which tended to wash out the image. Another twenty meters, another bend. The lights hung from the center of the ceiling. He didn't want to expose himself for the fifty feet it would take him to get there.

He pulled his 9 mm pistol, checked its silencer, leaned around the corner and drew a bead on the first bulb, hoping that one round would be enough to break the glass and send the titanium needle at the core of the bullet into the wiring, shorting it out. He drew breath to speak a word of warning to his team. So neither the pistol's muffled blast nor the sound of broken glass hitting the floor would surprise them. His world went to freeze-frame. At the slightest of sounds.

A distant soft scuff of bare feet on concrete.

Then more footsteps. Sandals flip-flopping. In the hall. Ahead of him. He heard the creak of a hinge. And the sound of distant gunfire. An opened door letting in battle noise from above. He smiled. The team outside had ambushed their quarry trying to leave the passage. Likely the very people he now tracked in the dust. And now one element of Al Qaeda fighters was retreating back inside. Toward him. He smiled.

The opened door let in the racket from outside, the rattling sound from the firefight again. Then the sound was cut off— the door closing—and he heard footsteps in the tunnel. Night Runner pulled the pistol back and holstered it.

"Four?" Poole wanted to know about the noise in his own headset.

"Bad guys," Night Runner said. "Bring it forward. On the double."

No need for silence now. They would need all the firepower they could muster once their enemy started back toward them. But they had an advantage now. Men retreating over ground they'd just covered would feel safe.

Night Runner detached the camcorder sight from his rifle and held the tip of it like a periscope to look around the corner. The video showed the others the hall, too. Five men at once peeking through the same periscope. With such high-tech wonders, the war should be over by morning—or at least that's what the government PR staff would like the American people to believe. And what the media expected. It couldn't happen, though. Not when a crude stack of low-tech dynamite could kill so many good men, and leave another a cripple.

The footsteps grew closer, both from behind Night Runner and ahead of him. He lay on the floor, his rifle set to automatic by his side, careful not to let its muzzle stick around the corner and betray his ambush.

He'd wait until they were midway down the hallway. Too far to attack into the gunfire, too far too run back to safety. Three to five men. Voices. He could hear voices now.

And he could feel one of his own men, kneeling at his hip. He would be the second man in the fight. A third man was positioning his feet so that he could stand and shoot around a corner. Night Runner could hear the breathing, smell the sweat, feel the shifting of knees and feet against his body, the sole of a Delta operator's boot pinching the skin of one elbow against the concrete floor. He recognized Foucault by his aftershave, Barret by his garlic-laced pepper smell, and Poole by his body musk. Michelotti, a bouquet of oregano and basil on his every breath, would have stayed behind, watching the last blind corner behind them, protecting their six. White men didn't like to be told he could ID them by their smells, so he never mentioned it to them. Yet, because of the odors, he knew without looking where they'd taken up positions. He knew what weapons were here with him. Foucault and Poole with their MP5 9 mm submachine guns. Michelotti with his M4.

With his left hand, Night Runner held the periscope sight and dared to wrap his fingers around the corner of the wall, ready to launch himself into the open. His right hand gripped his rifle. One finger probed the selector switch to confirm he had rotated it from safety, past semiautomatic fire, to fully automatic. A thirty-round clip was in the gun. He reminded himself that he had opened the bolt half an hour ago. He had seen the brass shoulder of the round as he pulled back the charging handle. He had pulled it back far enough to see the copper jacket of the slug. He was ready for his enemy. As long as—

Three men, armed with AK-47s stepped into view. They spread themselves across the hallway, as if standing guard. Getting ready to charge the position? *Damn!* Could they have seen him? *No.* No way.

No. Between their legs and behind them, Night Runner saw other legs moving. Two other men. Not dressed in uniform like the first three. They slipped past the guard force laterally, as if walking into the wall.

Into the wall? No. To the left of the tiny frame of his video

screen, he saw a door open. *Dammit!* A door that he could not
see until they opened it. They weren't coming toward the team,
after all, not walking into their hasty ambush. They were going
to escape down a second hallway, a second gopher's escape
route. *Damn!*

Night Runner let the video periscope slip from his fingers.
He hauled against the corner. Sliding his body into the open.
Swinging his rifle around with his right hand. Pressing the trig-
ger at floor level even before he brought it to bear. The floors
and walls would funnel his 5.56 mm bullets toward the target.
Even if the slugs spanged off the walls more than twice.

It was no act of panic, no blind blast of unaimed fire. He
knew how men reacted to gunfire. They would cringe, kneel,
flatten themselves on the ground. Right into the line of fire. Or
they would run. They would recoil from the chatter of gunfire,
as if the noise itself was deadly. They would flinch from the
sparkle of muzzle blasts. Their eyes would not believe the images they saw. Men shooting at them from within their own
sanctuary? Impossible. Then on second glance, they would see
an enemy soldier trying to kill them and flinch again at the audacity of it. Only then, after losing half a dozen precious seconds, would they return fire, focusing on their attacker lying in
the hallway. At first they would not see that two other fighters
had stuck their guns around the corner and began shooting as
well. A second moment of panic would put them to flight, unless they were as disciplined as Force Recon marines—or
Delta Force operators.

Even before Poole and Barret had cranked off the first
round, Night Runner had hit four of the Al Qaeda men. Two of
the sentinels in the legs, and a third man behind them, in the
ankle. A fourth man cried out from farther behind them before
he disappeared behind the door.

Before any of the Al Qaeda could bring their weapons to
bear, Poole and Barret had fired killing shots. Overkill, really,
and Night Runner redirected his unending stream of fire into
the open door, shooting through it, hoping to catch somebody
there who had paused, somebody who turned to fight, somebody who held the door for his companions, although that did

not seem likely. Panic was panic, and, beyond getting shot, the only thing able to rush more adrenaline into the Al Qaeda terrorists was getting shot at and missed.

The ambush lasted less than five seconds. Except for one short blast into the ceiling, the Al Qaeda shooters never put up a defense.

Rising to one knee in the center of the hallway, Night Runner ejected his magazine and swapped ends, inserting another thirty rounds. He saw two rounds left on the empty side, confirming his gun was hot, a round still in the chamber.

"Stay put behind cover," he said, making it an order. No time to debate rank now. It wouldn't do for all of them to be in the hall if an Al Qaeda opened up now.

He ran with his weight forward, up on the balls of his feet, ready to dive either way, keeping his footsteps silent. He leapt over the bodies of the dead. He picked dry spots for his feet, so he would not slip in blood.

He stopped at the end, stuck his back to the wall, and glanced down both hallways. To the right, nothing.

The left, a body, dressed in robes, lay in the doorway, propping it open. He saw footsteps in the post-bombing dust. Three, maybe four, Al Qaeda terrorists had escaped that way. Night Runner hopscotched from dry spot to dry spot until he could throw his back to the wall near the dead man acting as a doorstop. He called the others forward and studied the dust closely. Droplets of blood. One of the escapees was hit.

The team closed up and took positions back-to-back so they could watch down all three halls.

"Ideas?" Poole said.

Night Runner tossed his chin at the body lying across the threshold at his feet. The dead man was dressed not in a military uniform but in flowing robes bunched up over his face. "Not a fighter. Maybe Al Qaeda leadership. Two of the others were dressed like this."

Poole did a take. "Let's get a look at his face."

Night Runner knelt and pulled back the shroud of the man's own scarf. Not bin Laden, but a familiar face he'd seen in the pre-mission brief. "Leadership."

"Dead or alive?"

Runner felt at the jugular. "Dead."

Poole pointed his rifle at the man's head. He recorded a few seconds worth of digital video for later. If he had time, he would transmit it when they got back up top and in a direct line from his digital gunsight camera to the satellites overhead. "Roger. I remember the face. Definitely leadership. Right up there with bin Laden." He pointed his rifle toward the passage the other men had taken. "Let's go get-um."

Night Runner jumped into the opening, then back out. He slammed into Poole and ran by him.

"What the hell?"

"Let's go," Night Runner shouted into his radio but loud enough without it. "Everybody. Michelotti, forget the six and come on."

"What the hell?" Poole called again to Night Runner's back.

"Booby trapped. Let's go, let's go. On the double. Michelotti, catch up." Night Runner made it to the landing and jerked the door opened. He cleared it quickly, ready to sweep it with gunfire.

He saw nothing in the stairwell. But in his mind's eye was the blast at the gazebo, fresh as fear. *"Lessgo-lessgo-lessgo,"* he shouted to the team.

Ballard lay on his back, debating. Suicide. Well, not exactly. Hell, if he wanted to do that, he would take four—make that five—wraps around his neck. Nah. This was just combat surgery. A field expedient. To save a life, not take it. Quick and clean. He'd never stay conscious long enough to saw through both legs with a battle knife. And even if he did, he'd have to find the broken ends of bones. Not practical. Nah, this was the way to go. And if he did kill himself? What the hell.

The detonator in his hands, his life in his hands, his legs in his hands, his career out of anybody's hands. His wounds took care of that. But once he set off this charge, he was a soldier no more, all doubt gone for good. Maybe he could get a medical discharge, get retrained for a second career. As a surgeon. Doctor Det-Cord.

Wel-l-l-l, time to give it a go. He put thumbs to the buttons. He lay back to get his head and chest clear. A waste of effort, that. He would have mashed the buttons, too. But for a cry.

All that kept him from setting off the det-cord wrapped around his legs was a feeble call from the gazebo. Rather from the hole that was once the gazebo. A man from Team Two, the crew that had run face-first into the booby trap. Calling for help.

If the poor guy only knew. The only other guy on earth to hear his cry was a poor pathetic sonofabitch about to blow off his own legs.

Poole herded the team after Night Runner. They ran. God, how they ran. To the open door.

Night Runner spoke into each ear. "It's rigged. Like the gazebo."

The gazebo. All the men needed to hear. They had seen their pals vaporized. Poole made the first landing. He could not see Night Runner. Only the flit of a shadow on a wall above.

Poole heard the slam of a panic bar. Then urgent steps. He and the men tried to catch up.

Three flights up, their lungs burned. The fight close. Very loud. Shots. The angry song of slugs hitting off walls.

Night Runner. Again. Again he held a door for them. He pumped his fist in the air. Double-time.

"C'mon, c'mon, c'mon." he called. Urgent. *Gazebo.*

"Haul ass," Poole said.

The men didn't need the call. Or the sign. Let alone Poole's emphasis.

One word, *Gazebo*, was all they needed.

He led them into a hall. They stood in the dark, guns at the ready. A bank of windows.

"One sec," Night Runner said. "We need to go up half a flight."

Poole could see out, his eyes at ground level. Across the street to the west was the compound. The muzzle blasts sharp from just above them. He looked into Night Runner's eyes.

"Why circle up here?"

Night Runner shook his head. "We can't bust out. Our own guys. They might open up on us. And we can't wait in the stairwell. We need a sec here. To shut down our guys."

"Roger, Roger. I'll take care of that," Poole said. He spoke into his mike: "Task force Bravo, cease-fire. We be in the line of fire. Right at the six of the bad guys. Shutter down. We'll take-um down. Gimme a wilco on that."

The team waited for Knapp to cut off the Delta fire. Michelotti rocked from one foot to the other. Barret bit his lip. Poole waited. The worst thing for a Delta man to do—wait.

They'd have a go at the bad guys. They had an edge. The Al Qaeda would not expect it. Up the steps. Take them fast. From the rear. Not much of a planc. The booby trap. Damn it—

Night Runner's hand shot up. The marine put a finger to his lips. The men dared not breathe.

Night Runner waved them away from the door. He cupped one ear, then held up two fingers, then three. *Three men on the stairs?* Poole didn't hear a thing.

Night Runner slung his rifle. Pulled his pistol. Spun its qwik-fit silencer on. "Keep it quiet," he said into his mike. "Three men in the hall above. Knives or silencers only."

Barret pulled a bayonet as long as a short sword. He fixed it to the end of his rifle. Poole pulled his pistol, too, though he'd still not heard a sound. Not even a shot—

"Six, we're shut down." Knapp said into his ear. *Shitsakes, that was it!* The Al Qaeda had shut it down, too. He hadn't even heard the silence.

Night Runner yanked the door and flew up the stairs. Poole and Barret went next.

Night Runner waited at the top, his back against the wall. "Here they come."

They hit the wall beside Night Runner.

As the door burst open.

Two men ran on to the landing. One a soldier. A spot at the center of his shirt poked outward, like a tent. Then came the point of Barret's bayonet. Then a patch of blood. Barret lifted the man off his feet and pitched him down the stairs like a fork full of hay.

Poole took the second man, dressed in a gray cloak. He
grabbed his arm. Jammed the pistol into the base of his skull.
Let loose a round. The sound of a spit. The slug went up, away
from his own men, into the man's neck. Into his brain and out
his face above one eye. A jet of blood, stood up, fell back, and
lay over his own face.

"Shit!"

"Quiet." Night Runner hissed it. He held up one finger.
Night Runner jerked the door. A man's hand on the handle. He
let go. Too slow. Night Runner's hand struck like a snake. Into
the hall. It came back with a man's beard. He shoved his pistol
into a face. The silencer broke into the mouth. Night Runner
threw the man to the floor but did not shoot. Poole knew why.
His own bullet, if not fired up, might have hit one of the team.

Barret held the door open. Michelotti dived through, hit the
floor, rolled and came up on one knee, ready to shoot. Foucault slid past Night Runner to help.

"Get out of here," Night Runner said.

Still Night Runner had not shot his man.

Poole ducked into the hall. Still no spit-sound. What the
hell? The bomb. Get out of the—

He saw. The man that Night Runner was about to kill, the
man he held by his beard. It could not be.

But it was.

Osama bin Laden!

They had just taken the scourge of 9-11? Bin Laden?

Night Runner looked up into Poole's face. Asking for the
sign? Thumbs-up? Or thumbs-down? The marine didn't act as
if he cared about taking bin Laden alive. And bin Laden's eyes
were full of fear.

Poole didn't know enough to care. He had dreamed wild
dreams in his life, dreams about heroic combat. He had fought
off legions of enemy soldiers, usually rabid Arabs. But never,
not in his wildest dream, did he ever see Osama bin Laden
alive. In his hands. Never. Not even a fantasy.

"Bin Laden?" he said.

The Delta men could not hold it in. Each had his own curse
word for the name.

"Gazebo." Night Runner dragged the man into the hall and let the door go shut. "We have to get clear. This is still too close."

Poole was stuck on the one idea. *This? This was Osama bin Laden? The object of his hate? Taken? Bin Laden, for shit-sakes! Alive?*

Curses even came from Knapp's task force outside. *Bin Laden? You all got bin Laden?*

Nobody could believe it.

Least of all Night Runner. "It's not him." He pulled the pistol out of the man's mouth and ripped tufts off the beard. "Fake." The man cried out.

"But he yelled," Poole said. "When you pulled his beard."

"Good glue."

"It's not bin Laden?" *Say yes.*

"No. Too young." He pulled three more huge tufts of hair from the face. "Fake, fake, fake. This kid can't grow his own beard. He's a . . ."

Poole said the word first: "Double." He spat. "A fucking double."

Poole's heart began to beat again. But slowly. Bin Laden's body double. Maybe one of a dozen the CIA said he had.

"Kill him?" Night Runner asked.

Poole did not know. "I don't know."

"No time to think, boss." Night Runner cocked his head. *Gazebo.*

"Right." Poole tossed a set of nylon flex-cuffs to Night Runner. "Wrap him up. We'll take him with us. Maybe get some intel out of him." He could not hide the despair in his voice. Six men lost, five KIA and Ballard a combat loss. Nothing to show for it but a fake beard. They'd not done a thing over and above a simple bomb strike, which they could have done as well from a million miles away.

Poole called for the three extraction birds as they headed for the wall, back into the compound. Then remembered Team Two? There was no Team Two. He called off the third bird.

Leave no man behind, dead or alive. That was the romantic

notion of modern war. Hollywood loved it. Generals spouted it. Politicians glorified it. It didn't make a lot of sense. Risk live Delta Force men to pull out corpses? Pure bullshit.

A wounded man, okay. They did have to go back for Ballard. The others were dead. What else.

Their families would learn that they were lost at sea. Or in an air crash that consumed their bodies. Except for perhaps ashes or body parts positively identified in DNA reports, clearing the remains for cremation. Every Delta man gave DNA samples, blood, stool, urine, spit, nails, hair before his first operational mission. Delta stored the D-Packs so DNA tests could prove the bodies came back. Families would mourn over the burial or scattering of ashes of human remains. Bodies of men with no family to claim them. Anybody family that demanded a DNA test would get the real deal, proof to a certainty.

Poole tried not to visualize the Arabs pouring out of their hole in a neighborhood to the east. He tried not to imagine the last man out hitting a secret control panel and turning a timer switch to start the demo sequence.

His personal chaos matched the chaos in the streets, Arabs pouring out of homes. They knew to get away before a second round of airstrikes. They clogged the streets, keeping away any Taliban military reaction forces. As a good chaos should, this one had no direction. Rather, every direction, as people tried to get clear of the compound. Hell, what reaction force would want to try, after what Poole and his team had done earlier.

Poole scaled the wall and saw the figure of Simon Ballard. At first he thought it a good thing that Ballard was still alive, that he had not passed out in shock, that he sat upright, waiting for the group.

On second glance, he did not feel quite so sanguine. Ballard waved them away. Telling them to leave him behind?

No way.

"What's up, Simon?" He said into the mike. Thinking: *How in hell would they get a man's legs free of rubble? It would take a crane. Or a bulldozer. Probably both. Or worse. A double amputation.*

"Simon?"

"Stay away from me," Ballard said. He lay back as far as he could. "And get down."

Poole crouched. He zoomed in with his NVGs. What he saw he did not believe. The cord wraps. The detonator in Ballard's hands. Poole opened his mouth to call out, but not in time.

The blast lifted Ballard off the ground. It slung him into a backflip. Ballard knew he'd left parts of him behind. Head over heels, but without the heels. His last thought: *Too much det-cord, dammit. Should have left it at one wrap.*

Poole felt both explosions, the smaller one in his face and the larger one at his back. At first he didn't understand. Had the Al Qaeda planted charges in the wall beneath Ballard, too? No, the blast came from behind him. The escape tunnel going up. He looked over his shoulder at the building they had just left. In time to see all its windows and doors blown out by the flaming torch from inside. A flash caught his eye. Deeper into the city, about ten blocks away, another building erupted in a flash fire, windows blowing out, flames shooting out, air rushing back, the building collapsing in upon itself. The far opening to the escape tunnel. That's where Osama bin Laden had come up.

For one brief moment, Poole thought he might gather his team and go looking for the bastard. They still had a fighting force.

No, that would not do. He had to get his men away from the city under cover of the chaos. He had to get out before the Taliban got organized. He had the Blackhawks on the way already. As he thought it, he heard the radio call.

"ETA three-zero seconds," the lead pilot reported.

Poole found Ballard without his legs, the stumps tied off with nylon ties. He understood. The man had blown off his own legs so he would not hold up the escape. Amazing. What balls. Talk about heroes.

He ordered his team to load Ballard onto the floor of the Blackhawk. "Take care of him," he hollered to the onboard medic, a surgeon. He'd see to it that Ballard got the Medal of Honor in secret. Blowing off his own legs. That was heroism, right? Or was it just fear? Panic? Cowardice? He gave it a wry smile. It would be what he said it was in the citation. He would call it courage. Above and beyond the most far-flung boundary of the call of duty. One day a guy loses his head and kills another soldier in training—two-taps him in the head. Next day he blows off his own legs and goes up for a medal. War, man. It wasn't hell—it was fuckin' crazy.

The team picked up another man so badly burned that Poole could not identify him. A torso without arms and legs. Or clothes or hair. Or ears or nose. He let the men throw the remains onto the deck of the helicopter, although he did not want the body—what was left of it—to be there with the living. He refused his men's requests to search the area for more corpses. He decided. No more survivors. The rest dead. On his say-so.

He would not spend any more Delta Force blood this night. They'd created enough terror for one mission. On both sides.

"Un-ass," he ordered his pilots. "Get us the hell out of here." Before they could get caught in the next wave of terror, theirs or the enemy's.

They had cleared the area by no more than five miles, as the Blackhawk flies, when the pounding began behind them. Flashes of light heralded three waves of strikes like pushpins on the night sky.

First, cluster bombs to kill anybody in the open and to leave behind enough duds to create a lasting legacy of fear in the compound.

A second wave of bombs included white phosphorus mixed in with the explosive charge, so-called because it burned white-hot. Everything in the compound would burn, even bricks. Finally another round of cluster bomb units, leaving a full 40 percent of the bomblets as duds.

If any remains of the four and a half Americans were not

incinerated, nobody would go near enough to sort through flesh and bones until the rats and maggots had gorged all but the bright ivory of their bones and teeth.

"Hey, Mr. Taliban-man, you want terrorism?" Spangler had said at the close of his mission briefing to Poole, clutching the OPORDER to his crotch. "Terrorize this."

Poole looked at Ballard lying leg-less and unconscious and probably brain-dead on the floor of the helicopter. And the hunk of charred, dead flesh beside him, a man just an hour ago. Now just a DNA sample. No, General, terrorize that.

The Blackhawk helicopters twice refueled in-flight and landed on the carrier *Enterprise* in the predawn hours. It wasn't any easier keeping secrets aboard a small town at sea than it was keeping secrets in any other town of five thousand across America.

Still, the navy, practiced in handling its own SEAL force launches and recoveries, tried its best to accommodate the Delta mission. Elevators lowered the helicopters with crews below decks within minutes after the turbine engines cooled. Nobody could approach the craft. Nobody left the cordon thrown up around the Delta area. None of the Delta teams or their support force mingled with the crew. Fully a third of one hanger deck below was roped off. Army ground-handling crews hitched to the Blackhawks with tow bars and hauled them across the lower deck to a screened-off area. There, maintenance crews went to work preparing the five aircraft for their next mission. Two spare Blackhawks were also aboard, waiting. One for rescue, one a spare combat craft. All crews, maintenance, medical, signal, weapons, a mess, and other general support came aboard with the Delta fighters. Delta security teams kept watch at the curtains, and Marine Corps security forces from the carrier kept an outer perimeter, beyond earshot of what went on behind those curtains.

Poole stepped off his Blackhawk, feeling twice the usual gravity working on his body. Nothing could make him proud

of this mission. A few good men killed. One disabled for life.
Nothing to show for it but a handful of dead ragheads and one
teen prisoner, a damned kid. While the real bin Laden got away.

So it blew him away that Brigadier General Roscoe Spangler met him on a flight deck, his hand extended, his smile
wide. He snapped off a salute and took the hand because it
was there. Spangler was the last man he wanted to see. Now,
not only would he have to live with the disaster of the night,
he would have to relive it in debrief.

"Congratulations, Edgar, great job."

"General? I thought you were talking to me from the
Pentagon."

"Nope, I've been here all night. I watched the whole
thing—well, as much as we could see on SATCAM and the
drones. Good stuff, though, damned good."

Spangler turned his body to a stiff, sallow man at his right
shoulder. "Meet agent Brian Carnes, CIA."

Carnes's eyes flicked from Poole to Spangler to Poole.
Poole smiled at the man's unease. He didn't like the CIA part
of the intro. Funny.

Poole's smile evaporated. The night's disaster. These two
had seen it and more. By tomorrow, half the DoD—hell, the
whole administration. He'd never get work in Delta Force again.

"Nice job, LT."

Poole studied the CIA man's face. He was serious.

"How was it a nice job?" Poole said. "It cost me a helluva—"

"Not here," Spangler said, looking over both shoulders.
"As they say in the navy, the bulkheads have ears."

Inside a secure briefing tent set up on the deck, Poole took
off his gear, rechecking his weapon to make sure the chamber
was clear, the safety on. A nervous reaction. He didn't trust
Spangler and that amphibian smile of his. Nobody trusted the
CIA, of course, not even its own agents. Against a ridiculous
impulse that he might need a live round for suicide, he cleared
the chamber of his pistol.

"Let's have it," Spangler said to Poole. "Roll tape," he said
to a tech at the DVD player behind them.

As the images began to run, Poole filled in the blanks, the dead spaces in the mission that high spies could not see.

Spangler had not lied about being pleased, after all. And Carnes was not the prick that Poole had expected.

"A perfect mission," Spangler said after the follow-up questions had begun to repeat.

A perfect mission? Six combat losses out of seventeen? Five KIA? That was a perfect mission?

Spangler read the questions in his face. "And costly, yes. I didn't say it wasn't costly." He leaned across a field table, staring bullets into Poole's face, his hands clutching each other as if saying a prayer of thanks. Poole wanted to back away from the man. He was scary up close, freshly burned, with rumpled old scars beneath the new pink ones, his wide, watery eyes blinking behind those thick lenses. Caliban, one of Shakespeare's monsters came to mind.

"Perfect terrorism," Spangler said. "We paid a price, yes. But we hit Al Qaeda where they live. We hit their money. We destroyed a ton of their cash, maybe two tons. If we can do the same thing in Kabul—" He shook his head. "Well forget Kabul for the moment. You hit the Taliban. And Al Qaeda. And not just with bombs. A ground strike. You showed them we're not afraid of going into the center of their cities to ambush them. You took out one of the main safe houses of Osama bin Laden—hit him where he lives, literally—showed him it wasn't safe in the city." Spangler tapped himself on the side of his head above his heavy spectacle frames. Hard. "Think. Think what that does to a man like bin Laden. Hell, for all we know, you might have just missed killing the sonofabitch, maybe even put a stray slug into his bony terrorist ass. He's gonna have to go to ground."

Poole started to speak out, to say that he did not mean to imply that they had actually seen real evidence of bin Laden.

Carnes spoke up before Poole could utter a syllable. "Won't be long, and we'll know whether bin Laden was there. You brought me back a prisoner. An insider." Carnes licked his lips, actually licked his lips, and Poole felt a chill start at the base of his skull and run down his back. "I'm going to

visit with him. He's going to tell me whether bin Laden was
there." Carnes looked at his watch, a huge dial that kept time
in four parts of the world.

Poole gave him a weak smile. Not so much because he
knew the prisoner was in for a long night. Who the hell would
care what time it was in three other parts of the world?

"We have plans for Mr. I-wannabe-Osama-bin-Laden,"
Carnes said.

Poole didn't doubt it. Geneva conventions? Rules of war?
Civility? Ethics? After September 11—What was it? Just days
ago?—war wasn't merely hell anymore. War was terrorism by
another name. The hell he'd been through tonight? Leaving
the bodies of his men behind? That'd be nothing to what was
about to happen to the bin Laden lookalike. Poole didn't want
to watch, didn't even want to know what that guy'd be going
through. Screw Mr. Wannabe. Poole had his own hell to deal
with.

"And we're going after the king rat," Spangler said. He
pursed his lips. It tasted good. "That's what we'll call it. Operation King Rat."

Screw Osama, too, and the mule he rode in on. He didn't
even care about King Rat. The one thing Tyler hadn't trained
him for. The death of his own men. He cared about that.

Baker's Mother came to him in the morning with a bag of
powder, this one perhaps a full five pounds.

"Another antiseptic?" he asked.

She smiled at him, a little fire banked behind her eyes,
brighter then ever before. Without a word, she began changing
the dressing on his wound. He lay back, turning his head toward the wall so he would not have to see that stump again.
Bad enough that he had to look at a seeping bandage.

He turned back to look once, as she poured water into the
plastic bag and began making a mush of it. And again as she
turned down the top of the plastic bag. She took his arm and
made him relax, letting it drape over the side of his cot. She

raised the bag of cool mush until the arm was suspended in it. She held it in place. A poultice of some kind, he decided. It did feel good, too, the chill.

Brooding, he fell asleep, his face to the wall.

A bit later, how long he did not know, he came awake at a fresh, sharp, stabbing pain at the end of his stump.

She patted his forehead with a cool cloth.

"It hurts today," he said as she put on a fresh dressing.

"Rest," she said. "I will be back this evening."

She lived up to her promise, bringing back vegetables and a sinewy strip of fresh meat from the market. And in one bag, a package wrapped in brown paper. He was curious, but held his tongue. She saw him looking and read his face, but did not offer to explain, holding him off with that inscrutable smile of the Mona Lisa.

After a dinner of *mantu* rolls served in a spiced tomato sauce, the meat cooked tender and exotic, she began to remove his dressing.

He raised his eyebrows at her. "You changed it only this afternoon."

She smiled. "I want to try something," she said, and rubbed his wound with scented unguents.

She dried her hands and produced the mystery package, unwrapping it for him. In it was a prosthesis. A forearm, with a rigging and harness, and two steel hooklike appendages that opened and closed like a set of pliers.

She helped him into the rigging, considerate not to notice the tears welling in Baker's eyes.

"It fits," he said. "Perfectly."

"Of course," she said. "I made a perfect molding for it."

"Plaster of Paris."

"Plaster," she said, looking into his eyes. "From Khost. What is it to do with Paris?"

"Nothing," he said. "I thought it was medicine, an antiseptic, a poultice. But no. It was a plaster mold?"

She gave him a quizzical half smile. "Yes, a molding." She took a deep breath.

Don't ask, he pleaded with his eyes.

She didn't. She went to the cupboard. She brought back a platter. On it was a bowl turned upside down.

He shrugged. "I'm not hungry?" A question as much as a statement.

"What do you see?" she asked.

"A bowl and a platter?"

"And what is under the bowl?"

"Dessert?"

She lifted it.

"Another, smaller bowl?" he said. Again upside down.

"And what is under this bowl?"

He wasn't so sure. "The platter?"

She lifted it, and he jerked away in shock. As a rat scurried off the platter. He yelped, in English. Not a curse word but something worse. Just a name. *"Jesus Christ!"* He went to the Pashto the instant the word escaped his mouth. "Mother, pray God."

"God is not in need of our prayers, my son."

"But a rat?"

She didn't go for the change in subject. "Where are you from, my son? Truly?"

He gasped. Shook his head. Fell into his role of amnesiac. "I wish I could remember." And he wished he didn't.

He studied her face. Trying to decide whether he should kill her now, get it over with. She gazed into his face. *Go ahead.*

And he knew he couldn't.

Spangler called Poole for a short meeting. "You need to get your team some rest. We're working the intel from every angle, looking for a hot trail on bin Laden. You'll be the first to know when we get something out of the bin Laden double. I want you to know that replacements are already in the pipeline. A fresh crew from Tonopah." He shook his head. "Soldiers. They're calling it Area 52. A dozen more men are on the way. We're going to work in two teams as soon as we can."

Poole felt his face go slack.

Spangler answered his concern at once. "Don't worry, Edgar. We're not replacing you. You earned your chops your first night out. You'll keep your crew. At times you'll work with the other team in combined ops; other times you'll conduct separate missions." Spangler cleared his throat. "I'll have a good officer leading the backup squad."

Poole's eyebrows gave away his question.

"Tyler," Spangler said. "Now you go on and get a nap or something. You don't want to be around when Carnes goes to work on that kid you snatched."

"You might as well kill me," the young Osama wannabe said in Arabic. "I won't tell you anything."

Carnes smiled. The same light and gentle smile the Jesuits used to give him before they gave him a blow to the kidneys. He had urinated blood many a time in the aftermath of one of those smiles. He'd lived on both sides of the smile. He just smiled and smiled, the smiling villain.

It unnerved the kid. Tears began to flow. The kid slapped at his eyes. "Kill me."

"I won't kill you," he said. "Until you talk." Carnes could keep the smile going for half an hour, if need be. The kid seemed surprised. No wonder. Carnes spoke without an accent. Rather, with the same regional accent the kid spoke.

"I'll die first." Weakly. Already his resolve had thinned.

"Of course you will die." He put a sympathetic accent on his smile and a note of pity into his voice. "First you'll talk to me, then you will die. The only control you have is to decide in advance how much pain you wish to suffer."

The kid dry-swallowed.

"We have drugs. Very painless drugs. You will tell me the answer to every question. You will describe every time you fiddled with yourself in bed after dark."

The kid began to blink.

"You will tell me every time you mated with a dog or a mule," Carnes watched as it sank in, the disbelief, the confes-

sion in the eyes. "Every time you took a man's sex organs into
your mouth—or other places." A quick shake of the head.
Okay, so the kid had fiddled with animals, but not men. Too
bad. Carnes would love to have it in his confession that bin
Laden had queered him. Maybe, after a little prep time he
could plant the image. So realistic. Soon a reality in the kid's
head. Tape it. *Play that, Al Jazeera.*

Carnes picked the video camera up from the table and
turned the open LED screen toward the kid. So he could see
himself in the viewfinder. And went with the impulse of a moment ago.

"And when you tell me these things, with no marks of torture on your body, I'm going to send a copy of the tape to Al
Jazeera. So your mother will know. So Osama will know." He
opened a file folder and showed the kid a photo of a packed
feed lot in Oklahoma. "Then I will kill you." He tapped his
finger on the photograph, wall-to-wall pigs awaiting slaughter.
"Rather, they will kill you. They will kill you; they will eat
you; they will shit you; and they will trample their shit into the
ground. You're going to end up as pig shit. If I remember my
Islam correctly that would be the lowest thing on earth. Allah
won't even look at you. He won't even piss on your shit-dust."

The kid's full lower lip trembled.

"It's a simple thing," Carnes said. "The drugs get you to
talk. You tell all, including your sex with animals. Then we
photograph your body to prove that we did not use torture, and
we ask you on camera whether we used torture or drugs."
Carnes shrugged. "You tell the entire Arab world, including
Osama, that we never laid a hand on you. Then we turn off the
camera. Then we allow the drugs to wear off. Then we hurt
you." He tapped the photo. "Then we feed you to the pigs."

The kid's eyes flowed now. He would not look up into the
camera. "What do you want to know?"

"That's better. What is your name?"

"Aziz."

"Now, was that so hard?" Amazing what a little shame
could do.

As it turned out, the kid didn't know all that much. He

could only account for being within bin Laden's inner circle for a few days, once on 9-11, once this week, when bin Laden's people had Aziz made up to look like bin Laden and to audition for bin Laden.

The kid wasn't even a radical. Just a victim of his own accident of birth, the accident that he looked somewhat like the terrorist prince. The fake beard and a few touches of makeup sharpened the likeness. He was tall enough. But he was far too young and could not withstand close scrutiny. This kid was just a rookie. Still, he gave Carnes something to go on.

Bin Laden had gone to stay at the compound last night. For only the first time in six months. Even so, he would not leave the bunker below ground to visit his family in the residence. After news of the American attacks inside the city, bin Laden and his entourage went to the deepest part of the complex. He tried to leave right after the airstrike, grabbing up Aziz, who had swelled with pride that he could serve his prince.

"They led me in the tunnels," Aziz said. "In that itchy beard and makeup thick as mud, with one of his bodyguards at each shoulder. The Americans, they tried to kill me. Instead they killed the two bodyguards. Allah spared my life."

"Allah, maybe," Carnes said, "but sure as hell not Osama. He would have let you die."

"I would have gladly died."

"He left you behind to be killed or captured."

"I begged him to save himself, to leave me, even to kill me. If it would save his life, I would happily sacrifice mine, praise Allah."

Carnes let Aziz talk himself out, then invited a pair of medical technicians in. Five minutes after an injection, Carnes and Aziz went over every detail again. The drug was not a truth serum, strictly speaking. More a compliance serum. Once injected, a subject would imprint on another man, his handler, in this case, Carnes. He would do anything to please his handler. Anything. Carnes kept to business all the way through the interview. Then, he put some of the darker sexual details of the kid's young life onto the tape. It wasn't really so dark, more like shady. Still, that didn't matter so much. What mattered was the kid's state of mind tomorrow, after he sobered up. And the day after that. And the next day. And so on. And so on.

Baker had to learn to run all over again, but it didn't take quite as long as before. Because now the arm, properly weighted, gave him back his balance. The first time he went out, he thought he should keep running. Away. So his mother could not betray him to her husband. What was she going to do, for Allah's sake? Choose him over Mansour? Get real.

But he came back. She came to him. To help remove the wooden arm. She put a salve on his wound. Gently. No guile in her. She would not treat him this way if she planned to rat him out. Would she? Was she so full of guile he could not fathom her. He thought he'd test her.

"I need a weapon, a pistol at least, a rifle, if I can get one."

"Why do you need a weapon?"

"To fight, of course. To fight the infidels, the Northern Alliance, and the Americans."

She shook her head. Sadly. A look of, *You do not need to keep up the façade.* "You do not need to fight," she said. "You have proven yourself. You have your badge of honor in the loss of your arm."

He held up the prosthesis. "As far as any stranger knows, I am little more than a thief who got caught and had his left arm cut off in the soccer stadium in Kabul."

"No."

"Yes. If I have a weapon, they will know I am a soldier. And I can fight the people who do these things to us."

She shook her head, tears in her eyes.

"Mother. Please."

Aziz awoke with a throb in his left hand. He sat up, woozy, and nearly fell over. First from the dizziness. Then from the sight of his left hand. His thumb was missing. The hand and arm had swollen to his elbow. He saw that he was in a cage.

He had seen better pens for goats—dear God, goats. Had he talked about the goats?

"Yes, goats. And, yes, you did talk about them." The evil little man named Carnes stood outside the door to his cage. Had he said the word aloud? *Goats?*

"Yes, goats. And figs. Any number of times. About trying to mate with it. About not being able to. About getting kicked in the figs."

He had told about the goat?

"Yes, you told all."

The man was giving him that smile again, that tiny, evil smile.

"I'm not so evil," the man said. "You were the one trying to have sex with animals. What does the Koran say about that?"

Was he speaking his thoughts?

"Yes, you are. Every word. So, speak up. Since you can't stop telling me those thoughts."

Aziz held up his left hand and winced. "You lied. You said you were not going to torture me if I told you the truth."

"You did tell the truth. I'll admit that."

"But, why? Why then did you do this?"

"I did not." The little man held up a finger. He turned on a TV set.

Aziz saw himself sitting at a table, telling the truth, more or less. He would never tell all. He did not admit to having sex with animals, though. Never that.

Two men came into the room. He did remember them. He struggled too little as they gave him an injection. He should have fought them. Next time he would fight hard. Enough to make them kill him.

"They would not have killed you," the little evil man said.

He would have to keep his mouth shut.

"Yes, you will have to keep your mouth shut. So you can see this."

There he was, on the screen, jabbering like a songbird. He told about Osama. In much more detail than before. He left out nothing he knew. Anything he might have left out, the little evil man asked about. And Aziz kept talking, talking like a child, unable to stop himself. First telling the truth, then telling his fantasies, his dreams, his desires.

"That's true," the little man said. "I could hardly shut you up."

Then came a most horrifying moment. With no shame, Aziz told about the nanny goat. He told about trying to hump her. A kick in the gonads to go with a wet spot inside his pants. That kick stopped him from ever trying it again.

The Aziz on the screen told the story again. In great detail. In the cage, his stomach began to cramp. He could not hold his gut. It spilled his slop on the metal floor. Then he began to cry. He had never felt any deeper shame since that day of his greedy assault on the nanny.

A most horrible moment. But not the worst. That came next. A knife came into view on the table. The little evil man said, "Would you like to cut off your thumb in order to repent?"

"No," he said.

"Yes," said the Aziz on the screen.

Aziz watched Aziz saw the thumb from his left hand, at the joint, like a wing from a chicken. He and the other Aziz watched the bleeding, each with a dumb look on his face. He should have bled to death.

"No. We stopped the bleeding." The little Satan froze the screen. "We're not savages, you know."

Aziz looked up at his thumb, then the little Satan and his evil little smile.

"My head," he said. "I feel it now. It hurts." He put a hand to his scalp and felt a scab.

"You tried to stab yourself in the brain," Carnes said.

"I cut my own head?"

Carnes played more pictures.

Aziz began to weep anew. He felt new stabs of pain in his arm and hand and skull, but still not as much as the pain of his shame. Not as much as the regret that he did not take the knife and dive across the table at the little man. Not the regret that he should have spent on himself. He should have cut his own throat.

After they took the kid away, Spangler shook his head at Carnes. "You people are crazy. That's it, plain-and-simple crazy."

"Not so crazy. He's broken. He turned the corner to our side. He's ready to give us bin Laden."

"How?" Spangler squinted behind his thick glasses. "How is he going to lead us to bin Laden when he doesn't even know where the bastard lives?"

"It's a secret, General, but I'm going to let you in on it."

Mother would not speak to Baker for days, cool but not hostile. He used the solitude to restore his resolve. And to get into shape.

One night his heart stopped when she showed three men into her hut, then turned away without a word, but with an epithet pinned behind her thin lips.

A zigzag of a man spoke to Baker. "You want a weapon."

He bunched himself for a fight. The wooden arm lay on the cot a step away. It would crack a skull. He still knew how to fight with his feet. Even if Tyler had taken him on the plane that day this all began.

"Of course," he said. "What patriot doesn't want a weapon?"

"What for?"

"To fight. What else?" Maybe he could baffle them with bullshit.

"Against whom?"

"Against the invaders. Invaders from without, the Americans. Invaders from within, the tribes of the damned Alliance." Baker raised his stump of his left arm. With his right hand he pointed to the prosthesis at the end of his cot. "Do you doubt that I am a fighter in this cause?"

The zigzag man opened his mouth, but the words that came were not his. "Nobody doubts it." All four heads turned toward a gruff voice at the door.

Baker went weak in the knees. Mansour? He just called it the damned Northern Alliance. His last words? He looked around for Mother. She'd slipped out. He was dead.

The hulk of a man filled the room. "We meet again," he said. "You owe me a life. Yours, as it happens." He stepped between Baker and his arm.

"You let that bastard beat me with a whip." He didn't even have his arm now. All he had left was bluff.

Mansour shook his head. "No rose is without thorns." He raised his hands, palms up, in front of his face. "I had to let him. To prove I hate the Al Qaeda."

Baker held up his stump. "And what did you have to prove with this?"

Mansour shook his head. "That proved only the man is an idiot. I had not time enough to stop him."

Baker charged his mouth with obscenities. He held his tongue as Mansour raised a finger to the ceiling.

"Tut," the chieftain said. "A bad wound heals, but a bad word festers. I am sorry that you lost your arm, but pleased that you are alive."

So. A double agent, just as the CIA men said. And yet Baker's sworn enemy had saved his life. The life of yet another double agent.

"Thank you," Baker said, lowering his head. "Thank you for my life."

Mansour laughed. The others, seeing it safe to do so, joined in.

Mansour sobered up. "That stupid, mule-headed Powczuk. We have a saying."

Baker shrugged. *You're full of sayings.*

"A river is not contaminated by having a dog drink from it." Baker shook his head.

"But when a dog pisses in the well . . ." He roared with delight, as if hearing it for the first time. Then grew solemn. "This Powczuk. He is that dog who pisses in my well."

Baker nodded and closed his eyes. When his eyes flashed open again, they were angry. "I need a weapon. And one last favor?"

"You want to meet him again?"

"Yes. My arm for his head."

The giant chieftain shook his head. "No. If I lead you to

him, he will know that I saved your life. He thinks I shot you and had you buried in the wadi."

"He will know, but not for long. I take his memory with his head."

Another guffaw. "Perhaps later I will take you to meet him. But first, I have a good man for you to see."

Baker's heart began to hammer inside his chest. He fought down the impulse to ask who. "I don't want to meet a soul. I want to meet a heart and feel the beat of it in my hand."

Mansour stared. He looked Baker up and down. "You look strong. A bit thin, perhaps, but strong. As to a weapon, I will have to think." Mansour cocked his head. "How can I be sure you won't take out your vengeance on me? As you said, I let him whip you—"

Baker bowed deeper. "I have been ungrateful, sir. I should have thanked you for saving my life and let it to go at that. I will thank you again, if you allow me to return to battle."

"That's more like it." He lifted Baker's face with a finger to the chin. He studied his face. Still not trusting. A quick, fake smile. "I don't even know if I can slap you on the back. I'm afraid I will open another of your many wounds."

Baker laughed. He took the bear's paw and clapped it to his own shoulder. He held it there.

"I am at your service, my chief. You may pat me on the back. Or you may cut off my other arm. As you wish."

Mansour clasped him hard. "You are a good one. Strong of heart. Strong in body—what you have left of it. Let us see what kind of fighter you are. Tomorrow? Are you up to it? Perhaps you will at last shed the blood of somebody besides yourself."

Baker could not suppress a smile. The first genuine smile he had felt in weeks. "A fight?"

"I will arrange it." Mansour tweaked his face into a look of wonder.

"Against whom?"

"I am in a position to attack either side, as I see fit. What an insane world, eh?" He grew serious. "Let us see if your heart is as big as your mouth. Tomorrow."

Mansour produced a bottle. He found two glasses and poured them half full. He gave one to Baker and raised his in a simple toast. "Death is inescapable. Let us have a drink." They downed their drinks.

The fire in his throat left Baker unable to answer the toast.

Mansour swept out of the hut, drafting his men along in his wake. Leaving Baker elated, the warmth of the fiery drink spreading from his esophagus to his core to the rest of his body, dialing up his heart rate. A fight. On even terms? He didn't care who he fought with. Or against. As long as he was as well armed as his enemies. He allowed himself a grin at the pun. For the first time in weeks, he felt a lightness of heart. Only the promise of a fight could cheer him up? What did that mean?

Even as he asked, he knew. He wanted to hurt people, as people had hurt him. Make them feel pain as he had felt it. One man in particular.

"Aziz, we're going to take you back to your country."

"Do you mean it?"

"Indeed, six days is enough talking for you. One gets weary of hearing your fantasies. But I have instructions. You should listen."

"Instructions?"

Aziz could barely believe his ears as the man began to tell him how they were about to release him. That he could go anywhere and do anything. That he should tell anybody who found him and asked him about it that he had fought with the Americans and escaped the compound. Both things were true, the Satan assured him. And Aziz could see that was one way of explaining how he got away, that he did not surrender, that he did not see a need to kill himself, that he fought his way out and escaped that he might fight another day. That he might do something honorable for the prince.

Suddenly Aziz became aware that somebody had asked him a question. A question about the prince.

"Are you listening?"

"Yes . . . no, say that again."

"One thing you must promise. You must promise never to go looking for Osama bin Laden. You must never try to regain contact with him."

"Stay away from the prince?"

"I must have your promise, Aziz."

Aziz did not want to seem too eager to please. "How can I promise such a thing?"

"But you must. Or we will never let you go."

"Then I promise, of course."

"See? Now was that so hard?"

At the darkest hour of the night, midway between the setting of the moon and the rising of the sun, a black helicopter took off from an aircraft carrier in the Indian Ocean and became one with the void.

"Do you think he bought it?" Spangler asked, leaning into the stiff breeze off the bow.

Carnes shrugged. "Who knows?"

Spangler shook his head. "Are you sure you didn't scare him too well? What if he takes you seriously and avoids bin Laden like the anthrax?"

Carnes dragged deeply on a cigarette, showing off a broad smile, teeth glowing red in the light of the coal. "Then the King Rat will find him." He shrugged; smoke leaked from the spaces between his teeth. "The kid was willing to give his life for him."

Spangler shook his head. "Loyalty? You think bin Laden is loyal to somebody like that?"

"Don't be ridiculous. Bin Laden lives and dies by people willing to give their lives for him. He'll snatch up that kid, and keep him close. In case he needs to sacrifice him again someday."

"Ingenious," Spangler said.

"Devilishly."

"If it works."

"It'll work, baby." Carnes caught the hand on the general's shoulder. "And when it does, we will have bin Laden by the rat balls. Maybe we won't be able to drive a 747 up his ass. But we sure as hell can give him a 2,000-pound suppository from 30,000 feet."

Spangler was jealous. Someday maybe, as old men in the Old Soldiers' Home, he might have a talk with Carnes, maybe tell him about the stunt he pulled with General Bowers. That was still pretty damned good, too. But he dared not bring that up. Not yet. Maybe never.

These ruthless times demanded ruthless men, and Spangler was right up there with the best of them. He wasn't about to let some CIA spook out-ruthless him. Besides, by God, the defenders of this country, the real defenders, were the soldiers, the martyrs were soldiers, the brave were soldiers, the fighters were soldiers, the risk takers were soldiers whether they gave their lives on the battlefield or their careers in the court of public policy. By God, he was a soldier, and America was built by soldiers, not spooks. America, when it came time to be saved, would be saved by soldiers. He would see to it. Personally, by God.

Maybe tomorrow. When he went back to D.C. In and out. He had to drop in on his old buddy, his boss Randy. General Bowers. He might survive, the doctors said when he called this morning to ask.

"Wonderful," Spangler had replied to the news, barely able to swallow his vomit.

Week Three: October 2, 2001

Spangler did not feel as weary as he should. He checked his watch. Something like sixteen hours, fuel stops included to get here. He didn't even change the hands to the Eastern time zone. In and out. Catch a plane in an hour. Visit his pal. Do his deed. Bust outta town. Wait for the shit to hit the fan. Pray the death looked natural.

"General?"

"Yes?" *No.* That voice, so familiar. He turned to the woman. A nurse? Major Doctor Bitch. The one who tried to take Baker away from him in those first days of this campaign on terror.

"You," she said. She stood in the doorway, stunned. She looked from his face to his shoulders, starstruck. "You—"

"Yes." He tweaked the down-corner of his mouth. "Me."

"I see." Her face went stony.

If she made a fuss about wanting to stay in the room—

"You can see the patient now. Five minutes."

"Your patient, my friend. Randy Bowers. Old, old friend."

"Of course." She wheeled and left him standing in the wake of her sterile smell.

He caught the door with a foot, wary of touching it with a hand. Then gave a sheepish smile. Afraid to leave his prints? Funny. No prints would look worse than all kinds of prints. She saw him. She knew him. *And why did you not leave a single finger print, General? Don't be an idiot, Roscoe, you dumb somebitch.*

He put his hand on the door and pushed into the room. He dared to breathe now. The bitch didn't even ask about Baker. That's how much she cared. Baker—no way would he tell about that fiasco.

There he lay. Spangler's stomach turned. He remembered the smells. The pain. He, too, had laid in his bed like a piece of bacon once. God, the room even smelled like fried pork.

Randy. Poor Randy. Spangler felt weepy. If Bowers knew, he'd thank him for doing this. For putting him out of his pain.

He stepped to the bed. His knees wobbled.

Funny. All the things going on. He could Plan A a war on terror. And he could Plan B a shift in Plan A. But here he stood. No idea how to do it, this deed—

A hiss from the bed took him back a step.

He saw the open mouth. A mouth that would never shut again. No lips. The hiss had two syllables. *Hossss-coe.* His name, *Roscoe.*

The eyes were hard. The throat hissed. Sharper now.

"I know, Randy, I know. I'm sorry. I had to save the plan. You, I—" How did you tell a man? *I left you for dead. The OPLAN was worth more to the country.*

More hisses. Calling him ten thousand kinds of somebitches.

Spangler grinned. "Christ, man, I know what you're saying. You're going to get even. File a report. Bring up my ass on a general court."

The head dipped once with a hiss. *Yes.* More hisses. *You bet your ass, Hossss-coe.*

"Amazing. I get every word you're saying." Spangler leaned in. "What's that thing bolted to your head, Randy?" A cage with a bottle. Two drips. "I get it. Tears. They have to give you tears because you have no eyelids."

Hisses for two words.

"Such foul language, Randy." He sniffed. "It's time, old pal. I can't risk it that the doctor bitch ever learns to speak your lingo." He snorted to get the smell from his nostrils. "Jeez, Randy, how to do this? I never killed a guy before—oh, sure, I left you in the fire. But to outright *kill*? Not a single guy. Been in a war. Yep. Never killed a soul. Any ideas?"

Can you kill, Roscoe? Can you kill?

A catch of breath. Hissing on the inhale this time.

"I see you got no fingers to write a note. That's good. So no notes yet, either. I hear your wife won't come back to visit. That's not so bad. Time to let her go, Randy. Time to let it all go."

He looked around the edge of the bed at the machines.

Can you kill, Roscoe?

One loud hiss.

"So many plugs, Randy. Which one. Eenie, meenie, meinie, moe, catch a general by the toe—oops, that's right. You got no toes."

He leaned in close. "It's your duty, Randy. Good of the country. Purple heart. Flag folded into a triangle. Taps."

Can you kill?

He dipped his head in sorrow. "I'm sorry, my man. I truly am." He reached out his hand. "Bye, Randy. I love you, man."

The pain in Aziz's head had gone from merely painful to maddeningly itchy. An infection had set in among the stitches, surely. So he gave himself the day to look for somebody who could pull the stitches from his scalp.

He wandered through a bazaar, asking where he might find a doctor. "One who would perform a small task at little cost, for I have little money."

He found plenty of references for doctors, nurses, and healers willing to remove his sutures. But nobody willing to do it for nothing. He refused to scrub urinals, now that he had become so valuable to his prince. He would never scrub urinals again, not unless the prince asked him to. He was too precious now. The Americans had abducted him. They had tortured him. You didn't get any more valuable than that.

Aziz finally decided that looking in the bazaar was the wrong place. By definition, every mercenary in the marketplace wanted money for their goods and services.

So he went to find the nearest mosque. To appeal to one of the clerics for help. In the past, he hadn't found many who were willing to do anything unless you were able to listen to long diatribes about Islam. The itching was terrible. If listening was what he had to do to relieve it, he could.

He picked the first street he came to at the edge of the bazaar. Good as any. Just start walking. Sooner or later, he knew he would run into a mosque, every road led to one eventually. Before had traveled half a block, he felt somebody at his right shoulder, then another presence at his left. He waited for the fast-walking pair to pass by, but they did not. Instead they pressed in on him, each one taking him by an elbow.

He did not look left, nor right. In fear.

The voice at his right ear said, "You are looking for a doctor?"

No point in denying it. "A simple matter of removing sutures." Aziz lifted up his left hand. Without the last two bones of his thumb, the rounded stump looked like a tumor.

"As you can see, this wound has healed, but I have another in my head, and I am in danger of infection because the sutures have remained too long in place."

The voice at his left ear spoke up. "You are supposed to be dead. Why are you not dead?"

Ack! That voice! He could not stop himself from looking now, to confirm it. Yes, the evil bodyguard of his prince, Osama bin Laden, and his chief tormentor in the entourage of the prince.

"Ahmed Ali Kamel. How glad I am to see you."

"Why are you not dead?"

"A miracle?"

"No miracle." The man shook his left elbow hard enough for Aziz's vision to rattle around like the images in a kaleidoscope. "You ran away from the battle. Do you know what the penalty is for cowardice?"

"I did not run away," Aziz said, in the tone of: *Unlike you.* "I stayed behind to fight. I tried to give my life. The intruders never made it into the building where I was stationed. Yet, after you left, as I lay there fighting off the Americans, the building exploded."

The grip on his right elbow tightened. "What are you saying, you little bastard?"

Aziz no longer felt indignant. "The Americans. They dropped bombs on the building. I lost my thumb. And I was struck in the head." He tried to move his hand to his head, to point out the wound. But the pair were having none of it. By now they were carrying him, his feet off the ground.

"And how you know they were Americans?"

"The prince."

"Forget about the prince. What about the Americans? How you know?"

"The prince himself said so. Just before you—" *Just before the lot of you ran away, leaving me and the others to die.* But he dared not say *that.* "Just before you took the prince away to save his life."

"If they bombed the building, how come you are still alive?"

"As I said, it is a miracle of God." Tears filled Aziz's eyes, and they were not fake. "Everywhere the building tumbled down on me. For two whole days I remained inside, starving. Shitting and pissing in my pants. I had no water, nothing to eat. My thumb hanging by strings. But finally, after two days of crawling, I escaped the building and wandered into the neighborhood."

Kamel grabbed him by the wrist and stuck his injured hand under his own nose. "And you found a surgeon to repair your injured thumb?"

"No, I had no money, just like I have no money now. I cut off my own thumb. With a piece of glass. To remove the sepsis that had set in. A doctor in the neighborhood took pity on me and put in the sutures."

Kamel grabbed him by the hair and looked at his scalp. He came away with his face twisted into a grimace. "Putrid. Then why don't you have him remove them?"

"I cannot find him. He has left the city for safety in the mountains. In case the Americans bomb again. I removed the sutures from my hand. But I cannot seem to get them out of my head or to treat the sepsis."

The two men steered him to a car idling in the street. The doors opened, and they threw him inside into the care of two other men. As his car pulled away, Aziz looked out the rear window to see hs Kamel following him in a second car.

"Where are we going?"

Nobody answered him.

"Got movement," Carnes said, putting down his digital cell phone. "Aziz. The AWACS has him on the move."

Spangler, back aboard the carrier, was not impressed. The kid had wandered all over Kandahar in the days after his release.

"This time it's different," he said. "In a vehicle.

Spangler perked up.

"Doing maybe fifty."

Spangler sat up and put aside a crossword. "Do tell."

"Oh yes. North. Out of Kandahar."

"Toward where?"

"Kabul? Khost?"

Spangler went to his ops map. "Closer to whose AO? Tyler's or Poole's?"

Carnes put his finger on the spot. "Tyler's."

Spangler shook his head. "Launch Poole."

"By day? When Tyler's area of ops is just a hop away? The guy already on the ground?"

"Tyler's a good officer, but he's got a history, Brian. I want Poole and his crew on this one."

"It's a long flight."

"Then they'd better get going. Wouldn't you say?"

Aziz didn't need to use his feet. Kamel and the other one lugged him around like a goat carcass. From he black car into the inn at Dharzi. Once inside, they turned into a long hall and into an open elevator. Only on the way down did they rest his feet on the floor. The doors came open. They lifted him again. They swept him into a garage. To trade cars?

No. Into an office he glided. This time, when they let him go, his knees buckled. He went down to pray. For he was face-to-face-to-face with his prince—no, two princes. Just alike. Two Osamas. Other people stood in the room, near the walls, but Aziz did not even see them.

"Your worship," he said to one. "Your worship?" to the other.

Both smiled at him in that same slight smile. He wanted to go close to see which was the real one, but he dared not. Yes, he was stunned, but he had not lost his senses. To go near the prince? Kamel would kill him in two steps. Early on Kamel had given him many a punch to the kidneys just for looking at bin Laden too long.

As imposters went, this one—whichever was the imposter—might have been bin Laden's twin.

"You do not recognize me?" One of them had said.

So, that was him.

"You do not recognize me," the other said.

Aziz held his tongue. The voices were not alike exactly, but he could not tell between them.

He did the only thing he knew to do. He dropped his chin to his chest and covered his face.

"Your worship, I am not worthy to lay eyes on you." He shook his head. "Either of you."

Kamel picked him up and slammed him into a chair. They threw a bag of clothes at him, clothes exactly like those of the prince. Both princes.

"Put them on," said Kamel.

Aziz hesitated. For now he saw that one of the bystanders against the wall was a young woman. A kick to his ankle got him moving. A blow to the head stung his stitches. He shed his old rags and as much as threw his new clothing into the air and dived into it. Still he was nearly naked for moment. The young woman approached him, a kit bag in her hand. She opened it, and he knew what she was going to do. He settled into the chair, his chin erect, waiting for the rubber cement, the fake beard, and the makeup.

Kamel pulled up two chairs and settled into the one closest to Aziz. "Him first," he said to the young woman.

A man about his own age but the size of Kamel stepped away from the wall and took the third chair. The young woman began to apply makeup and before long, Aziz saw his worst nightmare coming into focus before his very eyes. The young woman created the very picture of another Kamel.

Then she went to work on him. She finished his face too soon. Aziz's tried to capture her every sweet breath for his own lungs. He could barely keep from crying. So pretty was she. But alas, she was done. She gave him an adoring smile. She handed a mirror to him, and he could see why she admired him. She wasn't admiring Aziz, but Osama. An artist who could make miracles. No wonder he couldn't tell the difference between one twin and another. When he turned the hand mirror so that both he and the other two reflected in it, he thought he was looking at identical triplets. All he could say for sure was he was not the real bin Laden.

Kamel snatched the mirror from Aziz's hands.

"Let's go, fool," Kamel said. "You're beautiful enough." He jerked Aziz to his feet roughly. Aziz had to wonder. Did the man resent the prince? Was he jealous of his power and money?

Kamel shoved Aziz through the garage beneath the inn. Aziz thinking. Before, when he was just an errand boy, Kamel treated him better. Now that he looked so much like—

"Hide that hand," Kamel said as they started to pass by a Red Crescent ambulance. "We can't pass you off as our leader if anybody sees you're missing a thumb."

Aziz planted his feet. He jerked his arm away and whirled on Kamel. "And neither can you pass me off as the prince if you push me around like a stable boy."

Aziz stiffened, waiting for one of Kamel's blows. But Kamel was confused.

"He's right you know," said a soft voice. It came from inside the box of the ambulance.

Aziz turned. There, in the darkness, sat the prince, looking at him, smiling his quizzical smile, looking through him and into the distance, seeing things that others did not even imagine. He felt his knees begin to buckle. For perhaps only the second time in his life, Osama bin Laden had eyes only for him.

Poole called his group into a briefing. Night Runner saw the huge smile and knew before Poole spoke the words. "Good news," he said. "We got us an Osama sighting." He shook his head as the members of his team laughed. "I hear ya, I hear ya. He's popped up in more places than Elvis. But this time we got A-1 intel. That kid we snatched from the bin Laden compound? They planted a passive GPS beacon on his ass. Somebody snatched him up again. Off the streets. He's on the wing. On a beeline toward Khost. We're gonna pay him a house call."

Less than an hour later, as they boarded their aircraft, Night Runner had to smile himself. Finally. A shot at making up for missing bin Laden that night at the compound.

They got an up-to-the-minute briefing in-flight. The AWACS processed and downloaded pictures to Poole's combat computer from both the overhead satellites and picture-taking drones. They showed glimpses of a black BMW sedan traveling in convoy sandwiched between a white Ford Explorer and blue Toyota 4Runner streaking north on the highway toward Khost. About an hour's drive north of Kandahar, at a town of perhaps twenty thousand, the convoy slowed and stopped beneath a drive-up canopy of the largest building in town. A voice from the AWACS said the building was a combination of an apartment, inn, and opium clearinghouse.

Aboard the Blackhawk, Night Runner and two other members of the team watched over Poole's shoulder. On screen the men saw every door of every vehicle opening. A clutch of men from each of the vehicles formed a small mob that moved inside the building, leaving a driver outside with each vehicle to shut the doors, check tires, look under the hood, and stand watch.

"That it?" Poole asked into his radio mike. "I can't make a mission outta that. What up? What you expect us to do? Kick the doors on a Holiday Inn? How we even know these are the bad guys? You got vid?"

The AWACS had answers within the minute.

A replay of the men dismounting their vehicles. In stills. Close-up mug shots of each. Poole recognized one he was looking for, Aziz, herded by a pair of thugs at the center of the mob into the inn.

The voice from the AWACS spoke out. "Our analysts say it's a rest stop, to get something to drink, eat, use the latrine."

Night Runner shook his head. "A pissbreak? After only sixty miles? I doubt it."

"Hell, the whole country is a bathroom," Poole said. "Everybody in it just pulls over and uses it anytime day or night."

"Something's up," Night Runner said.

A voice in their headsets rose an octave. "Something's up. Stand by for live feed in five-four—holy shit!" Poole's screen flickered. The AWACS voice came back, composed but still excited. "I apologize for the outburst. But look what we have."

Poole shook his head at Night Runner. *Apologize for the outburst. What kind of war is this?*

The parked convoy came into view. The lens zoomed in close, so fast the picture went out of focus. When the fuzz cleared up, Poole saw he was looking at the rear bumper of the black sedan, the license plate readable from space. The picture jiggled, and the lens panned from one face to another in the mob. Settling on one face in particular. A figure by now familiar to the world. A figure that had appeared on the cover of *Time* magazine barely three weeks after the strikes against America. Osama bin Laden. The King Rat himself.

"Holy shit is right," Michelotti said as the infamous head ducked into the sedan.

The convoy started off north, again toward Khost.

"Helluva head-fuck," Poole said.

Night Runner said. "A shell game?"

Poole had to agree. "They know we got the eye in the sky. They got to know. So, what? They sending the King Rat up the road in the convoy? Or is our good buddy Aziz, back in drag?"

He had his answer within seconds. "We don't have a signal from the planted beacon anymore," said the voice in the sky. "That isn't the double you guys picked up in the compound."

An image of bin Laden came up. The photo jumped into close-up. On the left hand.

"Besides. This guy's got both thumbs," the voice said.

One corner of Poole's mouth pulled back toward his ear. He looked at Night Runner, his eyes wide. "Okay. Roger, tell me about the beacon. You had it on the way up the road from Kandahar?"

"Affirm. Out the back window of the sedan. But who knows? Maybe it is our guy and his turban is wrapped with fabric that uses metal foil in the weave. That could cause us to lose the signal. Or maybe he is still inside the inn."

Spangler's voice came on the air. "I need a course of action, boys. You're the people on the ground—figuratively speaking."

Poole looked at Night Runner and exchanged facial shrugs.

"We *are* closing on the guy," Night Runner said tentatively.

Poole set his jaw. He had his course of action. "We haul ass. Lay in the weeds and take out the convoy," he said.

"Snatch the guy and get CI to tell us if he is the King Rat. Or else bring back his DNA."

"Stand by," Spangler said. "I'll get the final go."

"Don't Kneel," the prince said to Aziz. "As me you must do as I do. You must endure the adulation. And you must do it with dignity."

Aziz, at the rear of the box, turned to Kamel. He put a hand on the man's shoulder. "I forgive you, Kamel. With dignity."

Kamel bared his fangs. "For what?"

"You forgot to fake adulation."

Kamel gagged in his throat.

Aziz patted the giant shoulder. "Later, when I am Aziz again, you can beat your fake prince."

Kamel jerked away from Aziz's hand. "You are no fake prince."

Aziz spread his arms. *See?*

"You are a real prince. A prince of dunces." With a dog-bite grip on Aziz's elbow, he tossed him into the ambulance. He shut the first of the double doors. "And I will beat you. Depend on it."

Aziz sat on the bench across from bin Laden, his hands on his knees, his chin up, the picture of dignity, the mirror of his prince.

"Or perhaps I will have you beat," Aziz said as the second door went shut. Too late for Kamel to hear.

"My son," bin Laden said. "Thank you."

"Your worship?"

"You amuse me. A brief laugh feels good to my weary body."

Aziz sat stiff and silent. *What to say to that?*

The ambulance began to move. Once they were on the road, racing through the city under the wail of the siren, bin Laden said. "Forgive the ride." A shrug. "We have found this an effective way to get around a city without notice. Ironic, yes? To use a siren to remain anonymous?"

"Yes, Prince. Ironic. And brilliant."

Bin Laden gave a wry smile. "Don't flatter. Not me, not

anybody. It's not brilliant at all. Just pragmatic. We do it because it works."

The ambulance stopped and began turning and backing. Aziz looked to his idol. Bin Laden leaned across the opening between them and patted Aziz's knee.

"A hospital," he said. "We won't get out. Just to get a parcel." Bin Laden pointed at the bench seat. "If you don't mind, would you lie down and cover up with a sheet. They can't see two of us, you know."

Aziz stretched out. Bin Laden did the same. "In fact," bin Laden said through his sheet, "they can't see either of us."

Aziz could only listen and watch through his mind's eye. The rear doors came open. Kamel stood at the back and gave order. "In here. Be careful with that. Gently." Aziz felt the box shake as one or more men stepped in. A heavy parcel hit the floor. A curse from Kamel. A clearing of the throat by bin Laden. A murmured apology from Kamel. The rear doors shut and latched. And soon the ambulance on the move. Aziz, not knowing what to do, obeyed the last order his prince had given him.

They rode a distance on asphalt. Then at an abrupt edge, the pavement ended. He felt roads of sand and gravel. Dust began to seep into the ambulance, and Aziz coughed.

"Are you awake then, my son?"

"Yes, my prince."

"Would you like to sit up?"

"Very much."

Silence.

"Then why don't you?"

Aziz obeyed.

"Would you like to take off the sheet?"

"Very much."

"Then why don't you? We can talk, if you like."

"Very much."

Aziz pulled off the sheet and looked into the gentle, bemused smile of bin Laden. An awkward silence, because Aziz did not know how to talk to a prince. People of his station, men like Kamel taught, at the end of a stick or switch or boot.

Aziz nodded at the parcel on the deck. "This is what they put on?"

"Yes, for me."

"A refrigerator then?"

"No, my son." Bin Laden smiled his little smile. "It is a medical machine."

"For you, master?"

"To refresh my blood. About once a week." He dismissed it with a wave. "It is nothing. Let's talk about you. I admire men like you," bin Laden said.

Aziz's eyes went wide. The prince calling him a man? When the rest of the world called him a boy? *The prince admired him?*

"But why? I have done nothing of value. Next to you—"

"I am the one who has done nothing. I have been born to riches. Servants. Schools. Travel. Wealth." The last word he said with disgust.

"But look what you do to the enemies of Islam."

Bin Laden shrugged it off. "I give nothing but my words. And my wealth." Again the disgust.

Aziz opened his mouth to protest, but bin Laden silenced him with a limp wave. "Look what others have done. They have given lives, forsaken families, shed blood. I give only a small fraction of what I have and every day it amounts to less—I can't even spend my wealth faster than it comes to me." He took a deep breath. "But you. Look at you. Look at what you have given." He held up his own hand, the thumb hidden behind his palm.

"A thumb?" Aziz shook his head. "I run errands, master. And I dress up to look like you. Nothing have I given."

The limp hand reached out and took his. Bin Laden held up Aziz's wound. "You shed your blood in a fight for me. You gave your thumb for me."

Aziz felt a deep blush rising in his face. Not much of a gift. Since he did not give it in battle at all. But in captivity. At the behest of drugs. Cut off, not by the enemy, but by himself.

"I should have given my head." Tears leaked from his eyes.

"Such humility," bin Laden said.

Such shame. Aziz wished he could confess, own up. He began to search his limited store of words to find the right ones. Before he could speak, his prince spoke.

"And now you will give your all for me," bin Laden said. "And for the cause."

Aziz went speechless. Not merely for his lack of the right words, but in shock. *My all?*

"Men try to kill me, you know."

"Yes, master?" *My all?*

"Even my own people. The Saudis. And my family, the house of Saud. I would gladly let them take me, you know."

"No, master, you must live on. You are the life of the struggle."

"Sadly. As you say, I must live on."

Aziz slumped in relief.

"That is what makes me so sad now," bin Laden said.

"Master?"

"That others have to die on my behalf."

"Master?"

Spangler was back at Poole's team in half an hour. "Take down the convoy. If you can, take the King Rat alive. If you can't, bring back his body."

"Roger," Poole said. "This is the King Rat then?"

"98 percent sure," Spangler said. "We got a fix on his bodyguard, one Ahmed Ali Kamel. King Rat has not traveled without Kamel in the past year. Take him down."

"Wilco," Poole said. He and Night Runner exchanged stupefied looks. *98 percent?* Both shook their heads. Spangler had OD'd on wishful thinking.

Spangler went into the details. The team would carry out its mission under satellite surveillance, which Spangler would monitor. And the one-star would eavesdrop on the tactical radio net. In the oral histories of the Vietnam War, many a lieutenant and captain complained about trying to manage a firefight while colonels and generals kept butting in from their helicopter headquarters flying at fifteen-hundred feet above the action. Thanks to new technology, the colonels and generals could meddle in the action anywhere on earth but without the danger of getting shot down.

Baker found a new respect for Mansour's horses. For three hours they had climbed, picking their way in the dark on slopes of scree, broken, angular chunks of black basalt big as cinder building blocks. Switching back, slogging ever upward into air ever thinner and colder, until Mansour finally called a halt to his caravan of a dozen horses and riders and the thirty tireless men who kept up on foot.

Mansour's men each carried only a rifle and belts of ammo, a small skin of water, and a plastic bag of cold rice left over from dinner. When the men needed to, they ate on the march, biting a hole in the plastic and squeezing rice seasoned with curry, pepper, and animal fats into their mouths. If only the American army could travel so light. Even Delta men, lugging cell phones, NVGs, lasers, and other gadgets, couldn't match the lean Afghan fighters in the sheer simplicity of their logistics. When their ears got cold, they simply pulled their knit wool hats down over their faces. If they wore a turbanlike headgear, they rewrapped the wool, taking turns over their mouths and neck, leaving just a slit for their eyes. The cloak draped over one shoulder and across their bodies served as a pouch for carrying food and water. And became a blanket or sunshade, as the weather dictated.

Baker oozed off his pony and held on to the saddle with his good hand while he waited for his circulation to work its way back into his groin. He shook out his cramped muscles and past-numb knees to chase the tingling away.

"We climb the rest of the way on foot," Mansour said, bellowing into his face.

"Resting the horses?" Baker was glad for the chance to walk.

Mansour laughed. "These horses? They do not need rest for hours longer. The path from here to the pass. It is too narrow. We lose men on horses here every time we travel it. Even by day."

He leaned into Baker's face. "But you can ride, if you please."

"No thanks."

"We leave the horses here. All that running. I hope it made your legs strong."

"I need a weapon."

Mansour shook his head. "So eager to kill?"

Baker glowered at him in the dark.

Mansour shucked the sling off his own shoulder and handed over his own AK-47. "Here, take mine. And take care not to kill me. Strap it to your back and watch where you walk. A man cannot hold two watermelons in one hand."

Baker's head snapped erect.

"I regret saying that," Mansour said. "I did not mean to offend, to refer to your one hand. I only meant—"

"I know what you meant." *Like a man trying to walk and chew gum and carry a rifle at the same time.* "Forget it."

The spot for Poole's strike came right out of the ambush manual. A deserted stretch of highway between military outposts, a little more than halfway between Khost and Kandahar. At a spot where the road climbed up one camel-hump stretch of road, then dropped down into a wadi on the other side. Dark, desolate, defenseless.

The Blackhawks let them off two hundred meters downwind of the road so no residual dust thrown up by the rotor wash could drift into the headlight beams and give away the surprise. The helicopters went off to loiter, light on the wheels, engines running, three miles away.

Poole had briefed his plan in-flight. Two light squads of four men each took their spots on the slopes. The first one dug in where the road climbed the camel hump. The second lay on the slope on the down-side of the hump. Poole and six other men took the crest of the hill. They were to pull off the capture.

In some respects, the plan was almost too scientific. Poole asked analysts in the AWACS craft to tell him the interval between the three vehicles in the convoy, the dust-distance. On the paved roads, the three vehicles had traveled within a car length of each other. But once on the dirt track, they had to allow for the dust to blow clear of the road. So the drivers could see where they were going, when to swerve around potholes, and not risk crashing into each other.

In minutes, the boys from the AWACS came back at him. "Eighty to one hundred-twenty meters, depending on whether the road is crosswise to the window or quartering into it." The voice did not try to disguise a smug attitude.

So Poole gave it back. "I need something more precise than that. I'm going to throw up a fistful of dust. Tell me what interval they'll have at my position."

In thirty seconds, the voice reported, "Ninety meters."

The banter was light, but nobody doubted the stakes or made light of the ambush set. Each of the three teams crossed the road in the same set of footprints, to get on the upwind side for the attack. So dust and smoke would blow into the enemy's faces, and not the attackers'. One man from each team, using a piece of shrubbery as a broom, brushed over their tracks. Night Runner had taught that to them.

Night Runner surveyed the road at the crest of the hill. He was to set up for the capture of the men in the second vehicle, where the King Rat rode. On the west edge of road, less than a meter from the track, he stacked two stones and sprinkled dust on them so they looked natural. At the east edge, the same distance from the track, he put another, larger stone the size of a bowling ball. At the base of each stone he set a concussion grenade set to remote. After dusting off his tracks to make everything looked normal, he stepped off another ten meters and lined up the two stones before leaning on a foot-long stick to fix it in the sand. He then walked off fifty meters and began looking for the best cover on a perfect line to his three markers. It wasn't much. A pair of desert shrubs that caught the prevailing wind and raked out the sand, dropping it in a heap, like a mound on a fresh grave. Night Runner lay down behind the mound. He could see to line up his markers and yet stay hidden. He would strike King Rat from here.

To the south, perhaps five miles away, three sets of lights snaked across the landscape. They blinked in and out of his line of sight as the vehicles followed the uneven surface of the earth.

As his Blackfeet ancestors had two hundred years before him, and their ancestors a thousand years before them, Night Runner settled in to wait for his prey to enter the killing zone. Walking in on men asleep in their bunks. That was no decent way to kill a man. This was how to kill.

Spangler, operating out of a command center deep inside the ship, could not contain his euphoria. He watched in real time as Poole and his team set up. On another screen he kept tabs on the King Rat's convoy inching their dusty way to death. This was it. The moment of truth. Nothing could save the bastard bin Laden now. Even if he turned tail and tried to escape, he couldn't. That convoy wouldn't find a hidey-hole in fifty miles. Worst case, Spangler could order a strike, then send in Poole's team to sort bodies and find the rat bastard. This was it, the endgame.

The only thing that kept him from sending out for champagne was the reality check. He dared not declare bin Laden dead or missing until he had the proof. Absolute proof. He had heard the CIA brag about having bin Laden's family DNA. If they weren't blowing smoke, it might take a week to test, including travel time. Meanwhile, he could put the rest of his *Michael's Sword* task force on hold. Not risk anybody until he knew for sure.

He did not want to risk a man, not even Tyler, who had been bugging him all day to get into the action. Tyler knew about Poole's mission to ambush the convoy. Tyler was agitating for a strike at the inn, where bin Laden had stopped. Shake down the joint. Let people know it was not safe to harbor terrorists. Tyler thought they should pick up Aziz again, get some intel out of him, find out why bin Laden would risk driving to Khost.

A copy of the command center activity log showed Tyler

had called six times in the last hour. And six times Spangler had ignored him. That Tyler. Getting to be such a pain in the ass. Given his history, his marriage, his attack on another Delta Force operator, Spangler had begun thinking he should recall Tyler. Take him back to D.C., where he could keep tabs on him. Give him a job at a desk in the Pentagon, out of sight, if he was going to behave as if he were out of his mind. Maybe his old desk in the basement, where Bowers had put him to keep him out of trouble. Now that he was a one-star, now that he had a Spangler-type thorn in his own side to manage, the strategy didn't look as heartless as it did before, when he was the thorn instead of the side.

Even so—

One of the SigInt analysts, a buck sergeant maybe twelve years old from the look of him, stood in front of Spangler working a piece of paper in both hands like a security blanket.

Spangler looked at the name tag on the kid. "What is it, Beckwith?"

"We just picked up a beacon signal."

"And?" *So what?* The signal intelligence types kept track of hundreds of beacons inside Afghanistan, including one for every Delta operator implant. It didn't mean much. Hell, Baker's corpse was still transmitting from his grave. Creepy, that.

"It's the GPT-2242-104."

"In English, please."

"The one planted on the Afghan national."

Spangler held his breath. "Aziz?"

The youngster looked to his piece of paper. "Aziz. That's the one."

"He's at the inn." *I hope.*

"No."

"Where, then?" Spangler snatched the paper from the kid's hands. "Minutes, seconds? What the hell?"

"Latitude and longitude, sir."

"Goddammit." He sprang from his chair. "Show me. Not on a clock with your minutes and shit. On the map."

The kid drew a tiny electronic circle on the computer map.

A hundred miles north and east of where it had blinked off at the inn. Just thirty miles from the Pakistan border.

"This is his signal? The kid's?" Spangler said. "It can't be a mistake? A false positive?" The SigInt specialist shaking his head at each suggestion. "Atmospheric disturbance? Some goatherd playing his Game Boy on a mountaintop?"

"No, sir. We confirmed this signal every way possible. The clincher is, when we interrogate it, it responds. When we signal it to respond on a different frequency, it changes frequencies and responds on cue." The kid shook his head. "There is no other computer chip in the world that could mimic it—and there is no SigInt operator on the other side that could keep up with me when I run my confirmation tests. No way."

"Level of confidence?"

"A hundred percent." The kid put his hands on his hips. "That chip is an absolute singularity. Identical twins can have identical fingerprints—this thing cannot have a twin unless I invent it. And I did not. This is more positive than DNA. I am so sure that—"

"Enough," Spangler said. He shook his head. "Goddammit enough."

"I'm sorry to have to bring bad news, sir. You know it means—"

"I know what it means."

"Our implant guy is escaping into Pakistan."

"What'd I just say?"

A weak smile. The kid did not budge. "There is a bit of good news, sir. I mean, if you want Aziz back."

"Why the fuck would I?" Spangler was playing coy. Of course he knew why. Al Qaeda wouldn't smuggle a bonehead kid all the way across the frontier. They might put him in the back of a pickup and have him wave to the crowds to make the world *believe* he was taking a Club Med vacation into Pakistan. No, the terrorists were not sneaking Aziz out of the country. But they might be trying to sneak somebody else. Maybe the King Rat himself.

Spangler cocked his head as the kid put his finger on the map where the topographic contour lines were so closely bunched and irregular that it made the monitor screen look as rumpled as the ground. Under his fingernail, not far from Aziz's electronic circle was another mark less than fifty miles away from Aziz. "Right there, sir."

Spangler said, "Captain Tyler's team?"

"Yessir." The kid beamed a smile.

"And you think that's good news."

"Sir?"

"Never mind, sergeant." Connor Tyler his good luck charm? Connor Tyler good news? Maybe if he chanted the words like a mantra, they would come true. Even if Aziz wasn't with bin Laden, Spangler wanted him back. Send Connor Tyler in to snatch Aziz, who might drop yet another dime on King Rat? Connor Tyler? Hell, maybe that was simpler than socking him away in the Pentagon basement. "Get me Tyler on the horn, ASAP."

At the summit an hour after leaving the horses nuzzling around the scree for forage, Baker, his thighs trembling, felt a surge of relief as the steep trail widened, and the incline flattened out. Where earlier he had felt chilled sitting atop the horse, he was glad now for the cold breeze that swept clouds across his face. The fog left dew on his mustache. He licked the mist away, not daring to stop for a drink, and kept up to Mansour, who had not flagged a step. No wonder the man took such a dim view of exercise for its own sake. Half a dozen aerobics gym rats from LA, working in shifts, couldn't keep up with him on a trek like this. Baker, if he wasn't Delta Force, and even at that, if he hadn't jogged up the slopes behind Mother's hut, couldn't have done it, either. He would have had to stay back with the horses.

As they climbed the air began to bite at his ears, rough as dried potatoes, but sensitive. He pulled down the flaps of his cap to cover them.

Mansour did not even slow down at the summit. Acting as his own scout and point man, he began descending through the chill mist. Baker ran to keep up. He'd sit down if he lost Mansour. Rather than walk off a cliff, he'd wait out the fog. Until the sun burned it away. But when the clouds turned into a river of milk flowing in the moonlight over their heads, Baker had to work even harder to stay up, because Mansour became less than a shadow against the black backdrop of the valley at their feet.

Finally, Baker ran into the shadow, hard as Mansour's back.

"Sorry."

"Listen."

"What?"

"With your mouth shut."

Baker lifted one flap of his cap and heard it. The sound of distant shots. Automatic fire. Explosions. In the fog he could see nothing. After one last, huge blast, he couldn't hear anything either.

"Americans?" he asked.

"A tree doesn't move unless there is a wind."

Baker couldn't contain himself.

"What do you laugh at, Ramsay al Bakr?"

"Not a laugh. A shiver." He couldn't say what was on his mind. *Why don't you knock off the good-old-boy crap. You sound like Dan Rather going corn pone while doing the election returns?*

Tyler thought he was seeing fireflies at first. Rocketing past the open doors of the Blackhawk on final to a mountain LZ. Then a trail of sparks. RPGs. At close range. Too close for—

"*Ah,* fifty feet off the deck and taking fire," the pilot, his voice as calm as a drink order. *Vodka martini, straight-up, with a twist.*

Tyler felt a surge in his blood. Finally. Into the action. Moving on an Al Qaeda hideout, a tunnel complex. The spot where SigInt had picked up the bin Laden double. Snatch a body. In and out.

Taking fire. A good thing. The bad guys ready to fight.

"*Ah-h-h,* taking minor hits," the pilot said. "On the go-around here." *Make that a gin on the rocks.*

"Go-around to where?" Tyler wanted to know. *Go around on your own time. Don't you know this is my chance?* Even as he asked the question, he could hear small arms fire hitting the craft like hail.

"New LZ. *Ah-h-h,* about a klick from here."

A steep bank pressed Tyler into the deck of the craft. Then the nose tucked.

"*Ah-h-h,* major hit here." *And a beer chaser.*

The Blackhawk spun as if T-boned in a car crash.

"Going in. Going in hard. *Ah-h-h shit!*" *Gotta piss now.*

Tyler clawed at the dimpled deck of the Blackhawk. But the spin threw him. Too sudden. Too violent. Weightless, he flew away on his own. Out into a chill air. Spinning into the night.

Odd. To see the stars whirl. He felt cold. Not afraid, just utterly chilled to his core.

The Blackhawk hit the ground before he did, burning, tumbling, ejecting the burning bodies of his mates and the crew. *Ah-h-h, gotta die now.*

He hit the ground. Not as hard the pilot said, his impact cushioned by a bed of ground covering. Short, spiny trees. Hard enough to make him see a new constellation, stars in his head. Hard enough to rob his lungs. Thinking his last thoughts. How right he was about 9-11. 9-11 changed so much. Everything in his miserable fucking life. On 9-10, he's one of America's best. From 9-11 on, he's America's biggest fuck-up. Now this. *Fuck.*

Night Runner set off the Ambush. He let the first set of lights go by, a Ford SUV. King Rat's BMW sedan ran next. Then a Toyota.

When the bumper of the SUV came up to his line, he warned the others with a count: "Three-two-one." The bumper broke the plane. He ducked and set off two boomers.

At the cue, the trail team shot a pair of heat-seekers into the Toyota. The SUV burst into flames and rolled to a stop, its doors still shut.

The lead vehicle took off down the road like a rocket sled. A heat-seeker caught up and blew beside the hood. The SUV nosed into the sand. A hail of fire tore into the Ford.

Runner's boomers blew the BMW's left-side tires off the rims. The car tipped over onto its top, spinning. The doors popped, and bodies fell free.

Poole and two men ran to the road behind the BMW to take out any Al Qaeda who put up a fight. Nobody did.

"Sweep the kill zone," Poole said. At those four words his three men were to sort bodies and find King Rat. The helo pilots, a minute away, were to pull pitch.

Spangler's voice cut into the action. "I need a report on King Rat ASAP."

Poole shook his head. "What the hell izzat?"

Runner spoke up. "I have him in hand."

Spangler butted in again: "You have a visual on bin Laden? Confirm you have a visual on King Rat. Is he alive?"

"Stand by for an after-action report," Poole said. Damned staff officers. In the middle of a damned battle? "Rally."

His men ran the LZ to meet the Blackhawks. A perfect snatch. Except for Spangler. Goddamned staff officers. Take the fun out of a winning lottery ticket—hell, take the fun out of a blow-job.

After an hour the clouds parted, revealing half a moon. Compared to the darkness of before, this was like the glow of a street lamp. On this side of the summit, patches of vegetation came into view. Soon they were waltzing through pungent juniper shrubs. At first, an ankle-deep shag carpet. Then knee-high jumbles of bushes. And finally face-high conifers with branches like horse whips that Mansour kept flinging as he passed them, paying no mind to Baker a step behind.

Baker tried to memorize the terrain, in case he needed to pinpoint the locale for intel analysts, should he ever escape this place. Fat chance off finding it on a map. Hundreds of game trails crisscrossed the slopes. Goats and sheep, wild and domestic, had woven a web of tricky paths, and Baker soon gave up on trails. He tried to see larger details.

Patches of forest—those he could see. The peaks above he could not—the fog. A sheer cliff wall ahead, but with no features.

Before long, Mansour was walking along the base of that wall, in and out of the shadows among the boulders and outcroppings in the valley floor. Until, at a distance of less than three meters away, Mansour walked into one edge of a shadow but did not come out the other edge.

Baker stopped in his tracks. The man following him walking into his back and grunted an obscenity into his ear. Baker stepped aside. The man walked into the shadow and vanished. And the man after him. Baker looked in wonder. Here he was, just a few feet away from the fabled cave and tunnel system of Afghanistan, watching men walk into sheer stone like water whirpooling down a drain.

He stood back from the cliff wall as far as he could without slipping down the gravel slope. He put his head back and looked up. The cliff loomed over him at an angle like the Leaning Tower of Pisa. Then he walked up to the base of the cliff and looked out across the valley. Nowhere could he see the sky. Everywhere the peaks and ridges blocked a satellite's view of this spot. How many other tunnel entrances had the Afghans carved like this one? How many—?

"What in Allah's name are you still doing out here?" Mansour.

"Catching my breath," Baker said.

Mansour stepped up to his good shoulder and looked across the valley, just as Baker had done. "And what are you looking for? Or should I ask, who are you looking for?"

Baker caught a note of threat in his tone. "I'm looking for a place to hide."

Not the lie that Mansour had expected. It caught him off guard. "Oh?"

"I need a place to sleep."

"Come inside. You can sleep there."

"No."

"You defy me?"

"No."

"What then?"

Baker hesitated for effect. "I have something I must confess to you."

"Oh?"

"I am afraid."

Mansour laughed. "Don't be. There is no fight tonight. Not in the way you think."

"It's not a fight I'm afraid of. It's that." He inclined his head toward the shadow on the cliff.

"Now you talk nonsense. What am I to believe?"

"No nonsense. I am afraid of tight places. As I started to go in there after you, I experienced a memory returning. Something in our fight with the Soviets. I was in the place exactly like that, a cave. They dropped bombs and shot rockets into the mouth of it. The mountain collapsed over top of us. We had to dig out. The loose rock. The cave-ins." Baker shuddered. "I can see the bad parts too clearly."

"It's all right," Mansour said. "Nobody can drop bombs into this place."

"I know it," Baker said. "That's what I was looking for in the sky, a path for the bombs to fall."

"There is none."

"I am still afraid."

"I understand. Having been bitten by a snake, a man is afraid of a rope. Come on inside. Your fear will wait. I want you to meet a friend to us all."

Poole and Night Runner sat aboard the Blackhawk, their latest bin Laden POW between them. Poole played the beam of a penlight across the face, dusty, bleeding from the eyes, ears, and mouth. Shaken, but alive, his headpiece gone.

"Do you think it's him?" Poole asked Night Runner.

"Is it him? Is it really him?" Spangler. He had kept his mouth shut while the Delta team cleared the strike zone, but he could contain himself no longer.

"It looks like him," Night Runner said.

"It's him then?" Spangler again.

Poole took the man by the chin and tweaked the battered face left and right. "It does look like him," he said. "But then, so do the doubles."

"Is it bin Laden or not?"

"He's skinny, huh? Like a Somali."

"It's the television. They say the television adds ten pounds."

"Bastards. That's no help."

"And bald."

"Bald as an eagle. You sure don't get that picture of him in his publicity junkets."

"Vanity. It's the vanity."

"Damn you both. I have to know," Spangler said. "Is it him or not?"

Poole shook his head. "I don't think so, boss."

"How so?"

"Lips are too fat."

"The crash? Fat lips from the crash?"

"Hard to say."

"Bring him in for DNA."

Mansour took the leather sling of Baker's AK-47. Baker let the chief lead him into the cave.

Baker gasped in the dark, for Mansour's sake and for real. He did feel the rock walls close in on him. He had to skew his body to ease in. His cap brushed the stone. The walls were not vertical, either. As the entrance closed in, the crooked ceiling slanted down, too. Soon Baker had to walk in a crouch, like a duck, leaning to his left. A brisk wind shoved at his back as Mansour pulled on his sling.

Just as he thought he might have to go down on all fours, Mansour said, "Look. Here we are." The chieftain pulled aside a blanket, and Baker stood bathed in an orange glow.

"Don't make me go there again," he said.

Mansour just shook his head. "An Afghan afraid of a cave?"

"Not this cave," Baker said. He tossed a look back. "A path as tight as a coffin." He looked into the glow. "The cave is better than my home."

The interior of the mountain radiated with light, warmth, and the murmur of a hundred men standing in groups, mostly around small cooking fires, in a room the size of a gym. The talk was animated, loud, punctuated with laughter. Baker picked up snatches of it. War stories. These were fighters from the battle he had heard from above.

Baker stood in the doorway, the ventilation draft pushing at him from behind, looking into Mansour's face. He returned the smile, the feeling his face go a bit wild. Here he was—among the Al Qaeda. In one of their dens. The clubhouse of the bastards who made 9-11 a day of infamy. It made his blood run hot.

"See?" Mansour said. "It's not at all cramped."

Baker looked up at the orange glow on the slanted stone ceiling, perhaps fifty feet up. "It's like being outside," he said. "At sunrise."

"What did I tell you?" Mansour's proud smile faded. He squinted into Baker's face. "Why do you look so vicious?"

"I had hoped to join the fight we heard," Baker said. "We missed it. The shooting is over. These men are full of joy. I am full of anger."

"I have a thing better than a fight." Mansour beamed an orange smile, firelight reflecting off his teeth. "Come."

He led the way through the small throngs of men, trading greetings along the way. Baker watched the smoke arising from the small fires. Gentle breezes swept it up, up into a far, dark corner of the ceiling. Somewhere up there, a vent released the heat and smoke into the air. If he ever got out of here, he might tell the intel guys to look for—

"Here," Mansour said. He pulled aside another blanket.

Some time ago, parts of the cave ceiling had flaked off and fallen. New slabs lay flat on the cave floor, slabs bigger than most driveways where Baker had grown up. The jumble formed a series of rooms. Mansour led him through two small compartments. A pair of men in each stood up. Sentries. The third room was the size of a living room. The Al Qaeda had arranged the rubble as furniture, a slab for a table, boulders for chairs.

At the stone table, against the wall, sat three men.

On his far left, Powczuk glared at Mansour. His wrists were tied. At the sight of Baker, his eyes widened. *Didn't I just cut off your arm? Didn't they bury you just—? You're not dead?* Powczuk's shock was short-lived. He directed his hatred anew at Mansour, the last piece of his puzzle of betrayal now in place.

Baker dropped to his knees, partly in his role as Al Qaeda warrior, partly in shock. At the near end of the table was the core reason for his head wound, his missing arm, his plight, this war. There he sat, his very reason to be.

Osama bin Laden. Washed out, weak, and worried. Hard to imagine the vile extremes of that terrorist mind behind the wan face.

"Prince." He bowed deeply. *What now?* Roberts had said he knew bin Laden. *How the hell could he lie his way out of that?*

Between the two of them sat the third of his earthly demons. Just a bare glimpse was enough. The bloody, the bruised, the man who'd first tried to kill him. Connor Tyler. The first time he'd seen him, he thought him too pretty to be a terrorist. Until he saw the hatchet in his hand. Now, even beat up, he looked too Hollywood to be Delta. But . . .

Tyler. There he was. Would he blurt? No, in that fleeting moment before he lowered his head he saw that Tyler had no idea who he was looking at. Of course not. His own father would not know him.

Baker felt dizzy. One of Mansour's sayings came to mind: In an ant colony, the dew is a flood. He shut his eyes against the flood of new data, barely able to process it. His head cleared, but not his heart. He felt an urge to kill. He could do it. In his right fist was the AK-47 sling. He opened one eye, looked at his one good hand, and gave it the command to pull down the rifle, to slide to the pistol grip and slip off the safety, to lift the rifle and begin firing on auto, sweeping the stone table and the cave interior with bullets. *When in doubt empty your magazine.* He'd get bin Laden first, then Tyler, then Powczuk. *You bastard, you beat me when I was unconscious, not so I could feel it but so you could enjoy it.*

Then Mansour, if he had time, then the bodyguards—no. He wouldn't have time for them. They'd get him first. An act of suicide. But what a result. In one blast of gunfire, wiping out the scourge of the Western World and his own personal demons. If he could, in one blast—

He opened his other eye. And saw Mansour's hand on the grip of his pistol.

Mansour. The man didn't trust him yet. Why would he? He had lived so long not because he trusted, but because he never trusted in full. A wrong move now was a suicide, all right. With no other result. He'd have to wait.

"My prince," he said again. God. He kept his head down. He knew enough to do that. What else to do? He did not know. Yes, yes, he did. One word from bin Laden. Any hint of *I never saw this man before* and—

"I am told of your bravery in the fight against the infidel." The voice sounded as frail as the body, a young man already old, weak and tired. "You gave up your arm, to the enemy." Bin Laden took a deep breath. Baker got ready to pull the AK-47 down. "My dear friend, Mansour, has given these men to me as a prize in the war against the infidel. And he has warmed my heart with the stories of your courage."

Was it possible? Could he lie his way out of this? "My prince is too generous," he said. "My bravery had less to do with it than my head wound. It has made me forget things. I had no information in my brain to surrender to the enemy. I was not so much a hero as a mindless idiot."

"Amnesia?"

"Perhaps. I do not know this amnesia, and I am no doctor." He glanced up beneath one eyebrow.

Bin Laden gave him a lame smile. "This amnesia can be a terrible thing. Do you suppose it is contagious?"

Baker felt his heart lurch. "Prince?" *Here it comes.* He saw Mansour's hand tighten on his pistol grip, and behind bin Laden, his surly bodyguard tensed. Baker lifted his head. He smiled broadly. Stupidly. He'd die with an idiot smile on his face. His cheeks ached with the effort. His rifle felt as heavy and useless as an anvil. He wasn't going to be able to throw down on bin Laden before the others got to him. He put his hand to his hat. "No, I don't think my failed memory is contagious." End of bluff. End of story. He saw Mansour's pistol come out. He'd never act in time. Now. Not a suicide. Just a death. Wasted. Useless. Pointless. Death.

"Then why is it that I do not recall that you are a member of my inner circle?"

He gasped. Chocked down a swallow. Spit up a word. "Prince?" *Dead. He was good as dead.* "I do not recall it, either."

"And yet, Mansour tells me that you were so." Bin Laden lifted his right hand from the table, palm up. "I must have contracted this amnesia, too. For I do not recall meeting you until this very moment."

"I never said such a thing."

"Out from under the leaking roof and into the rain, eh?" Mansour pulled his snub-nosed pistol and jammed it into Baker's ear. "Liar."

"You are the liar." Baker pulled off his cap with one hand. He used it to lift up his hair. To show the hatchet scar at his hairline. He knew how ragged and angry the wound looked. "Think, Mansour. And tell me when I told you I was close to the prince."

"Roberts, the CIA man told me you said it."

Baker growled. "Tell me the moment you heard *me* say it."

Mansour scowled at him. He flushed to bright red under his tan. He worked his mouth in the forest of his black beard. But he said not a word.

"No," Baker said. "You can't. The first time you heard me speak, I was screaming under his whip." Baker pointed at Powczuk. "Did I say it then?"

Mansour's pistol hand wavered. Baker could feel him tremble through the muzzle, still against his head. *Could he pull this off?*

"He cut off my arm. Did I say it then?"

Mansour shook his head.

"When I was under the care of your wife, did I say it then? Did she tell you I said it? Either in my delirium or to impress her?"

"No, only the CIA man said it."

"Yes, only the CIA man."

"He said—"

"Yes, he did. Because I did tell him. Not you, but him."

Mansour raised the pistol again, but half-heartedly. Baker shoved it away with his wooden arm, pushing the muzzle toward the floor of the cave. He got to his feet.

"I told the CIA man a lie to save my own life." Baker spoke to Mansour but for bin Laden's benefit.

Mansour cocked his head.

"After he captured me, I thought he was going to kill me outright. I thought if I sounded like a great man, I could impress him. My sin? I wanted to live. I thought to escape. To get back my own. I lied to the CIA. But I did not lie to you."

"A good strategy, it seems," bin Laden said.

Baker shrugged. He caught a glimpse of Tyler. The head came up. He saw it dawn on the Delta man at last. He had pulled off his cap. He showed off his ears. Tyler might not recall his face. But those damned ears of his. Had he just saved his own life? Only to lose it to Tyler again?

Tyler forgot the throb in his head. Forgot the dull ache in his ankle. The sting of the wound in his left eye. His disgrace as a POW. His imminent death. Hell, he even forgot his utter failures of the past weeks.

All was gone. The instant the one-armed man pulled off his hat. The head wound, angry as the Arab man's eyes. That would have tipped him off in time. But not like the ears. Those ears—rough and formless as dirt clods. Once he had seen them as huge spiders clinging to the sides of the man's head. Aboard an airliner, on America's most fateful day. His most fateful day.

The glittering eyes flicked from bin Laden to him and back again to bin Laden. *Baker.* Army Captain Ramsey Baker. A Delta man, for God's sake. The eyes, yes. The wound, yes. The ears, for certain. The whole package of hatred so profound it couldn't be just the ideology or the hatred. Hatred for him. Personal.

Tyler's heart went on a rampage, a kids' rhythm band, out

of tune, out of time. *Ramsey Baker had infiltrated Al Qaeda?* Spangler must be having wet dreams. *Spangler put a Delta guy inside Al Qaeda? And not just inside, but at the top?* That Spangler. Talk about an evil genius.

He studied the eyes without seeming to. What was he seeing here? Ramsey Baker infiltrating Al Qaeda? Or Al Qaeda infiltrating Ramsey Baker? And what had happened to his arm? Tyler didn't remember cutting off Baker's arm, too. Breaking it, yes, but—

Chrissake, would he have that to atone for, too?

Baker broke eye contact with Tyler.

"Your blessing, my prince." He dropped to one knee, his head down. His eyes flicked left and the right, looking for a chance to strike. Mansour's hand still gripped the pistol, and to his right, bin Laden's bodyguard dropped the tip of his AK-47. But he still stood at the ready.

He could still try. He might even get away with it. He might kill just one sonofabitch before they got him, but if it was the right sonofa—

He felt a hand on his head, a gentle touch. The feet were long and bony and thin, too thin for his sandals.

Bin Laden. Touching him. Standing right in front of him. Too close to swing the rifle on him. But not too close, if he could get to his dagger in time. He closed his eyes. Give me the courage. The will. The energy. A knife to the groin. *Jesus-Allah-Christ!*

He felt the whisper of a breeze. A strong arm took his left shoulder.

"He's gone," Mansour said. "You can get up now."

Stunned, Baker looked around him. Bin Laden gone as yesterday.

"Was I dreaming?"

Mansour pulled him to his feet. "No, that was him. I think he likes you." He shrugged. "What's left of you." He shrugged again. "I confess I have grown fond of you, too. I'm glad you did not get caught in a lie." He Blushed. "Listen to me. An old porcupine speaking to his baby, calling him a child of velvet."

"I wanted to—" Baker cleared his throat. "To talk to him, to tell him things."

"Never mind. He has a mission for you. Accomplish this, and perhaps I can arrange a private audience."

Baker's head snapped to attention. He looked into Mansour's eyes. "Do you mean it? Do you really believe he will see me again?" There was no fake thrill this time.

"Perhaps. But first." Mansour looked to the stone table. "I want you to dispatch these two heathens to hell."

A smile creased Baker's face. "Do you mean it?"

"Of course."

He studied Mansour's face. He felt Mansour studying his face. The chieftain was wary. So was he. Still, the smile he gave was not fake. "With pleasure," he said. He had to say it, but did he have to mean it so?

He pulled the sling of his AK-47 free of his right shoulder and draped it across the crook of his left arm where wood turned to leather and leather to skin. He slipped the lever from safe to single-fire with his good hand. He had practiced this a hundred times. In Delta training. But not with one arm. He took too long.

Shit. He would not have got off a quick shot at bin Laden, after all. Next time he would use the dagger. To the groin.

He aimed for Powczuk's head. Powczuk cringed, but he did not close his eyes. Obscenities formed on his mouth, but he did not flinch or speak to the muzzle staring at his head.

Once he had him in his sights, Baker did not want to kill the guy. Not really, although the sorry bastard had cut off his arm. That was bad enough, but Powczuk beating him while he was unconscious? He could kill him for that.

He dared not flinch, either. If he did not kill these two, Mansour would know he was one of them.

All his talk about the infidels. Spouting all that hatred. He had to kill them. Powczuk and Tyler had to give their lives for their country. Or else all three of them would.

And bin Laden would get away. He—

Baker felt a trembling in his arm as he raised the rifle. He had to do it before his anxiety gave him away. He had to. He squeezed the trigger. A metallic click. Was that his heart or the gun?

Powczuk finally did flinch. He blinked rapidly. Curse words streamed from his mouth, not aloud, but in vile whispers. *Get it over with, you bastard.*

Tyler's eyes went wide. *Was this a game?*

Baker pulled the bolt back, clearing the dead round. His mind raced to keep up. No, to get ahead. What the hell was going on? He raised the AK-47 again. Again he pulled the trigger. Again the click.

"What is wrong with my rifle?" He looked to Mansour. Mansour, who was holding out his black 357 Magnum. The snub-nosed pistol that was at his ear a minute ago.

No. Busted! How did Mansour know?

Baker shifted his grip and his weight, ready to jab the butt of the rifle into Mansour's face.

"There is nothing wrong with the rifle," Mansour said. "I arranged for the dead rounds to be put into my clip even before we left my camp. It was as good as empty when I gave it to you on the other side of the mountain."

"Bastard."

"I'm sorry."

"A sorry goat-lover." Baker felt a flash of anger and knew it was the right response. "You don't trust me." He shook his head. "Child of velvet. I despise you for this."

"I trust you in full." He put on a lame smile. "Osama. He trusts nobody. Nobody gets a visit with him carrying a loaded weapon." Mansour handed over the pistol.

Baker took it. "Nobody?"

Mansour gave a crooked grin. "I am somebody. Do not forget it."

With an expert motion, Baker pushed the release and gave a flip of the wrist to unhinge the cylinder. Five of the six chambers were filled. He looked to Mansour.

"I always carry it with a hammer on an empty hole," the chieftain said.

"I'm not worried about the empty spot," Baker said. "What

about the rest of the rounds. Are the five real? Or are they fake as well?"

"You will see soon enough." Mansour turned and pushed through the curtain into the main cavern. Before the blanket fell back into the opening, he turned back. "After you are done, come join us for dinner."

Baker looked around the room. He was alone with the two Americans, Powczuk still cursing him under his breath, sweat beading on his forehead now, no longer so defiant. That pair of metallic clicks had unnerved him. For a moment Baker felt sorry for him. For a moment, he tried to think of a way to spare the man's life. If there was a way for him to arm the other two, the three of them might fight Al Qaeda to the death.

He looked toward the blanket, and beneath its bottom hem saw the toe of a left boot. Mansour's boot. *The walls have mice, and the mice have ears.* He'd heard the man use that one the night they left his adopted mother behind.

He had to be quick. For his own survival. And to extend the mercy of a quick death to Powczuk.

A flip of the wrist closed the cylinder. As he lifted the pistol, he pulled back the hammer and stepped forward. As soon as the sights lined up, centering on Powczuk's forehead, barely six inches away, he pulled the trigger.

This time nobody could hear a metallic click, for the blast that rocked the room and stopped up every ear. Baker felt the warm spray of the blow-back.

Powczuk's head exploded, his hair flying, spouting and spray-painting the wall, leaving a brief, sheeny rainbow in the air. One eye bulged from its socket. A torn hole began seeping at the points of the star on his forehead.

Tyler gasped. Curse words leaked from his lips, too. Baker stole a glance at the space beneath the curtain. The boot was gone.

He stepped up to Tyler, pulling his dagger. He glanced at Powczuk, his stomach cramping. He'd just killed one of his own. Not just an American, but a soldier and a Delta man. If Tyler was a bastard for attacking him by mistake, what was he now? Killing one Delta Force brother in cold blood? And now a second.

"No," Tyler said in low but shaky English. "Use the pistol, not the knife. Do it quickly. Please."

Baker locked eyes with him.

"Ramsey Baker, isn't it?"

"Quiet. If they hear us speaking English—" Baker leaned across the table and put the knife blade on the American's face.

Tyler spoke in Pashto, his words a murmur. "I'm sorry for taking that hatchet to your head. Believe it or not, it was an honest mistake."

"Shut up," Baker said. "I don't have time to talk."

"I know you have to do this, Ramsey, to stay close to bin Laden. Just get him. Get the sonofabitch." Tyler's words sounded brave, but his voice trembled, and so did his body.

"I said, shut up. This is going to hurt. A lot." Baker looked over at Powczuk's pulverized head, still dripping a black puddle on the chair behind him. He put his keen blade to the American's forehead, cutting a vertical slice through the skin, down to the bone with no pressure at all. The American barely moved. He didn't even close his eyes as his blood began to pour along the knife blade and each side of his nose, down his cheeks, around his mouth, across the chin into separate streams, and down his neck and into his shirt collar.

"How did they get you alive?" Baker asked as he shifted the blade and cut a horizontal slit. In the tone of: *Tell me you didn't give up.*

"Blackhawk crash." Tyler said. "I was out cold. I never had a chance to fight."

"I smell the fuel on you."

Tyler blinked as if in Morse code, as blood flowed into his eye sockets. "When you get back—"

"Shut the hell up, I say."

He turned the knife a quarter turn and pressed another slit into the head, then turned to again and cut again until he had cut an asterisk into Tyler's face, a fair copy of what the bullet had done to Powczuk.

"Find my wife. Tell her I said I'm sorry. I love her. I—"

"Shush, someone's coming."

He got up onto the table and put the night to Tyler's throat. He drew the blade, cutting into the skin. The blood flowed into Tyler's collar. Suddenly, he glanced back toward the door.

To see Mansour's face, peeking between the blanket and the stone slab. "What's keeping you? Oh, I see. A bit of entertainment, perhaps?"

Baker smashed his wooden prosthesis across Tyler's face, forcing him to turn his head away so that Mansour could see only the slice forming at his throat.

"I took the other one in anger, too hastily." He waved the wooden arm, leading Mansour's gaze away from Tyler. "Because he did this, I let my hatred get the worst of me. This one I want to suffer."

"Even so, hurry. We will eat. Then perhaps arrange a meeting for you."

The blanket flapped shut.

"You're right," Tyler whispered. "It does hurt."

"You know, it wouldn't take much for me to put a little force behind this knife blade. If it would make you shut your fat face."

"Dammit, give me my one last wish," Tyler said. "Promise me you'll find my wife, Amy."

Baker finished making the shallow cut around Tyler's throat, keeping the blade above his Adam's apple. "What makes you think I'm going to get out of this alive?"

"I don't care if you do. Just promise me, you bastard."

"All right, if it will shut you up. But you have as much chance of getting out alive as I do." He smiled. "Which is to say, very goddamned little."

"Say the words."

"I promise to find your wife, Amy. Now will you please?"

"And?"

" 'I love you.' "

"And?"

" '*I love you I love you I love you.*' All right?" He shook his head. "If bin Laden walked in on *that.*"

Tyler closed his eyes. A look of peace eased across his face as he waited for whatever Baker had in store for him.

Baker grabbed Tyler by the hair on both sides of his head. He took a deep breath and put his open mouth over the star that he had cut into Tyler's forehead. He sucked hard, pulling blood into his mouth. Then he draped Tyler's head back over his chair. He stepped around the stone slab and blew a spray of blood against the cave wall, spitting and hacking. He compared his work to the first pattern of blood spatter he had made with the 357 Magnum slug. Again, passable likeness. He wiped off his mouth and continued spitting blood, this time in disgust.

He pulled Tyler's hands off the table and positioned them in his lap. He cut the rope around his wrists and left the dagger

As he walked around the table, he heard the scuff of a boot step again. He saw the toe of Mansour's boot, threw up the pistol, shot it into the wall, in the center of the blood spatter.

The blanket came opened, and Mansour stepped into the room, shaking his head.

"Loud, isn't it?" He held out his hand for the pistol, barely looking at Baker, but surveying the damage with a quick eye. "You've made quite the bloody mess."

Baker didn't release the pistol right away, not quite trusting Mansour. If he knew. If he suspected. He might turn the pistol on Baker.

Mansour tugged. Still Baker could not bring himself to let go. Mansour released it. "If you like it so much, perhaps you should keep it. Personally, I find it too heavy, like carrying around a shank of lamb."

"If you mean it, I will take it." Baker gave him a meek smile. "The rifle is a better weapon, but hard to work with only one hand. And this"—he waved the wooden arm at his bloody work—"The pistol is a nice token to keep this night near to my mind."

"Keep it then." He held the blanket for Baker. "Come on, you have missed your meal. We have a report of more helicopters coming. The Americans. You know how they are about picking up their dead bodies."

"A weakness."

"To be sure."

"The prince?"

"The prince. I'm sorry to say, you will not get to meet him."

Baker cursed in Pashto and grabbed Mansour's jacket with his hook. "You *promised*."

Mansour pulled free. "He has to escape. And so do we. We must climb again, back up and over the pass before first light."

Tyler waited as long as he could before he dared to take a breath. It wasn't long. His heart beat too hard. It needed oxygen, and in no more than a minute, he had to take it in. He'd had too much. Not the pain. Not the brush with death.

No, his pulse raced because now he had a second chance at bin Laden now. He had no weapon but a hand-forged dagger. It would have to do. He used it to cut away the ropes around his ankles. As he worked, the blood kept flowing from his neck and head wounds. He cut a strip of cloth from his camo trousers and tied it in a tight wrap of his head. He gave a small grin at the idea. Rambo. He looked like Rambo. Forget the slice at his throat. No way to tie a tourniquet around his neck.

Outside, in the larger cavern, he heard a roar rise up. One huge booming voice. Then cheers. Men looking for a fight.

Tyler had seen bin Laden go out the back of the little room. They had used that way to bring him here. He bent over and slipped through the tiny space between rocks. On the other side, the path opened up. He saw his combat pack where his captors had dropped it off. He fumbled into it quickly, and took out two boomers, the concussion grenades. He stuffed them into his shirt pockets and took two more. Those he put into his pants pockets. And found the final pair. *Now*.

Now he was not helpless. Now he wouldn't have to get close to bin Laden. He could toss the grenades and get him. Or find the sonofabitch and cram it up his ass.

The going was dark now and slow. His ankle was weak. He should stop to haul his laces tight. But he did not want to waste time. He'd just limp his way along. Later, he'd get to a chopper and get out. He had to smile. Tall odds of that. If the Al Qaeda didn't get him, the Delta men would.

Tyler kept to the litter of boulders at the edge of the cavern. Like a mouse, kept to the faint path. Where shafts of light cast shadows, he could see the way worn smooth in the sandy floor of the cave.

In only minutes, he found the exit, not as much by sight as by the flow of fresh, cold air blowing in his face. He eased into it, using his hands to trace along the wall, letting the breeze guide him to the opening. Soon he had to bend at the waist, then crawl on all fours. This was not a main path. He ended up on his belly, low-crawling out of the cave.

The blood seeped from his rag, and he had to wipe it away on his sleeve. He had to keep the flow out of his eyes. So he could see.

Finally he was free of the cave. Ahead of him at about fifty meters, he saw an vehicle. Men milled around outside it. A panel truck. *No!*

An ambulance! Bin Laden prowled Afghanistan in a Red Crescent ambulance? Why not? A perfect hiding place. Mobile, able to store supplies for his ailing kidneys—even a portable dialysis machine. Sure. A mobile hospital. He could have a generator, a bed, a surgeon. Most of all the smug knowledge that Americans would not bomb the Red Crescent. He'd armor it for extra protection. And the armor would shield a signal from a beacon like the one in the head of the bin Laden double, the kid.

Tyler felt the urge to act. A soldier thing, to attack. But not across fifty meters. Too far to run without getting shot down. Too far to toss a grenade and be sure of getting it close enough to bin Laden. Somehow he had to put one inside the box. He had to get closer.

There was cover enough for a sneak. Some patches of brush and some boulders. He began working his way from one

to the other, ignoring the wet, cold chill on his chest and neck,
trying not to let his mind's eye picture his cut throat, keeping
his mind off the loss of blood. Daring not to dream he could
kill bin Laden. His mind giving a nod to Baker.

Ramsey Baker. One of his great sins was trying to kill
Baker. Baker had forgiven him. The other great sin the betrayal
of Amy. Baker again. Baker could make that right. If he—

He put his mind back to work. He had to kill a man, just one
stroke to win all wars.

Finally, he got within range of a grenade toss. A thrill ran
through him. He might just do it. With luck, he might land one
inside the open doors. He took one of the boomers out and began working his fingers across the tiny buttons of the digital
control panel. He could adjust the delay. But—

Chrissake. The door of the ambulance went shut. Just one
black cube. A box of darkness in the night, dark figures standing around outside.

Maybe if he tossed it low. Maybe roll it under the box. It
might, *might,* go off in the tight spot. Maybe start a fire. Then
he might run up and maybe chuck a second and third grenade
to finish the job, maybe get away. He shook his head, slinging
blood droplets off his nose.

Too many mights. Too many maybes.

An engine roared to life. Then came the dim glow of black-
out traveling lights, ultra-low red beams that reached out to no
more than three meters. Enough for a slow night drive, but not
enough to give away a vehicle to the naked eye. Very low-tech.
And pointless in the age of night vision bomb sights. What the
hell were they thinking? An ambulance with tactical lights?
Bin Laden would be better off traveling with headlights and
flashing emergency signals, sirens, the whole works. The
only—

The rear doors of the ambulance opened again. Tyler read-
ied himself for one last chance. He drew back his throwing
arm and pressed the arming button with his thumb. But he did
not throw it. Because a body flew out, landing in a heap on the
ground behind the ambulance.

In the white light that escaped the interior before the doors chunked shut again, he saw bin Laden lying on the ground.

Bin Laden given the heave-ho?

No way. The figure rolled over and leaped to his feet. Too athletic, too limber, too young. This was not the wan kidney patient he had seen back in the cave. One of the lookalikes, one of the doubles, perhaps that kid that they had been chasing all over the country. What was his name? The one with the passive GPS in his head? Aziz?

Aziz. Sure. They'd leave him behind for the Americans to find, while bin Laden, prince of a guy that he was, slipped away.

Bad for Aziz. But good for Tyler. Very good. Now Tyler knew. The bastard was in the box.

The floor of the little valley had come alive with an army of men like ants. Their shadows appeared in the backlighting of caves and tunnels. Men shouting in Arabic to each other. *Helicopters coming. Save the prince. Hold the landing zones at all cost. Keep the heathens away until the prince escapes.*

The box rolled from beneath the overhang of the cliff. Tyler surveyed the road, barely a ribbon of sand in the moonlight. The track curved left, swooping his way before dipping into the valley and the darkness. He could cut it off. His way littered with boulders, crisscrossed by waves and heaps of gravel washed up in the rare flash flood. But he could get there first.

He dared not run. Dared not draw an eye. He walked, one boomer in each fist. Each thumb ready to arm each boomer. He picked a spot where the track bent to him. A walk in the park. In the dark and amid the chaos. He did not try to sneak.

Twenty seconds. That's all. Give him twenty seconds.

He might have a function in life, after all.

All these weeks of futility. He might have power. Power to serve his country. To avenge Michael Woodrow. A gift to all who had died on 9-11. An act of—

His heart stopped. As a pair of Al Qaeda fighters ran at him, he dropped the grenade from his right hand. Found the dagger. Drew it behind his hip. A thrust to the gut of one, a slice—

They ran by him. They didn't care about him. They raced each other to their deaths. *I will die first,* said one, *for the prince.* The other giggled. *No, I will die first.*

Tyler gasped for breath. Afraid he might die before either of them. He cringed behind a boulder. He'd not armed the grenade. The one he dropped. *Right?* The old Delta joke: *Once it's dropped, Mr. Grenade is not your friend.* Three seconds later, when the boomer still lay silent, he knew he hadn't.

A final indignity. To blow up his own ass.

The clock in his head started up. What was it now? Fifteen seconds? He gave himself that much. Bin Laden would pass by in fifteen seconds. He put his knife away.

He bent over to pick up his boomer and let another pair of fighters run by, this time running away. *We'll hide out in the cave and watch to see how the fight is going,* said one. *And join it if it goes well,* the other said. *Or run away if it goes badly,* said the one.

Bin Laden came at him, his ambulance laboring in low gear.

Ten seconds more. And he could put a dent in the world of terror. With his left thumb he armed one boomer and tossed it to his left. Far enough so blast would not take him out. In the road. To blind bin Laden's driver. Blind him with the flash. Or even a shower of glass.

Seven. Tyler lay down behind a gravel bar, his fingers jammed into his ears, one boomer still in his right hand, and his eyes shut, hard.

The grenade blew, spanking him with concussion. He kept his head. He armed the second grenade and kept the arming button down. So the timing sequence could not start until he threw it. He got to his feet.

At five seconds.

To see the vehicle bear down on him.

He tried to leap clear. Tripped. Fell on his face. He saw his end now as the front tires hit the gravel bar. They raised like the hooves of a pony. He waited for them to come down, to crush him.

It fell short. All four wheels ground at the packed sand. The right front tire spun, an inch from his boot. The vehicle stuck on the gravel bar. The left front tire clawed at the hem of his shirt.

Zero seconds. The driver kept his wits about him. Back and forth, he drove, grinding gears, trying to get free.

Tyler rolled clear.

And ran, bent-legged to the rear of the box.

He grabbed for the doors. Locked. Back and forth. He shrieked. He smashed his boomer into the glass. In rage. A hammer. A curse. A string of curses.

Safety glass. It did not shatter. He drew back and tried again, as hard as he could. Again and again. Still the grenade did not break through. His fingers smashed. His thumb slipped.

Armed.

He'd armed the boomer.

Less than three seconds. Then, out of time, out of tries.

He smashed at the glass once more.

Twice.

As he drew back his arm again, a rifle went off inside. On full auto. Slugs tore through one door. Slugs tore at his left arm. His left leg.

An odd thought. Odd, that. Why armor-piercing slugs? For the choppers? *Yes.* To bring them down. *Yes, yes.*

Slugs tore through the glass.

He brought his fist forward. Punched through the glass. At last.

Slugs hit him like somebody tap-dancing. On his chest. Across his gut. The teflon slugs passing through him without blowing him off the rear bumper.

He held on. *Yes.* His fist was in. *Yes, yes, yes.* His arm.

He knew he was dead. Even without the slugs. The grenade in his hand would set off those in his pockets. One last thought.

Ironic, that.

Connor Tyler.

Spangler's ultimate terrorist weapon.

America's own. Suicide. Bomber. *Yes, yes, yes, yes. . . .*

Amy Tyler held her phone to one ear, Brendan to the other. One a source of distress, the other comfort. Until finally he came on the line.

"General Spangler speaking."

"Roscoe, Amy Tyler."

"The sergeant told me."

"Roscoe."

"I can't tell you anything, Amy. You know that. I wouldn't even take the call, except that it's you. Out of respect for you. Because you and Connor and me, we go way back."

"Can you get a message to him at least? Can you tell him I love him? That I don't want a divorce?"

A long, long pause. Too long, until Spangler said, "I, uh, can't. I'm sorry."

"You can't even get a message to him?"

"You know how this works, Amy. I can't confirm, can't deny. You know the business he was . . . you know the business."

"*Was in?* The business he *was* in? Roscoe?"

"Shit. Good-bye, Amy. Somebitch, I'm so sorry." The line went dead.

Even before she could hang up the phone and redial, she could see them coming. Two men. Soldiers in uniform. One a black man, an officer. The other a one-armed officer with disfigured ears.

The worst fear of every army wife. Uniformed visitors in a time of war. That's why Spangler was so hesitant just then. He knew they were coming, thought they'd aleady come and gone.

She thought her knees might buckle, but she locked them up, walking stiff-legged to the door.

She thought she might cry out, even scream, but she set her jaw against hysteria.

She opened the door before either of them could ring the bell. Their bars and nametags identified them.

She spoke before they could. "Captain Poole. Captain Baker. I already know you have to tell me lies about the way he died."

They stood there blinking in the shade.

Baker held out a parcel to her.

She shook her head. She wasn't going to take it. "Just tell me the truth about two things. Did you know him?"

"Yes, ma'am," they said as one.

"Did he say anything?" She'd begun to tremble so hard her knees literally knocked. She had to clutch Brendan with both arms.

"Yes," said the one-armed officer with hideous ears. "He asked me to tell you—"

"Captain Baker?"

"Yes?"

"The truth, Captain. Promise me that this is the truth and nothing but, or so help me, God, I will swear a curse on you, the curse of a widow and a son left without a dad."

Baker gulped. She could not stop glancing at his ears. "He spoke to me before he died. He made me promise to take a message to you."

"So help me—" She shuddered, sending a sprinkle of tears from her hawk eyes. "I'll know if you're lying. If you're feeding me some Pentagon line of shit, I'll know. I swear."

"It's no line of . . . bull, ma'am."

"Then what did he say?"

" 'I love you—' "

"Bullshit! He didn't say that. He loved somebody else. Did Spangler put you up to this bullshit?"

"I wasn't finished, ma'am. What I told you is true, straight from his mouth, but you have to let me finish. Before you decide, hear the rest of it."

She lifted her head, waiting, looking down at him with those eyes of the hawk. Ready to go at him, talons first. To tear off those mangled ears, if she had to.

So Baker gave it to her. First the truth, the line Connor Tyler had spoken to him that night in the cave.

" 'Tell Amy I love her.' He made me say it. 'I love you I love you I love you.' "

She balked at that, stiffening, ready to go at him. But she stayed within herself and waited, giving him his say.

So he said the rest, the line from Spangler, the Pentagon bullshit, just as she had called it.

" 'I love you more than Laren. Chrissake, Amy, I always loved you more than Laren.' His exact words. Swear to God. His dying words."

She shut the door in their faces. Not a slam, just a shut.

Before she disappeared, Baker saw it in the body posture, the dam breaking, the flash flood of emotions bursting free.

Mostly relief, he could see that. Even in the soft keening from behind the door he could hear the relief. He heard the child start up, too. The child, knowing nothing of the news, but crying in sympathetic resonance with his mother. He put down his parcel on the mat. Inside was a tricorner box with the folded flag. No remains would come back. The only personal effects were some clothing from the carrier and Tyler's cell phone, the personal phone he'd left in his duffel on the carrier. Spangler would summon the DNA proof, if Amy wanted proof.

She wouldn't. She had the lie to cling to.

Spangler did right to tell him to tell the lie. And Baker felt better about passing it along. Now that he saw that she needed just those words. She'd have the lie for life. For two lives. Hers and the kid's.

The two captains turned away and walked back to their sedan without a word between them. Baker thinking: *God forgive me.* He gave it a second thought: *Not Spangler, though. Christ, don't forgive him.*

Baker knew that Poole was thinking the same thing: Spangler. Without 9-11, he'd never have existed. But because of 9-11, he flourished. Before long Amy Tyler would come to the door again, to claim the box there. She'd find the phone. Soon after, she'd wonder. Not long after, she'd play the messages in her husband's voice mail. She'd not find the voice of Laren, his lover. She'd know Tyler had not saved the words of his lover. She'd know he loved his wife more than Laren. She'd know it for the rest of her life. And her son's.

He'd erased it, all right. That Spangler. Exactly the kind of evil genius Amy Tyler needed in her moment of grief. Exactly the kind of dark wizard the country needed in the aftermath of its.

Courtesy of Al Qaeda. Terrorists had created a new Spangler. Once a toad, now a prince of evil up there on a level with bin Laden himself.

Baker shook his head. No wonder they called it terrorism.

IV   Aftermath

Baker. The invisible Delta fighter. Thought dead and buried. If he could find his way out of that godforsaken country, he'd be the second coming of himself. He made it out. After all he'd seen, it was so simple. Drop out of the march. Work his way to the troops. Announce himself as a Delta man to other Delta men. Let them rescue him.

Aboard the carrier, Carnes hugged him, and Spangler actually gave him a kiss. On the cheek but chilling anyhow, slobber-lip wet and cold. Then, later, they gave him a medal. Secret, of course. The country's highest, MOHTNES. The Medal of Honor That Nobody's Ever Seen, they called it. Still, it was nice. He'd get a few extra bucks in his medical retirement packet. A heckuva reward for being the object of so many beatings and hatchet blows.

Debrief after debrief later, they let him go with all his honors. His last duty the call on Amy Tyler. He insisted on that.

No debrief could make him tell one thing, though. About Mansour.

Before he dropped off the trail, he pulled the pistol, the

man's own gun. He put it up to the warlord's head, a bare six inches away. The sometimes Northern Alliance chief, sometimes Al Qaeda lieutenant had eyes in the back of his head.

He stopped. And let the barrel touch his skull.

"Think, Bakr," the warrior chief said. "Think a moment and you'll see you must spare me."

"You're my enemy," Baker said, "because you are the friend of my enemy. I have to kill you." He should have done it already. Without a word. Shoot and run.

Mansour's very next words: "You won't now. Because you have thought on it a moment too long already. And now you are being too polite."

"When you kill a man it costs nothing to be polite."

Mansour laughed. "You're beginning to sound like me. Even so, you will not kill me. You owe a debt."

"You think because you saved my life? You think that means something? You thought I was an Al Qaeda. If you had known I am an American, you would have killed me with your own hand."

"Your life, my life. Neither means a thing. A wolf's pup will grow into a wolf, no matter if you raise it in the city."

"Wolf pup? What the hell does that mean?"

"A leopard cannot change his spots. You think you're a soldier. You think I'm a soldier. We are not soldiers. Neither of us. If you think otherwise, then perhaps you *should* kill me."

"What the hell are you talking about? Of course I'm a soldier."

"No. You are too decent to be a soldier. Like me, you are a humanitarian."

"Where the hell did you get an idea like that?"

"From your mother."

"What?"

"My wife, your mother. If she is right, you won't thank her in this vile way. Spare my life and you spare hers. Spare hers and you spare yourself a life of hell on earth."

Silence. Mansour cleared his throat. "Bakr?"

"What did she say about me?"

"She told me to ask you."

"Ask me what?"

"If I should ever come into conflict, she said to ask you: What is under the bowl?

Silence.

"What did she mean?" Mansour asked.

Silence. "Bakr?"

But Baker was gone.

Later, aboard a Blackhawk on the flight to the Indian Ocean, he let himself smile on it. Mansour. True, he was a bastard Al Qaeda part-timer. But, thing was, once you got to know him—

He began to laugh. The mirth grew hysterical. He saw the other Delta men staring at him. Hell, he didn't care. He had a secret. Only he and Mansour would ever know it. And maybe his adopted mother, the Al Qaeda woman who saved his life by not telling Mansour her suspicions about him—not suspicions—he'd said the name that betrayed him: Jesus Christ. He wondered why, but only for a moment. Somehow she must have known he would not kill her husband. But . . . oh, the hell with wondering about it. She was right, wasn't she?

Talk about surreal. They gave him the Medal of Honor. For all the beatings he took, which took no courage at all. When push came to honor, he tried to give up everything, tried to tell Powczuk who he was.

Powczuk. He'd killed another American? A Delta Force American to boot? Shooting him square in the face? Where the hell was the honor in that? After all his own obsessing about what Tyler had done to him on 9-11. Shit.

Honor. The only honor he felt was in not killing Mansour, his sworn enemy. If he ever got to heaven, they'd have some questions for him. Lotsa questions. If he ever got to hell, they'd crown him king of the damned.

September 11, 2003

The world's most ruthless terrorist. The King Rat himself, Osama bin Laden the Notorious.

The rumors about bin Laden crop up all the time, like torn

petals tossed from a daisy. *Is he dead? Is he not? Is he dead? Is he not?*

The argument never stops in the intel community. Of course the American public *thinks* it wants him dead. And the world of terror knows it wants him alive.

Even if the terrorist world has buried the body, it will keep the man alive anyhow. They not only want him alive, they *need* him alive.

Most Americans in the know believe bin Laden is dead.

Then again, many in the CIA part of America do not want him *completely* dead. Better to keep his fate obscure than to show the Arab world a body, a martyr's body. Most of the terror world would not even believe it anyhow, even with DNA tests. They'd have reason to doubt, too—not even a DNA test was trustworthy anymore?

The audio tapes that turn up from time to time? Sure, it could be him. Maybe not. Could be him. Maybe not. Why give the terror world comfort? Hell why give the terror world closure. No man, even if he had bin Laden's charisma, can step up to the leader's role. Not when there's the slightest doubt about bin Laden's death. The man who steps up as much as tells the whole world that the King Rat is dead. So. A vacuum. Not a bad thing.

Even within the CIA, there is no consensus on how to report the King Rat's fate. It's a good thing to let him live in the minds and hearts with never a body to show for it. That makes him a coward, fearful of showing his face.

Or, if need be, they can claim to kill him at any moment and produce the body of Aziz. Delta Force picked him up that night in the valley. If they needed a body, the CIA had one. Someday bin Laden might even die of old age, his reputation cold, long-dead before him, the absolute worst fate of an egomaniac like bin Laden.

September 11, 2004

And the world's second most deadly terrorist, though nobody yet knows his name: Spangler the Obscure. He never needed the accolades to do a job. No charismatic, he. Only to work behind the scenes. For the good of the country.

Nobody needed to tell him he was a shit. Nobody needed to tell him he was a good man. For he knew he was both.

The good man in him rose to his moment in history. The country needed him for a single task, and when he'd done it, they gave him a pat on the back and let him go. The eagle had ceased to scream, but now the parrots began to chatter. He'd won the war of the giants. And lost the war of the pygmies. Like his idol Churchill, banished, but happily, and without the public humiliation.

Oh, they had called him back for one brief tour of duty in Operation Iraqi Freedom. Then set him free again.

So, he could watch from a distance as those in the press, the parrots, found fault with first the peace, then the war. As the peace-at-any-cost types, the political pygmies, tried to appease the America haters in Europe and in the Mideast, feeding the crocodile, hoping it will eat them last. Like Spain after the terrorist train bombings.

They'd never get it, the parrots and pygmies. Fighting terror was like playing in goal in a hockey game. A hundred saves, and you're a genius. But just let one get by in a sudden-death overtime of the seventh game of the Stanley Cup championship, and you're a goat. The army, the CIA, FBI, and the rest of the alphabet soup agencies had made a thousand saves a year before 9-11. And a thousand since. Saves they couldn't even brag about. But what did they want to talk about? Who was to blame for not foreseeing the events of September 11, 2001, the press riding down from the hills overlooking the battlefield, riding about willy-nilly, shooting the wounded where they lay. *Shee-it.*

The army kept his many secret plans, but let the man go. Retired as a colonel after the war in Afghanistan. Better than he'd dreamed, better than even he thought he deserved. His plans would speak for him in the wars to come against terror. The nation, once wounded, had shown the heart of a lion. His plan but the roar. So he left.

His pride intact.

As well as his shame.

Leaving the body of Randall Bowers in the fire. Walking over him to save the OPLAN.

Of course that was not the shame. That was a necessary evil. Killing Bowers on his hospital bed? That was something else.

He'd stood there deciding which plug to pull.

He overheard himself recite his daily prayer: *Can you kill, Roscoe? Can you kill?*

For as long as he was a soldier, he'd never killed. This was his chance. Not an enemy, to be sure. But surely for the good of the country. Not just to save himself but to keep the plan intact until—

A nurse had walked in on him at his moment of truth. *No! Major Doctor Bitch!*

"What are you doing?" she wanted to know.

He worked the electrical cord through his fingers. "Saying the rosary?"

"Get out," she said. "I'm calling security to have you arrested."

"For what?"

"Messing with these machines? That might be construed as attempted murder."

"Try to prove that, why don't you. He's my friend. He's—"

A sharp, high electronic tone drowned him out. Then another tone, like a siren. A light flashed. The Major Bitch grabbed a phone and hollered into it. Medical gibberish. *Code Blue.* He recognized that term from the television.

"Get out, you bastard."

He did step off a ways. He hung around, of course. For the sake of his friend, of course. To see General Randall Bowers IV wheeled out, a sheet over his head. He stood by Esther Bowers's shoulder when the intern gave her the sad news. Of course. Major Bitch, outraged, looked on, but from a distance. He looked into Esther's eyes: *Sad, very sad.*

"Stroke," said the intern. "Coupled with a heart attack. He didn't have a chance with the infections eating at him."

Spangler had to stifle a grin. At himself. What a bonehead

he was. Trying to figure out which plug to pull. Or whether to use the cord as a garrote. When all he had to do was jump up into Randy's seeping excuse for a face and yell, *Boo!* Maybe take off his own glasses and look him in the eye. Put him over the edge and into the eternal abyss with a scary look.

All the killing he'd asked men to do, he could not deliver the goods himself. A rabbit telling others how to hunt. *Shee-it. For shame, Roscoe. When push came to shove, you couldn't kill. At least not on purpose. Accidents? Accidents don't count, Roscoe. For shame.* Still.

Even Esther wasn't all *that* broken up. More relieved than sad, in fact. Later, when they were alone in the hospital cafeteria line getting coffee, she looked into Spangler's face—tried to look into it. She glanced at all the scars and averted her gaze from the reflection in his glasses. "I'm ashamed to say it," she said.

"What?" He tried to give her a pat on the shoulder, but she cringed away from his hand.

"I'm ashamed to say that it's a blessing. That he didn't live. The constant care. And that he might live to . . . to look like—"

Don't say *You.*

"*That.*"

"There, there." His hand shot out like lightning and took her shoulder before she could duck away.

"I'm so ashamed. I prayed, oh, I prayed he'd die. Oh—" She stood up and pulled back before he could embrace her.

"Now, now, Esther, don't blame yourself," Spangler said.

"Roscoe, I didn't just pray for God to end his suffering," she said.

"I understand."

"No. You don't. I prayed God to end *mine.*"

"Oh, I think I understand your thinking there." In spades.

He lunged and hugged her shoulders, in his hands, at arms' length because she went stiff and held her coffee as a shield when he tried to take her to his chest. "It truly is a blessing, Esther." And proof, too, after all.

There truly is a God.